Mothers
and
Sons

Mothers and Sons

A Novel

Adam Haslett

LITTLE, BROWN AND COMPANY

New York Boston London

Copyright © 2025 by Adam Haslett

Little, Brown and Company
Hachette Book Group
1290 Avenue of the Americas, New York, NY 10104
littlebrown.com

First Edition: January 2025

Little, Brown and Company is a division of Hachette Book Group, Inc. The Little, Brown name and logo are trademarks of Hachette Book Group, Inc.

The publisher is not responsible for websites (or their content) that are not owned by the publisher.

The Hachette Speakers Bureau provides a wide range of authors for speaking events. To find out more, go to hachettespeakersbureau.com or email hachettespeakers@hbgusa.com.

Little, Brown and Company books may be purchased in bulk for business, educational, or promotional use. For information, please contact your local bookseller or the Hachette Book Group Special Markets Department at special.markets@hbgusa.com.

Book interior design by Marie Mundaca

ISBN 9780316574716
Library of Congress Control Number: 2024940326

Printing 1, 2024

LSC-C

Printed in the United States of America

For Dan

Likewise the imaginative woe,
    That loved to handle spiritual strife,
    Diffused the shock thro' all my life,
But in the present broke the blow.

—Tennyson, *In Memoriam*

Once Jared's car has vanished down the driveway into the darkness, there is nothing to do but turn and face the rectory. The only light on is the bulb above the front door, as if my mother and sister have already gone to bed. But that can't be, it's too early. My sister must be out, like I have been, fleeing this house of the dead. It's summer—August—but I'm shivering.

I have to find my mother. I must tell her what has happened with Jared. But where can she be? Inside, the house is quiet, the front hall and the living room dark. I head toward the kitchen, glancing into her study as I go, and that's where I see her, standing there in the gloom with her back to me, silhouetted by the window, looking out over the drive. She's been watching. She's seen Jared drop me off, she's heard me enter the house, heard me enter this room—she must have. But still, she doesn't move. My mother the priest. My mother the widow. Yet is she really that? Or is she relieved to have my father gone?

Through the window screen, the cooler night air flows past her into the space between us. She doesn't switch on a light, she doesn't ask where I've been. She just remains there, motionless. Is it that she knows already about Jared and me? Is that why she doesn't turn to face me? As if her silence could prevent what I have to tell her from being true. As if her not hearing it could make it not so.

I

Judge Manetti calls out a name, 'Dovgal, Matvey,' and a white guy—mid-twenties, gray sweatshirt, gold chain—makes his way into the enclosure. He's got a Legal Aid lawyer with him. The home address is Staten Island. His lawyer concedes his client received his notice to appear. He concedes he's removable. Declines to specify country for removal. Why make the government's job any easier? Judge Manetti designates Belarus. He's claiming asylum; failing that, withholding of removal; failing that, Convention Against Torture. Callahan, the Department of Homeland Security lawyer, points out Dovgal has a theft conviction so he's expedited. Manetti leafs through her calendar, a sheaf of wrinkled dot-matrix-printer pages stapled at one corner. Silence in the courtroom as the judge peers through her reading glasses searching for a date for the merits hearing. He will need an interpreter. Manetti's got a Russian booked on a Wednesday in three months. The lawyers consult their phones. June 8, 2011. Agreed.

The courtroom is windowless. They all are. There are the fluorescent lights flush to the dropped ceiling. There is the judge's miniature dais, the lawyers' tables in front of it, the low bar with the hinged gate, the dark pink carpet. Respondents and their counsel cramped on benches either side of the gallery aisle, awaiting their turn. No one's allowed to use their phones. All we can do is watch and listen.

Beside me on the bench, Sandra Moya whispers something in the ear of her fourteen-year-old son, Felipe. 'Ask Mr. Peter,' she says.

Then Felipe whispers in mine. 'How much longer will it be? My mom can't be late to work.'

He and his little sister, Mia, are citizens, but Felipe has told me that if his mother is sent back to Honduras, he wants to go with her. I know Sandra will never let that happen. She will make them both go to relatives.

'They don't tell us the order,' I say. 'We just have to wait. Soon, I hope.'

Next up, Fatima Saleem, Long Island high-school student, Pakistani, not present. The attorney making the appearance for her asks for a continuation pending family court proceedings. Files proof of the girl's school attendance. Copy to the judge, who stamps it entered, copy to Callahan. Silence as everyone reads.

If she goes to school in Nassau, why was her first court appearance in Suffolk? the department wants to know. Her lawyer has no idea. Manetti agrees it's a question. What's the path of the application? Educate the court. She allows thirty days to submit. Callahan doesn't object to the adjournment. The attorney shuffles out.

Neto, Winston. Black man in his early thirties, jeans and a white button-down, Legal Aid at his side. Application for cancellation of removal to Angola. Citizen wife, two citizen children. He was ordered removed four months ago.

Callahan is in a theatrical mood today. He waves a letter, issued this week, from the chief counsel to the whole Department: the hardship that a removal would cause must be stated at the time of application. 'Your Honor,' he says, 'he's in violation of a final order. We're in overtime. Let him state his hardship.'

The Legal Aid lawyer says there's no requirement to establish the nature of the hardship at a scheduling hearing.

'What does that mean?' Callahan asks. 'He needs more time to invent it? He doesn't know what his hardship is?'

Legal Aid repeats herself: No requirement. Manetti agrees. Callahan moves to put his boss's letter in the record. Accepted. Thirty days to submit the reason for the hardship. The judge returns to her calendar. A Thursday in April, six weeks out. Agreed.

The older woman on my other side wearing a hijab leans forward and glares at Felipe, who gets the message and stills his bouncing legs. Instead, he crosses his arms tightly over his chest. He's his mother's timekeeper, there to hurry her into our office or court or out again to her job. The one she puts on the phone when I call asking for documents and usually the one who gets them to me.

'Moya, Sandra,' Manetti calls. Finally.

I shuffle past our disgruntled neighbor and lead the Moyas to the front. Callahan nods hello as we enter the enclosure. Pats Felipe on the shoulder, all buddy-buddy. As if he is anyone's friend here.

'Good morning, Your Honor. Peter Fischer for the respondent.'

'Good morning, Mr. Fischer. Your client's conceded service, she's conceded she's subject to removal, declined to designate a country for removal, the court designated Honduras, and she's already scheduled. So what are we doing here this morning?'

I gesture for Sandra and Felipe to sit at the table, but Sandra shakes her head, and taking his cue from her, Felipe remains standing also.

'Your Honor, my client's requesting an adjournment. I have here an affidavit she's signed attesting to the impediments she's encountered trying to collect documentation to support her asylum application, most importantly witness statements. I'd request the affidavit be made part of the record.'

'So ordered,' Manetti says, taking the paper from me. Callahan doesn't look up as I place his copy down on his table. He's hunched over the file, flipping through it no doubt for the first time. He's only halfway through the scheduling slog, but he's sick of it already, all this procedure and delay. He thinks Manetti's a soft touch, that most all the New York judges are. He's bored and restless. It's just a question now of where his eye happens to fall.

'Does the department have a view?' the judge inquires.

'Well, Your Honor,' Callahan says, still reading, 'it seems Ms. Moya has been in this country quite some time, long enough to have given birth to her son here. She apparently did not come forward voluntarily. No record of an interview. And'—he flips another page—'she's been given one delay already. So, no, the department does not support the motion, and objects.' With that he closes the file and leans back in his chair, his duty temporarily done.

'As you know, Your Honor,' I say, 'the length of time my client's been in the country has no bearing—'

'You're right, Mr. Fischer, it doesn't. But the fact she's already on a continuance does, and she's scheduled three weeks from now, so I'm disinclined. Who are these people she couldn't reach in eight months who she's supposedly going to reach if I grant your motion?'

Out of the corner of my eye, I see Felipe tilt his head back to glare at the ceiling instead of Manetti. He knows as well as Sandra does that this judge is most likely the person who will decide his mother's fate.

'One of the people,' I say, 'is an eyewitness to the events in question, a family relation we're still working to contact, who we were recently told moved to Tegucigalpa.'

'Oh, well, that narrows it down,' Callahan says.

'What it does,' I say, ignoring him, 'is confirm that Ms. Moya's cousin is alive and that we have a chance to present her testimony in this case.'

For whatever reason, it's now that Sandra chooses to sit. She rests her elbows on the table and clasps her hands together as if in prayer, though her expression couldn't be further from worship. She wants this done. It's not she who asked for extra time. I'm the one who told her it was needed. She told me the statements might never arrive. But with another couple of months they just might.

'Your Honor,' Callahan says, 'if the court waited for everyone who is merely *alive* to testify, we'd all be dead before anyone had a hearing.'

'All right, that's enough,' Manetti says. 'Mr. Fischer, what you're giving me just isn't sufficient for another continuance. Motion denied. We'll see you in three weeks.'

Felipe barrages me with questions as we exit the courtroom and head down the corridor. 'Why did you ask for that? Does that woman hate my mom now? Did that make it worse?'

'We needed to try,' I tell him. 'But your claim's still strong,' I say, addressing myself to Sandra. 'You put in the work, you're ready.'

Felipe goes quiet in the crowded elevator but as we squeeze out of it into the lobby, he's back at me. 'That judge hates us now,' he says. 'I could tell.'

'No,' I say, leading them toward the exit. 'Manetti's not going to count it against your mother.'

On Duane Street, the cold drizzle of early March has the lunch crowd sprouting umbrellas as they file past us out of the federal building.

Felipe wants more from me, some further assurance. But Sandra is past it, gazing off into Foley Square, where lawyers and staff and jurors scurry up and down the steps of the courthouses towering above them. I could have kept us in the lobby to debrief further but I'm already late for our staff meeting.

'Remember—three weeks from tomorrow, meet here, one thirty.'

'Sí,' Sandra says, 'lo sé.' She turns and begins walking toward the subway entrance, Felipe stepping quickly behind her.

The line at Pret is to the door so I get a coffee and falafel from a food cart on Chambers and eat my wrap on the 1 train listening to voicemail: Joseph Musa's wife, Jasmine, saying detention isn't giving him his blood pressure meds. When am I going to visit him? Then the pro bono coordinator from Cleary, Gottlieb, hoping she can refer a Russian Baptist couple they don't have room for in their program, so sorry to have to ask. And one from my older sister, Liz, complaining about the cost of health care for her foster dogs, one of whom is now apparently receiving radiation treatment, and that her almost-four-year-old, Charlie, still doesn't shit on the toilet, but that's obviously not *your* problem, and anyway, why do you never call me?

I get out at Houston Street, across from another federal building with another immigration court, and hurry to the office, where I finish my coffee in the conference room listening to case updates.

Monica has been at detention in New Jersey. A lockdown the night before means she saw only half the people she had scheduled and no intakes. She is unfazed by this, as always, and proceeds without complaint. Three Laotian women from the same job site in the

Bronx have been in the Bergen County ICE facility for thirty-eight days. The department says they're still waiting on records checks. Which is either nonsensical or true. The interpreter got more family cell numbers and will help with documents. Lucas Montes is the Brazilian father of four with the possession conviction in Elmont, which his lawyer pled out with no explanation to him of the immigration consequences. His daughter answered the door when ICE knocked. This morning Lucas told Monica about a fight he was in maybe eight years ago in Tampa that the police broke up, but he doesn't think there was any record of it and doesn't remember signing anything. So one conviction, not two—he might be okay.

Our director, Phoebe, begins to speak, but Monica cuts her off. 'Don't worry,' she says, 'I'll call down to Tampa, I'll make certain there was no charge.'

Phoebe has a cold and is less chipper than her usual self but no less vigilant. And no less put together, her gray hair clasped neatly in a silver barrette that matches her silver bracelets, her delicately wrinkled white skin freshly moisturized. It's the basement of her town house that we work in, converted into an office decades ago, the garden glassed over to create this conference room.

Winston, the basset hound she is forever trying to cheer up, sleeps at her feet. Now that her husband, Jack, is retired, he is available to bring her tea.

Monica runs through a few more cases. Mostly Central Americans, mostly asylum seekers, the work Phoebe founded the place to do back in the '80s. Plus a detainer for petty theft. It's just a gloss, a check-in on a fraction of the fifty-odd clients that she, like the rest of us, is juggling. Carl and I don't have much to add. Monica knows her business. She took the warden at detention the latest John Grisham novel for his birthday. He always tells the guards not to give her any trouble.

'And I'm out next week,' she concludes, flipping through her notes, 'so I need someone to cover an intake, young Albanian guy, sexual-orientation claim.'

After a brief, avoidant silence, Phoebe says brightly, 'Peter? You don't do many of those, would you like to cover?'

'He doesn't do any of them,' Monica says.

'That's not true,' I say.

'Yeah, it is,' she counters as I turn from her stare to give Phoebe a little nod, accepting her request.

Up next is Carl, our crusading cofounder, old enough to have represented Czech dissidents and Russian musicians and organizers fleeing Pinochet—the old Left of the Cold War, a child of Jewish Communists turned conservative intellectuals, all of whose politics he rejected in favor of civil rights.

The pencil he's forgotten is behind his ear, the one he's found is pressed to his legal pad. Today he wears his gray cotton suit, the least worn of his three-suit rotation. He does a bit of everything now, but it's the political claims that still matter most to him. They're the ones he ticks off his list.

Giorgi Abasi, son of the Georgian newspaper editor murdered in his office, interview date set for December; the family has moved out of Tbilisi and he hasn't heard from them in a while but he's still thinking they'll get him a police report, for what it's worth.

Daniil Timirov, the blogger who covered protests at the Russian nickel-mining plant who's living with his cousin in New Jersey; he'll need to show the threats from the oligarch's henchmen had some government nexus, which shouldn't be hard, except it's Judge LaRouche so it probably will be. The oligarch is in New York at the moment, so Daniil is not leaving his cousin's house.

Mourad Gamal is proving to be a real problem. Or is in a lot of trouble. It's difficult to tell which. He's not responding to messages at the moment. The claim is that he has two brothers in a Cairo jail for putting together a strike. But there's only one affidavit and it's meandering. He's skipped an interview prep already. Outlook guarded.

Carl checks off the names as he goes.

Javad Madani is new, an Iranian businessman who entered the U.S. via Italy on a false passport after learning the regime intended to imprison him. He's still trying to get his family out, which is the priority for now, the asylum claim a comparatively easy lift because — Iran.

'A businessman,' Phoebe says. 'Any chance he's covering fees?'

She's an old hand at the grants and the fundraising but is tired of it. She would close the place before declining anyone who can't pay, but it doesn't hurt if they can.

'I gave him the sheet,' says Carl, who couldn't be less interested in the question.

Phoebe is the one with the wealthy friends. Carl regales them twice a year with his courtroom war stories only because Phoebe tells him that he must. Monica and I are better about it. We get the drill, the ways of the little nonprofit, while Carl remains offended. He's lived in the same rent-controlled walk-up on West Twenty-First Street since the '70s. The richer his neighborhood gets, the more derisive of it he becomes.

'Either the man's paying or he isn't,' he says. 'Look at the sheet.'

Phoebe makes a note on a Post-it, then turns to me.

I used to prepare for these meetings. To have a list at the ready of cases it would be useful to get input on. Now it's just pieces of the list in my head. I tell them about Sandra, the denial of the continuance, her hearing in three weeks. About Girvesh and Feba Rijal, the Nepalese couple who've promised me documents. If the claim fails, their daughter might still get juvenile status but they don't want to think about that yet, having to leave her. Joseph Musa, the truck driver from Sierra Leone — I'm due at detention on Friday to see him and four others. Abraham John, the Ivorian with the election-violence claim who got caught up in a DUI. And there is my Sahrawi client, Hassan El Moctor, who needs to know if he can visit his sick mother in Rabat given that he's seeking asylum from Morocco. I pause for a moment, trying to think past this week, but can't.

'That's what I have,' I say.

Phoebe's smile is mildly disappointed but still somehow approving. She wants more. Not names, but texture. Still, I am forgiven for now.

She herself goes last and speaks the longest. She doesn't need us for issue spotting. What she wants is to talk a particular case through. Not the law of it, but who her client is and what she's experienced. After ten years of working for her, I keep thinking that at some point she will no longer want to do it this way, that it'll be easier for her to run through files like the rest of us. Yet still every week she does it.

Her clients are mostly children now. The longer she's done the work, the more this has been so. As if all along she's been moving toward the keenest hardship, the least protected of the insecure, with whom, somehow, despite a caseload as heavy as any of us and the organization to run besides, she's able to slow down. To dwell in the particulars of a given child's circumstance and imagine a way forward. The law being just a piece of it.

It drives Carl mad. He fidgets and scribbles like a child himself—an elderly child gaunt with impatience. Sometimes when he can't stand it, he bursts out: 'Yes, yes, the suffering, the suffering, we get it, but who's the judge, what can you appeal? It's one case, Phoebe, one case.' And like an old married couple they'll bicker quickly and efficiently and she'll return to her narrative as if he'd never spoken.

Today it is the recent life of an eight-year-old girl named Ana Andino. How two years ago, in her village north of San Miguel, she saw her father shot to death on the street in front of her; how she didn't want to leave her grandmother and friends and schoolteacher but her mother said they had to go north; their journey through

Guatemala and Mexico; the border crossing where the men held her mother back but took her into the desert; her detention in McAllen, her detention in Nashville, her transfer to New York. The HHS placement into foster care. The apartment in Washington Heights where a seventy-year-old woman takes care of her and five other children. The van that arrives early in the morning to take them to the shelter in East Harlem where the little ones sit in a roomful of teenagers trying to learn English. And finally the conversations Phoebe has with Ana in the shelter's kitchen, learning about the girl's favorite food and how she prays all the time under her breath. The actual content of those prayers. For her mother in the desert, for her older brothers, for her grandmother to get her diabetes medication.

Carl is beside himself.

Monica, herself once a client of Phoebe's, having come from Nicaragua as a teenager, just drifts off, as she always does when she has to listen to these stories.

'This girl,' Phoebe says, 'she has enormous eyes, almost too large for her head. I get lost in them just hearing her speak. Don't sneer, Carl. It happens to all of us, even you, even if you don't want to admit it. Some clients get under your skin. I'm saying it so it doesn't just pile up inside. That's how we shut down, that's how we become bad lawyers.'

On the top page of his legal pad, Carl has sketched the planet Earth with a large rocket aimed directly at it.

'That's one theory,' he says, 'the other being learn to live with it. But hey, I'm not in charge of the emotional gestalt around here, so far be it from me to comment. I do however have a hearing to be at.' And with that, he stands up to leave.

Back in my office, I open my laptop, click on the client folder, and a blizzard of new messages fill the screen. When I began the job, I replied to the emails of the people I represented the day I received them. But that was a long time ago. Now the task at hand is the task at hand. And this afternoon that's the Rijal application, on which I am behind.

The documentation I have for conditions in Nepal is from an old case and needs updating. Girvesh and a group of other boys were kidnapped by the Maoists when he was eighteen, during the civil war. They were trying to recruit him but also wanted him to be their soccer coach. Neither of these qualifies him for asylum. But when his captors found out he belonged to the Nepal Student Union, they let the others go and kept him, so he's got a political claim. The civil war is over, which doesn't help, but the Maoists are in power, which does.

I read State Department reports, NGO reports, newspaper articles, expert witness testimony scraped from filings in other cases, anything I can vacuum up off the internet before having to email experts myself and begin the process of cajoling and bargaining and scheduling them.

Monica is the only one still there when I take a break around eight o'clock. I ask her if she wants barbecue again, and she says yes, so I order it, and when it arrives I eat mine standing in her office doorway.

'What's this with you being out next week, anyway?' I ask.

'I'm going on vacation.'

'That's funny,' I say.

'No, I'm serious, that's why I'm out next week. I'm going to Vermont. I've decided I want to learn how to ski.'

'You're going *skiing*?'

'Why, you think a brown woman can't be into that?'

'No, I just can't believe you're into it. Did you get a Groupon or something?'

'Fuck you,' she says.

For a moment, I picture Monica in a rental car, on her way

to some ski resort, driving up the hillside past my mother's retreat center, but then I doubt that she will go that far north.

After ten years of working with her, what I know of Monica's life outside the job is that there isn't a great deal of it. She lives in a rent-stabilized apartment in the West Nineties with her mother, whom she brought over from Nicaragua after Phoebe helped her through college and law school. Her father was disappeared by the Somoza regime during the revolution. Once on a winter evening in the car as we were on the way back from detention, she told me, apropos of nothing, that for a long time she'd hated her father for what his idealism had cost their family, but eventually she'd understood. She'd never meant to be an immigration lawyer. It was just a start after law school in the office of the nonprofit that had helped her. What she meant to do was get a corporate job and buy a house in Jersey where her mother could have a garden and grow vegetables. But that was twenty years ago, and here she still is.

'I don't see you taking any vacation,' she says.

Which is true. I don't.

'But at least you'll be here to cover the Albanian,' she says. 'Now that Phoebe forced you to. I take every other Nicaraguan who knocks on the door but you're the gay one and leave all the gays to me and Phoebe.'

'No, I had Afsana Ravani. I took that all the way to appeal.'

'The Baloch woman? It was a political claim. She was incidentally lesbian. You didn't even argue that.'

'Are you giving me this person's phone sheet or not?' I ask.

She looks across the stack of files on the floor beside her desk, finds what she's after, and holds it out to me.

'Here you go,' she says. 'I tried to reschedule but he didn't answer.'

Monica stays till nine, and I leave a few minutes later. Out on King Street, through the parlor windows of Phoebe's town house,

I see her husband, Jack, in the comfortable amber light of the wood-paneled living room, stirring a drink at the sideboard. A tax partner now retired from Davis, Polk. Past chair of the Bar Committee on Professional Ethics. The old epitome of trusted counsel to major concerns. He wears cardigans and collects Art Deco clocks. If Phoebe's fundraising now and then runs short, Jack is always there, proud sponsor of his wife's good works. He has more faith in her than in his itinerant children and their romantic dramas. Finished stirring, he places two glasses on a tray and carries them deeper into the chandeliered parlor.

I get a seat on the train and scroll through news—'Gaddafi's Forces Bomb Misrata,' 'Obama Signs Bill Preventing Government Shutdown,' 'Heroin Distribution Network Raided'—until we reach High Street–Brooklyn Bridge. On the stairs up to Cadman Plaza, I consider calling my sister back but text Cliff instead. By the time I reach my lobby, he's texted to say sure, he'll come by in an hour.

Which gives me a chance to pull a few more quotes for the Nepal synopsis.

He arrives with three beers in a canvas bag and offers me one. White, thirty, Nebraskan, a web designer of some kind. It's been three months now that he's been coming over like this, once or twice a week.

I close my laptop for the day and join him at the other end of the couch.

'How's that deranged schnauzer?' he asks.

The woman in the apartment next to mine, at the end of the hall, is unwell and treats her animal poorly. It whimpers and barks all hours of the day and night. But she's an owner and I'm a renter and the noise isn't as bad for the others on the floor and they are scared of the woman so don't want to get involved.

'I guess it's fine,' I say. 'I haven't noticed it tonight.'

He takes his shoes off and swings his legs up, then touches the balls of his feet to my thigh. 'You look tired,' he says.

'Thanks.'

'I didn't say you looked *bad*,' he says, grinning. 'I like you in a shirt and tie.'

He's found a song, an Elliott Smith ballad, and sets his phone down on his chest, pointing the little speaker in my direction. I close my eyes and rest my hand on his shin. It's wrong to call him inno-cent—he's been in the city a while, getting by—but when he's here he acts it, as if he's a wide-eyed ingénu and I, ten years older, am somehow impressive. I don't know if he has a real boyfriend or not, though I doubt it. In any case, it's not something we've discussed.

'You could tell me things,' he says. 'Like about the work you do.'

'I've told you about my job,' I say.

'No, actually, you haven't.' When I make no reply, he takes another swig of beer and says, 'But it's okay, you can be a mystery.'

He prefers the light on in the bedroom but doesn't object when I turn it off. Once, on a weekend, he slept over. But it's a Tuesday, and when we're done he doesn't ask. He just dresses and checks his phone. By the time I say good night to him at the door, the dog down the hall has begun to bark.

Ann reached for her water glass on the bedside table, Clare still asleep beside her. Coming upright, she took a sip. The solid weight of the clear glass. The mineral taste of the settled water. First gratitude of the day.

Through the window's unshaded panes she looked down into the twilight. Mist shrouded the remnants of snow in the yard. The branches of the old apple tree were still bare. No morning birdsong here in late winter, but in its place the blessing of silence. Inviting her to notice the dark streaks of moisture on the smooth bark of the tree, its trunk coming slowly into focus in the gathering light. And its gnarled branches also, perfectly motionless, perfectly indifferent to human hurry. The second gratitude of the day: to be present to this and not only to herself. How was it that she had ever prayed thanks to God for granting man dominion over the earth? Or what she'd once called praying. Not yet knowing there could be this receptiveness to an already existing prayer. The warmth of the bed, the warmth of her body in it, the warmth of Clare beside her, the coolness of the air on her neck and face and eyes. And none of it belonging to anyone. And so the third gratitude: for life.

She made up her thermos of tea, put on her boots, and set out for the studio in the still-gray light. All was quiet. Down the drive and across the road, fog blanketed the valley. In the other direction, up the slope of the yard, the curtains were pulled over the floor-to-ceiling windows of the center's meetinghouse. And in the little windows of the converted barn where the retreatants slept, no lights yet. For all that was here, she was grateful, too. The intentional community that she and Clare and her old friend Roberta had founded together more than two decades ago now. They had left their previous lives behind to move to this hillside in Vermont not far from the Canadian border. A farmhouse, woods, and a dilapidated barn was all the property had consisted of when they purchased it. Their first guests had simply been their friends. Women who believed in what the three of them were doing: trying to create a place for women to talk amongst themselves about the direction of their lives and their spirits. A ministry of hospitality, they called it. Ann was the only one who had been a minister, but still the notion made sense. Clare was a religion professor, Roberta a therapist, and the three of them had met in fellowship at St. Stephen's Episcopal, Ann's old parish in Massachusetts. Two decades now of gatherings and circles. Of discussions and occasionally arguments about how to run things, how to extend their welcome beyond only white women and those with the means to donate even the center's modest suggestion for room and board. And somehow, chipping in what savings they had, asking here and there for contributions from women with more means, they had done it: fixed up the barn into sleeping quarters, had the meetinghouse built, added a work shed, and welcomed guests from all over the country. Some older, like them, some younger. Some who came once, some who came every year. A community—Viriditas, they'd named it—built up out of friendship.

As she headed up the slope, the only sound in this stillness was her boots crunching against the granulated snow. She reached the meadow and entered onto the path. All around her, the high stalks lay flat. There was no mist up here, just the brightening light of dawn picking out the beads of moisture on the coned tips of the dead grass. In the cluster of Scotch pines at the edge of the woods, the air grew dim again, then brightened once more in the clearing. The studio was a small shingled structure, gable-roofed, with a short metal chimney in the middle and sash windows either side of a narrow, dark green door. A gift from Clare is how Ann thought of it, though it wasn't only that. For years Ann had meditated each morning and evening in their guest room, until seven or eight years ago Clare had taken it upon herself to raise the money and organize the donated labor of the center's friends to put up this little building in the woods. A place for an even deeper quiet. Others used it, of course—Clare or Roberta occasionally, guests quite regularly—but every morning at this hour, and every evening after supper, and now and then for a week at a time, it was Ann's alone.

Once the fire was going in the stove, the chill in the room receded. She knelt and tucked her low bench beneath her thighs, keeping her jacket on, then opened the little wooden box on the table beside her and took out the index card on top of the pile, one of the hundreds she'd written quotations and notes to herself on over the years and added to still. Reminders, really, callbacks to the insights that she spent her days forgetting. *We must be saved from immersion in the sea of lies and passions which is called the world. And we must be saved above all from that abyss of confusion and absurdity which is our own worldly self. The person must be saved from the individual.* Thomas Merton. An old one, clear back to divinity school, faded ink on brittle card. Oh, the self-seriousness of it! The male absolutism. The Catholic disdain for the fallen world of the everyday. And yet the truth in it, too. Persons must be saved from individualism. The capacity for experience rescued from the fear of vulnerability. Merton, her first guide on the long road out of the organized church.

She let the muscles of her throat slacken, and as she did this her head floated slightly back and up, coming to rest with more ease atop her spine. The little discomforts—the ache along the rim of her hip, the tightness between her shoulder blades—never vanished but the need to fix them had diminished over time. She started to sense her breath in her belly, and the gentle repetition of the widening and narrowing of her ribs that went along with it, and the joints of her collarbones as the air reached the top of her torso. And as she noticed all of this, a stream of association set off by the Merton quote floated past her inner eye: the arched entrance of Episcopal Divinity School, walking on Cambridge Common in full sun, the four-story brick building on Garden Street where she'd shared a top-floor apartment full of library books and houseplants, the row of brass mail slots in the lobby where she'd turn the key to find another admiring, even worshipful letter from her then-boyfriend Richard—the man she would soon marry, father of her children.

The ache in her hip asserted itself again, followed by the blistering of a log in the stove; the fact she'd forgotten once more to order wood; that Clare would sigh at her for this oversight. On and on, the ordinary noticing of the unstill mind. We're like movie projectors, one of her meditation teachers had said, loaded with an endless reel of film, and our minds are the bulbs that light the frames. Get some popcorn, take a seat. The movie has no plot. Eventually it will bore you. Then maybe you can begin.

The stream began to slow. Thoughts still occurred but took up no more space than the sunlight visible now on the floorboards or the dust floating in it. Her mind settled. And soon feeling arose, as it often did, given room. This morning it was sadness. A warm, objectless softening that she sensed throughout her body, her body ceasing then to be a collection of isolated complaints, becoming whole. She welcomed this. And right away, too, she wanted to hold on to it, like a dreamer grabbing at the memory of her dream. It was a state that seemed so much truer than her thoughts, deeper and more resonant. A kind of accession to meaning. Not of anything in particular, just meaning as such. And so all the more seductive, all the better at convincing her that there was a plot to her life after all, a heroic journey that had led to this very point. Oh, the feelings you'll have! Tomorrow the feeling would be jealousy, and she would berate herself for it, or joy that she would long to bottle and preserve. But for now the sadness felt good. She kept breathing, and then this feeling too faded into the quiet.

The less her mind held on to feelings or stray thoughts—whether of Clare's irritation with Jeanette, the caretaker, or the family history questions her daughter, Liz, kept asking, or why Peter, her son, had stayed away from this place for so very long—the less her mind possessed. And without possessions, what was there left to narrate? But still the need for narrative remained. The urge in its raw form, stripped of content. To tell a story, any story, if only about the merest scrap of sensation. And yet it turned out that even this habit was no more capable of life without sustenance than any other living thing. Unfed, it too starved, leaving in its absence, if only for a moment, peace.

Monica's intake looks like a kid. A kid brother accompanied by his older sister, her in navy-blue sweatpants and a bright yellow puffy, him in a pale gray windbreaker zipped to the chin. They're smiling at something on her phone in the little reception area at the front of the town house's garden floor, their heads almost touching. His mouth is wide with amazement at whatever she's showing him, but as soon as he spots me, the light in his face goes out. It happens in an instant. The hardening of his expression, as if I've caught him at something.

Vasel Marku, Albanian, twenty-one. Entered two years ago on a false passport; could have sought juvenile status if he'd applied earlier, but he missed that deadline, then applied for asylum without a lawyer. The only evidence he provided was a cursory letter and a dated newspaper clipping about a gay bashing in Tirana, which clearly didn't impress the USCIS officer who interviewed him, denied him, and referred him to court. What's more, he didn't get a lawyer for his first appearance in front of an immigration judge and now he's wasted seven of the nine months he had to prepare for his merits hearing. He has a filing due in eight weeks and a story that needs a ton of work. It's a reach, even for someone as relentlessly efficient as Monica.

I signal for the two of them to follow me into the conference room. They are my last appointment of the day, and the mid-March light coming through the glass ceiling is already beginning to fade.

The young woman — not his sister, it turns out — introduces herself as Artea Dodaj. Says she comes from the same town, no blood relation, she's here to translate. Which suggests she understands how family sponsorship works and wants to make clear she can't help him that way. She's in her late twenties.

'Vasel lives in my apartment,' she says. 'He works at my uncles' market and also downtown for those people who sell the 9/11 things.'

Vasel says nothing. He sits with his arms crossed, impassive.

I give them the rundown on the process, the fraction of people we're able to represent, the caveat that I won't have an answer for them today, et cetera, then explain the posture of the case, namely, that his application left out a whole lot of what he would need to file before his hearing. Then I ask him to tell me what happened, why he left. He's been in the U.S. a while so I assume he understands most of what I've said even if he isn't fluent, but I wait for Artea to translate anyway.

Instead, she leans forward, places both hands flat on the table, and says to me, 'What you need to understand is, where we come from, family is the most important thing. Nothing matters more than this, nothing. Children, they keep living with their parents when they grow up. They have no choice, they can't afford anything else, thirty years old, forty years old. If you don't have a family, you have nothing, you have nowhere to go. That is Vasel. He cannot go back to his family. You want to know why? Because there was a rumor. At his school, they say he kissed another boy — it is a lie. But like they say a girl isn't a virgin — the truth, it doesn't matter. No one will believe her, the thing is done. You understand? And in the north, where we come from, people can kill you for this. The police, it is not their business. Now they try to say that it is, because they want to join the EU, but it's bullshit. In the north, in the villages, they do what they want, no one interferes, no one ever has. A thousand years they have not interfered. It doesn't matter what the EU says. So there's a rumor, and these men, they follow Vasel in a van, they are going to hurt him. Only there is an older woman who comes by and they will not do it in front of her, so they leave him there. That's the only reason he's alive. If he goes back, they will try again. It doesn't matter where, they will find him.'

My phone rings. It's Jasmine Musa, Joseph's wife, probably about his medication again. I send the call to voicemail.

Politely, I tell Artea that I need Vasel's version of events, not hers. She raises an eyebrow at me and sits back in her chair. Her bit was supposed to suffice. I'm about to become another useless bureaucrat in her eyes, someone who doesn't get it.

Reluctantly, she speaks a few sentences to him in their mother tongue, then leans back and waits. Vasel has kept his eyes on me from the moment we sat down, monitoring my reaction to the story being told about him. When he speaks in Albanian—brief, uninflected words delivered without uncrossing his arms—it's with none of Artea's passion. As she translates what he's said, he scans my face more intently still.

'It began at school,' she says, remonstrance in her tone, as if to say, *See, it's just what I told you.* 'Some younger kids, they are trying to make trouble, they want to impress their older brothers, so they tease Vasel in front of them, about him and a friend of his. And that's it, that's all it takes. People talk. You have no idea what it's like,' she says, apparently unable to refrain from unleashing her commentary. 'They're so fucking bored—the kids and the parents too. The parents, they sit in their front rooms talking about everybody's business. People here, they gossip, but it's nothing like this. There it is like religion, like sports, every day. A girl walks two minutes down the street with a boy and that's it. Did they have permission? Will they marry? On and on. So this? Vasel—the talk about him and this boy? It's like the Super Bowl. Like Easter. They go crazy for it. Only they don't tell Vasel's family, certainly they do not tell his father. This is important, you must understand this. That would be a dishonor to his family, and unless they are absolutely sure, they will not say this to his father, because if they are wrong and they have spoken against his son this way, he will have to protect his honor against them, he will have no choice. But everybody else, they hear it, they talk about it.'

When Artea is done, Vasel speaks again, longer this time but in the same blank tone.

'What he's saying,' Artea continues, 'is that at school, after this happened, they treated him like shit. They took his books, they hit him. The teachers, they didn't say anything, they laugh too. And I will shut up in a minute, but let me tell you, what he is saying — it's true. The way the teachers are. You know if I want a good grade, I have to pay them. I am not lying. You bring the money, you get the grade. Okay? That is what we are talking about. So, boys and girls, here is your lesson on how to succeed. Think about that. People say I hate my country. I don't hate it. I just don't lie about it. Anyway. Sometimes Vasel, to get away, he doesn't go to the school, he goes for a walk instead. On the little roads up in the hills. It is very beautiful where we come from, that is true also. He does this for a few weeks. But then those younger kids, they see him there, they know that is where he goes. And afterwards, that is when these men in the van follow him. They take him to the woods, to the stream. And they beat him. They tell him he should pray to God, that they are going to kill him, that he will die. There is a path there along the stream — I know where he means — and the woman is on it, she sees them, and she says to these men, What are you doing? And the men say it is not her business, but she stays there, she doesn't keep going. Then they push him in the stream, and they tell him today he is lucky.'

As I listen to her tell this story — a boy pushed into a stream, a boy beaten—I both hear it and don't. My eyes drift to the far end of the conference room to rest on the houseplants that sit on the low filing drawers. Their leaves have begun to fade. Is this because they need watering, I wonder, or is it a natural part of their life cycle? In which case, why have I never noticed it before, in winters past?

'These men,' I say, 'the ones that attacked you. Who were they? Did you know them?'

Before Artea finishes posing my question, Vasel's expression changes, his impassivity pierced by interest. He's curious about what I've asked, or maybe that I would ask it at all. But then the spark goes out, and his look of indifference returns with all the precision of an actor communicating as much with his face and eyes as with words. For an instant, I have the uncanny sense he and I are onstage together, as I haven't been since high school, the two of us scene partners; he's in character, but I'm not, and so am about to be embarrassed. And then, just as quickly, the impression is gone, and he's an intake again, interpreting my question as doubt. Which isn't wrong. His application, Artea's summary, his own retelling—they track too neatly, the way rehearsed stories often do.

When eventually he answers my question about the men, he speaks only a few words.

'They were from the town,' Artea says.

'So you recognized them?' I say.

'No,' she says without posing the question to him. 'They weren't people he knew.'

'Could you say how old they were? How they were dressed?'

She asks him this and he considers it for a moment, then says something brief. Artea chuckles. 'About your age,' she says. 'Forty-ish. And they dressed badly, like they all do.'

'Okay,' I say, playing along to see if it will get me somewhere. 'What about the older woman? Did you know her? Was she badly dressed too?'

As Artea puts the questions to Vasel, it's clear he doesn't like them. I've misspoken somehow, misunderstood the joke.

'Like the men,' Artea says after he speaks. 'He doesn't know her either.'

'Would you be able to get in touch with this woman if you had to? Would she give you a statement about what she saw?'

They discuss this briefly. 'No,' Artea says when they're done. 'He doesn't know where she lives.'

'That kind of statement would help a lot,' I say.

'He cannot find her,' Artea says.

'Did you report the attack to anyone? To the police?'

'Are you crazy?' Artea says. 'They would do nothing except laugh at him. He would be lucky if that's all they did.'

I tell her again that I need Vasel to answer.

She spits my question at him dismissively and Vasel shakes his head.

'And what about your family? Did you tell anyone in your family?'

'Aren't you listening?' Artea says. 'Didn't you hear anything I said? You expect him to bring that shame to his family? Is that what you would do?'

That I would be a bit drowsy now, at the very end of the day, is hardly unusual, but what comes over me in the face of Artea's interrogation is more than mere sleepiness. It's a fatigue that arrives all at once, strong as a potion.

'Okay,' I say, willing myself to attention. 'So you didn't report what happened. You kept it to yourself. But you'd been beaten up. How did you explain it? What did you tell your parents?'

Artea translates, but her derision for me is open now.

Vasel doesn't answer right away. He considers the question, no longer looking at me but over my shoulder, already glancing at the exit.

Without his eyes on me, I can gaze at him directly for the first time. A narrow face angled down to a slightly dimpled chin. Eyebrows nearly flat. Jet-black hair, short on the sides and longer on top. A bit of product in it to hold the wave of his bangs in place. A Euro kid, we would have called him in high school.

When eventually he answers, it's a single sentence, spoken practically under his breath to Artea.

'He told his parents it was the older brothers at school,' she says. 'That they were the ones who did it.'

The next yawn I can't stifle, but I at least cover my mouth. I'm suddenly wiped. Which is probably why I'm doing this intake wrong, starting with the assault rather than the background material, a beginner's error. By the looks on their faces, the two of them can't wait to get out of here.

'Okay,' I say, shifting gears. 'Your trip to the U.S. The passport—how did you obtain it?'

They discuss this longer than should be necessary. 'He bought it in Tirana,' Artea says finally.

'That would be ten thousand dollars, wouldn't it?' I ask her, no longer bothering to address him.

'I helped him,' Artea says, more defiant than convincing. 'But why does it matter? Gossip, that's the problem, okay? I should know. That's a longer story, I won't tell you that story, it doesn't matter here. But believe me, I should know. It is lies and gossip. And it gets people killed. That's why we came here, because you are supposed to help him.'

By the time I get home and go out for my run that evening, it's already late. I head down the hill to the park being built along the Brooklyn waterfront. The piers are dark squares protruding into the East River. Only the one with the soccer pitches on it is lit, teams running in packs back and forth across the bright turf. At the bottom of Atlantic Avenue, the gates to the beer distributor are all locked up. Columbia Street is quiet. The homeless man who wears ten or more layers in all seasons sits at his encampment at the end of Kane Street, reading a newspaper by streetlight. There's no stench from the poultry slaughterhouse at this hour, just a lowered grate. Around the corner, a minivan backs its food cart into the overnight garage already full of them. The container port is idle, its giant cranes outlined in safety lights against the night haze. Beyond them, pools of lamplight lead down to the trucks backed up to the mouths of the warehouses. Past these is the cruise ship terminal, its vast parking lot empty. The water moves unbothered through the channel. Across it, Governors Island is all darkened trees.

There's no traffic along Conover Street. Kids smoke and pose on a bench in the park by the mouth of the canal. The fencing is covered in vines. Behind a stack of cinder blocks, MTA vans fill the lot where the grass stops and the tail end of Columbia reaches . the water. The wind gusts up off the harbor. A night fisherman stands at the railing alone, the Bee Gees playing from the tinny radio perched on his cooler. He doesn't see me in the dark.

At the gate of the auto pound, I turn to start back. And there, north across the canal, is the old grain elevator, massive and derelict, a structure I've passed by on this same run hundreds of times without much noticing. But tonight, in the murky yellow light of what passes for darkness in the city, that row of huge silos—mottled gray and white—appears to me as a series of giant x-rayed spines, as though the aging structure were being held upright by creatures long dead. And then, out of nowhere, I think of the Albanian kid. What didn't he tell me?

It's only when I reach the door of my building back at the northern tip of Brooklyn Heights that I realize I've forgotten my keys. This seems impossible. I've never forgotten them, not in the ten years I've lived here. Someone exiting the lobby lets me in and I ride the elevator up to my floor, imagining without believing that maybe I somehow decided to leave the apartment unlocked. But of course I didn't. Behind the door at the end of the hall, the schnauzer yaps. Its owner, my neighbor, comes out only at night and only occasionally to buy groceries that she wheels in a cart. The way she treats that animal is cruel, I've heard others on the floor say. I hardly ever see her or the dog. Certainly she has no key to my apartment, nor I to hers.

I go back to the lobby, call a locksmith, and order delivery. When a half hour later neither has arrived and I've sated myself on the news, I scan my list of voicemails and notice my sister's from last week. I'm not sure what it is that inclines me to call her, but I do.

'This is late,' she says when she picks up. 'I should be asleep. I told you Nor-person has one of those breathing machines now, right?'

At some point in the last year, for reasons unclear to me, Liz began referring to Norman, her husband, as Nor-person.

'The sound that thing generates,' she says, 'it reminds me of global warming. Like the air has gotten that bad and Nor-person is filtering it out, which means that I'm not. Does that make sense?'

Little that my sister says makes sense to me. It hasn't since we were teenagers. For a long time, she lived in Seattle, as far away as she could get, working in bars and coffee shops, dating a series of men she went on about ad infinitum, back when we spoke more often—a bike mechanic living in his parents' attic; an aging grunge-band drummer; a tattoo artist who, to our mother's fury, Liz allowed to practice on her—one long antic narration, as if her life were a screwball comedy that sent her into stitches. At some point, she became a tarot card reader, later a Reiki practitioner. Then one day in her early thirties, she announced she was marrying a software engineer named Norman who played in video-game championships and fostered large dogs and that they were moving to Portland, Maine, to be close to his ailing mother. More mysterious still, four years ago, having until that point in her life expressed only animus at the idea of children, she decided to have one of her own. Her latest enthusiasm, and gig, is helping to stage cosplay conventions. Norman, Charlie, and the dog all travel with her. I can't picture this, or the events, or what compels her about any of it, but then we talk less than we used to, and I often find it hard to follow what she tells me. I haven't seen her in a year and a half or more, not since the three of them passed through the city on the way back from one of her gatherings in Philadelphia.

'Anyway,' Liz says, 'what's the occasion? You never return my calls.'

'That's not true,' I tell her.

'You're a terrible liar. You always have been, you know that? You couldn't even lie about your homework. But then I guess you always did it. Anyway, what are we talking about?'

'Your voicemail.'

'Jesus,' she says, 'you sound like Nor-person. So *literal*. I've put him on a personality watch. He's not allowed to bore me. But I can't say anything bad about him right now because he's taken night duty for the little shitter. You wouldn't even believe it. My son shits like a Great Dane. It's weird. It's not even diarrhea, it's just the sheer *volume*. Like a bull in a pasture. Nor-person says it's psychological, as he would, which is whatever. I'm just like, where does it all *come* from?'

'I'm sorry to hear that,' I say.

'Meanwhile, Maisie, our actual dog—the shelter knows we won't be able to stop ourselves, so they push all the sick ones on us—she's got a kidney tumor. What are we supposed to do, let her die? But why am I talking about this? We're going to visit Mom and Clare, that's why I called.'

'Weren't you just there?' I ask.

'Your sense of time's all fucked up,' she says. 'That was

34

Christmas, when normal people—unlike you—visit their families. Anyway, what I wanted to say is you should come with us. You know, spend time with your nephew? Actually see Mom? It's been, like, *years* since you saw her. Which is frankly messed up. So maybe you could make an effort for once? You could help me get more genealogy stuff out of her. I told you I'm mapping the family, right? So the little shitter will understand where he came from. Dad's side is pretty uneventful, all German and Irish laborers in Minnesota—beer and cows. But did you know Mom's great–great–et cetera–grandfather was a captain in the British expedition that took Manhattan from the Dutch?'

'No,' I say, mystified by my sister's interest in the subject. It's entirely unlike her.

'But you remember Dad calling Mom a snob, right?' Liz says. 'That was because of her family—Colonial, Anglican, all buttoned up and snooty. She'd tell him he was being ridiculous, that all that history had nothing to do with her, but I realize it's because she didn't want to talk about it. Her ancestors don't fit her politics. She doesn't want anything to do with them. Which is probably why she doesn't help me when I ask her questions. You're the immigration guy,' she says. 'Aren't you curious how we got here?'

Across the lobby, a white man, a decade or so older than me—gay by the exactitude of his cropped hair and tightly fitted suit—turns his key in a mail slot. I've seen him before a few times, always alone. His mail is junk. He pulls one bill from the stack and tosses the rest into the recycling.

'Hello?' Liz says. 'Are you there?'

'Yeah, I'm here.'

'The point,' Liz says, 'is that you have a whole month. We're not going until the middle of April. I'm giving you notice so you have plenty of time to get your little duckies in a row and you can't invent some lame excuse.'

'Okay,' I say. 'I'll think about it.'

'No, you won't. You never do.'

Through the glass door, I see the delivery guy approach. The locksmith is right behind him.

'I have to go,' I say. 'My dinner is here.'

'You're an odd one.' my sister says. 'You know that, right?'

As kids, we hated the sermons. They were the longest, most boring stretches of those long, boring services. Our mother went on forever. Two lessons, the Gospel reading, then up into the pulpit she climbed, and we were doomed. Always she started by making fun of herself, some little everyday thing that received a smattering of laughter and my sister's whispered derision: She didn't burn the pancakes, she didn't even *make* them.

Then she would say, *In this morning's lessons,* and I'd begin counting the stones in the gray wall behind her, losing my count every time Liz knocked me on the shin to entertain herself. Eventually would come the Christ-is-not-a-stranger-He-is-us bit, signaling what our father called the Guilting of the Liberals. These were the longest passages, about poor people in other countries, or children sick from lack of food, or our government's policies in Central America, the subject we knew irked our father the most because he'd bow his head as he never did when it came time to pray. He hadn't wanted to move his family and his business from Virginia to Longfield, that town west of Boston — a stuck-up place, he called it, but that's where St. Stephen's was, the one Episcopal congregation my mother had found willing to hire a woman to lead it. And so we had come, when we were still in elementary school, and he had rented an office and a warehouse to store all his lighting fixtures and wires, and he'd started his wholesale business all over again, and though it had never done as well, he mostly didn't complain.

When at last our mother intoned from the pulpit the words *And all of us here in this church,* we knew we'd reached the beginning of the end. Her voice would slow and deepen. And then I would actually listen to what she was saying because that slow, deep rhythm matched what I imagined to be the rhythm of her thoughts as she read her books in her study, and I wanted to understand what it was that absorbed her to the point of not hearing our voices in the house.

'This form's blank,' Monica announces, standing over my desk her first day back from vacation. 'What's with that? You didn't meet with the Albanian?'

I'm gazing at a picture of Vermont on her phone that she's handed me: a field of bright snow, a strip of evergreens, above it brilliant blue sky. I hand it back and ask what she's talking about. She holds the form out to me. There's barely a word on it.

'I guess I took my own notes,' I say. 'Anyhow, it's a pass. What was his name?'

'Marku,' she says. 'Why's it a pass?'

'His story,' I say, trying to remember it. 'It didn't add up.'

'Meaning your gaydar didn't go off? Or you actually did an intake?'

'I did an intake.'

'Then fill the form out,' she says. 'And send him the referral list.'

Once Monica's gone, I stare again at the sheet. *It began at school*—those are the only words written on the page. I flip through my own notebook, but there's no record of our conversation there either. I start rummaging through my desk for a legal pad where I might have jotted down something further, but then Jasmine Musa calls to say a bunch of the detainees where her husband is being held are being transferred somewhere, they won't say where, and she's afraid she'll never see him again if he's sent to some other state and then back to Sierra Leone, where the police in Freetown want him dead.

'He's not going anywhere,' I assure her. 'Not while he's got a hearing date in New York.' Which is what I tell Joseph, too, that afternoon when I get out to detention at Bergen, in the little windowless room off the rec area in the men's pod. He's a broad-chested, round-faced man in his thirties whose scalp was shaved clean when I met him but is now rimmed with scraggly hair. His skin has gone sallow since he got in here. Jasmine says he can barely eat the food. The department has no good reason not to parole him out before his hearing—they still might; it just hasn't happened yet. Jasmine has been collecting statements from his mother back in Freetown, his cousin, and a coworker, all confirming he testified before the anti-corruption commission about a tax agent who had demanded a bribe from him and that after testifying he was arrested and detained for two months and came home with a fractured skull and lacerations on his back. She's working on the doctors' records, too, which I keep telling her have to be correctly dated. Before ICE picked him up, he had a job earning decent money at a logistics company in Teaneck, but that's gone now.

We have to start putting together his own affidavit, which is why I'm here. We move through the basics quickly enough but when we get to his appearance before the anti-corruption commission, he talks on and on about one particular commissioner, who it turns out is the brother of the tax agent who demanded the bribe and who Joseph says was trying to discredit the inquiry from the inside by making him look like a liar. The story only gets more convoluted from there—the tax agent co-owns a business with the cop who arrested him—and soon I've lost the thread.

Through the doorless doorframe, out in the rec room, I can see three other men lined up on plastic chairs waiting to talk to me: a client—Kabir Nath, Bangladeshi, twenty-eight, detained after a conviction for petty theft—and two intakes, one older, Balkan or Eastern European, the other a Latino man in his thirties dressed, incongruously for this place, in bright red cotton pants and a canary-yellow t-shirt.

If I am going to speak to any of them what I need from Joseph isn't the internecine politics of Freetown but what government officials did to him in prison. Yet this he doesn't want to discuss.

'I'm not saying the commission doesn't matter,' I say. 'But the story we're telling is about you. How you did the right thing, and they tortured you for it.'

'What they did to me is not torture,' he says, clasping his hands together on the table and resting his weight on his forearms. 'I heard the ones they tortured.'

'The point is,' I say, 'we need to be very specific about what happened at the prison. Don't worry about the definition of it right now.'

'You want to be specific?' he says. 'Okay, then. I wasn't in a prison. They didn't send me there. Because there were no charges.'

'Where were you taken?'

'A room in the building next to the station. In my own neighborhood, near my house. I recognized the dogs that barked. I thought I heard Jasmine, too, because I knew she'd be coming to yell at the policemen, but I couldn't be certain, and of course I hoped it was not her, because if she got in their face—the way she would—they wouldn't hesitate, they would hit her, or worse. And she could never have enough money for a bribe to get me out. So I didn't want her to come. This, if you want to be specific, this is where I was. Not in the prison.'

'Okay,' I say, noting this down on my pad, trying not to repeat my error with Vasel. Though soon my attention wanders again, back to the men waiting for me or, more precisely, to the chairs they are sitting on—beige plastic, chrome-legged chairs I've seen here countless times but only now remind me of the nearly identical ones that filled my high-school cafeteria, the seat and back one rounded mold, their round metal feet fastened to the legs by a single ball bearing that let you lean backward without falling, which was what I used to do, copying Jared, the boy I loved, who I have not thought of in I don't know how long. These are old chairs now, sold off by the local schools, perhaps, only to appear in another public facility. A county jail taking ICE money to house Joseph and Kabir and all the other detainees loitering in cells just beyond this room.

'Are you listening?' Joseph asks.

'Yes,' I say. 'I'm listening.'

It's a guard I know who comes by an hour and a half later to say, 'Time's up.' Like Monica, I try to be cordial to all the staff for whatever advantage it might get me, and when I ask for just five more minutes, he walks off without saying yes or no, giving me time to finish explaining to the fifty-year-old Bosnian-Croat convicted of tax evasion that given the years that have passed since the Balkan wars, it will be hard to show a fear of persecution upon his return and that he's better off arguing his family would suffer extreme hardship if he's sent back but that I'm sorry we won't be able to argue that for him. He curses—at me or his circumstance, it's hard to tell. As the guard leads me out of the rec room into the green-lit corridor, he says, 'That one's a slimeball, went after a kid in the shower,' which is the kind of thing he's said to me before about my clients. He offers it without aggression, less a warning than a chance to register his disgust at the job he finds himself doing before he waves to the control room to let me out.

* * *

It's nine thirty by the time I get back to Brooklyn Heights and text Cliff. He comes anyway, a half hour later, smelling faintly of pot, and flops himself down on the couch to watch me eat my takeout at the dining table.

'What are you doing over there,' he asks with a lazy grin. 'Silverware, a napkin, wine? Are you celebrating something?'

I look down at the napkin—a limp square of faded blue linen. I must have gotten it from the rectory when my mother left her job and cleared things out. Come to think of it, these may be the only napkins I own. Which is itself strange. Why I bothered to use one of them tonight, I don't know.

'Maybe next time you can invite me for dinner,' Cliff says. 'We could talk, even.'

He's lying with his arms stretched behind him, head resting in his interlaced fingers, his t-shirt riding up off the waist of his jeans, leaving a few inches of his belly bare.

As Jared once did.

Does Cliff come here to feel younger? I wonder. Is that what I give him? Wearing a shirt and tie, living in a staid neighborhood. Some version of an adult.

'For example,' he tells me, 'we could cook a meal and set the table. I could say to you, *Hey, honey, how was your day?*'

His tone is half irony, half endearment. As if he wants to say *honey* but knows he can't. As if pretending, just for a moment, that he's spent his day here without me, making a home for us.

My eyes fall again on the bare strip of skin his raised t-shirt has left exposed. I empty my wineglass, cross the room, and get on my knees in front of him.

'And then you say, *Well, sweetie, my day was great, I did all these interesting things that I want to tell you about.*'

'You're baked, aren't you?' I say.

'Only a little,' he says.

He props his head up from his supine position to watch as I unzip his jeans.

'Then I tell you all the interesting things I've done,' he says, 'and even the boring things, and you listen, and we go back and forth like that.'

He wants to watch as I take his dick in my mouth, but I reach my hand up to block his sight, and his head lolls back. And then I can close my own eyes, and I see myself as if from afar, in an earlier life, resting my cheek against another boy's stomach.

When I was little, if the weather was good, I'd go to the end of our street to meet my father on his walk home from work.

As soon as he saw me, he'd lean his head forward and peer in my direction, and when he got to the stop sign where I waited for him, he'd say, 'Are you Peter Fischer? Are you the boy I met at breakfast?'

Then I'd take hold of the corners of his briefcase and he'd tighten his grip on the handle, tugging it back away from me, that hard black shell with the shiny strip of chrome down the middle that held all his papers. We'd tussle over it, his grasp unbreakable until eventually he'd let go and allow me to carry it for him the rest of the way home.

If I asked, he'd describe for me once again the forklift at his warehouse hoisting the big wooden boxes out of the trucks, the boxes full of the little pipes and wires and bulbs his company sold to builders and hardware stores and sometimes shipped to other countries, where he now and then traveled to sell them, all this activity somehow controlled by the papers in his briefcase. Each morning he'd be clean-shaven and each evening he'd have just a hint of the black stubble that on the weekends made his cheeks feel like sandpaper. He wore a suit to work even in the height of summer, came home with his jacket slung over his shoulder, the underarms of his shirt soaked through, his tie loosened and top button undone just below his Adam's apple.

I'd accompany him from the end of the street back to the house, less than a quarter of a mile, four driveways and a short stretch of woods, wishing it would last longer, knowing that once we got home we wouldn't be alone together anymore and that after dinner he'd spread the papers from his case out on the kitchen table and stare at them as intently as our mother stared at her books.

Sometimes as we walked I'd ask him questions about earlier things, about his life before we were born, which I had trouble imagining, and running a hand through my hair, he'd say, 'You don't need to worry about that.'

It was only from our grandmother, on one of our rare visits to St. Paul, that Liz and I learned how after graduating from high school our father had gone to work on a pipeline in the North Woods of Minnesota.

Our grandmother still lived in the house where my father had grown up with his five siblings, at the end of a street by a big chain-link fence covered in vines, which meant you heard the nearby highway but never saw it. The house had a wide front porch and eave windows in the little attic bedrooms where Liz and I slept. She would make us waffles with mushy fruit on top and smoke as she watched us eat them, the wall behind her covered with pictures of her children and grandchildren arranged beneath a black lacquered cross.

'Oh, yes,' she said, 'your father cleared a way right through those woods. Four men to a hut with only a privy and a washbowl between them. That's where he broke his arm. That was the thing, you see, because if he hadn't broken his arm, his life would have turned out very differently. He never would have met your mother, or a woman like her—from the east. You two wouldn't even exist. He was only a kid himself then. He said he'd do that job in the woods just for a summer, but of course he was good at it, worked hard like his own father. They kept paying him more, put him behind the wheel of a bulldozer, and that was it, he thought he was the cat's pajamas. Building the future is what he called it. But there was a bad apple up there, a fellow who gave everyone trouble, and they got into it, he and your father, they fought. A bad fight. And I think they shipped that fellow off somewhere, but your father got that broken arm. That's when he came back here and started doing those classes of his through the mail, for people who wanted to be in business. Right in there,' our grandmother said, pointing with her cigarette to the front room. 'He'd stay up half the night. Didn't talk anymore about going back to the pipeline. Just studied those workbooks. And somewhere along the way he got this idea in his head—I certainly didn't give it to him—about making that trip of his all the way over to Europe. This was '60 or '61. Said he wanted to do it before he tied himself down with a job. He'd saved the money, nothing to spend it on up in the woods, so that was it. He wanted to see the place where his father fought in the war, he said. I thought it was crazy. People didn't go to Europe, not back then, not like they do now. But he never would have met your mother other-wise. All because someone broke his arm. Don't get me wrong,' she said, taking our plates. 'She's an admirable woman, your mother, always has been. It's just one of those accidents of fate.'

Headed to the meetinghouse for that morning's circle, Ann saw Roberta getting out of her car and waited for her in the middle of the yard. Her friend always had a smile for her at the beginning of a day, a gladness upon seeing Ann. This morning it came from beneath one of the red and white wool caps that she knit by the dozen and gave out freely. It didn't matter how well or poorly Roberta had slept or what trouble her arthritis was giving her; whenever they saw each other, her face lit up. And gladness is what Ann felt for Roberta. A thankfulness for her constancy and care. She had been the head of the vestry that had hired Ann at St. Stephen's all those years ago. She had believed in Ann from the time they'd met and kept believing in her right through the troubles of her leaving Richard and being with Clare. And she was the first person Ann had taken into her confidence back then about what she and Clare had begun to discuss—the idea of this community. Right away, Roberta had understood it. And more than that, to Ann's surprise, she'd desired it. All three of them, in moving here, had been required to break with how they'd imagined—up through their forties—the course of their lives, but Roberta perhaps most of all. A straight, more or less happily married woman, a therapist with a full practice in the suburbs of Boston where she'd lived most of her life and where her parents and siblings still lived then. Yet nonetheless, in the span of the two or three years it had taken for their idea to go from a daydream to the purchase of land, she had lovingly communicated to all these people, including the vestry of St. Stephen's, that she planned to leave that life behind. Her marriage, after considerable work, had survived—Gavin had come with her—but what Ann marveled at still was how, even through the uncertain early days of Viriditas when they didn't know if anyone but their friends would actually show up, Roberta had never second-guessed her decision. She missed having family close. She didn't love the long winters. But she believed in the work the three of them did—then and now.

They hugged—no need for words—and proceeded together up the grass still spotted with snow.

Once inside the meetinghouse, Ann turned on the lights, and Roberta fiddled with the electric heaters.

'Remind me who we have this morning?' Ann said.

'Deborah Weber,' Roberta said. 'The hospital chaplain.'

'Right, of course. With the Pittsburgh group.' A white woman in her late fifties, here for the first time. In the discussions thus far, she'd said very little.

'She's the only one of them without a food allergy,' Roberta said, 'thus my fondness for her.'

They took turns helping their guests prepare meals in the barn kitchen, a chore only Clare seemed to derive any pleasure from.

Ann crossed the big open room to the far wall and pulled back the heavy curtains they had hung for extra insulation. Looking through the plate glass, she could see the rear of the property, up to the meadow and over the vegetable patch. There, despite the cold, Jeanette, their caretaker, in her usual jeans and plaid overshirt, was already at work spreading mulch around the rhubarb and asparagus beds. Everyone imagined that Ann and Clare and Roberta, founders of a women's retreat in rural Vermont, must be amazing gardeners, but it couldn't have been further from the truth. Clare had blamed the tomato plants when they failed to thrive the first summer. Roberta had become a decent lay carpenter but gardening she left to her husband. And Ann had simply never done it. Had never had the inclination, much less the time. Without Jeanette, the property would be a field of weeds. A local woman now in her late forties, she had appeared eight or nine years ago, first a drop-in at their Sunday gatherings, then a volunteer helping with the yard, and soon enough a full-time employee with her own room in the barn. Of the three of them, Ann was closest with her, and the most glad for her presence.

'Hello there,' Clare said, coming up beside Ann to give her a kiss on the temple.

'I didn't hear you come in,' Ann said, looking away from Jeanette.

Clare wore a scratchy wool sweater, dark blue with holes at the already darned elbows, and over it her black wool coat. Her breath smelled of coffee.

'Did you sleep all right?'

'Well enough,' Ann said.

'Okay, you two,' Roberta called out. 'I can't move this myself.'

'Sorry,' Ann said, stepping away from Clare to help lift the low table. They set it down in the center of the four chairs arranged in the middle of the room.

They used to spend time preparing for these circles, asking each woman to write in advance a brief statement, which the three of them would discuss the night before, deciding how to approach the conversation. But Ann had come to see this practice as more of an impediment to spontaneity than an aid to depth, and eventually Roberta and Clare agreed. Now they just took things as they came.

The knock on the door was faint but audible. Roberta went to open it and welcomed in Deborah Weber, who apologized for being late, which Clare promptly told her she wasn't. After leading her to the assembled chairs, Roberta indicated for her to sit. Sunlight streaming through the plate glass lit the loose strands of the woman's graying blond hair, creating a faint halo about her head.

A calm spirit, Ann thought, at least outwardly so, but tired.

Deborah smiled at them with watery eyes.

'Thank you for coming,' Ann said. 'We're glad to have you here. We'll begin with a period of silence.'

Deborah nodded and the four of them went quiet.

Early on, they had worried over the length of this opening moment, using a clock on the wall (which was all wrong and came down quickly), then a little timer one of them would keep, as if the ritual they'd invented required rules to legitimize it. But none of them experienced any such bother this morning. It was simply a matter of when the room and the people in it had settled. Once that happened, one of them would speak, and the circle would begin.

The vision object Deborah had brought to share was a rock, a clean beige oval with a pale blue core, the granite perfectly divided from the sandstone surrounding it, as if placed there by an artist. She set it down on the coffee table, beside Roberta's multicolored beads and Clare's copper amulet and Ann's silver, flat-topped ring, which she'd had made for herself sometime after Richard's death.

Deborah began by speaking about her job. Most people did. The concrete thing. She had gone to seminary imagining herself becoming a parish priest working with a congregation and eventually leading one. But her chaplaincy internship had changed that. She'd thought she would find the hospital depressing and want to be done with it as quickly as possible, but then she'd started tending to the dying, and the depth of the work had stunned her. Everything else fell away—the doctors and machines and grief-stricken relatives—and she felt as if she were at work in a field of almost pure spirit, overcome with thankfulness for the intimacy with which the dying entrusted her.

There was no need for Ann or the others to smile in acknowledgment or even nod in understanding at what Deborah was saying. They were already offering their full attention. *We are grounded in the decades-long friendship of our three founders,* the center's website said. *This friendship is what we offer to our guests as a source of guidance and renewal.* Which was true. Their strength was intimacy. And trust. Because they could be present to one another, in difficulty as well as in ease, they could as a group be present to others. Most all the women who came to the center felt this. They intuited it, especially in the circles. And so the social niceties could fall away, and along with them the surface insecurities. The three of them didn't need to signal to Deborah that they were listening. She knew.

She'd stayed at the hospital and taken a job as the assistant chaplain, she said. A decade had passed, and then most of another, and for years already she had been the head chaplain herself. What had begun as a revelation became, inevitably, a routine. Her kids were teenagers now. They respected what she did but didn't much want to hear about the sick and the dying. And though she had denied it throughout her divorce, she understood now that her work had gotten in the way of her marriage. Her husband, even if he couldn't bring himself to say it—and this she still blamed him for—could never feel as important as the people whose final hours were her daily concern. At the beginning, the hospital had been a nonprofit but then was sold. There were assistants to train, and now cost cuts to fight, insufficient hospice care, needless suffering. She felt less present to others. Increasingly, she couldn't rid herself of the conviction that in the most important aspect of her job, she failed people precisely when they needed her most.

It was in these moments, after a person finished her first unburdening of why she had sought out the center and the circle, that the urge to soothe came most strongly to Ann. To minister and to mother. She knew well, after all, how it was to be married to a man who felt slighted by his wife's work. But to speak immediately would be to glide over the heaviness in the room. In this case the passage of time and the aging of a vocation. Nothing the three of them could say would reverse these. And nothing said without acknowledging that fact would be worth the breath of its utterance. People barely had room to grieve the loss of others, let alone pieces of themselves. And yet, unmourned, such fragments were bound to haunt. Clare and Roberta would put it differently, but they agreed. The urge to solve people's problems was one of the greatest obstacles in their work. Which was what made allowing for silence in these particular moments so important.

Clare spoke first, as she usually did. It was her way, having been a professor and later a dean. A certain kind of authority came readily to her. Mostly this was just a fact, not a problem. A habit acknowledged between the three of them, to be discussed when it impeded things but otherwise cherished. And mostly Ann loved her for it. She had from the beginning. This bold woman, who'd nonetheless come to Ann for solace.

'You're describing a kind of contact,' Clare said, 'a communion, which clearly means a lot to you. But the institution gets in the way, it's suffocating. The space to do the work is shrinking, it's already shrunk. Maybe it's been that way for a long time. I don't need to tell you all this. But this is how we start, letting you know what we're hearing from you. It sounds like there was at least a partial container before, but now you're supposed to be the container as well. Which is pretty much impossible — for one person to hold the outside space and the inside. So you've been assigned an increasingly impossible thing but you do it anyway, which is not uncommon. We're given these unattainable assignments and we make them ours. And then we blame ourselves when things break down.'

Roberta waited to be certain Clare was through before leaning forward slightly in her chair. 'The number of years you've been doing this,' she said, 'even before all the changes you're describing—that's a lot of death. You have patients who get better, there's that, too, of course. But still, over time, it's a lot of death. Where does the weight of that go? How does it move through you? Can it move through you? I'm not asking for an answer. We all know the pastoral advice. It's just that listening to your voice, this is what I find myself wondering.'

Ann watched to see if Deborah would follow the natural inclination to respond right away, to do her own comforting of Roberta and Clare by telling them they were right, that they understood, that yes, this was exactly it. But she didn't. Mostly, Ann imagined, because she was herself so practiced a listener that she too had learned to resist the first anxious urge to reassure, which hid more than it helped. But also, she thought, because Deborah had quickly picked up on the rhythm of the energy in the room, the rhythm the three of them brought to the circle. They made silence okay. Deborah recognized this. And she seemed glad for it.

From across the low table, Ann sensed Clare wanting her to speak. It was her turn, except they didn't really have turns anymore, they spoke when moved to. But Clare had her expectations, she always had, her strong view of how things should go. They'd struggled with this over the years, the three of them, but also the two of them, very much so, because there could be a violence to how Clare spoke about what needed to be done in any situation, a force of presumption that bordered on dismissal, and which she acknowledged was at odds with the mutual discernment and group process to which they had committed themselves from the beginning. That being the foundational commitment: to not replicate amongst themselves the structures of power they had created this place to be free of. So even when a want of Clare's might be nothing more than that, there was an added step for Ann of noticing whether she felt pushed by her partner, commanded even.

'She'll never have your skills of spirit,' Roberta had said to Ann once. 'No matter how hard she tries, and that will always make part of her jealous. But you know that already—you just wish you didn't.'

'I think I'm still just listening,' Ann said now, her eye catching again on the nimbus of light glowing around Deborah's head that gave her the appearance of an angel in middle age. 'But I am curious about something. You were doing chaplaincy before you had children. And you've done it ever since. Did the work change for you after they were born?'

Deborah smiled, meekly but with apparent pleasure. 'Do you know,' she said, 'that's something I've been thinking about. Probably because they're almost grown, and they'll be gone soon. I must have thought of it when they were little, how it was affecting us, but there was always something else to be done, other people to care for. I guess I mostly just carried on. My husband wanted me to stop, or at least take a year off. After each baby he thought I wouldn't want to go back. But I'd been made head chaplain, and I got to arrange things the way I thought they should be. So I wanted to stay, I did. But I've been thinking about it for a while, because there's something to what you say: Every day, people at the very end of their lives, dying people, and then suddenly there were these little creatures, ravenous for life, taking everything I could give, with no pasts, no regrets, no thanks. Like beings from some other universe. Maybe I should have taken time off. Maybe my brain just couldn't live in both places at once. Am I going on too long here? I can stop, if there's an order I should follow, in what I'm telling you.'

'No,' Clare said, 'you keep right on going.'

'Thank you,' Deborah said. 'I'm always the one leading groups myself, so I'm out of practice, speaking like this.'

'Which is why people come here,' Roberta said.

Deborah smiled again, less meekly this time. 'I used to be so much more reflective about these things,' she said, turning inward. 'It's amazing how much I've forgotten.

'Did the job change after the kids?' she went on. 'I guess the answer is I don't know. The hospital hadn't been sold yet, and those were good years generally. Was it different at the bedside? I don't know why I say this now—I don't have a particular memory—but I do have a sense that I was more confident, for a while at least. Maybe after the children, the hard parts of the job didn't throw me off the way they did before, like I was protected from them by what I went home to. But I might be making that up. Because I was tired all the time, obviously.'

She's arrived now, Ann thought. She's here. It didn't always happen. Some people remained on their own surface, enumerating frustrations. Others, for good reason, found the space hard to trust—three older white women with their first-wave feminist vibe, their church roots and women's lib. Some of the younger women who came, some of the women of color, they were skeptical, as they were right to be, and the three of them had to try harder to discern what kind of welcome would let these women drop into themselves. That was the work. To let a person *be* in their presence, so that she didn't just describe her uncertainties but experienced them. It was then that the befriending could begin.

Roberta and Clare clearly sensed the moment, too, which was why they said nothing to fill Deborah's pause.

'We talk a lot about the bad deaths,' Deborah said. 'Bitter people. Aggrieved people. The lonely, though that's different—they're often the kindest. Sure, at the beginning those deaths were difficult. Because you're right there, and often you're the last one, so they want to wrestle you to the ground, wrestle your faith to the ground, however ecumenical it might be. They're trying to win some old fight, prosecute some grievance, but the people they need to hear it aren't there. You are. Which can enrage them, just the fact that you're willing to stay. And I was willing,' she said, looking down at the four objects arrayed on the table. 'I always was. My supervisors would joke about it. Send Deborah!

'I was glad for the peaceful ones, obviously. The ones who

wanted me to sing to them. They're the people who are taking care of *you*, showing you how to let go. Of all your ideas. You can't do it for long if you don't experience some of that grace. But with the hard ones, the bitter ones, I found that once you strip yourself away, until part of you isn't even there—the ego part—and you're just a funnel that can take it all in, then it's like the invisible world becomes visible, like all the suffering we don't want to touch—at the end it flares up in these bright colors because it's being forced out of them. It's losing its host, losing the body. No one wants to be bitter. It's a kind of exorcism, I suppose, or the attempt at one, not because of anything I do, but you're a witness to it. And it changes you.'

'How?' Ann said, after a moment.

Deborah considered the question. She took a clip from the pocket of her cardigan and gathered her hair up at the back of her head and fastened it loosely, leaving a few strands still hanging behind her ears in the light. There seemed nothing timid about her any longer.

'This will sound weird,' she said, 'but I think it made me believe too much. The hard ones wore other people down, but they fed me. It was like I was a warrior, fearless, and I am, part of me still is. I do the bureaucracy because I have to, but it's like Clare said, I want the communion. And I know it's real. So, yeah, it's true, other things feel less important—that's one way it changes you. And I guess my husband became one of those things.'

She pursed her lips and shook her head very slightly back and forth as if saying no to some question she'd posed to herself. Then a smile flashed up, an apology of some kind, and just as quickly disappeared.

'Did I do the same thing to my kids?' she said. 'Make them feel less important? Probably, and I can't undo that. I go to work, and put out fires, and feel like I'm always too late now with the patients. I haven't spent enough time with them before the end, always trying to catch up, which is its own kind of sin, not to have paid enough attention. So the thing that made everything else make sense, it's not gone, but—I don't know. I just don't know.'

Ann could feel Clare's urge to jump immediately in but also her restraint of the urge. There was practically nothing at this point that the two of them, or really the three of them, didn't intuit or love or at least tolerate in one another. Resting on Clare's chest was the necklace she wore every day, and hanging from it the pendant that bore a little silver version of the symbol they had adopted years ago as the guiding image of the center, an oak tree with its deep system of roots visible. Clare was the one who had suggested it. As well as the name for the center, Viriditas, meaning greenery and lushness and the spiritual force of renewal intrinsic to all living things, a word central to the thinking of Hildegard von Bingen. Without Clare none of them would be here. She had been the one to take Ann's idea of a ministry of hospitality for women and galvanize the three of them into the belief that it could actually come to pass, that they could leave their jobs and homes and make this intentional community real. Whenever Ann felt tempted to call Clare out for decisions she'd made without discussion or the preemptory way she sometimes spoke to Jeanette or some of the other local women who occasionally helped out, she did her best to remind herself of this. A small price to pay for this whole life she wouldn't otherwise have.

'There's this myth,' Clare said after a judicious pause, 'that we're endlessly elastic. It's propaganda. Capitalist, patriarchal propaganda. Stay positive! Work hard! Find that extra little efficiency that lets you do more and more in less time. What if you don't want to do more things? What if it's inhuman? But that's the myth. That doing one thing doesn't mean not doing another. Because if you try hard enough, anything is possible and we're never going to die, so there's always time. But there isn't. That's what your work's all about—finitude. Facing it, being right there in the very teeth of it. Such a powerful acknowledgment. So brave of you to live in its presence every day. But that doesn't dispense with the myth. You walk out into that hospital hallway and there it is all around you. And when you get home, oh, boy, it's there. Husbands, children. It's in their eyes, their mouths. Sure, you work, sure, you're great at your job, but you're a *wife*, you're a *mother*. You can add things on top of that—of course we're all modern—but you can't subtract from it, can you? That would make you a bad person. Even if it's what allows you to be a person at all.'

Roberta didn't have to glance at Ann for Ann to read the thought on her face: Deborah had gotten somewhere particular, somewhere subtle, in what she'd shared with them, in her not-knowing. But then—Clare's speech. And with it, they were back to generalizations, to ideology. To which Clare would have said, *Stop being an intimist, there are no unconditioned subtleties.* Roberta the therapist, Clare the professor. Over the years, Ann had done her best to surrender the role of mediator between them, but there remained the instinct to marry their visions and thus dissolve their conflict. Which wasn't wrong in principle. It was the slogan of their youth: The personal is political. And yet, in this instance, Ann understood exactly what Roberta was thinking of Clare and didn't disagree: *You misread the moment.*

'This stone you brought,' Ann said, 'I'm wondering what its meaning is for you.' She was skipping ahead, to where they might end up, but it felt right, to get them back to where Deborah was.

'Oh, it's silly,' Deborah said. 'I read what you wrote about bringing a significant object, but when I looked around my house there were only photographs, and I couldn't think of anything else. I saw this on my bureau, I remembered the trip I got it on, so I threw it in my bag. I'm sorry, I should have given it more thought. I ask families for this kind of thing all the time, what they could bring in to comfort their loved one. My kids wouldn't know what it is for me, and I guess I don't either. Is that sad? I suppose maybe that's sad.'

'You mentioned a trip,' Roberta said. 'What kind of trip was it?'

'Just a conference,' Deborah said, 'in Houston. It was actually kind of dreadful. I hadn't paid attention to what it was about. It turned out there were all these administrators there, and one afternoon I just decided to blow it off. I drove down to the coast and walked for a few hours. It's just a stone I picked up there. It's pathetic!' she said, laughing. 'Some middle-aged lady wandering a beach collecting stones. How clichéd can you get? But there it is, that's my meaningful object.'

'That's pretty harsh,' Roberta said. 'It sounds to me like you were giving yourself a break.'

'I agree,' Clare said.

'So why don't you indulge us,' Roberta went on. 'Go with the cliché. You're on the beach, there are lots of stones. Why this one?'

'I just have to say,' Deborah said, 'this is a very weird experience for me. It's good, I mean I'm glad I'm here, I'm glad we're doing this, but I keep having this double take, like you're three chaplains and I'm the patient and—I'm sorry, I don't mean any offense by this, but I'm thinking, Is this what I do? Is this how I sound? And then I'm thinking, Have I ever helped anyone? I mean, actually. Or have I just convinced myself I did? That sounds terrible, I know, like I'm saying you're not helpful, but in fact I think you are, it's just—the whole thing's very strange.'

'Yes,' Ann said. 'To follow your analogy, it's almost as if you are the one who is dying.'

When the room went quiet this time, it was different than the previous pauses. Deeper and more sudden. And in this tenser quiet, it occurred to Ann, as it had more and more of late, that somewhere along the way she'd stopped observing the barrier between thought and speech. She should have held on to this thought and better considered the placement of her words, as she often imagined Clare should. But after most of a lifetime of viewing careful consideration as an ethical necessity, she no longer believed in it. Besides, the concern wasn't even accurate. There was no thought to hold back because no thought had existed before she spoke.

Meditation had done this for her, effacing her self-consciousness, leaving less of her to get in the way of perception. Deborah Weber's spirit was dying, incrementally. Knowingly or not, Deborah sensed this and was afraid. Which was why she'd come here. The three of them could listen to her as generously as it was their habit to do, but if they didn't bring the reason for her journey into this room and befriend it, she would leave unseen.

At first, Deborah went very still, and there was a flash of defiance in her eyes. But it melted quickly, and after a moment she uncrossed her legs and leaned farther back in her chair, as if she herself were melting.

'But I'm not dying,' she said, more to herself than to them. 'Not the way my patients are.'

'Exactly,' Ann said. 'And that makes their suffering more important, doesn't it? More important than you.'

For a few moments, Deborah ignored the tears that had begun to leak from her eyes, but when she was unable to any longer, she took a tissue from her pocket and swiped it across her cheeks. Then she wadded the tissue in her palm and closed her hand into a fist. 'I'm such an idiot,' she said. 'It's so basic.'

'What is?' Roberta asked.

'To hide in other people's pain,' she said.

'That's not basic,' Clare said. 'For women, it's practically mandatory.'

To this, Roberta nodded.

'Send Deborah—isn't that what your supervisors joked?' Ann said. 'It's hard for any of us to see what's going on when we're in the middle of it. And you aren't only hiding. You know that, we know that. Just in speaking to you now, I sense the spirit you give the people you care for. And the fear about your children, and your husband before them. All of us hear what you're saying, believe me. But you have to matter, too. If you don't, there's only sainthood or misery.

My mother read all the time when we were kids. In her study in her office at the church, at the breakfast table, on the couch in the living room after supper, sometimes even while walking. Her books weren't trivial, like television. We understood that. They contained important things. The divine, for one. That's what I thought the invisible world was—the world that lived in books. Each time she used the word *faith* in a sermon, I knew she meant faith in books, and I knew hers was strong because she read so many of them. They had small print and no pictures and when you opened one, it would part to a page with whole paragraphs that she'd underlined in blue ink.

'The world would stop,' my father said, 'if everyone read as much as your mother does.'

Her books were like another member of the family, with their own room and share of her attention and power to cause arguments between the two of them.

'Your father's being a Philistine,' she said before I understood the word and knew only that it meant he was being stupid and somehow male.

'Mom thinks men are the devil,' Liz told me. 'Except Jesus. And maybe you, but you're not a man, you're a boy.'

'What about Dad?' I asked.

'Don't be stupid, of course he's the devil,' she said. 'He voted for Reagan.'

She was only half kidding. She pretended to hate both our parents, but our father in particular, because he teased her about her grades and her piercings and her choice of friends, as though she were less his daughter than a kind of daily entertainment. He did this because it was another way to needle our mother, who found his lack of worry over my sister's troubles at school infuriating. What is it? he'd say to her at the dinner table, with Liz right there. Are you worried she's not going to make it to divinity school?

But whenever they fought, it would always come back to politics. Our mother was outraged that he could support a president who funded death squads in Central America. He told her he was trying to keep sixteen people employed, himself included, and endless rules and taxes didn't help. She said that had nothing to do with death squads.

'Except,' he answered, 'that you care more about the fate of socialists half a hemisphere away than your husband's livelihood, but I guess that's your job, to care more about strangers.'

It was the only time I saw either of them lay a hand on the other. My mother slapped him, once, hard.

And then he looked at her with a grisly smile and said, 'Watch now, children, I am going to turn the other cheek.'

To stay out of the drizzle, I wait for Sandra Moya just inside the security tent at Federal Plaza. I should have told her 1:15, not 1:30, as the line's long, and they are running late. Eventually, I see her and Felipe crossing Worth Street, Felipe holding an umbrella above the two them. Sandra wears a long black raincoat belted at the waist. After spotting me, Felipe speeds up, then realizes his mother is no longer beside him and reaches the umbrella back to cover her. They walk another few yards up onto the plaza, until Felipe's impatience yanks him forward again and he's once more left her in the rain. Sandra notices neither her son's movements nor the weather, it seems, her pace unchanging.

When they reach the entrance of the tent she looks up and says, 'Mr. Peter,' as if surprised, though not much, to find me here.

She's had her hair done, but the rain has tamped it down, and along the side of her face, her mascara has begun to streak. She's younger than I am but appears old enough to be her children's grandmother. Mia must be in school, but Felipe would never let her come here alone.

Once we are through security and up the elevators, we huddle outside Judge Ericson's courtroom. Judge Manetti has been out sick for two weeks, which is why Sandra got moved onto Ericson's docket. He's a long way from the easiest judge in the building. Certainly harder than Manetti. Ornery and impatient, an old-school white guy nearing retirement. Not the best draw for Sandra, but unpredictable. He grants on cases I think he'll deny, and now and then denies a slam dunk. None of which would have been helpful to share with Sandra. I simply called Felipe to ask him to inform his mother about the switch. He had lots of questions; she didn't seem to care.

Rather than getting into any of this, I use the few minutes we have to remind Sandra that she's well prepared for this hearing, that she has worked hard at it. She understands but Felipe translates anyway, and his mother nods.

I've never seen her in a dress before. She's always worn tight jeans and flowing shirts to our office, clothing that made her appear almost carefree. The dress is navy blue and goes down past the knee, and over it she wears a navy blazer. She's followed my advice, dressing as the version of herself a judge is most likely to trust.

Hugo, the interpreter, is on time. Once we're in the courtroom, he joins us at the respondent's table, sitting on the far side of Sandra. Felipe is in the front row of the empty gallery.

It's Sievers for DHS. White, early thirties, clean-cut in a young Republican sort of way. He nods hello to me and smiles at Felipe, all jocular, just like Callahan. We stand for Judge Ericson, who welcomes us.

'Peter Fischer for the respondent, Your Honor,' I say.

'Alex Sievers for the Department of Homeland Security.'

Judge Ericson can't get the audio recorder to work. He fiddles with the software, speaks into the mic, tries to play it back. Sievers is doing what is likely his only prep for the hearing, leafing through the three hundred pages I filed.

'Well,' Ericson says after another minute, 'just speak loudly and we'll see how it goes. For the record, I have familiarized myself with the filings in this case and am ready to proceed.'

I turn to face Sandra and, to let her get settled, begin with the easy stuff, first asking her to describe Potrerillos, her hometown in Honduras. The store her father kept in their house on the square. What they sold. Who the customers were. The men who came to drink beer and play pool in the front room. Question, translation, answer, translation, next question. Step by step through her affidavit. The school she attended, how she worked in the store after school, the date she graduated, which she nails just as it is in her statement. Sievers follows along on the page at the table across from us, scanning for the tiniest inconsistency. I move onto the arrival of the mara. How the shopkeepers had to pay the gang members, first whenever they happened to appear, then, later, every week.

'And did your father pay them?' I ask.

'No,' Sandra says. 'Le rogábamos, para que se protegiera, porque todo el que tenía tienda pagaba, pero mi padre siempre decía que no. Él dijo: Si les dejo hacer esto, estoy muerto antes de que disparen.'

'We pleaded with him,' Hugo says, 'so that he would protect himself, because everyone with a store paid, but my father always said no. He said, If I let them do this, I am dead before they shoot.'

'So your family was known, in the town and to the mara,' I say, 'as a family that was not paying la renta?'

'Sí.'

'And what did they do to people who didn't pay?'

'Los mataron.'

'They killed them,' Hugo says.

'And did the mara kill your father?'

'No, no era así con él,' she says.

'No,' Hugo says, 'it wasn't like that with him.'

'Why not?' I ask.

In our sessions in the conference room, Sandra would get this far willingly, and then her mind would drift and she'd look away, up through the glass ceiling, and I'd have to repeat my question, sometimes twice, before she swam back to the present.

'Why didn't they kill him?' I ask.

'Mi padre les daba de comer cuando llegaban a la tienda,' she says, to the judge, not to me, just as I told her. 'Eran adolescentes, entonces tenían hambre, porque incluso en la mara, los más jóvenes, no tienen tanta comida. Y mi padre les daría cerveza. Comían, bebían y jugaban al billar. No se inclinó ante ellos, pero los trató como clientes. Sólo que no tenían que pagar. Así fue como fue.'

'My father fed them when they came to the store,' Hugo says. 'They were teenagers, so they were hungry, because even in the mara, the younger ones don't have so much food. And my father would give them beer. They would eat and drink and play pool. He didn't bow down to them, but he treated them like customers. Only they didn't have to pay. This was how it went.'

'And so your father,' I say, 'how did he die?'

'Su corazón,' she says, 'his heart. Él tuvo un ataque al corazón.'

'He had a heart attack,' Hugo says.

'And after your father was gone, did the young men come back to the store?'

'Leading question, Your Honor,' Sievers says for no other reason than to break our rhythm.

'If he's leading her,' Ericson says, 'he's not leading her very fast. Proceed, Mr. Fischer.'

'After your father died, what happened then?'

Sandra gazes down at her hands but then remembers what I told her in our prep sessions and lifts her eyes again to the judge.

'Volvieron los jóvenes,' she says, 'pero con ellos venían los mayores, algunos con máscaras. Dijeron que les debíamos lo que nuestro padre no había pagado, entonces se llevaron todo lo que teníamos en la tienda, toda la comida y las otras cosas que vendíamos, se las metieron en su camioneta. Vaciaron nuestros almacenes. No quedaba nada.'

'The young men came back,' Hugo says. 'But the older ones came with them, some of them in masks. They said we owed them for what our father hadn't paid, so they took everything we had in the store, all of the food and the other things that we sold, and they put it into their truck. They emptied our storerooms. There was nothing left.'

'And while these men were in your house doing this,' I say, 'where were you and your brother?'

At this, Sandra's gaze slides away again, coming to rest on the flag hung on the freestanding pole beside the judge's dais. I lean forward, trying to get her attention, to track her back in with my eyes. She looks at me as if to say, *Do I have to?* All I can do is wait. I cannot coach.

'Ma'am,' Ericson says, 'you need to answer the question.'

Sandra nods, then speaks her reply in a monotone. 'Estábamos abajo junto a la mesa de billar. El de la cabeza, le dicen el Fantasma, tenía un cuchillo, un cuchillo grande, lo puso en el cuello de mi hermano. Se cortó un poco el cuello, se podía ver que había un poco de sangre, para mostrarnos lo que haría. Hicieron esto. Lo habíamos visto una vez. Un cuerpo sin cabeza, al borde del camino. Uno de los más pequeños, uno de los que alimentaba mi padre, también tenía un cuchillo, lo sostenía contra mi vientre.'

'We were downstairs by the pool table,' Hugo says. 'The head man is called the Ghost, he had a big knife, and he put it to my brother's neck, cutting it a little—there was a small amount of blood—to show what he would do. We knew they did this. We saw once a body with no head. One of the younger men, who my father used to feed, had a knife too, and he held it to my belly.'

'Se reían porque estaba embarazada. El Fantasma hizo que mi hermano dijera que era su hijo. Todos se rieron cuando dijo esto, y el Fantasma dijo que si eso era cierto, ambos iríamos al infierno. Pensé que iba a matar a mi hermano. Pero no lo hizo. Lo tiró al suelo y lo pateó.'

'They were laughing because I was pregnant,' Hugo says. 'The Ghost made my brother say that it was his child. They laughed, and the Ghost said if this was true, we were going to hell. I thought he was going to kill my brother. But he didn't. He pushed him onto the ground and he kicked him.'

'How long were these men in your house?' I ask.

'Media hora, tal vez, tuvieron que sacar las cajas.'

'Half an hour, maybe,' Hugo says. 'They had to carry the boxes out.'

'How many men were there?'

'Seis tal vez siete,' she tells Hugo.

'Six, maybe seven,' he says.

Sievers marks his copy of the file. Her statement says nine. I could try to cure it, get her to tell me how many were in the front room, how many were loading the truck, and I might get her back to nine, but it would take time; Sievers would object, Ericson would get impatient. So I move on.

I have her recount how, four days later, she went to the police station with her brother Ernesto to report what had happened because she decided that this was what her father would have done. If a thief comes to your house, you tell the police. And besides, they had nothing left to sell. She describes how the police said maybe people from her own family had robbed the store because they had heard her father was greedy, and when she told them that this wasn't true, they said they were very busy and that it was best to do things without the government. Maybe her brother, if he didn't have one, should get a gun.

'Which is why, Your Honor, there is no police report in our filing—about the robbery or any of these events. The authorities' refusal to protect the respondent was explicit and repeated.'

'No report,' Sievers says to no one in particular. 'How convenient.'

'Carry on,' Ericson says.

'Can you tell us what happened next?' I ask Sandra.

She can no longer manage to look at the judge. Instead, she glances behind her at her son, as if he might somehow absolve her of the need to answer. Felipe sits on his hands on the gallery bench, biting his lower lip.

Sandra turns back, wiping at her eyes with the tips of her fingers. When she begins, her voice is quiet. Hugo knows she'll go longer here than before, so he scribbles notes.

'Yo fui el que lo reportó. Mi hermano no quería. Pero él vino conmigo, para protegerme. Nos vieron ir a la comisaría. No los vimos, pero sabían, tienen ojos. Al día siguiente mi hermano desapareció. Sabía dónde ir a preguntar por él, dónde pasaban el rato en sus camionetas. Pero dijeron que no sabían de lo que estaba hablando. Dijeron que era una chica loca y que debería irme a casa. Uno de ellos llevaba la gorra de béisbol de mi hermano. Pero me dijeron que me vaya a casa, que no nos moleste. Mi primo lo vio primero. Lo habían puesto atrás, en el callejón. No podías ver su rostro. Su cara ya no estaba allí. Le habían cortado la lengua. No tenía ropa puesta, estaba desnudo. Todo esto fue mi culpa. Solo vino conmigo porque estaba preocupado por mí. Pero él es asesinado, y yo estoy aquí.'

By the time Hugo speaks, Sandra's fingers no longer hold back her tears.

'I was the one who went to the police,' he says. 'My brother didn't want to, he only came to protect me. The mara saw us going to the police station. We didn't see them, but they knew. The next day my brother went missing. I knew where to find those men, where they hung out in their trucks. But they said they didn't know what I was talking about. I was a crazy girl and I should go home. One of the men was wearing my brother's baseball cap. But they told me, Go home, don't bother us. My cousin is the person who saw Ernesto first. He was in the alley at the back of the house. You couldn't see his face, his face was not there anymore. They had cut out his tongue. He had no clothes on, he was naked. This was my fault. He only came with me to the police because he was worried about me. But he is murdered, and I am here.'

I let Hugo's words settle for a beat.

'If you are returned to Honduras,' I ask Sandra, 'do you have reason to fear you will be persecuted or killed?'

'Sí, porque denuncié el asesinato de mi hermano también.'

'Yes,' Hugo says, 'because I reported my brother's murder also.'

'Thank you,' I say, then turn to Ericson. 'That's all, Your Honor.'

Slowly, Sievers rises. 'I'm sorry for your loss,' he says without looking at Sandra. This would be terrible lawyering if he were in front of a jury, to be so perfunctory. But there is no jury, and he's uttered this rote line before Ericson and every other immigration judge so many times already that sincerity would only seem false. His words are the ritual transition to the task at hand.

'This was what,' he asks, checking the dates in the file, 'fifteen years ago? A lot to remember, from a long time ago. So I just want to make sure we have everything straight.'

He doesn't wait for Hugo to translate; Hugo just speaks into Sandra's ear as Sievers carries on.

'So when the men came to rob your house, how many men were there?'

'Creo que había tal vez ocho,' Sandra says.

'I think there were eight,' Hugo says.

'Oh,' Sievers says, all mock surprise. 'Eight men? Because just now you said it was six or maybe it was seven, but in your statement you said it was nine. So which was it: six, seven, eight, or nine?'

Sandra whispers something to Hugo, which he doesn't translate.

'What's the respondent saying?' Judge Ericson asks. 'Please explain to her that the court needs to know.'

'She's asking why it is so important, the exact number,' Hugo says. 'A group of men came to the house. That is what she remembers.'

'It's not up to Ms. Moya what questions she's asked,' Ericson says. 'Ms. Moya, you must answer the department's question.'

'Creo que eran las ocho.'

'I think it was eight,' Hugo says.

'Okay,' Sievers says, 'so we have at least four different answers to that question. Now, some of these men were wearing masks, is that right?'

'Sí.'

'Was the man you call the Ghost,' Sievers says, 'was he wearing a mask?'

In our prep, I never asked her this. Which is unforgivable. I asked where the Ghost stood in the room, where she was standing in relation to him, what he was doing when the younger man held the knife to her belly, but never *Did the Ghost wear a mask?* Sandra shakes her head. 'No,' she says, and I breathe again.

'Okay,' Sievers says. 'Let's say he's not wearing a mask. Had you met him? Had he come to your father's store before?'

Hugo speaks into Sandra's ear. 'No,' she says.

'So how did you know he was the Ghost?'

'Todos lo conocían.'

'Everyone knew him,' Hugo says.

'Sorry, maybe I'm missing something,' Sievers says, 'but I don't understand. You're saying you'd never met this man, you'd never seen him before, but you right away recognized him? Did he introduce himself? Did he say, *Hello, I'm the Ghost?*'

'Objection, Your Honor. Badgering.'

To my surprise, Ericson sustains it. Sievers bows his head and smiles.

'Let me rephrase,' he says. 'You've just said you'd never met this man before. How did you know he was the Ghost?'

'Todo el mundo hablaba de él,' she says. 'El camión que conducía, los muchachos con los que estaba, no era solo yo, cualquiera
hubiera sabido que era él, así es. Son como cantantes o estrellas de
cine, simplemente en el pueblo. Lo reconocerías, si vivieras allí.'

'Everyone talked about him,' Hugo says. 'The truck that he
drove, his men. Everyone knows him, that's how it goes, like a
singer or movie star. If you lived there, you would recognize him.'

'Well, that's the problem, Ms. Moya,' Sievers says to the judge.
'I wasn't there, and neither was Mr. Fischer or anyone else in this
room. All we have to go on is your word. About something that
happened fifteen years ago. And it's hard to make sense of some of
what you're saying.'

Sievers is better put together than Callahan, thinner, wears a
better suit. He's not a lifer, not in this unit. He's the kind looking for
some multiagency task force, some high-profile enforcement where
his bosses will get promoted and take him with them. Until then he
just needs to rack up as many denials as he can. Nothing personal,
he said to me once after a hearing I lost. And I'm sure it isn't.

Now that he's got Sandra off balance and worried, he speeds up
and goes for the hard stuff. The kid who supposedly had a knife to
her belly, had she ever met him before? How tall was he? Was he
thin or fat? Did he wear anything on his head? Did he have a beard,
an earring, tattoos? Did he stand on her left side or her right side or
behind her? Who laughed at what joke when? As quick a barrage
as he can manage with Hugo's translations, which he cuts off as
soon as he has what he needs. Sandra doesn't look at the judge at all
now. She speaks in a low, shut-down voice. *They will never believe
me,* she said the first time I met her. I can't tell her not to look
defeated. All I can do is object and give her the few seconds it takes
for Ericson to overrule me before Sievers presses on. 'You say you
went to the police to report your brother's death,' he says. 'What
happened after that? Did the Ghost show up at your house? Did the
young men come back and threaten you?'

'No,' Sandra says after Hugo whispers in her ear.

'Oh,' Sievers says, 'I see. You understand why that might surprise me. Because you're telling the court that you can't go back to Honduras because you reported your brother's murder to the police and this gang will harm you for doing that, but when you were still in Honduras they didn't actually harm you.'

'Hijo de puta,' Felipe spits from the front row of the gallery.

Sievers chuckles. 'Would the court like that one translated, Your Honor?'

Ericson can't be bothered but must be bothered. 'Young man,' he says, 'you have no role in this proceeding, you understand? You can't talk to an officer of the court or anyone else here that way, and if you do so again I'll have you removed.'

'I don't blame him for his frustration, Your Honor,' Sievers says, playing Felipe's outburst for all it's worth. 'It turns out this is a difficult story to understand. Ms. Moya doesn't seem to know how many people were in the room when her brother's life was being threatened. The man who supposedly held the knife to her brother was not someone she'd ever met, but her testimony is she knew exactly who he was. And hardest of all to overcome, the very danger she's asking the court to protect her from never materialized. The Ghost didn't return. And I would add to this, Your Honor, even if you do find this story credible, it's well understood by respondent's counsel and this court that the gangs operative in Honduras fifteen years ago are not the same ones operative today, and there is no evidence to prove that the particular actors who supposedly threatened the respondent have any power today or are even alive. In the department's view, this isn't a hard determination. The respondent's testimony doesn't add up, and the claimed fear of harm is contradicted by the record and by the country conditions.'

Ericson has been leaning back in his padded swivel chair listening to Sievers but comes forward again now, forearms resting on his dais. 'Anything further, Mr. Fischer?'

'Yes, Your Honor.' I try to remind Sandra with my eyes alone that we have practiced this. I played the other lawyer, I poked holes in her story. She didn't like it, no one does, but she got through it. Calm and steady now. Question, answer, translation.

'When the young men first came to your family's store and demanded la renta,' I say, 'and your father gave them food and beer instead, was it always the same boys who came?'

'No, a veces había muchos de ellos, ahí era cuando bebían juntos.'

'No, sometimes there would be lots, when they drank together.'

'And each week did you count how many there were?'

'No.'

'On the day in question, to the best of your memory, how many men were there altogether?'

'Ocho o nueve.'

'Now, this man called the Ghost. You said he was like a celebrity in the town, like a rock star. Did people gossip about him? Did they describe him to each other? Did they describe how he dressed?'

'Si todo el tiempo. Era como el alcalde, pero siempre en su despacho, siempre dejando que sus personitas hicieran su trabajo. Todos sabían qué camión conducía, con la oveja cornuda en la parte delantera, y que era muy delgado y tenía bigote.'

'Yes, all the time,' Hugo says. 'He was like the mayor, but always in his office, always letting his little people do his work. Everyone knew what truck he drove, with the horned sheep on the front, and that he was very thin and had a mustache.'

'Had you seen his truck before?'

'Si muchas veces.'

'Yes, many times.'

'So that day, did you recognize the truck?'

'Sí.'

'I want to go back now,' I say. 'You reported the robbery four days after it occurred, is that right?'

'Sí.'

'And how long after you and Ernesto went to the police station did you find Ernesto's body in your backyard.'

'One day,' Sandra says.

'So one day after you went to the police station, your brother's maimed body was dumped at your home?'

Sandra nods.

'Ms. Moya,' Judge Ericson says, exasperated, 'you have to answer the question out loud for the court!'

'Sí.'

'Yes,' Hugo repeats.

'That much I get!' Ericson says, sighing. 'Carry on.'

'And how long after your brother's murder did you report it to the police?' I ask.

'A la mañana siguiente, fui a la mañana siguiente.'

'The next morning.'

'And after you went this second time to the police station, how long after that did you leave Potrerillos?'

'Cuatro días. Tuve que pedir prestado el dinero, no lo tenía.'

'Four days. I had to borrow the money first.'

'To the best of your knowledge, based on your communications with your relatives in Potrerillos, do the maras still operate there and in all of Honduras?'

'Sí, es peor, mucho peor.'

'Yes, it is worse, much worse.'

'Do you have any reason to know or believe that the Ghost is dead?'

'No.'

'That's all I have, Your Honor. Ms. Moya's testimony is consistent. She had a clear means to recognize her assailants. As for the department's suggestion she never suffered the harm she seeks protection from, I'd argue her brother's maimed corpse dumped in her yard is both a harm and a threat. And that, as she has just testified, she fled from the only place she had ever lived as soon as she had the means to do so. Finally, submitted with her application is ample evidence that while criminal organizations operating in Honduras have evolved since the respondent's departure, retaliation for reporting to law enforcement, such as it is, is ongoing.'

Judge Ericson takes off his big rimless glasses and rubs the skin between his brows, eyes closed. Silence.

'For the record,' he says, picking up his pen and beginning to mark his file, 'I find the respondent, Sandra Moya, to be a credible witness. I believe she and her family suffered the harm she describes, and that she therefore meets the subjective prong of the well-grounded fear test. However, the department argues that there are changed country conditions, that the criminal organization at issue is, by our government's account, no longer the dominant organization committing these crimes in Honduras. So her problem is the objective prong. Is her fear objectively well grounded? I need to consider the full application to determine that. The court will not issue a ruling today. Written opinion to follow, notice to counsel will be given.'

When Hugo finishes whispering the judge's words in Sandra's ear, she looks at me, stricken. She's not shut down anymore. She's terrified she's going to be dragged from the room this minute and put on a plane, never to see her son again—her fear from the very beginning.

'Come on,' I say, 'let's talk outside,' and the four of us leave the courtroom and go out into the foyer.

Felipe is the one whose expression is frozen now. The anger is gone, and he is gone with it.

Hugo says he's sorry, but he has another hearing. He shakes Sandra's hand and wishes her luck.

I usher her and Felipe to the bank of chairs in the hall but they don't want to sit.

'You did great in there,' I say. 'I mean it. And the judge believed you. You heard him say that.'

'Yeah,' she says, already retracting from her fear, back into resignation. 'Pero a quién le importa, él no me da nada.'

'Nothing today,' I say. 'But he didn't rule against you. Which is a lot. I know it doesn't seem like it, but believe me, with this judge, that's good.'

'¿Pero ahora?' she says. 'What happens?'

'We have to wait,' I say. 'It could be a month, it could be two. But there's no order, no one is going to deport you.'

'Are you lying to us?' Felipe says, leaning in toward me.

My son has no idea what it is like there, Sandra said to me when I asked her about Felipe's notion of returning with her if things came to that. *He says it because he wants to be brave.*

'No, I'm not lying,' I tell him.

We crowd again into the elevators, and I walk them out onto Duane Street, where it has stopped raining. If she'd been given a final order, I would sit with them longer and go over the options; losing is what takes the longest. But we are not there yet, and I'm already late to meet another client at the office.

'Él piensa que el Ghost está muerto,' Sandra says, putting on her black raincoat. 'He thinks I'm afraid of the past.'

'Come on,' Felipe says to his mother. 'Let's get out of here.'

'It won't be much longer,' I say as they turn to leave. 'I'll let you know as soon as I hear.'

The next day, I forget my keys again. This time, I realize it standing beneath Phoebe's stoop at the locked front door of the office.

'Welcome to middle age,' Monica says after she lets me in and I explain. We're standing in the dimness of the little reception area. Despite her quip, her voice is unusually mild, even slow. Still, I expect her to turn quickly back toward her office, but she doesn't. Something has changed in her since she got back from her vacation, which I'm still amazed she actually took. Something subtle. How strange her week away must have been for her — not the skiing, but the not working.

'Is forty middle-aged?' I ask.

'Maybe not in America,' she says. 'But where I come from, we're getting old.'

Around noon Monica asks if I want a sandwich from the deli, I say I'll walk with her, and she looks at me as if I might be unwell. 'Why would you do that?' she asks.

I don't answer. I just grab my jacket and we head out together. We walk up Sixth Avenue in the cold bright day, picking our way through the line of traffic backed up across Houston.

'How's your mother?' I ask. 'You haven't mentioned her in a while.'

'I didn't know that I ever did. But if you're asking, she's not great. She hardly gets out of the apartment anymore. She says she isn't in pain, though she is, but she won't see a doctor because she thinks of them as officials, so she doesn't trust them.'

'That must be hard.'

'Peter, what's up with you?'

'What do you mean?' I ask as I hold the door of the deli open for her.

'You never talk like this.'

I follow her to the counter, where she puts in her order and Carl's, then I give the guy mine, and we step aside to wait.

'It's fine,' she says to me. 'It's just weird.'

'Well, I guess you never say much. About personal stuff.'

'*I* never say much. We've worked in that basement together how long? And what have you ever said to me about dates, or a boyfriend, or anything? For all I know, you could be in the closet.'

'Wow, really? The closet?'

'How should I know why you never take the gay claims?'

She's standing in front of the glass case stacked high with Boar's Head meat, her arms crossed over her dark green parka.

'What does that have to do with anything?' I say.

'You tell me,' she says.

The sandwiches are done in what seems like no time. I carry the paper bag, and Monica carries the sodas. A breeze swirls up the sidewalk, lofting dust and candy wrappers, while high above, bright pillowy clouds scud across the blue sky.

'I don't mean to get after you,' Monica says. 'I sound like my mother. Every night she used to ask me, *Where is the man in your life? Are there no men at all?* One day I told her I'd turn off the cable if she didn't stop. So now she doesn't ask.'

'You don't have to tell me anything you don't want to,' I say.

'It's all right,' she says. 'But what is there to say? The white guys are either ignorant or they pity me in their tender little hearts, and I can't stand that. And the Latin guys, they're like my mother. *How come you're forty-two and don't have kids?* They don't say it, but they think it. Sometimes I sleep with them, sometimes I don't.'

It's when we turn right off the avenue onto King Street that I see the Albanian kid, leaning against the railing of the forecourt of Phoebe's town house, earbuds in, staring at his phone. He's dressed in the same gray windbreaker from our first meeting, again zipped to the chin. Seeing me, he takes a few steps toward us, removes his earbuds, then stops, still yards away.

'Monica,' I say, 'this is Vasel Marku.'

She steps forward and shakes his hand. He glances at me, then back to her, and I realize he's stuck. He has no interpreter, no Artea. But then, in accented yet perfectly understandable English, he says to me, 'Can I talk to you?'

When I make no immediate reply, Monica looks at me sideways, then says, 'Yes, you can talk to him.'

Vasel waits for me to confirm this, but his sudden appearance has thrown me off and I say nothing.

'I'm sure Mr. Fischer would be glad to speak with you,' Monica says, boring her eyes into me now. 'You'd be happy to, wouldn't you, Peter?'

'Yeah,' I say finally, 'sure.'

Carl is in the conference room with a client, so Monica escorts us to the door to my office. 'Nice to meet you,' she says to Vasel, extra-polite, as if showing me up for my hesitancy toward him.

I indicate for Vasel to go in ahead of me, then follow Monica down the hall. 'He didn't speak a word of English to anyone when he came in,' I say in a low voice. 'There was this whole rigmarole with his friend doing all the talking. And now this? There's something going on here.'

For the third time that day, Monica beholds me as if I've lost my mind. 'Since when *isn't* there something going on?'

In his lap, Vasel holds the decline letter and referral list that I sent him. He keeps his eyes on the papers, the white wires of his earbuds draped around his slender neck.

I don't have time for this, is what I'm thinking. I really don't have the time, and yet the need to know why he's come back is palpable. 'So,' I say, 'you wanted to speak.'

He holds the papers up. 'This means you don't believe me, right?'

'It's not that simple,' I say, 'we only have—'

'You are right,' he says. 'I did not tell you everything. Artea, every day she is messaging people. Friends back home, people that know me, know my family. Anything I say, she tells them. If she knew the truth she would tell her uncles, and then I would not have my job at the market. But she is the one who heard about this place, that maybe I would not have to pay, so I came with her.'

The question intent on his face now is one I see all the time: Am I safe? Can I trust you? Because no one in an office or with any kind of power has ever been someone to trust.

You don't wait for a question like that to be spoken aloud—it might never be. You clock it and respond. You reassure. Yet in this moment, I don't. I let it hang there between us. Then I open my laptop and click on Google Maps.

'Remind me,' I say, 'the name of your town.' He tells me, and I bring up a satellite image of what looks like a nearly empty landscape, then turn the screen so we can both see. 'Why don't you show me around,' I say. 'Show me where you lived.'

He glances at the screen, hesitant.

'It's okay,' I say. 'I should have started here last time.'

It's not an answer to the question still in his eyes, but it's a concession of sorts. And apparently a sufficient one for now, because he reaches for the track pad and zooms down into the basin of the valley. He drags the viewer over fields of pasture until the houses and outbuildings become less occasional and the edges of a town appear. After enlarging the image again, he points with the cursor at what seems to be a courtyard. Along the top of it runs a thin, stable-like building that connects a large red-tiled roof at one end and a smaller gray structure with an unfinished upper story at the other. In the paved yard stands a flatbed truck.

'Here,' he says.

'A farm?'

'No. My father's father, he was a shepherd. Now we have only a few animals. My brother,' he says, wobbling the cursor over the stable building, 'he fixes cars in there where the animals used to be. He's shit at it. They come because he makes them pay only a little.' Vasel zooms out and pans to the right, closer to the center of town. 'There,' he says, moving the arrow over a black rectangle along the main road. 'This is my father's store.'

'What does he sell?'

'Everything. No food, but everything else. TVs, tools, stuff for kids.'

He seems intrigued by the picture on the screen and I wonder if he's ever bothered to look at his home this way, from the distance of space.

Out of my desk drawer, I dig a pen and take a pad from atop a stack of case files. 'Your parents,' I say. 'What are their names?'

Instantly his guard is up. And why shouldn't it be? Why part with anything when anything can be used against you? Soothe, reassure, redirect. These are basics of the job.

'It's fine,' I say. 'I don't need to know them right now.'

'Jozif,' he says after a moment. 'Everyone calls him Zef. Marta — that is my mother.'

He watches me write the names down.

'You mentioned a brother,' I say. 'Any other siblings?'

'My sister, Pera, she is the first.'

'And your brother's name?'

'Why do you need it?' he asks.

I tell him what I tell everyone: It's helpful to get a full picture of things. As if I didn't already fail to do this with him the first time.

'We call him Arbi,' he says dismissively.

He leans away from the computer then, back into the chair, crossing his arms over his narrow chest. Everything about him seems tight: his rigid posture, narrowed eyes, pursed lips. He's forced himself to return here. After a moment, he reaches for the track pad again and scrolls north, away from the town, up the narrowing valley, eventually letting the cursor rest on a brown smudge along what looks like a bluff.

'What's that?'

'Cisteau,' he says. 'In English, I don't know—little army building? They are everywhere. The Communists, they made everyone build them. All over. They are empty now, farmers store things in them. Kids drink there.'

'Is there something special about this one?'

'The other kids, they use ones closer to town. No one else goes here. The farmer is gone and you can see down the road if someone is coming. At night, too, you can see headlights before anyone gets there. A bunker, that is what you say in English, a bunker.'

The silence that follows is long enough for me to notice the fan of my laptop and the car horns still bleating in the stalled traffic out on the avenue.

Again, the question is there, implicit in his eyes: Am I safe? Again, I don't answer it.

His gaze drifts off, to the shelves behind me, the rows of binders stacked up the wall. There is a spray of freckles across his nose and cheeks and a slight gap between his two front teeth that I didn't see before.

'So this bunker, you hung out there?'

'Yeah,' he says, more muted. His phone chimes. He takes it from his pocket, glances at the screen, then texts something back. 'I should go soon,' he says.

'Wait,' I say. 'You showed me this place here for a reason. Did you go there with someone?'

His eyes flash up at me. 'You want his name too?' he says, energy flexing back into his voice as quickly as it vanished. 'Armend,' he says. 'His name is Armend.'

He watches me write that name down too.

'You know him from school?' I ask.

'You don't get it,' he huffs. 'Everybody is known. I have known him my whole life. The only people are people you know. Unless they are outsiders. It is nothing like here.'

I feel an urge I haven't felt in years—to justify myself. To tell him I've represented hundreds of people from places not so different. But I don't. It will do this intake interview, which I've apparently decided to conduct over again, no good.

Repeat back, confirm, listen.

'So you've known Armend your whole life,' I say, 'and this is one of the places you hung out with him.'

'He had songs,' Vasel says, gazing at the floor now. 'Songs on his phone, to dance. He wanted to dance in videos when he got out. With Beyoncé or Rihanna, he practiced the moves. He said it was like football, you need practice. He wanted me to do it with him but I just watched.'

'Okay,' I say, careful not to interrupt whatever tentative flow he has entered.

'His father has money,' Vasel goes on. 'They had an SUV, he got clothes in Tirana, he had an iPhone—that was why he thought he could do anything. He wasn't stupid, he knew, but he pretended. Like it was just a joke, everything we did was a joke, just funny. He called it practice for when we would be with girls. Not faggots.

Just playing. He didn't believe it. But he thought if he didn't say it, I would stop coming.'

'So this bunker is the place you'd go when you wanted to be together,' I say.

'It was stupid,' he says, 'the way he always played the music too loud. I told him, *Turn it down,* but he didn't care. Maybe the kids saw us biking there, I don't know, but we didn't hear them. I just saw them on the steps looking in one time, little shits. And they saw us. And they ran off.'

'And these kids, are they the ones who started the rumor?'

'What I said before, it's true,' he says. 'I could not go to school. Armend's father is with the smugglers, everyone knew that was where their money came from. So nobody touched Armend. They wouldn't talk to him anymore, but they didn't fuck with him. It was my fault, people said, I was the sick one. I told everyone, these little shits, they are liars. I said they were lying because *they* were like that, *they* were the faggots. Some of my friends believed me—it was okay, they told me, just talk—but the older brothers, they believed the rumor. They were the ones who started trashing me, started fucking with me. People saw I was treated that way. Pushed around. The teacher, he saw. Everyone did. They were waiting, like shqiponjat, like the birds that wait for the animal to fall down.'

'So your teacher saw you being harassed, he knew why you were being harassed, and he did nothing to protect you, is that right?' When Vasel doesn't answer, I look up from my pad.

'Yeah, but so did others,' he says. 'Why does the teacher matter?'

'Well,' I say, putting down my pen and paper, 'in a case like this, one of the things you need to show is that people in authority threatened you or failed to protect you because of your orientation.'

Vasel is listening carefully to me now, more attentively than to anything else I've said thus far, and not just, it seems, to my meaning but to how I speak.

'You are gay, aren't you?' he says.

To my astonishment, I blush. Up to my ears. Which is ridiculous.

'I *knew* it!' Vasel says, sitting forward in his chair, coming suddenly to life. 'That's why I came back. I knew it. You have a boyfriend, too, right? Is he your age or is he younger?'

My cheeks burn with something close to shame, as if in the space of an instant I've become an awkward teen again, caught naked by a stranger, while Vasel's whole manner—aggrieved and reluctant only a moment ago—has been transformed in the other direction, his face now bright and open and full of expectation.

'We're not talking about me right now,' I say, then take a breath. 'We're talking about the actions of your teacher and their relevance to your case.'

'I bet you two live in one of those towers in Hell's Kitchen, don't you? All the rich gays live over there.'

'Like I said, this discussion isn't about me.'

'What?' he asks. 'You think I'm rude? That I shouldn't ask this? I tell you everything, but you say nothing?'

'With a lawyer, that's generally how it works,' I say, hearing the hardening in my voice, as if I'm butching it up for him. It's close to malpractice, not to grant him the reassurance that it is safe to be honest with me.

'Ah,' he says, 'you are not out. White guys like you—downtown—I thought you were all out.'

'Listen,' I say. 'As it happens, I am gay. And I am out. And if that's one of the reasons you felt okay coming to talk with me, then good. But what we're doing here isn't about my life. It's about yours.'

'How old is your boyfriend?' he asks, as if I haven't spoken a word. He's up on the edge of his chair now, his legs bouncing. 'All the young guys, they seem to be with older guys. I think thirty is a good age—for me—someone who is going somewhere, but not rich like they are buying me things. Guys hear my accent and they think that is what I am looking for, that I am trash. But whatever. It doesn't matter. The cute ones don't like me anyway, even before they speak to me.'

'Vasel,' I say, using his name for the first time, which he clearly notices and which causes him to pause, as if I've called back his former self. 'I don't mean to be rude. But I didn't schedule for us meeting like this. And there are questions I still need to ask, to evaluate the situation you're in.'

His legs stop bouncing. And as quickly as his energy erupted, it is gone, his burst of fun spoiled. He wants to play, but all I want is his past.

'So,' I say, getting my composure back. 'You were talking about your school.'

His eyes glide off to the side and he slumps back in his chair. 'Yeah,' he says glumly. 'I stopped going to school. My grandfather, his fields in the hills are empty now. I went there instead, during the day. I told Armend we could not meet anymore. But he texted me all the time anyway, said he wanted to see me. He told me he hated the ones at school who fucked with me, that he could protect me, but it was stupid, he couldn't, no one could.' He pauses to pick at the cuticle of his thumb, his jaw tensing as he does it. 'Next to us,' he says, 'there was a wedding—the neighbor's son. We all went, my mother and father, Pera, Arbi. Weddings go on forever there, all day, all night. After the big meal, when people were dancing, Armend texted me, said he wanted to meet up. I told him no, that it was crazy, with people talking about the rumor—about him and me—we couldn't risk it. But he said he was already there, across the field, at our gate. Just come down here, he said. Just let me in.' Vasel's hands go still. Almost imperceptibly, he shakes his head.

I see regret on the faces of clients all the time. But I've never seen it so clearly on the face of someone this young.

'It was dark already,' he says. 'I didn't think anyone would notice me leaving the wedding. I went to the gate and let Armend in. He was drunk, and I guess I was too, a little. I didn't want to be in our house with him, that felt too weird. We just stayed in the courtyard and smoked cigarettes there. Armend was trying to be funny, to do his little dances again, to the wedding music across the field. Like nothing had happened, and we could still do everything we did in the bunker. But that asshole Arbi, he saw me go, and some evil piece of his little brain made him follow me. The whole time he was there, in the dark of the stables off the courtyard, sitting in one of his shitty old cars, watching us. The sick fuck. He probably liked it. The next morning, Arbi said to me, like a gangster — that's what he wants to be, a smuggler, a big man, not just fix cars — he said, You are not human, you are garbage. But he is the garbage. Everyone knows he can't get a wife. My father's store, it should be Arbi's when my father dies. Arbi is the oldest boy. But everyone knows my father doesn't like him. It's always been that way. So people know there is something wrong with him. And families don't want their daughters to marry him. The first son should be favored, but my father likes Pera better. And me too. When he came home from the store, he always put his arms around us, he kissed us. My mother told him he was being like a woman, but he didn't care, he laughed, that's how he is. Or how he was.'

'So your brother saw you and Armend?' I say.

'Yes,' Vasel says, still gazing at his hands, which are gripped together now on his lap. 'And he told my father about it the next day. He was glad to tell, to fuck me. But it didn't go like that. My father hit him in the face. *Never speak this filth in my house, ever,* that's what he said. *You disgust me.* My mother, my sister, they were watching. Arbi called him an old fool. He said everyone knew, that it was not the first time, people were speaking behind our backs, I was a dishonor to our family, to all our relations. But my father wouldn't believe it. He told him never speak it again. Or he would leave him *nothing.*'

I realize that once more, while listening to Vasel, I've stopped taking notes. But it's all right, I tell myself. I will not forget this.

'And that is how it was,' Vasel says. 'But only for a little time. I could not fool my mother, she knew, and she worried about me like crazy, like she was sick. She cried when my father was not there. And it was crazy in the house anyway because she was getting ready for Pera's wedding. All the dresses, all the gifts, the things she had made for months, stuff everywhere. It was a family near Shkodër, a much bigger town, on a lake, a place with things to do. Pera wanted to go. She met the guy there when she visited our cousin. They decided themselves to get married. And my mother was glad too because Arbi has no wife, and she was worried Pera would not have a husband. She was already twenty, maybe she would have to go over the mountains somewhere, to some old man my father would find for her. Not because he wanted to. But a daughter with no husband is almost the worst.'

Vasel has slid lower in his chair now, his attention no longer in the room at all but on the images circling his mind.

'Then people in the town started coming less to our store,' he says. 'The men, they said to my brother, *We respect your father, we don't want things to go bad for him, but he must speak about this thing with Vasel, or take care of it.* When Arbi told my father this, my father shouted at him again, he hit him, said it is his fault for spreading lies.'

Raising his eyes now, Vasel glares at me.

'I told you the truth,' he says. 'These men that talked to my brother, they stopped me on the road, like I said. They told me, *Armend is gone.* I knew it already, that he went to Tirana, because the rumor was worse. His father has connections, he could go to Italy, they can travel. But these men—not the older brothers anymore but the fathers of the boys at school—they joked that Armend was dead, that something should be done with me now. What was I supposed to do? I had to tell my father. But it would be okay, I thought. I would tell him and then I would leave. You don't understand how crazy it was. My mother was so scared of what would happen, she started speaking only in English to me, trying to hurry up and teach me everything I would need if I had to go. To give me this language she learned in Pristina before her parents matched her with my father. She always wanted us to learn English.'

Beneath the weight of the memory, his agitation has faded.

'So I decided to do it,' he says. 'To tell my father the truth, then leave. But before I could, these two old men came to the house. I had never seen them before. They had come to see my father. They were not from our town, they just showed up, and he took them into the front room and my mother brought them food and closed all the doors. Pera and my mother, they sat in the kitchen, waiting. They knew something, but they didn't tell me. When the old men left, my father came to me and said, *Go outside,* and he went into the kitchen and I heard my mother crying. The men were from the family in Shkodër. They had come to tell my father they could not be joined to our family. There would be no wedding.

'That is what I did,' Vasel says. 'I killed my sister's life.'

The rest of that afternoon, no matter how I try, I can't focus. I begin emails and forget who I am writing. Reading a report, I lose my place again and again. At six o'clock, I give up and wander out to the subway.

It occurs to me I could text Cliff. I could even—at the last minute—invite him over for dinner like he suggested. Set out napkins and silverware, open a bottle of wine. The image of it all is there in my mind, and then it's not, and I'm looking up from the pavement to realize I've walked right past my stop at Spring Street and am already at Sixth and Canal, in front of the steps to the train. Instead of descending them, though, I cross over and continue down onto Church, as if headed back to Foley Square. Only that's not where I'm headed either, so I don't turn east but keep south, on past Chambers, where the sidewalk traffic thins out.

At the clearing of Ground Zero, flags sway from the tops of giant cranes, the half-built tower looming over the half-filled hole. I haven't been down here in ages. Not since I left the firm where I worked to pay off my law school loans.

Seventy-odd hours a week, that job was. Sorting through tens of thousands of business records and drafting memos about their airless content, all to prepare for trials between corporations that everyone understood would never occur; yearslong litigation aimed at the inevitable settlement that rendered the work null. I think very little about that time. It is itself a kind of void. Late each evening I would come down into the lobby of the skyscraper, move past the line of town cars waiting to ferry the partners uptown, cross Zuccotti Park, and head south past the American Stock Exchange, down onto Rector Street, and into the lobby of my own building, the old headquarters of U.S. Steel, where I'd nod good night to the concierge and ride up to the cubicle of my studio and without turning the lights on go to the big window and gaze for a while down into the darkened graveyard of Trinity Church.

'Your father would be proud of you,' my mother said to me once. 'At least I imagine he would be—you working with all those big companies. But I hope for your sake you won't do it forever.' I couldn't imagine my father being proud of me, even in this narrow ambit. More likely, he would have thought I'd rented myself to the monopolists, to the elites who would have gladly crushed a business like his if it earned them a fraction of a point. My own walk at the end of the day—or the night—wasn't a walk to a home, like his, but to an apartment with no one in it, carrying a briefcase full of papers I couldn't care less about. I'd backed into going to law school for its promise of security, with the excuse I might one day be able to help people. And there I'd taken a course on the law of citizenship and asylum taught by a man who'd spent most of his life traveling to refugee camps and detention centers to gather evidence of mistreatment and harm. If you have to work at a firm to get out of debt, so be it, he said to me. But use them for what they're worth—learn something. My supervising partner was happy for me to do as much pro bono representation of asylum seekers as I wanted, as long as I understood it would be in addition to, not instead of, my work for him.

It was in my second year at the firm that I met Tesfay Kidane, my first real client. An Eritrean journalist, mid-fifties, lithe and fine-featured. He dressed in a black turtleneck and black leather jacket, looking every bit the Marxist intellectual that he was. At the beginning of each of our meetings, he would remove a hand-rolled cigarette from his pouch and hold it between his index and middle finger as we spoke, as if our conversations were a mere interruption in a single action that would conclude with him stepping back out on the sidewalk and striking a match. He spoke about his mistreatment by the Afwerki regime as though it were a crime of taste. As if his captors had more than anything made an aesthetic error. Twenty years fighting in the war for independence from Ethiopia, and instead of the humanist democracy they'd dreamed of in the field, they got dictatorship.

The first time I asked him to detail what had been done to him, he smiled. 'Don't worry,' he said, 'I understand. I am to be the victim in this particular morality play, begging mercy from the great power. We have been Christians far longer than you, so yes, the righteousness of suffering in the eyes of a merciful God, I understand. I will do my best to play my part.' His sarcasm so courtly it hardly seemed directed at me at all, or at anyone other than himself, as a kind of quiet entertainment still available to the completely disenchanted. His case was the only thing I wanted to work on. Three more years it took to pay off my loans and, with the help of a lot of other lawyers I met in the process—Phoebe being one of them—to win Kidane the right to remain.

On the sidewalk now in front of Century 21, a few late-in-the-day tourists still mill around the vendors hawking 9/11 memorabilia, models of the Twin Towers and t-shirts with images of bin Laden's head centered in a rifle's sights.

Which reminds me now of what Artea said. Vasel's second job—selling the 9/11 things. And all of a sudden I wonder if when Vasel left the office he came here to work, and if this is the reason that I've wandered down here myself, to these blocks I used to haunt.

I look around, from cart to cart. The vendors are beginning to pack up their wares, hitching their wagons to the backs of vans, but none of them is Vasel.

Before he left, he assured me he would return soon, to answer the rest of my questions, to begin the work he and I now have ahead of us.

'This is what I am curious about,' Tesfay Kidane said to me once, standing out on the sidewalk after lighting his joint-like little cigarette. 'Why do you—who has comfort and a job and a place to live—why do you do this work? What am I to you?'

The first time I got to touch Jared we were pretending to fight. It was in theater class, an improv the teacher had the two of us do together. Acting out an argument without words, only our bodies. At first, Jared laughed. He wouldn't take it seriously. Then the teacher said to him, 'This makes you nervous—use your nerves.' And so he did. By the end, he was holding me to the stage floor as the others watched, my face pressed into the hollow beneath his collarbone, the thick funk of him flooding my nostrils. So this, I thought, this is wanting.

After Deborah Weber's circle, it was Ann's turn to do the grocery run. She drove into town, did the shop, and stopped in at the hardware to pick up a list of things Jeanette had given her. By the time she had returned, unloaded all the food into the fridge and cabinets, and helped Roberta cut vegetables for that evening's soup, she had time for only a short end-of-the-day walk, this one out past the near end of the Tibbett farm, then down the hill to the intersection and back. There was light in the sky now that daylight saving had come, but the air remained winter cold. On her return, she found Jeanette still at work in the yard. She was crouched alongside the barn, clipping at an old vine that had grown over the lower panes of one of the windows.

'And how were the three magi today?' Jeanette said without looking up. In one gloved hand she clutched a thorny stalk and with the secateurs in the other sliced the base of it clean through.

'Oh, as wise as ever,' Ann said.

Standing, Jeanette tore the long tentacle from the glass and shingles, leaving behind the spidery black outlines where the vine had gripped. 'Glad to hear it,' she said.

Several times the three of them had asked Jeanette if over the winters she would prefer to help out with the scheduling and meals and so be in from the cold, but each time she'd declined, opting to be outside in anything short of a storm, and even then she would retire to the new shed to work on maintenance and repairs. Other women from nearby had also become part of the community at the center and joined the regular Sunday-night gatherings, but they were mostly couples who'd moved up from Boston or New York. Jeanette was the only one born and raised here. Ann had liked her from the start, her cynicism and wit. Clare, not so much. She thought Ann romanticized her. Being working class doesn't excuse being difficult and rude, Clare had said without needing to add that, being the daughter of a mechanic, she ought to know. And yet Clare was not an undifficult person herself.

What Ann wanted to say when Clare complained about Jeanette was that her guarded way in the world might have more to do with being the survivor of a rape. But in the eight years since Jeanette had revealed this, she'd never given Ann permission to share it with the others.

It made Ann uneasy, keeping it to herself, here where everything was shared with Clare and Roberta and most often with a larger group as well. Openness was their ethos. But just before Jeanette had spoken about what had been done to her, she asked Ann to swear she would not talk about it with anyone else, and something in the force of the request—the totally uncharacteristic desperation of it—uttered in the twilight of the car as Ann drove her home on a late-winter afternoon not unlike this one had remained seared in Ann's mind. And so for years now the two of them had lived with this understanding, which Ann had grown used to and which no longer troubled her as it had. She'd given up some time ago on the script of confession and catharsis. If Jeanette's suspicion of the center's ways was what allowed her to be here, then so be it. Doctrine was for cults.

The two of them could be like this together, Ann thought,

comfortably silent. Jeanette appreciated her presence but would never say so, and that was fine too. In fact, Ann found it to be a relief. Something about being around Jeanette allowed her to think.

That Thomas Merton quote had stuck with her. Divinity school was a lifetime ago. She thought of it rarely. She'd been so determined back then to make the institutions of power recognize her and to win some share of that power for herself, but this was a notion she couldn't be less interested in now. What a waste of spirit it seemed. *That abyss of confusion and absurdity which is our own worldly self.* She'd read the line originally as pleasure denying, which it was—a denial of the body, women's bodies in particular. But it struck her differently now that she no longer struggled with that. Now it seemed less about the confusion and absurdity of the worldly self than of the self per se: the stories people told themselves about themselves, ad infinitum. That concatenation of who they'd been told they were and who they styled themselves to be, willingly or not, in order to get by. What labor went into the sustenance and reinforcement of these self-told tales: This is who I am. Unbinding people from these stories—that's how she had come to think of the work she and Clare and Roberta tried to do here.

Not that people ever managed to do this altogether. Even now Ann herself was recalling that first misplaced gesture of hers with Richard: giving him a book of Merton's on his first visit to Cambridge. And with that remembrance she linked herself back to her own tale of the young woman she'd been then, still wed to the story of marriage. Such was the snare of memory.

And yet what did this past matter now as she watched Jeanette cut the bramble off at its roots. The air here in the yard was raw, the light beginning to fail, the edge of the meadow becoming indiscrete against the edge of the woods. Jeanette was beside her. Soon there would be dinner with her oldest friend and her partner and the women in the group and Jeanette too in the unlikely event she was inclined to join. What story was there to tell about any of this other than gratitude?

'You planning on just standing there?' Jeanette said, her arms full of the unruly scraps of vine. 'Or are you going to help me move some of this crap?'

Ann smiled. 'You always ask so nicely,' she said. 'How can I resist?'

Later that night, in bed, after she'd finished reading, Ann snuggled up against Clare, who still had her reading light on and an open book resting on her chest. She smelled of the eucalyptus and menthol cream she used for the soreness in her wrists, a scent once medicinal but now so familiar as to be lulling.

'You were good in the circle this morning,' Clare said, still reading. 'It meant a lot to Deborah, what you said. I could tell.'

Ann rested a hand on the softness of Clare's belly. 'Maybe,' she said. 'But tears aren't a plan, as you like to say.'

'True. But it was more than tears,' Clare said. 'You let her discern something about herself.'

She was being generous. Ann could hear it in the gentleness of her voice, and it felt good.

'Maybe that's right,' Ann said. 'But you know it only works with all of us in the room. I wouldn't have gotten there without you and Roberta.'

Clare turned the page of her book, and for a while they were quiet.

What floated up into Ann's vision then, as it hadn't for a long time, was the very first moment the two of them had met, down in the parish hall at St. Stephen's, Clare in her black turtleneck and gray cardigan and silver cross on a silver chain. Right as they were being introduced, their eyes had joined for just a beat longer than nicety required, not in a romantic swoon but in a recognition strangely immediate. Clare, who'd been out for years and married only briefly in her twenties, would later say Ann was just waking up to actual desire, which wasn't untrue. But it wasn't all of it either. Their recognition included something more particular. Ann saw a woman who didn't give a damn what other people thought of her, and in that moment—without a word, and in the space of an instant—Clare told Ann that Ann didn't either, whether she knew it or not. In the months after that, as they got to know each other and fell in love, even as Ann was still married to Richard, the only image Ann could summon to make sense of that first moment was a muscle deep in the gut, letting go. How could Ann have gotten to the age of forty—a feminist since her teens and a crusader since divinity school for the right of women to be priests in the Episcopal Church—and not have seen her own near constant need for the approval of others? In fact, it was more than that. She hadn't just failed to see it. She'd imagined that she had already overcome it. Until Clare took one look at her and without the need for language, even, said, *Come on, now, I know you're stronger than that.* How *couldn't* Ann be attracted to her? She was the door into a world freer than Ann had imagined possible. Their sex, when it began, was revelatory, not just of pleasure but of what felt at the beginning like an almost wild detachment from the strictures of her life. The question wasn't whether she should separate from Richard but when, and how to do it in the least disruptive way for Liz and Peter. There were plenty in the congregation of St. Stephen's who despite their liberalism made it clear this went well beyond anything they could approve. But by the time it had all come into public view, Roberta, the former head of the vestry no less, had joined Clare and Ann's conversations about a women's retreat, and Clare, with her administrative instincts, had begun calculating start-up costs and looking into the price of land.

Clare closed her book now but rather than putting it aside rested both her hands on it atop her stomach. 'The question you asked Deborah,' she said, 'about how having kids had affected her work. You were remembering being her age, weren't you? You were thinking of Liz and Peter.'

Ann was still lying on her side facing Clare, her forehead resting against Clare's shoulder. 'Not particularly,' she replied. 'Why?'

'That's just how it sounded to me, the way you wondered aloud about it.'

'I suppose I might have been,' Ann said, rolling back onto her side of the bed. 'Is there anything wrong with that?'

'No, of course not,' Clare said.

Richard had never been a threat to Clare. It had become clear early on that at some point Ann would leave him, so Clare had no reason for jealousy. But Liz and Peter were a different matter. Their claim on Ann was far greater. Clare had tried to get to know them better than she did just from church, but at the worst time, when they were teenagers and their parents were separating. And she had responded to their lack of welcome by pushing back, defending Ann, lecturing Liz and Peter on the importance of the retreat center the three of them were planning to create. To the kids, Clare would always be the woman who'd bullied her way in when they least wanted anyone else around. And Ann had done little to help the situation. She'd had the congregation to care for, the parish to run. Besides, part of her welcomed Clare's defense. Richard had never defended her when the kids complained about how much she worked. Nonetheless, she had let that seed of animosity establish itself, and had been reckoning with it ever since. She had no doubt this was one of the reasons Peter had stopped visiting the center early on—having to contend with that tension. And here Clare was, in her veiled way, still at it.

'You still think I have regrets,' Ann said, surprising herself with her own directness. 'When have I ever told you I regretted anything about us?'

Clare put her book aside now and removed her reading glasses.

'You never have,' she said. 'You're very good at protecting me from that.'

'*See*, it doesn't matter what I say,' Ann said, snuggling a little tighter, her tone half playful—the child's voice they sometimes used with each other—and half exasperated. 'You're just convinced.'

'That's not true,' Clare said, her own voice gentler now, satisfied enough it seemed to have gotten a little rise out of Ann, a little assurance of her devotion.

To move here, each of the three of them had given up different things. Roberta her practice and proximity to family; Clare her tenure and status. And Ann? In a sense she'd given up the least. After ten years at St. Stephen's, even if she hadn't been fed up with the organized church, it would have been time to move on. And yet to say it had been easiest for her missed something. True, when the moment arrived to pack the rectory up, leaving was more a deliverance than a sacrifice. Where else would she have gone? But the fact was the three of them had been planning the center for several years by then. The promise of it had already been there when she asked Richard to move out. By the time he got sick and had to return, the property up here had been purchased. And then the year after he died, while Peter finished high school, Ann had driven up frequently to work on the renovations. During that whole period, when Liz's and Peter's world was being turned on its head, she had possessed a kernel of hope that had nothing to do with them. And she had held on to that kernel, as she had held on to Clare. Despite the mess. It wasn't regret that she had felt about that, but guilt. For having a hope unconnected to her children. And this was what Clare had always misinterpreted. She had taken Ann's occasional remorse about the effect on Liz and Peter of her moving here as a sign of Ann's misgivings about *her*. And so even now, two decades into their no-longer-new life, a question in a circle about children could become something between them—something that it wasn't.

After turning out her light, Clare rolled onto her side to face

Ann. In the sudden darkness, sensing her closeness, Ann lay with her eyes wide open. She found herself picturing Liz and Norman in their bedroom. Its closets overflowing with the costumes Liz wore to those festivals of hers, a dog or two slumbering on the rug beside their bed, and behind that long ranch house the big backyard, fenced for the animals to roam by day, empty and quiet by night. And from that imagined silence in that little town west of Portland, her mind drifted farther south, down over the darkened coast to New York, where she saw Peter at the back of that apartment that she had visited only once, soon after he moved in, the one with the fractional view of the Brooklyn Bridge—Peter alone, as best she knew, in the bed set in the corner of that room facing the wall of the building next door. She tried figuring out in her head precisely how many years it had been since she had seen him (and only then for a meal in the city when she and Clare had gone down), but whatever that span of time was—six years? Seven?—it remained oddly vague, and her effort to calculate it came to nothing. She had, as she did every year, invited him up to Vermont for Christmas, and he had, as he did each December, offered his excuse: work. *The courts only close for a day* is what he wrote.

Picturing her children where they slept—a habit of motherhood that had long since fallen away. But tonight her mind didn't stop with them; it drifted back up the countryside again, to this hillside and to Jeanette in her room in the barn. The twin bed, the raw-pine side table, the low bureau backed against the pitched roof. When she came to live at the center, she had brought so little with her in the way of personal effects, and had accumulated barely any since. She didn't care for comfort. And yet Ann had always wanted to offer it.

'Good night,' Clare whispered. 'I love you.'

'I love you, too,' Ann replied.

On the anniversary of my parents' wedding each year, my father would talk about the trip he had taken to Europe to see where his father had fought in the Second World War. He had a ritual—he'd make a reservation for them at a fancy restaurant, buy my mother roses, and before they left the house, he'd sit with us as we ate our supper and tell the story of how they'd met. It happened at a youth hostel in Paris. He was there only one night, on his way back from the Ardennes Forest, when he spotted her in the courtyard. She was writing in a journal and paid him no mind.

You didn't see many girls traveling on their own back then, he would say. She was different, I could tell that right away, her own person, and I wanted to know what she was writing in that book of hers. So I asked, and what do you think she said to me? *Observations.* I knew then I wasn't likely to meet anyone like her back home. And of course your mother was beautiful, is beautiful, she absolutely was. She said if I wanted to talk to her, I'd better come back in an hour. So I did. We had a coffee, she agreed to a meal. And the whole time she looked at me like she knew my kind coming and going and didn't care for any sort of flattery. A girl from an old New England family. What did she need with a lumbering guy like me? I got one kiss before I left for the station, that was it.

Each year, the same story. For my father, their having met in Paris never stopped being a romantic fact. That somehow, despite the odds, he'd managed to capture my mother's imagination. It was a glow cast forward over their marriage. A moment to be recounted and believed in as something fated.

Then one year, not long before they separated, my mother said, 'Stop it, Richard. They've heard it all before.' And he did. He stopped, right then. He didn't say another word.

For days Vasel doesn't respond to my emails about coming in for his next appointment. We have only six weeks left to file. I need documents from him and an affidavit; I have to prepare him for court. Finally, he responds to a text. *I need to see you anyway,* he writes, *I will be there in an hour,* along with a smile emoji. My schedule doesn't work that way but as it happens, I don't have to be in court, so I tell him, *Fine.*

He shows up in a brand-new outfit. A pale blue Members Only–like jacket over a white button-down and black jeans. His hair's been cut, too, even shorter on the sides, and there's more product in it, sculpting his bangs. He could be auditioning for Eurovision or a boy band. He's even applied a touch of makeup to smooth over his freckles. It isn't just his appearance, either. His whole demeanor, sitting across the conference room table from me, is brighter and more confident.

When I begin by asking him how he's doing, he seems to have been waiting for the question, and his answer comes out all in a rush. He is about to start a job at a newly opened restaurant, high end, modern, a very cool space, and close to here, only a few minutes away, clearing tables and supplying the bar, but the owner says if he is good, they will need more waiters soon, so he's started looking at listings for roommates, not in Pelham Parkway but Brooklyn, with Americans, he says, not Albanians.

'But anyway, the legal thing, now is not good for that,' he says, 'maybe later. It is not why I am here. You seem like a good person,' he adds, 'a good professional person. I get it, in New York, how it goes, to make things work you have to know people, not just for favors, but maybe favors too, because you never know in the future, things you might want to do or people they might know. That is why I came today, not for my case. I need to know: Will you be in my network?'

At first, I think he's kidding. And then, worse, that he's making fun of me. But by the time his burst of words is over, his ebullience has turned to nerves, and I realize he's serious.

One thing we never do, Phoebe said the day she hired me, is condescend to a client. It clouds your judgment. To which Monica added sometime later: She should know; the only people who worry about condescending are the ones who do it.

'If what you're asking me,' I say to Vasel, 'is whether, once we've worked together on your case, I could be a reference — sure, that's something we do for people. But you need to understand, you're already in proceedings. You can't just put this off. If you don't show for your hearing, you'll get a deportation order. ICE could pick you up. They could detain you, they could put you on a plane. I'm not saying that'll happen, there are a bunch of steps, but you don't want a final order. That's not a good place to be.'

He bows his head, his legs starting to bounce, the same nervous tic as last time. 'That is not what I am talking about,' he says. 'I did not have to come back here. I came because—because just how I said it, you are a good, professional person. And I am going to be doing good things, better things. These guys I met, out, I told them about you. And they said he sounds good, you should ask him. That is why I am here. ICE doesn't care about me. For Albanians, they want people they think are the gangsters. Me, Artea, her uncles—it is not like that.'

He isn't wrong about this, and yet still.

'Whatever you want to do in the future,' I say, 'a final order is like a sword over your head. After that, when you want to fix it one day, it's more than twice as hard. I'm not saying a judge would issue a warrant, but they could. Which would make you a fugitive. People you live with could be charged with harboring you.'

'You're trying to scare me.'

'No, but I need you to understand the situation you're in. That's my job.'

He stands suddenly, the speed of the motion pushing his chair out behind him, and walks to the far corner of the conference room, where he gazes up through the glass ceiling at the neighbor's ivied brick and the bright sky above it.

'I meet with a lot of people,' I say. 'Nobody wants to go through all this, talking about the worst things that happened to them, to strangers. But right now, it's the chance you've got.'

'So that is it,' he says. 'If I do my case, you help me, but if I say no, you will not.'

'Help you with what?' I ask.

'Why do you think this restaurant is hiring me?' he says. 'Because I know someone. The gays, they are like the Albanians, they gossip and give each other jobs. But whatever, it's stupid, I'll find some other way.'

'Another way to do what?'

He punches himself hard on the side of his leg. 'I am an idiot!' he says, scrunching his eyes closed. 'In one hour, I have to be there, at the restaurant. They said everything is fine. Just bring a letter from your office job, then everything is fine. What do you think I told them? That I work at a fruit stand? That I sell shit to tourists? It is high end, the people are beautiful. I told them my day job is I work for a lawyer.'

'Ah,' I say.

I have had clients ask for loans, co-signatures on leases, even help getting a fake Social Security number, and I explain to them why I can't do these things. What Vasel is asking me to do is lie—on our letterhead, no less. It's not a hard call.

My phone pings. A text from my sister. *So I guess you're not coming to Mom and Clare's? Thanks for thinking about it—liar!*

I click the phone dark and put it aside. When I look up, Vasel is headed to the door.

'No,' I say, 'wait.'

If he leaves now, he won't come back. He'll have no chance at all.

'Supposing I write this letter,' I say, 'will you work with me on your case?'

'Yes,' Vasel says, nodding vigorously.

'We don't have much time. We need to work quickly.'

'I promise,' he says.

I open my laptop. Vasel watches as I type. 'So,' I ask, amazed at my own behavior, 'how long have you been working here?'

He waits a beat to make sure I'm kidding, then allows himself a smile, almost demure. 'I don't know,' he says, brightening. 'What do you think is good?'

'Usually the truth,' I say. 'But in this case, let's say six months.'

When I go to fetch the letter, Phoebe is at the printer.

'Is that the fellow you were so concerned about?' she asks without looking up from her document.

I turn to see if I left the door of the conference open, if Vasel can hear her question. 'Was I concerned about him?' I ask.

'He's the only person you talked about at the staff meeting.'

'That's not true,' I tell her. 'But, yeah, that's him.'

'Good,' she says, glancing at me over her half-glasses. 'I'm glad he came back.'

The day that Liz, Norman, and Charlie were due to arrive at the center, Clare announced she would cook a big dinner for them all. Given how erratic Liz's timing could be, Ann usually just fed them out of the refrigerator the first night.

'But we have to give them something,' Clare said. 'Why not enjoy it?' A group had just left, it was a Friday; if Liz was late, they could always have the food the following night. And so Clare spent much of that afternoon in the kitchen preparing a stew and a salad and baking a pie, while Ann got the house ready for the arrival of a four-year-old and waited for the call she knew would come, and which did, at a little before six, when they were supposed to appear. They hoped, Liz said, to make it by eight thirty.

When Ann suggested they eat, Clare said, 'Don't be silly. We'll wait.'

They showed up after nine. The first member of the party to come through the back door was the foster dog, a boxer with a limp and protruding lower jaw, who barreled to the center of the kitchen and promptly shat on the floor. Liz traipsed in next, guiding a sleepy Charlie with one hand and hauling a bag of dog food with the other. When she saw the steaming mess, she broke out in laughter, and then so did Jeanette, who'd seen them pull up and had come to greet them.

'Sorry!' Liz called out, dropping the dog food where she stood, then steering Charlie to Ann. She crossed the room to give Clare a hug.

Ann noticed a second sharp smell, this one coming from her grandson, who'd apparently had an accident in his pants while dozing. Last in was Norman, dressed, as always, head to toe in black, toting two video monitors, which he took right past everyone and up the back stairs to the guest room.

A half hour later, after the mess had been wiped up, Charlie had been cleaned, and Norman had emptied the car of his gaming equipment, they finally sat down to eat.

Jeanette hardly ever joined Ann and Clare for dinner when there wasn't a group around, even lately, when Ann had invited her to more often. She preferred to fix something for herself in the kitchen in the barn. But over time she had become quite friendly with Liz and often joined in when she came. In fact, she got on better with Ann's daughter than she did with most women at the center, apparently enjoying her as a kind of antidote to the seriousness of the place. Whatever the reason, Ann was glad to have her there.

Clare stood at the head of the table dishing out her bean medley and braised tofu and then everyone set to eating. It turned out the three of them had driven not from Portland but from one of Liz's festivals in Rochester, which had taken longer than expected to wrap up. Ann didn't really know what these events consisted of other than being large and involving fantasy. Liz herself was still dressed in what looked like either a Victorian nightgown or a particularly elaborate negligee. Apparently Norman didn't participate—he was child- and pet-care—but then again, he appeared costumed at all times, gothically so, in his black sweaters and black nail polish and unruly black hair. He'd always struck Ann as a kind of mild-mannered specter. That he remained generally mute in her presence did nothing to cut against this. After Charlie was born, she wondered if his father's lugubrious appearance might actually scare the boy. Liz's choice of him as a partner had mystified Ann. But then, ever since her adolescence, when her voracious appetite for boys and drugs had driven Ann to her wit's end, Ann had found much about her daughter indecipherable. In the eight years that the two of them had married, though, she had come to see that Norman did offer a stability Liz had never had before. And she and Ann got on better now, an improvement for which Ann was grateful. However cynical her daughter had been about Viriditas at the beginning, when it was the reason for Ann giving up her job and the rectory, she had come around and was full of enthusiasm for it now. Liz would tell Clare and Roberta how she bragged about her mother's spiritual retreat in the mountains, and how everyone she described it to wanted to come. If they would just add art classes and theme weeks, she thought the place would really take off.

Through most of the meal, Clare listened patiently to Liz regale the table with the story of a man dressed as King Tut marrying a furred leprechaun on the convention floor. Jeanette seemed richly entertained by this, which didn't, Ann could tell, make the recounting of it any less difficult for Clare to endure. She wanted to welcome Liz—she always did, for Ann's sake—but she'd never found it easy.

As the tale of the nuptials unfolded, Charlie, past any reasonable bedtime, rolled on the kitchen floor grasping a giant stuffed hamster to his chest and mewling for his mother's attention. Norman, in the middle of dessert, got on the floor and rolled around with him, wrestling him for the creature.

'Oh, what fun to be a kid!' Clare bellowed, at Norman not Charlie.

* * *

Upstairs in their bathroom, she didn't mince words. 'They aren't adults,' she said as she and Ann stood in front of their sinks. 'You agree with me, you just don't want to.'

'She admires this place now,' Ann said. 'Can't that be enough?'

Clare turned off her water and put down her toothbrush. 'That child was beyond exhausted, it's no wonder he can't hold his bowels, to say nothing of the dog. Who travels with such an animal?'

It would do no good for Ann to say they would have been better off putting something in the microwave, so she didn't. Instead, she said, 'I agree, it's a lot.'

'It's not your fault,' Clare said as she applied her eucalyptus cream. 'Some people just don't want to grow up.'

'That's being a little harsh, isn't it?' Ann replied, brushing her hair out, down over the nape of her neck, feeling a pull at the roots.

'It's just the effort we put into creating a certain space here. It's as if they run right over it.'

It would do no good either for Ann to say it amazed her how long such antagonisms could last. Or that it still surprised her that Clare, after all this time, hadn't reconciled herself to Liz's way of being, even when it seemed Liz had long ago given up her adolescent resentments of her. But then Ann had never had to try to be a stepparent or to contend with all that Clare did when they were first together — being with a married woman, having to stay in the background, present but not cloying, while Richard was sick and then dying. Ann had never forgotten Clare's devotion then. And she reminded herself of it in moments like this, as she watched Clare's mottled hands in the mirror smooth the dark gray length of her hair down over her ears. They had been in love once, passionately so. It wasn't over — Ann didn't think of it that way — but it was different, naturally. In the beginning, their disagreements had seemed only to goad their desire for each other, whereas for so long now they had been simply familiar.

She splashed her face with cold water, then dried it with her towel. Turning to Clare, she opened her arms and Clare accepted a hug.

'It's only a few days,' Ann said. 'And you have to admit, you don't actually dislike her.'

'I know,' Clare said, kissing Ann on the forehead, as her extra inches had always allowed her to do. Ann could feel her softening in her arms. 'I'm sorry if I sounded harsh,' Clare added.

She pulled her in more tightly. When a moment later she loosened her grip, they rubbed noses and kissed, lips pursed. Then, surprising themselves, they kept kissing, open-mouthed. Pressing her hands down over Clare's hips, Ann grasped her close. Through Ann's nightgown, Clare cupped her breasts. These moments came much less often now but not never. Moving her hand under Ann's gown, Clare took the weight of Ann's belly onto her forearm and reached between her legs, making Ann inhale and then let go, inhale and let go, the two of them up against the bathroom door, comfortably and familiarly undone.

And yet, still and all, amid the flush of giving up, there was in Ann an old shiver of guilt—at the escape of it.

Maisie, the boxer, in addition to her limp and underbite, had a hairless black scar on her flank, apparently from a BB-gun wound. She was the latest in a long line of troubled dogs Liz had tended after meeting Norman. Ann didn't quite understand the term *fostering*, as they seemed to keep them for years at a time, and add others as the need arose, and she generally preferred not to think about the reasons for their identification with these creatures. But truth be told, within a day she had grown rather fond of this one, whose protruding teeth and alarmed, pleading expression made her hard not to pity. The dog stuck close to Charlie as he careened over the wet lawn in his little blue jeans and hooded winter jacket, Maisie only now and then running off to chase squirrels to the foot of the apple tree or the side of the barn.

'These two seem to get along,' Ann said to Liz.

'Charlie likes her more than us,' Liz said.

They stood side by side wrapped in their puffy coats and knit hats, the latter courtesy of Roberta from one Christmas or another, watching Maisie run circles around the boy.

'I've been reading some of those Buddhist books of yours that I borrowed,' Liz said, 'when I can't sleep at night. They help chill me out.'

'I'm glad to hear that, though not that you can't sleep.'

'They all go on about the preciousness of being born in the first place. Like how easily we might not have been. I think about that when I'm doing the genealogy stuff. How just one thing going differently—someone getting sick, someone not getting married, their child not surviving and marrying—if everything hadn't gone exactly the way it did for hundreds of years, you and me and Charlie, none of us would be here. So much chance. You never told us anything about that history. Dad thought you were embarrassed by it. All those colonizers.'

'I wasn't embarrassed,' Ann said. 'I just never paid much attention.'

'I don't believe that. Most of what I have is straight out of Grandpa's closet.'

'Well, if he told me, I certainly didn't retain much.'

'So you never heard about Daniel Brodhead, the general in the Revolutionary War?'

'The name's vaguely familiar.'

Charlie ran into Liz's legs and threw his arms around them. She seemed barely aware of his arrival, only belatedly putting her hand over the top of his head, a mother's idle notice of the omnipresent child. Ann didn't agree with Clare that Liz hadn't grown up, but in appearance it was true she wasn't greatly changed — the substantial makeup, the little diamond nose piercing, the dyed-jet-black hair, and now the costumes. She had, in one sense, been playing dress-up for a long time.

'I guess, like those books you've been reading,' Ann said, 'I just put more stock in the present. It's our only usable life.'

'I'm not sure what that means. Dad is pretty much in the past, being dead and all, but he's still part of me.'

'I didn't mean — '

'I know you didn't. I just think it's good to know about your past. To keep it in mind. I've got the stuff on Dad. I'll show that to Charlie too, one day. But there were things going on in your family. This Brodhead guy, he was kind of a big deal. He's got his own Wiki page. You should read it. He's your ancestor.'

The dog had followed Charlie to his mother and now tried nuzzling her way between them, wheedling for whatever affection might be going.

A while later Norman and Clare joined them for a walk out along the ridge trail, which crossed through the back of the center's property. As they moved through the woods, low clouds came and went, hiding the valley below from sight, then letting the sun back in across the path. They turned west, down toward one of the highland fields, Liz and Clare moving ahead with Charlie as Maisie ran in front.

Ann, who was almost never alone with Norman, walked beside him now.

'I've been meaning to ask how your mother is doing,' Ann said.

'Oh,' Norman said, taken aback, it seemed, that she had spoken to him at all. 'She's okay, I guess. I mean, she's been sick a long time, she doesn't move around so well, and I can't get her to quit smoking, but somehow she's still alive.'

'You being nearby must have something to do with that.'

He nodded very slightly, his hands buried in his oversize black hoodie, his shoulders pulled forward. 'I don't know,' he said. 'Maybe.'

They walked a few more paces.

'Liz keeps telling me how helpful you are with Charlie. I don't know if I've ever said this to you, but you know she is happier with you than she's ever been.'

'That's okay,' Norman said. 'You don't have to say that.'

'I'm not just saying it, I mean it. She's found something with you she didn't have before. Which I realize doesn't mean she's always happy. But still, I just wanted you to know that I see that.'

Norman had no response to this, which wasn't a surprise.

'What Clare and I do here,' Ann said eventually, 'it's strange in a lot of ways. People come to take a pause from their routines. And we're the pause. It's just that we're here all the time. What I mean is, it can leave you a little out of practice with ordinary social life, so forgive me if I'm intruding.'

'I don't know anything about ordinary social life,' Norman said. 'It's always been weird to me. How people talk about stuff. Liz just says what she's thinking more or less always, you know? I guess that's one of the reasons I like her.'

'That's true,' Ann said. 'She and her brother are very different that way.'

For a fugitive instant, she had the urge to ask: *Do you ever speak to Peter? Do you chat?* But then, why would Peter speak to Norman? What would the two of them have to say to each other?

'Why are you two dawdling!' Clare called from down the slope.

Behind her, the fog had floated in again, obscuring everything beyond, such that it appeared she stood on the verge of a great blankness.

The visit seemed to pass in no time at all. On the morning of Liz's departure, Ann went looking for Jeanette with a question about the retreatants' rooms and found her in the shed with her daughter. Jeanette had the riding lawn mower on its side and was removing one of its blades. A space heater whirred in the corner, and on the workbench the little transistor radio played Neil Young. Liz, smoking, sat cross-legged in an old wingback chair that had come with the house and which they'd never gotten around to donating anywhere; when Jeanette showed up, she took it as her own.

'I see my daughter is being a great help to you,' Ann said.

'Stop being so friendly, Mom,' Liz called out. 'She'll think you're acting weird.' Jeanette slid the last bolt off and, breaking the seal of grime, lifted the blade from the deck. 'She's witnessing my work,' Jeanette said, smiling slyly at Ann. 'You always talk about the importance of witnessing, right?'

'See, Mom? I'm a witness.'

Liz took a drag of her cigarette and blew it upward. Slouched as she was in the chair, wearing the same historical undergarment as she had on the day she arrived, though wrapped now in a tweed jacket against the chill, she looked like a slattern at the end of a long night.

'Well, you're doing a great job of witnessing,' Ann said. 'I'm sure Jeanette feels very seen.'

Jeanette laughed. She seemed to enjoy being included in their familial jibing. She was probably a decade older than Liz, but when the two of them were together she seemed younger, as if they were siblings. She was never so playful as she was in Liz's presence. It was enough, at times, to make Ann jealous.

'I came to ask you something,' Ann said, 'but now I can't remember what it was.'

'You guys need to put in a Jacuzzi,' Liz said, 'warm your bones up.' She stood, slid her cigarette into her empty Pepsi bottle, and screwed the cap back on. She would be off to the house to pack, and then they'd be leaving.

'Well,' Ann said, 'when I remember my question, I'll come

back.' She followed Liz out, and was two steps behind her on the lawn when she said, 'Dear?'

'What?'

'I just realized you haven't mentioned Peter at all.'

'*I* haven't mentioned him?' Liz said, coming to a halt, though not turning around.

'I suppose neither of us has,' Ann acknowledged. 'I was just wondering if you'd spoken to him.'

'Ah,' Liz said, 'I see. Now that I'm leaving, you're wondering.'

She turned to look at Ann now, sober-faced, no more play-acting. Ann was reminded that part of her had always been a little scared of her daughter, of her mockery.

'All right,' Ann said, 'fair enough. You're leaving, and I'm asking.'

'Well, as you may know, he works as a lawyer in New York.'

'Oh, please!' Ann said. 'Really.'

'Please what?' Liz said, opening her arms out to her sides, the wings of her jacket rising behind her in the breeze.

'It's not as if he and I are total strangers,' Ann said. 'We email now and then. It's just that he never visits.'

'So then what are you asking me?' Liz called out.

'I invite him here every year,' Ann said, her own voice rising to be heard. 'For Christmas, in the summer—you know that.'

'Yes, I'm aware.'

'And he could come anytime he wants, besides.'

'That isn't strictly true,' Liz said, 'for him, or for me.'

She was being obstinate now. A stickler, a debater.

'Fine, then,' Ann said. 'Whenever I'm not on a retreat. Which to be clear is most of the time.'

'I'm still waiting for your point,' Liz said. 'Or your question, or whatever it is.'

'You don't have to be harsh about it,' Ann said, more loudly than she'd meant to. 'I'm just asking if you've spoken to him, and how you think he is.'

She'd let herself be riled, and Liz knew it.

'Weird, isn't it?' her daughter said after a moment's pause. 'He's the one you're always curious about. Yet look who's here.'

Girvesh and Feba Rijal have been waiting in reception forty-five minutes by the time I get back from court. I apologize for being late, but Girvesh brushes it off with a tilt of his head, anxious to move on. I escort them into the conference room, checking my phone yet again to see if Vasel has responded to my latest text. He got the letter he wanted, but the better part of a week has passed and he's failed to make good on his promise.

The Rijals are in their mid-twenties yet fuss at each other like an old couple over the opening of the envelope containing the papers they've brought with them, mostly news clippings about the Nepalese civil war, along with the translations I requested. There's an article about Maoists shooting police in the rural districts and stories of forced recruiting in the villages. Given the country's poverty and unemployment, many did support the rebels' assault on the monarchy, but those who didn't, like the Rijals, were frequently tortured or killed.

Feba holds one sheet back, then hands it to me after I've glanced at the others. It's a 2005 piece in the English-language daily that mentions the abduction of a boys' football team in the Dang district.

'This is Girvesh,' she says emphatically, pointing at the document. 'This is his team.'

Girvesh mutters something critical to her in Nepali, which Feba shuts right down, prompting him to close his eyes in forced patience.

He's unusual for not having made the journey on his own, as most young men do. Feba and their five-year-old daughter were with him the whole way: from India to Peru to Mexico to Arizona, Chicago, and Jackson Heights. Feba wasn't pregnant when they left, and now they have a six-month-old too. The ladies at the Sherpa Association temple help out with babysitting, though the Rijals aren't Sherpas. Buddhists, yes, but from the lowlands. Do they go to the temple because I told them community ties are important to show in their application? I don't know, and don't ask.

I tell them the articles will help. After they left Nepal, Girvesh's mother moved to Katmandu but still has his soccer jersey, which she's promised to mail. There is some confusion as to whether it is the one with the team logo on it or not. For the next hour, I question Girvesh regarding the details of what he experienced: the number of men who stopped the bus; the number of boys they separated out as Maoists and released; the layout of the farm where they kept him and the others; the frequency and duration of the interrogations; his admission that he belonged to the Nepal Student Union; the frequency and duration of the beatings that followed this admission.

I hear what he says—I am listening to him—but when I look up from my notes, what draws my attention again is the houseplants at the far end of the conference room on the low filing cabinets, three of them in large terra-cotta pots. Their long, narrow leaves aren't just faded now. Many of them have withered and fallen off. When Vasel and Artea were here, I thought it was the changing leaves that I hadn't noticed. But now it occurs to me that I don't recognize these plants at all.

When Girvesh's voice draws me back, I see that Feba is holding her husband's hand in her lap. He has gotten to the hardest part now, describing precisely what was done to him by his captors, how they cut at his limbs, how they urinated on him. In the midst of this he tries, instinctively, to withdraw his hand from Feba's. But she doesn't allow it. Not until he's finished. Only then does she let his hand go and rests hers on the middle of his back, like a mother might comfort a son.

Later, after they've left and Phoebe has gone upstairs for the evening, Carl is the only one still working. On my way out, I stop by his office. It makes mine look practically vacant. A narrow path between document boxes and files piled in listing stacks leads to a single chair behind a desk so covered in papers there is barely room for his computer. On one wall is a poster for an anti-apartheid protest from 1989, on the other a framed, autographed photo of Václav Havel.

'I don't want barbecue, if that's what you're here to ask,' he says, without looking up from his screen.

'Those plants in the conference room,' I say. 'Have they always been there?'

Carl tilts his head. His reading glasses rest so close to the tip of his nose they seem on the verge of falling onto his keyboard. 'Plants?' he says. 'What plants?'

'You're not helping me, Carl.'

'I have no idea what you're talking about,' he says, going back to his document. 'But I'm always glad to be of service.'

I'm about to step away, but then pause. 'I'm curious,' I say. 'That Egyptian guy you mentioned in a staff meeting a while back—the one who started a strike, the one who wasn't getting back to you—did you ever hear from him?'

'Gamal? No,' Carl says. 'For all I know, he's moved to Toledo, where I will be driven to spend the rest of my *godforsaken life* if I cannot reformat this *fucking* footnote!'

'So you just leave it at that.'

'Leave what?' Carl asks. 'You can't chase clients. If they don't show up at the beginning, how're you going to get the rest of it done? Is this about that Albanian kid?'

'Yeah,' I say, embarrassed to admit it. 'I guess everyone's noticed.'

'The trouble with young people,' Carl says, 'is their optimism. They think time's plentiful. It's a dangerous quality when it comes to the law. If he figures himself out soon, he'll cooperate. And if he doesn't,' he adds with a shrug, 'long may he elude our glorious system of immigration enforcement. Meanwhile, you need to drop it.'

'But he hasn't finished telling me what happened.'

Carl strikes a key on his computer like the final note of a concerto, holds a breath, then shouts, 'I did it!' And with that, he leans back in his ancient swivel chair, clasps his hands behind his head, and gazes at me with a pitying look. 'You sound like Phoebe,' he says. 'You don't want to go down that road. You'll get nothing but lost.'

'You think Phoebe is lost?'

'It's different,' Carl says. 'She's got Jack. She's got her whole world. You're more like me—a weapon for your clients. But you get too involved, and you're a tank in the mud. Trust me, it'll only come to grief.'

* * *

That evening, heading down Sixth Avenue, I once more walk right past the Spring Street stop as if it weren't there, though this time I catch myself, and, rather than drifting south again, I turn around and get on the train where I'm supposed to. And yet, when I reach High Street and climb up the steps to Cadman Plaza, it's as if my body refuses to turn toward my building and carries me instead across the median into the park, up past the row of empty benches toward the War Memorial. I see this path every morning and night but never have reason to walk it. A slight sweetness perfumes the slightly warmer air, from the sprouting grass or the buds of the plane trees, I can't tell.

I could text Cliff. He could come to the apartment to fill this little gap between work and sleep and I could half pretend along with him that I am something more than impatient for the gap to simply close. But tonight, that isn't enough. I need to talk to someone. A friend. An urge that only reminds me how bad I've been over the years at staying in touch with people—from college or law school or any other time. There are some. Dinners that used to be every few months but are now once a year. People I would have to begin with by explaining too much. And what is it that I would explain to them, exactly?

Instead, I take out my phone and call Liz.

'What are you—in the hospital?' she asks as soon as she picks up.

'No. Why?'

'This is the second time you've called me in a month. It's almost like we're siblings. I'm telling you, you missed a real party up at lesbian camp. They've installed an amazing sound system. Mom's become a dancing queen, it's all coke and hustlers now. Coke, hustlers, and knitwear.'

I want to ask her to stop turning everything into a joke. But the truth is, I'm just glad to hear her voice.

'Where are you for real?' she asks.

'Do you remember how Dad used to walk to work?' I say. 'Even if it was snowing or raining. Every day, no matter the weather.'

'Of course I do. He walked in blizzards, he walked when it was ninety-five out.'

'And he had that perfectly good car. *Who wants to be a softy?* Isn't that what he used to say? That he did it to stay strong.'

'He did it to piss Mom off. To see the look on her face when he refused to get in her car with us on the way to school with the rain pissing down. But what *Twilight Zone* episode are you in anyway that's got you remembering this?'

'I don't know,' I say, turning around on the oval lawn and looking back at the massive stone memorial at the center of the park. 'I just thought of it. He used to do it even when Mom was away. When she went off on those mission trips to Honduras with Clare in the summer. I remember him coming up the driveway in some heat wave with his clothes soaked and just wanting him to stop, to drive like a normal person. I don't think I realized it back then, but when I remember it now, I think: I pitied him. That's what I couldn't stand. That's what made me want to flee. I didn't want to pity him.'

'Peter, I'm having this sense that you're going through some kind of *experience*,' my sister says. 'And if I didn't have an aging infant refusing to use the toilet, I might even ask you about it, or even—who knows?—tell you how it went for *me* visiting Mom, which, PS, you haven't asked about. But nature is again calling my son, so really, I have to go.'

'Okay,' I say, 'sorry. I'll try you soon.'

'Yeah,' she says. 'You do that.'

I wander toward a row of benches and take a seat on one. On the far side of the park, the stone and glass facade of the federal courthouse looms up over the tops of the trees. On the rare occasions that a case of mine is both strong enough and hangs on an unsettled question of law, it's to that building or the federal courthouse downtown that I get to bring it. Those are the moments we are supposed to be most excited about, because on the even rarer occasions that they go our way, we help not just one person but hundreds, even thousands. A legal standard gets tweaked; a rule of timing is modified; the precise quantity or quality of what one subset of asylum seekers must show to remain out of danger is slightly adjusted.

But Vasel's case will never make it into that building. Not a year from now, not five years from now. At the moment, it's hardly a case at all. I should follow Carl's advice. I've been doing this long enough to know that he's right. But I can't help it. I take Vasel's file from my satchel, look up his phone number, and dial it.

He picks up on the fourth ring.

'You promised,' I say.

'Okay, okay,' he says.

Two days later, we meet at the nearly empty diner around the corner from the office. Despite showing up late, as soon as Vasel sits down, he starts typing on his phone, apologizing as he does it, saying he will be done in a minute. I don't chastise him for this. And when he finally puts his phone down, I don't dive right into my questions, as I'm tempted to do. Rather, I start off easy, and ask about his job.

He tells me the restaurant is very good, very professional. His second night, a supermodel came in, someone he hadn't heard of but now understands is famous. The bartender told him, 'That's nothing, just wait.'

'What people spend there,' Vasel says, 'it's crazy. The money — for me, it's the most ever.'

I set my notepad down on the table between us.

'I take classes, too, you know,' he says, as if my question about his work suggests I underestimate him. 'The ICE woman who interviewed me, she didn't believe me, she said I needed a letter from the school. But I started when I got here. Artea showed me. Two more required, and then I can do the ones I want.' He hesitates, deciding on something, then reaches into his jacket and takes out a notebook. 'Business,' he says. 'I will do a class for that, and also graphics. You want to see?'

He leafs through the pages, worrying over which to show me, then flips the notebook around and slides it across the table. The drawing he's selected is a densely patterned bull's-eye in fine black pen, each concentric ring composed of a different repeated shape, hundreds and hundreds of tiny geometric forms, as precise as can be.

'This must have taken a long time,' I say, amazed at the level of detail, the exactly replicated interlacing of the shapes along the border of each ring.

'I have much bigger ones,' he says. 'I can fill a whole wall when I get my own room. These are just tests. But it will be a business, too, like logos for companies.'

'This is great,' I say, 'the classes, all of it. Good things to tell the judge.'

He looks away dismissively. 'I don't do it for that,' he says.

'Of course not. I'm just saying it helps.'

The diner's owner, who in the late afternoons is also the waiter, approaches to take our order. He knows all of us at the office as the ones who come at odd hours with clients, spending little but tipping well, so when Vasel asks for a coffee and I order a corn muffin, he gathers our giant menus up with a forgiving bow of the head.

In a booth against the far wall a young woman in an oversize headset is bent over her laptop, oblivious to the intense whispering of the nearby elderly couple, the only other customers at present, first-generation Village gentrifiers by the looks of them, black-clad but shabbily so, who often come here to argue, or continue their argument.

'Your boyfriend, he is a lawyer, too?' Vasel says, his tone an uneasy mix of surly and playful. 'Is this what you guys talk about—what judges like?'

'You mean in the tower in Hell's Kitchen we live in?'

He grins at this, against his will, it seems. (I've remembered something he said.) 'Yeah, in your tower,' he says.

I haven't seen him smile this broadly before and am taken aback at how immediately happy it makes me. As if I've already succeeded. As if he could walk out of here right now and our meetings would have been somehow worth it, regardless of what happens with this case.

He's still grinning, but covering his mouth now, as if he shouldn't be. 'Once,' he says, 'this guy, he took me to a musical, and he knew all the words, and after, we went to a bar, and everyone there, they knew the words too! Everyone was singing! You know this place? It's crazy.'

'If it's the one I think you mean, yeah, I know it, it's not far from here.'

'The people there?' he says. 'In Albania, they would not be okay. But this guy, he came from Texas to see Broadway and Ground Zero. That is where I met him, down there, selling that shit. He talked to me — he was a customer so I couldn't tell him to go away. He said, I have a ticket, do you want to come? So then I knew he was gay and probably he wanted sex, and I told him I don't do that. And he looked at me very sad, like a kid, like I hurt him or something. And he said no, that's not what he meant. He was older, like you. And he seemed okay, like he was just lonely. So I made an excuse to Artea and I went with him. Everywhere, at the show, at the bar, the other gays — none of them were my age — they looked at me like I was some kind of animal, like the guy I was there with owned me.' He pauses and gazes out the window, at the passersby. 'Armend,' he says, 'he would be jealous. Me seeing that show, seeing the dancers in New York.'

The owner appears with the coffee, the muffin, and a check. I write *V. Marku* and the date on my pad and underline it.

'Are you still in touch with Armend?' I ask.

He shakes his head.

I'll need him to be but don't want to go there yet.

'The way those men looked at me,' he says, 'maybe it was because they wanted to fuck me, I don't know. Or maybe they just thought I was trash. But the weird thing? It was the same as those men back home, the ones who talked shit to me. They looked at me the same way—like I wasn't really a person.' He lowers his eyes to the coffee in front of him but doesn't touch it.

'When we spoke before,' I say, trying to lead him back into the story, 'you were telling me how the old men came to your house, and your sister's wedding was called off.'

'I need to ask you something,' Vasel says, very seriously. 'Will you be honest, you promise?'

I nod.

'Am I too short?' he asks. 'Online, everyone, they want tall guys, tall white guys. I am too short, right? Don't lie.' He scans my face as vigilantly as he did on the day we first met.

'I'm not being rude,' I say, 'but we really need to focus.'

'See,' he says, 'it is true. You are not denying it.'

'I'm not here to comment on your appearance. You seem like a perfectly normal height.'

He shakes his head. 'That's what tall guys always say.' He leans toward me across the table. 'You are bullshitting me,' he nearly shouts, flinging the words in my face. 'You're a bullshitter!'

Suddenly everything is vivid: the sea blue of his eyes, the bright white of his shirt, the glowing red neon sign in the window behind him. Blood thuds in my ears. My nostrils flare to the scent of cheap coffee and Clorox and Vasel's astringent aftershave. This young man—he wants to fight me. And in the flood of his aggression, I am disorientingly alive. As if wrenched from slumber.

Either I give in and tell him what he's demanding that I tell him—that he's unattractive, unlovable—or I'm a liar, not to be trusted, in which case he will walk out of here right now and I'll never see him again. It's a diversion, I know that. A way to ward off my questions. I've been here before. A client trying to conscript me into condemning him, into agreeing how selfish he is to have left his family behind, or how deserved his wretched treatment was. And each time I've said, *No, you're wrong,* with compassion or pity, however fleeting or dutiful. But what I experience now with Vasel is neither of these. It's contempt. A roiling, visceral contempt. Look at him. So naive, so insecure, so vain.

If I'm not careful, I'll give him all the judgment he's asking for.

He leans back against the banquette, moving his face away from mine.

I take a breath, dizzy almost. 'I'm telling you the truth,' I say. 'Honestly, there's nothing wrong with your appearance.'

His aggression isn't gone, but it's smoldering now. He stares again at the dull white coffee cup in its dull white saucer. 'Whatever,' he says. 'It doesn't matter. You just want to know if we lied, Artea and me, right?'

'If I'm going to help you, what I need to know is what actually occurred.'

'My mother, she was the one who gave me money for the passport, not Artea,' he says. 'Money from what she saved for my sister, so she could get married. She put it in an envelope and handed it to me. I went to Tirana, to my aunt's. Her husband knew a person in one of the offices. He didn't want to help me, but my aunt made him. I stayed at their apartment. For a few weeks. Until I got the plane ticket.'

'Where did you fly?'

'Germany. I slept on a bench in the airport. They woke me with dogs, but they didn't smell anything, so they just checked my ticket and let me go.'

'Why the U.S.? Why not somewhere else in Europe?'

'My aunt is related to Artea's family through her husband. She knows that they are successful. Anyway, it is better here. There are too many Albanians in Europe. And for people like me—like you,' he says sardonically, 'New York is the best, right? But not my neighborhood, I hate it. Every day people are watching. Artea, her uncles, the people in the store, the idiot guys with Hummers. Why are you never around? they ask. Where do you go? I hate it.'

I give his frustration a moment to settle, then try once more to circle back. 'So the wedding was canceled. Then what? Is that when the men attacked you?'

He slouches further into the banquette. 'No,' he says, slowly. 'That is not how it works.'

I wait for him to go on but when he says nothing more, I ask what he means.

Another long pause. Using his thumb and middle finger, he slowly rotates his coffee cup in the saucer, as if hypnotizing himself. 'For these things,' he says, 'it is not other people who decide. It is up to the family.'

Again I wait. And after a moment, he goes on.

'There is a field,' he says. 'In front of our house. It goes down to the road. There is a big rock in it. We used to play there, Arbi and Pera and me. That was where I went. After the old men left. I couldn't go inside. I could not stand to see Pera. Arbi and my father—they were arguing, drinking and arguing in the front room. So I sat there. I don't know how long. A long time, I guess. It was dark when my mother came out. She had my schoolbag. Clothes and books in it. Her English books. That was when she gave me the money. She just said, *Take it*. And told me to sleep in the front room, not upstairs in my bed. Because we will leave early together.

'So I did. I slept there that night. The neighbor's goats, they have bells on them, they are always moving around. I never really listened before, but it was the only sound. I thought, I need to remember this, I will not hear it anymore. When Arbi got me up, it was still dark. And I thought, Okay, we are leaving, I am going. My father was in the van, he was still drunk. I never saw him so drunk before. And my uncle too, my father's brother, he was there, he was driving. He didn't make any sound with the van, he let it roll down to the road, quiet, so we wouldn't wake anyone.'

As Vasel speaks, I take notes but try as much as I can to keep my eyes on him, to keep him going.

'There is a stream,' he says. 'Near my uncle's house. You hear it everywhere in spring, like a river. But it was summer, there was not much water, you could only hear it if you were close. It's not really the woods. Artea said the woods, but it is just some trees and bushes by the stream, near my uncle's barn.'

He pauses, turning his cup in the saucer, inch by inch.

'My father is not to blame,' he says, glancing up at me. 'You understand? Arbi, he is the one that dragged me out in the dark. He smelled like shit. Drunk, but dirty also, like his cars. He doesn't change his clothes hardly, and he thinks women are bitches for not wanting him, but who wants that? He is gross. He always hit me anyway, when I was a kid, so whatever, that was what he did, when he got me down on the ground. Only more. He started kicking me. He said, *You need to die, you bring shame, say your prayers.* Like he is some movie-star gangster. That is all he wants, for people to think he's hard.'

Vasel shifts his eyes across the diner to the woman in the head-set and the bickering couple, peering at these people as if trying to discern if they are real or a mirage.

'The stream, it was in my ear,' he says. 'Not the water, the sound. I guess I was right next to it, on the stones. And cold. The air wasn't cold, but I was. I didn't see my father, not his face. He was standing in front of the headlights. I only saw his shape. The way he holds his rifle when he is shooting birds. He told Arbi to stop kicking me. His voice was weird, I guess because he was cry-ing. I am not sure, I'd never heard him cry. He came up close and said to me, *You are not my son.* He didn't mean it. I know he didn't mean that. But he had to say it. He said I would go to heaven with the angels, and one day I would see my mother and Pera. But not him, and not my brother, they would go to hell. Arbi shouted at him then, but he told Arbi to shut up.'

Vasel sits up in the booth, bowing his head slightly. He's sweating now, his forehead glistening with moisture.

'My father tried to leave too, you know,' he says. 'When I was young, and things were bad everywhere, and there was no money. He went to Durrës and took a boat to Italy. Lots of the men did. But they sent them back, they didn't let them stay. That's what he wanted for me, too. He never said it, but I know. It's not his fault, what happened to me. He had to do it. To save my family's honor.'

After a pause, he says, 'My father put his rifle up to me. I am not sure where my uncle was. Watching, I guess. Arbi too. But then there was this voice, like a dying person's, like someone who's angry to be dying, shouting my father's name. I never heard my mother's voice anything like that. Like she was God out of the Bible. She rode her bike there maybe, I don't know. She must have heard us leave. And she knocked my father down. He was so drunk, it was easy. Knocked him down right next to me. He was lying there. I could smell him. And Arbi shouted at her, *It is none of your business*. He shouted that I am a curse on all of them. *Djall*, my mother called him—demon. *I will slit your throat*. She yelled that at my brother. *I will cut it with my hands*, she said.'

He lifts his coffee cup from its saucer for the first time now and takes a sip. Sirens blare out on the avenue.

'So, there,' he says. 'This is what you wanted, right?'

II

'Sir, you forgot this,' the owner of the diner calls to me on the sidewalk after Vasel walks off, holding out my satchel with my laptop in it, and client files, and the notes I just took. He hands it to me, and I thank him, twice, and he bows his head the way he does and walks back into the restaurant, turning to gaze at me curiously from behind the glass door. Which is when I realize that I'm not moving. I'm standing stock-still in the middle of the sidewalk, facing the booth Vasel and I were just sitting in, pedestrians passing me by.

I should be returning to the office, catching up on other work. But instead I head south, against the traffic, and I don't stop, walking all the way down through Tribeca, across the park in front of City Hall, and up onto the Brooklyn Bridge, toward my apartment.

Down the clear sky the sun is setting over Bayonne, its last rays still shimmering on the facades of the towers past Brooklyn Heights. Words from a poem I haven't read since college float up out of some occluded region of my mind: *The City's fiery parcels all undone.* A poem about this bridge. Hart Crane, the one who jumped from a ship after a sailor he had made a drunken pass at beat him up. *Only in darkness is the shadow clear.* Or a phrase like that. Cryptic language, but somehow thrilling. If only in the sudden recall of it. As if of pleasure.

Below, the East River disperses into the harbor, past the green of Governors Island, into the gray waters flowing out toward the Verrazzano, and beyond into the ocean in the distance, the vista opening newly before me, as though despite its near daily familiarity, I'm seeing it for the first time.

I wasn't the only one who found Jared Hanlan beautiful. Most people did—kids, teachers, parents. Though his beauty also unnerved them. Because he wasn't just handsome, he was pretty. Too pretty, almost, for a boy. There was a fineness to his looks, his heart-shaped face and dark green eyes, a slight androgyny, accentuated by the New Wave clothes he favored, the fitted black pants that barely reached his ankles, the flowing white shirts, his luxuriant blond hair buzzed at the sides. He'd modeled, that was the rumor, for teen-clothing catalogs, and it wasn't hard to believe. Girls were entranced by him. Boys were jealous, or thought he was a fag, or both. He was in the class above me, a junior, inaccessible, guarded by his cool, jaded companions, Stephanie and Brett.

In between classes, I'd spy on the three of them from an upper-hallway window as they smoked in the courtyard. Or I'd sit on the bench outside the cafeteria so I could watch them leaving campus for lunch, which they weren't supposed to do. I joined the drama club because they were all in it. In the one class Jared and I had together, I sat as close behind him as I dared. Sometimes looking at him felt too exciting to bear, the churn in my chest and head so violent, it seemed on the verge of spinning out into the room. At other moments it was like hypnosis: the past, the present, everything around me disappearing, except him.

For my photography class, I started to snap shots of our play rehearsals, pictures Jared supposedly just happened to be in, that I supposedly just happened to be taking. Then pictures of the three of them off in a corner during the breaks, Stephanie usually in one of her sleek black dresses, wearing dark lipstick and dark eye shadow, every bit a match for Jared in the precision of her outfits, while Brett, the most conventional of the group, made up for the sloppiness of his attire — his ill-fitting jeans and faded polos — with the volume of his cynicism, always trying to outdo the others when it came to disaffection.

In the safety of those theater stairwells or up in the balcony with no one else around, the three of them would indulge me, gazing into the camera with their looks of elaborate boredom. And when they went out onto the back steps to smoke, I'd follow and take yet more pictures.

'What's your damage, anyway?' Jared asked.

'Nothing,' I said. 'I just have an assignment, to do portraits.' Which was true.

Brett and Stephanie chuckled.

'Sounds pretty gay to me,' Brett said, 'but boy model here probably likes it.'

'It's not my fault your mother dresses you like a sixth-grader,' Jared retorted. He was posing a bit now, in front of the brick wall, one foot up against it, his head rolled back. He knew how to flaunt himself in a way neither Brett nor any of the other boys at school did.

'But is this really the exposure you're looking for,' Stephanie asked him, 'at this point in your little career?'

They mocked each other like this constantly. Deriding each other's clothes, looks, odor, choice of music, choice of words, one put-down after another. It was a kind of joint performance with Jared in the lead. And the more I hung around taking pictures of them, the more they seemed to accept me as their audience. If I got too close to Jared with the camera, crouching down to get a shot of him lighting a cigarette or leaning in as he lay back across the hood of his car in the school parking lot, he'd say, 'Okay, weirdo,' to prove to Brett and Stephanie that he wasn't that into it. And they'd smile at my little shaming, and I'd back off.

Jared was the only one of them with a car, putting him even more in charge of their movements, and one day, instead of leaving me in the lot after school, he let me go with them in that blue coupe of his, with the plush blue seats and wide middle console that let you see the driver in full profile.

'You're becoming an actual person,' Stephanie said to me across the back seat, amused that I had been promoted into their company.

She'd lived in London for a year and was always reading books no one had assigned her. She did this even in the car, seemingly oblivious to the despondent pop Jared blared from the speakers up front.

'You put your camera away,' she added, not looking up from the page, 'what will Jared do without his paparazzi?'

Stephanie was the one who'd taught me how to be with them—find the thing I could be superior about. When they cut you, never defend yourself, only cut back. If you get the laugh, you win. I was a better student than either Brett or Jared. It wasn't much to work with, but the first time I dared taunt Brett for getting a D on a history paper, Jared cackled. And not at me.

Some afternoons, he'd drive us out past the edge of town and turn along a road that stretched into the woods and down to the lake. He'd pass around a joint, I'd smoke more than I knew how to tolerate, and while Stephanie sat in the car reading, Jared and Brett and I would tear off into the woods and whip branches and stones at one another, missing most often by a mile.

But the closer any of us got to landing a blow, the harder Jared and Brett laughed, their mockery physical now and chaotic. I'd never been so exhilarated in my life. To be violent with them, to compete not in some dumb sport but for the most absurd attempt to injure each other. The thrill of it was overwhelming. I hurled the largest branches I could lift, threw rocks inches from their heads, whacked them in the legs with a stick as they whacked back at me. Then whacked harder still until even Brett shouted, 'You're insane,' which was the most thrilling of all, to sense that I existed enough in their eyes to almost scare them.

After we exhausted ourselves, we'd lie on the pine needles by the shore of the lake, tripping on the light in the trees. There by the water I'd close my eyes and let myself imagine Jared leaning down over me to touch his lips to mine. *The language of love slips from my lover's tongue*, that song went, *cooler than ice cream, and warmer than the sun.* And still he'd be there when I opened my eyes again, this gorgeous boy. The one who had just hurt me for fun, and let me hurt him back.

The sun is down but the streets still light as I descend the steps that lead off the bridge and walk up toward my building. In the elevator, I get a text from Cliff. *So have we like broken up?* If I could hear his voice asking the question, I could gauge the level of irony in it. Whether he's playing with the notion that we are even together enough to break up, or if he's actually wondering. But the typed words are mute. He's soliciting a reaction. To find out what's safe to ask and what isn't. But rather than answering, as soon as I get in my apartment, I put my phone aside and begin my research.

The State Department's country conditions report on Albania is mixed. Homosexuality was decriminalized in the '90s. An anti-discrimination bill, recently passed, includes sexual orientation. These are facts that Homeland Security will rely on. An improving environment in the country of origin. Fledgling rights groups in Tirana are allowed to operate without interference from the state. *You see, Your Honor, there are protections. Even a small parade.* But in the same report there is the Albanian deputy defense secretary stating, 'My only commentary on this gay parade is that the organizers should be beaten with clubs.' And there are the groups of young men who then in fact throw tear gas at the participants.

And the politician who, on national television, tells the activist, 'If you were my son, I would put a bullet in your head.' All of which will be helpful. As will the NGO reports of a gay man who went into hiding for over a year after death threats from his family; the lesbian woman beaten by relatives and confined to her home; a student prevented from attending school by police harassment and, according to a local source, torture.

These reports will be useless, however, if the judge doesn't believe Vasel is gay. If his story can't be at least partially corroborated. I start an email to him about the documents he needs to collect, then realize I'm hungry and that the takeout I ordered as I began to read has already gone cold. I shut my laptop, microwave the food, and return to my seat.

The table I'm sitting at is made of dark lacquered wood, a higher-end IKEA model that I put together the day I moved here ten years ago, its bolts still tight. It's not a thing I notice from one day to the next, but it occurs to me now that it has remained all this time in exactly the place I positioned it that first evening. As has the sideboard across the room, the one I found on the street in the snow. On the sideboard is a green and beige lamp whose origin I don't remember, two tiles I bought on a solo trip to Portugal, and in either corner a small black speaker wired to a subwoofer on the bottom shelf. A sound system that was once crisp and resonant but now cuts in and out and needs to be either repaired or thrown away. The overstuffed gray sofa, the silver and white standing lamp beside it, the vaguely modernist metal coffee table—all remain where they have always been.

I put my plate aside and keep reading. It turns out Artea is right. The government is seeking to get Albania into the EU, effectively requiring the country to pass human-rights protections to show fealty to official Europe's idea of tolerance. But the reports suggest that local authorities have taken little notice of this or any of the laws intended to satisfy Brussels. In the north, there are still blood feuds over land and honor, killings between families that by custom must be avenged. Boys and young men are forced to shelter in their homes or risk being murdered in cycles of reprisal that go on for decades. These too are considered family matters, not subject to police interference, adjudicated by the traditional law of the kanun, a custom suppressed but never eliminated under Communism, practiced in the shrinking towns and villages of the highlands. Perhaps so, the department will say, but the applicant could live in the capital. There's no right to asylum from your hometown.

But everyone knows everyone, that's what Artea said. People from the towns and villages have family in Tirana. Vasel won't be safe. This too will require corroboration. News articles or analogous cases, a submission from an academic who studies the region.

It's after midnight by the time I get up and take my food containers to the kitchen, too late to reply to Cliff's text much less ask him over. In my bedroom, after I've turned out the light, I lie there with my eyes wide open and begin to shape in my head the argument I must now make.

The day my parents sat Liz and me down to tell us they would be separating, my mother tried to make it sound almost inconsequential. 'He'll be very close by,' she said, 'he's not going far at all.' As if he were doing nothing more than moving to a different room in the rectory. Maybe one of those curtained rooms off the upstairs back hall used to store boxes of old hymnals or sets for the holiday pageant. My father sat like he did during my mother's sermons, his elbows on his knees, head bowed.

'So are you going to tell us why?' Liz asked.

My father lifted his gaze then, not to my sister, but to me.

'You want to know the reason I'm moving out?'

We were in the living room. It was a few weeks before Thanksgiving, that same fall that I'd begun hanging out with Jared and the others. The two of them sat on opposite ends of the long, low couch. Behind them was the table of houseplants, their dark green leaves dull beneath a coating of dust. We knew the reason, but we weren't supposed to know it.

'Well, I think your mother can explain that best. Can't you?' he said, without turning to face her.

His words were somehow physical. As much objects as sounds. And he was using them to squeeze my mother. To force her to say:

Clare. Clare is the reason. To make this hard thing harder for her. Mostly, I felt bad for him. He hadn't wanted to come to this town in the first place. He loved our mother and often told me and Liz that. And now he was being asked or told to leave. But still, something about the way he spoke that day, the way he tried to force my mother to speak, scared me. He watched me watching him as he did it—this little act of violence, open and veiled all at once. It seemed like an initiation almost, as if he were revealing to me the way of the world. *You see, Peter? This is what people do to each other.*

An apartment was what he got. In a white brick building, next to the fire station, with a cracked concrete patio that none of the residents used. It had a spare room meant for Liz and a foldout couch for me, though neither of us stayed there much, with the rectory being only a bike ride away.

In the months after he moved, the way he spoke to me began to change. He'd always lectured us at the dinner table about politics and the news, but now that he was living on his own, and with Liz hardly ever visiting him, I was the only audience left, and his lectures became angrier. He admired Ronald Reagan, but couldn't fathom him not punishing Iraq for killing thirty-seven American sailors on the USS *Stark*. 'You can't project weakness,' he told me. 'It only invites people to harm you.' The same with Hezbollah in Lebanon. 'We never should have pulled those Marines out. You never run from a fight. You need to understand that, Peter.' But this didn't mean the government was the answer to everything. Businesses like his were being drowned by the government.

'Most of your friends' parents, they make money off money,' he said, 'or they get paid with donations to some do-gooder charity. But they don't handle things, they don't touch things. I'm not saying they're bad people, but there's a difference. It changes what you know.'

He would point at me as he spoke with a fork or a pen. Liz said it was because he didn't have our mother to argue with anymore, that spending time on his own was making him crazier, and that this was why he'd gotten so thin and pale.

At the Howard Johnson's where he took me for breakfast on Saturday mornings, he asked once out of the blue if I was dating anyone. 'Don't look so surprised,' he said, 'you're sixteen. You'd tell your mother, so tell me.'

My mother was gay, apparently. Or at least, she wanted to be with a woman. If it had been another man, my father would have exploded. But Clare being a woman had denied his fury a target. He'd always proclaimed that all he wanted was for our mother to be happy. But now he didn't know if she ever had been.

Me wanting a boy, though. I knew, somehow, that would be worse. Women were mysteries. Which was what made the way he'd romanced my mother a sort of miracle to him. To have solved a mystery so many men never did. Men themselves were animals. Common, obvious creatures. When it came to the men he employed, the men he did business with, the only thing you could trust was their desire for money. If my mother loved a woman, she would still be a woman herself, just more inscrutable than he had imagined. But a man wanting another man was an appetite gone wrong. He never said this. When AIDS came on the news, he didn't mutter disgust or claim they deserved it. His face just grew tense with impatience for the broadcast to move on.

'No,' I told him, 'I'm not dating anyone.'

'Oh, come on,' he said, 'there's tons of girls at your school.' Something seemed to catch in his throat as he said it, and he started coughing and then couldn't stop, slugs of saliva and masticated food blowing onto his napkin, until finally he took several sips of water to calm his throat. He was, as Liz had observed, thinner and paler. And now he seemed sick as well.

'You must like someone,' he said eventually.

I shook my head and kept eating.

There is the Rijals' application to complete, and Joseph Musa's, and Hassan El Moctor's, and dozens of others besides, but in the days after meeting Vasel at the diner, it is to his case that I return each evening. Even after I have the two hundred pages or more of supporting materials a strong submission needs, and after I've emailed an anthropologist of contemporary Balkan societies and an Albanian sociologist who's testified in British asylum cases. Still I go back over my notes, reviewing each element of Vasel's account.

The bunkers—he wasn't making them up. Enver Hoxha, the Stalinist dictator who ran the country for forty years and turned it into one of the most isolated nations in the world, believed Albania was in perpetual danger of invasion. His generals advised the building of a modern army but instead he insisted on the construction of thousands of domed pillboxes, in city squares and village centers, in fields, on beaches, in backyards. From these concrete forts, he was convinced, an armed citizenry would fire at the enemy, as he and his partisans had in World War II, first at the Italian Fascists, then the Germans. He banned religion, private property, and travel abroad. Khrushchev and then Mao were deemed insufficiently doctrinaire, and relations were cut first with the Soviet Union and then

China. Albania became the North Korea of Europe until Hoxha finally died, and his successor floundered. The sudden end of the one-party state brought chaos, food shortages, and land disputes, as everyone tried to reclaim what had been theirs sixty years earlier. But the bunkers remained. Too numerous and substantially built to demolish. Littering the landscape, in the towns and on the hillsides.

Vasel mentioned a period when there was no money, which I took to mean in his family until I read about the Ponzi schemes that swept the country in the '90s, hundreds of thousands of people giving all their savings to newly privatized banks offering absurdly high interest rates. People selling their land and borrowing cash to get in on the bonanza. When the swindle was up, and their money gone, they revolted, attacking offices and government buildings, bringing the country close to civil war.

Even what he said about his father trying to leave the country himself as a young man—there it is in the news archives: Albanians fleeing to escape economic collapse. The most notorious episode of this being a cargo ship commandeered by migrants in the port of Durrës and forced to sail across the Adriatic carrying ten thousand or more people, some clinging to boarding ladders for the duration of the journey, only to have the authorities in Brindisi refuse to let the ship dock. They sailed up the coast to Bari, were confined in a stadium, then sent back.

With one of the articles, there's a photograph: the ship after it arrived at its second port. Every square inch of the aging vessel's deck is jammed with people, a town's worth on one boat. Yet on the dock beside it, there is a still vaster and denser crowd that has already disembarked, though it seems impossible these people could ever have fit on the ship already dangerously overfull. These men stand packed against one another, with no room to sit, most shirtless in the heat. The photograph is shot from a vantage in the port overlooking the scene, at too great a distance to discern any individual's face. It's the kind of picture that rights groups use to prick the consciences of their donors and that nativists employ to stoke fear and panic.

I gaze at it, enlarged on my computer screen. The gray ship *Vlora* lists toward the shore, weighed down by men gathered on the near edge, trying to join the others confined on the dock, against the literal edge of the country, their backs to the sea. Any one of them could be Vasel's father. A man sent back to his country, a man who opened a store, had a family. Then found himself one night at that stream with a gun to his son's chest.

The photograph has no bearing on Vasel's hearing, but I print it out anyway and add it to the file.

With each breath, cool air freshened the lining of her nose, the same air warming the same flesh as it flowed back out into the quiet of the studio. The iron of the stove ticked as it heated. Outside, a breeze moved high in the firs. These sounds less heard than felt, the membrane between Ann and the world loosening.

But what for? Simply to cease thinking? To rest in equanimity for her own peace of mind? No. Meditation was a means, not an end. Compassion, that was the gift, to be gained and given. To allow it for oneself, yes, because without it you only spread the poison of its lack, but to direct it toward others, too. This was the real purpose of all the various practices.

One of them being to envision, first, a person for whom you felt the most direct affection, to breathe in whatever suffering the person might be in, and breathe out what amounted to a prayer for that suffering's end. For Ann, this first person was nearly always Roberta, for whom she felt such ready gratitude. Her warmth and understanding and generosity. She summoned her friend now, her gray-green eyes and round face and sun-mottled cheeks, her joyful smile, and she drew into herself the arthritic pain Roberta often lay awake with in the night, the fear she lived with that her breast cancer might return, the loneliness she often felt in her marriage, holding these tensions in her own spirit for a moment, then offering back to the summoned spirit of her friend all the lightness and ease that she had to give. An offering that brought gladness with it, joy even, in the felt reminder of the love she bore Roberta, which would be more present to her now throughout the day.

Second, a person you encountered but did not know, for whom you felt neither affection nor animosity. Today the person who came to mind was the woman who ran the shipping-and-variety store in town. Pleasant, helpful, though never forthcoming, a woman of thirty or so, whose mother had been the mailwoman for years, who had kids of her own now who often played in the back after school. Ann pictured her in her denim shirt and jeans and brown boots, her long brown hair done up in a scraggly bun, letting her mind rest on this picture, then breathing in whatever it might be that weighed on this woman, the stresses of running her business, the stresses of child-rearing, any heartache or pain there might be, gathering it into herself, and offering back in its place gentleness and calm.

It was so basic a practice, such an ordinary part of her former life—to pray for others. And yet when she'd been a priest with a congregation, reciting those prayers and exhortations, she'd longed for some means to experience rather than just rehearse this giving of spirit. To embody the offer. There was the work of charity, and she had done it. Down the street, in the parish, in Boston soup kitchens, in a Honduran village helping to build houses. But always present in her had been charity's companion, pity. Pity and the distance it secured. This being the moral architecture of liberalism (about that Richard had not always been wrong). Which wasn't to say the Gospels weren't still with her—the necessity of love and generosity for those in need was simply the truth—but that in meditation she'd come to see the fear that lay behind pity and had found a way to let go of both.

Third, a person for whom it was hard to feel compassion. Gathering that person's suffering into you as you had for the others, and offering in return your own well-being. However many mornings Ann had trained her mind along this course, she always stumbled at this point, if only for a moment, not so much in the doing of it as in the choosing of the person. Would it just be Mitch McConnell's vacant soul she'd carry again for a few moments, offering him in its place her most universalized love? Or, closer to home, Gerry Connor, their neighbor up the road who their first month here had warned them in the supermarket he didn't want dykes going near his kids, had never talked to them since, and now had an image of Obama in the crosshairs of a rifle on the back of his truck? Or, closer still, would it be a woman staying at the center who'd, knowingly or not, insulted Ann or triggered her anger or resentment, someone she'd be glad to see gone? And when, fleetingly, she couldn't decide, the whole exercise would suddenly seem absurd, just so much self-absorbed Western Buddhist bullshit — sitting alone in a cabin in the woods picking which person you couldn't extend your heart to — until she recognized for the umpteenth time the purpose of these accusations shouted at herself in the silence: to distract her from the unwanted realization that on some days, this third person was Clare. Or, worse, this morning, her son.

There was nothing to the summoning of Peter. She didn't need to picture his willowy frame or once freckled cheeks or hazel eyes or any particular at all. He entered her as unseen as he'd grown in her — a living presence. Not hers but of her. From the utterly dependent infant, to the restless boy, to the melancholy adolescent in whom she had seen her own younger self. There had been moments when Richard was sick and Clare was pressing on her that she had wished she could be an adolescent herself again, as if she might have hidden from her own life in her son's body, a reverse birth, to freeze time before he got older and they were separated.

This was the thing about observing your thoughts rather than controlling them—they flew off in all directions. Peter. She summoned Peter. Working, always working. In that city he'd moved to at eighteen for college and never left. Where for years she'd worried he would be one of the young men who got sick and died of AIDS. He was so serious already, by then. The boy who used to sit on the braided rug laying his head against her thigh as she read in the living room after dinner, asking what her book was about, or, earlier still, lie transfixed in his bed as she read him story after story. Even if much of the texture of his life now was a blank to her, she could imagine some of what had to weigh on him. The fates of the people he spent his days helping. That most of all. He'd stopped going to church in his teens and had never gone back, as far as she knew, and yet daily he did the work of welcoming strangers. Then there was his being on his own. Was he still? She imagined him so. And wouldn't Liz, despite her resentment of Ann's curiosity, have said something about Peter having a person in his life? Did his being alone pain him as much as it pained her? That a child of such deep affections was without someone to offer them to? Of course she could feel compassion for him in these things. How could she not? So why not Peter first in her practice, welcomed in, like Roberta, with gladness? Because he had taken himself away from her. Closed himself off. What cold shoulder had she ever given him? What failure of welcome? No, it was his father's death, the whole confusion of that period in his life, and Clare being there through it all when neither he nor Liz wanted her around. He'd sealed himself off from that time and, with it, her.

In the beginning, she'd understood. She hadn't wanted to pry. He was young, he was in college, he needed to be in the world and enjoy it without her reminding him of what he'd been through. Don't force it, Clare had said, even when he started going to his grandmother's house in St. Paul for Christmas instead of coming up to Vermont. Ann hadn't complained or demanded his presence as some parents might have. Instead, she paid for his plane tickets and spoke to him while he was there. And after that, when he visited the center only once a year, in summer, and then not even every year, again she told herself he was working, he had friends, it was a long trip up from New York and back. But that was long ago now. And still the pattern held; according to him, he was just always busy. The few times she and Clare had gone down to New York, he had met them only for a meal. Just enough contact to ward off the kind of formal break that would require an explanation, if not to her then to his sister. His sister to whom he spoke not frequently but far more than he did to Ann.

So, yes, small though it made her feel that any of this stood in the way of her compassion for Peter, it did. Which was yet another reason she was thankful for this practice. To help quiet her own grievance and the self that fed it. Letting her breathe in all that troubled her son, without resentment, without bitterness, taking it into herself, and letting out toward him her wish that he be free of it.

The rapping of knuckles on the door caused Ann to flinch. Everyone knew not to disturb her here. She rose, crossed the room, and lifted the latch.

Roberta stood before her wearing neither a coat nor a hat despite the cold. 'It's Jeanette,' she said. 'She got in a fight.'

'What do you mean, a fight?'

'I mean a physical fight. With the repairman—they were talking in the driveway. I don't know what it was about, but she's hurt.'

Ann pulled on her boots, grabbed her coat, and led Roberta fast along the path back to the house. She went straight through the front door, which they never used, into the living room, where

Jeanette lay on the couch with her eyes closed, unmoving. Clare was leaning over her with a damp cloth, cleaning the abraded flesh along the side of her neck.

'She was awake a minute ago,' Clare said, 'but now she's out again.'

'Have you called an ambulance?' Ann asked.

'Of course we have, what do you *think*?' Clare said.

Kneeling by the couch, Ann took the cloth from Clare and pressed it gently against Jeanette's forehead. Her fleece and shirt had been torn at the neck, her right cheek was red and swollen, and from the ear above it came a small trickle of blood already beginning to dry. As Ann wiped at this residue, Jeanette winced and her eyes blinked open, then closed again.

'What on earth happened?' Ann said.

'It was the man who came for the water heater,' Clare said. 'I was just putting my things on to go out. Jeanette was in the yard, they were talking, I figured she knew him. Then suddenly she swung at him with a rake and they were on the ground, he was hitting her, it was horrible. I yelled at him, and when he saw me coming, he went to his van and turned out over the lawn.'

Ann brushed the hair matted to Jeanette's forehead back behind her ears and asked for a new cloth.

By the time the ambulance arrived, Jeanette had come to and was mumbling that she didn't want to be taken anywhere.

'You are going with these people,' Ann said. 'And I'm going with you.'

Greg Palmer, who worked at the town dump, was one of the EMTs. He and the other medic strapped Jeanette onto the stretcher. Greg put an oxygen mask over her face, which made her condition appear even more dire. All the retreatants were out on the lawn watching as she was carried into the bay of the truck.

Ann climbed in with her and told Roberta it was okay, she didn't need to follow behind, she'd call when she knew more.

The drive down into the valley seemed to take forever. Ann leaned over as far as she could toward Jeanette so that when she opened her eyes now and then, it was Ann's face she saw.

Jeanette clawed at the mask several times and Greg gently guided it back in place.

'Just a precaution,' he said, 'just breathe with it.'

Greg, Beth the librarian's son, had been a toddler when Ann and Clare first moved up here, playing behind his mother's desk, but unlike most of his classmates, he'd stayed, doing a bit of everything. Jeanette would know him, his family, his aunts and uncles and cousins. Even if she could have spoken, she wouldn't have said a word in his presence.

At the hospital, the waiting went on and on. For the nurse, for the doctor, for the paperwork, for the scans. Three hours of people milling around telling Ann things would happen soon. Finally, as they waited for the results of the tests, it was just the two of them, with at least the privacy of curtains on either side. Jeanette gazed fixedly at the clock high on the wall opposite the bay in which they'd been parked, oblivious, it seemed, to everything: the endless beepings, the bleached air, the whole anonymous continuance in which hospitals drowned you.

'This is bull,' she said, 'I don't need to be here. I should just leave.'

She wasn't serious and didn't need dissuading, so Ann didn't bother. 'Who was it?' she asked.

'It wasn't him,' Jeanette replied, 'if that's what you're thinking. He's long gone. It was his brother. I thought he'd gone too, but apparently he's back. He looks just like him, like they're twins. Those fat little eyes.'

'Did he say something to you?'

'I was telling him to leave,' Jeanette said, 'that was all. To just get in his truck and go. I was going to walk away. But he said, *You don't get to tell people where they can be.* And then he went off on me, shouting. Saying I'd ruined his brother's life. With what I'd said about him. How he couldn't live here anymore. How I'd ruined his parents' lives too. He started calling me a bitch and a liar.'

Her eyes remained fixed on the clock, on the smooth sweep of the second hand.

'It was like it was him,' she said. 'That voice. Like he was the one yelling at me. I guess I just lost it. I don't care. I hope I hurt him bad. Maybe he'll fuck off again.'

A nurse came into view, smiled, and kept on, headed for another patient.

'But you don't need to sit around and listen to this shit,' Jeanette said. 'You've got women with way more interesting problems waiting for you. I've got people I can call.' This was Jeanette all over, fending off help lest she be denied it.

'You're out of luck,' Ann said. 'I'm not going anywhere.'

Jeanette made no response to this. She pushed aside the metal tray that had been rolled in front of her. She fidgeted with her wristband, trying to slip it off, and with the bandage on her neck. Whatever advice the nurses might give her, she was sure to ignore. Which Clare would no doubt comment on as self-defeating. Rationally, Ann agreed. Yet she couldn't help but admire Jeanette for it. How little she cared for her own comfort. She was like Richard in that way. He'd infuriated her at times, his pigheadedness—walking to work in a downpour—but that was also his eccentricity, his obscurely principled way of being, the very thing that despite herself had intrigued her about him. And about Jeanette, though strangely the similarity had never occurred to her before this moment.

'You're going to tell everyone now, aren't you?' she said to Ann. 'You want to get me in one of your sessions and feel it all out. Now's your big chance.'

'No,' Ann said, 'I have no such designs.'

'Where do you get off being so *calm*?' Jeanette said. 'So *understanding*? It drives me crazy.'

Ann smiled.

'You don't have to put up with me,' Jeanette said. 'You could just leave me in the shed.'

'True, I could. But I don't want to. I never have.'

'We don't need that asshole to fix the water heater anyway,' Jeanette said, ignoring the thickness in Ann's voice. 'I can do it myself.'

'I'm sure you can.'

Sandra Moya texts: *Can I talk to you? Mia will call.*

I'm standing in a small crowd outside Judge Manetti's court-room with Abraham John, an Ivorian in his early thirties with a tattoo of a cross over his throat and clavicle. It's midmorning but Manetti is already running late, entertaining some kind of emergency petition, and the doors haven't opened yet.

Before texting her back, I scan my email and other messages. Nothing from Vasel. A week has gone by now since he met me in the diner and still he is dragging his feet about the documents I need from him.

Okay, I write to Sandra, thinking I'll just tell her Judge Ericson hasn't issued an opinion in her case yet, and that will be that.

But when Mia calls—she's a girl of nine or ten—she starts right in about how Felipe is all messed up, he's flipping out about their mother getting sent back, he doesn't go to school, he just stays in their room.

I can hear Sandra in the background, frantic, telling Mia what to say. The call is a last resort. It must be. I'm not someone she would talk to about her son.

On the far side of the waiting area, Carl appears with Javad

Madani, the Iranian businessman, and nods hello to me. He's in his blue wool suit this morning, the oldest in his rotation, his jacket hanging to one side, as if the garment has suffered a mild stroke.

'Felipe thinks it's his fault,' Mia says, 'because the cops stopped him and looked up his ID and then Mom got told she had to come to court.' She pauses, waiting for the next torrent of her mother's words to subside. 'Mom says it's too much,' she continues. 'Felipe's going to hurt himself, she doesn't trust that judge, what's Felipe going to do if she gets sent back? So unless you got some other thing, we're going to Uncle Herman's in Florida because Immigration doesn't have his address.'

The courtroom doors open and whoever the emergency petitioner was leaves with his lawyer. People start filing in.

I ask Mia if I can talk to Felipe.

'Nope,' she says, 'I already asked him, he doesn't want to talk to you, he doesn't talk to me except when he's yelling, *Get out of my room,* but it isn't just his, it's mine too.'

There's a rustling, then a thud, then Sandra's voice comes on. 'You understand?' she says.

'Yeah,' I say, 'but I have to tell you, it's not a good idea. If you get denied, we can still argue extraordinary hardship, that your kids need you in the country. You've got a pretty good chance with that. But if you leave, if you don't appear when we try for that, it's bad.'

'What about my son?' she nearly shouts, more in fear than anger.

I nod to Abraham to go ahead into the courtroom without me.

'That's why I want to talk to Felipe,' I say. 'His stop had nothing to do with you getting your notice.'

More shuffling. I hear her walking through the apartment.

'Felipe!' she shouts.

A door opens. There's bass music, which ceases, more rustling, then Sandra's voice in the background again. 'El abogado, escúchalo,' she implores. Followed by silence.

'Felipe?' I say.

Nothing in reply. I'm picturing him on a bed in the corner of a room he shares with his little sister, face turned to the wall, cradling the phone to his ear. Already taller than his mother, gangly, morose. With no way to save her.

Finally, I get a grunted 'Yeah?'

'Felipe, listen,' I say, 'they didn't come after your mother because you got frisked. I promise, that's not how it works. It takes way longer than that.'

'Un-huh,' he mumbles.

Why shouldn't he be depressed? Even if he believes me, what difference does it make, if they take his mother in the end?

A department attorney, Janice Lee, one of the supervisors, wheels her cart of files down the gallery aisle and into the enclosure.

I want to ask Felipe to tell his mother not to go to Florida yet, but I hear Phoebe's voice: *You don't conscript a client's kids to get what you want, they're not your helpers.* Still, I need him to feel not quite as bad right now so I'll have more time to convince Sandra to stay.

'I'm serious,' I tell him, 'you didn't do anything wrong. You didn't cause this. And there are things we can do if the decision doesn't go in your mom's favor. They're not taking your mother this week, or this month, I promise you. You understand that?'

'Huh-uh.'

Manetti is already done with the first respondent.

'Okay,' I say. 'Now, look, I'm not anyone to tell you what to do, but your mother's worried about you, and if you go to school, she'll be a little less worried, right?'

Again, there's a shuffling sound, the movement of bodies in the apartment funneled into my ear.

Then Sandra is speaking in the background, and Mia's asking me, 'Did you tell him?'

'John, Abraham,' Manetti calls from the bench.

'Yes,' I say to Mia, 'but I have to go. Tell your mother I'll call her.' I hang up, hurry into the courtroom, and look over at Abraham to indicate that he should join me at the lawyer's table. 'Peter Fischer for the respondent,' I say.

'Good morning, Mr. Fischer. Does your client concede service?'

'He does.'

'Does he concede he's subject to removal?'

'He does.'

'Does he wish to specify the country he'd be removed to?'

'No.'

'For the record, the court is designating Côte d'Ivoire. So what are we doing here this morning?'

I take the file from my bag. Which is when I realize it's the wrong one. I must have pulled the wrong file last night at the office while gathering more articles on Albania. What I have in my hand isn't Abraham John's folder but an old Uzbek case. I've got nothing for him, not even a case number.

'Mr. Fischer? Are we keeping you?'

'This is a visa overstay,' I say.

'Thanks for the enlightenment,' Manetti says. 'It's also a guilty plea to a DUI. My question is, What's he asking for?'

Abraham glances at me sidelong. He's a slender man, my height, wearing a Jets sweatshirt and red puffy jacket, his hair braided tight to his scalp. Referred from Legal Aid. A political claim. I remember that.

Janice Lee looks up from her copy of the file. She's been here forever, seen a thousand lawyers flounder, but she's surprised that this morning it's me.

'Do it,' Abraham whispers. 'Tell her.'

'I'm already running late, Mr. Fischer,' says Manetti. 'Consult with your client on your own time.'

Her clerk stops typing and stares at me over her reading glasses. My eyes float to the DOJ seal on the back wall, which appears all of a sudden brighter, as if spotlit, but also hazy, the blue and yellow braided circle beginning to blur, the eagle's mass of brown feathers and hooded eye dropping out of focus. The room is stifling, the air parched. I fight to swallow a wave of nausea. It seems as if I'm tipping forward and will have to break my fall with my hands, but I manage to steady myself.

'You don't remember facts, you remember stories,' Carl said once—Carl, who is behind me in the gallery this very minute, watching. But the story filling my head now isn't Abraham John's, it's Vasel's, the part about Arbi sitting in the shadows of the courtyard eyeing Vasel kissing a boy.

Finally the eagle and the arrows go still again, the air becomes breathable, and I hear myself saying to the judge, 'Mr. John's applying for asylum.'

'Okay,' Manetti says, *'and?'*

But nothing comes.

I hear Abraham say, 'What is this?'

Then one bare fact returns to me. 'The contested elections,' I say. 'My client was persecuted by the security services in the wake of the contested elections. He has a well-grounded fear he'll be harmed if returned.'

Janice Lee's eyes narrow. She knows I don't have the jacket with me. Callahan or Sievers would rip me for the sport of it. But Lee knows Manetti doesn't punish respondents for their lawyers, or their lack of them. All she'd get from showing me up is delay. So when Manetti asks if the department has anything to add, Lee places the John folder back on her metal cart and says, 'No, Your Honor,' and Manetti begins flipping through her jumble of a calendar.

'What was that?' Abraham says back in the hallway. 'Why didn't you tell her my circumstance? How come she didn't say anything?'

It's easy to be a bad lawyer to poor people. *This is just how the system works,* you can always say. No matter what you've failed to do. And to my disgust, it's what I say to Abraham John now. 'This is how it goes. We've got your date for the hearing.'

'I have to come all the way down here just for that?'

How could it be that I didn't explain this to him already, the pro forma nature of today's proceedings? I spell it out now. But he's suspicious, knows something's off.

'What's up with you?' he says. 'You on some kind of drugs? You were weird in there.'

'I didn't have my notes,' I say. 'I needed a minute to remember.'

'Are you *kidding* me? Like, remember who I am?'

'No—the details,' I say.

'So you did fuck up.'

'I should have had my notes, I'm sorry, but it didn't hurt your case. The hearing's what matters.'

'I guess you get what you pay for,' he says. 'And you're free.'

By now his story has come back to me: The job with the delivery service, driving a van all over the city, a Sunday barbecue in Van Cortlandt Park, his pregnant girlfriend, a sudden pain, needing to go to the hospital, the bullshit traffic stop, Abraham raising his voice at the cop, saying they're in a hurry, then the breathalyzer, which led to the DUI, which led to someone, probably the cop, alerting ICE to the conviction, and then a year later the notice to appear.

He half turns as if to leave but doesn't, his protest unspent, however futile he knows it to be.

What do I know of Abraham John? That he didn't want to apply for asylum to begin with but that he qualifies for no other status. That a lane change without a blinker and a hard-ass in the system turned a life of getting by into the fear he'll never see his daughter again.

I have the urge, absurd on its face, to ask, *Are you all right?* As if the question or the answer could do him the least bit of good.

167

In the elevator, he leans his head against the wall, eyes closed, no doubt wanting more than anything just to be gone.

'So I get no answer?' he says down in the lobby. 'And I have to wait *ten months*?'

The absurdity of it is fresh for everyone but the lawyers. If he hadn't said anything, I wouldn't think anything of it. It's a good outcome, after all. A reprieve.

When we get out of the building, he heads down the sidewalk without saying goodbye. Instantly, I check my phone again. Still nothing.

After Jared had let me into the group, I got invited to hang out with him and Stephanie and Brett not just on weekday afternoons but weekend nights too. That spring, the four of us spent hours in his blue coupe, a kind of floating living room with one seat for each of us, Jared always behind the wheel and in charge of the music, the rest of us passengers who could bitch or complain or criticize all we wanted but who in the end went along with whatever his plans for us were—a movie or a party or a night swim at the lake. I felt almost as if I belonged.

By then, my father had started to look worse. He'd lost more weight and coughed all the time, and he kept getting paler, but he told us it was only his chest acting up, no reason for him not to keep walking back and forth to work, even though none of us were there to witness the discomfort of it, and certainly no reason to go to doctors, whom he had always disdained. When I'd tell him I was worried about him, he'd say to quit being a softy. Clare hadn't quite taken his place at the rectory yet, though she might as well have, for all the evenings she was there. Liz had no interest in spending time at our father's apartment, whatever his condition, and now she didn't want to be at the house either. So she simply fled. In the end, I did the same.

Because of how effortlessly detached I imagined Jared and Stephanie and Brett to be—indifferent to the petty concerns of ordinary high-school students—it took me a while to understand they had their reasons, too, for not wanting to be at home. I'd thought Stephanie's parents were cool for letting her spend her freshman year living with an aunt in London, but actually they had been away together on some research trip in Southeast Asia and were glad not to have their daughter on their hands. And it turned out they didn't deplore the semi-gothic way she dressed like most adults would—they just didn't notice. Brett's situation was more obscure to me. Stephanie said he had an older brother who'd gone to college, then to a psych ward, and then returned home, but Brett never spoke about him or anything to do with his family, and theirs wasn't a house we ever hung out at. As for Jared, his parents, who were friends with Stephanie's, had divorced several years back, and his father had moved to Chicago to be with another woman, leaving Jared to live with his mother in a house that Stephanie called the orphanage for how little his mom was ever there.

Some nights, if Jared happened to drop the other two off first, it would be just him and me alone together in the car. Without Brett and Stephanie to joust and banter with, we'd go quiet. And in that quiet my fear of what he really thought of me blossomed, and I'd pray that he didn't see when I blushed in the dark.

On one of those nights, as we approached the rectory, he asked if I would help him with an English paper. I thought he was joking, like he always did, getting one of us to assent to something only to mock us for being eager. If I agreed, he would laugh. And yet the chance that he actually meant it, that he actually wanted *me* to help *him,* was too thrilling to pass up.

'Whatever,' I said, as he pulled into the drive to drop me off. 'I can if you want.'

He didn't reply, just came to a stop by the front door and let me out.

A couple of days later, in the hallway between classes, he said, 'So, yeah, that thing I mentioned, it's due.'

Behind the facade of his mother's red Colonial, the decor was plush but sleek, an expensive, modern look, all solid beiges and whites and light grays, that couldn't have been further from the rectory's jumble of old wooden furniture strewn with books. His mother had a job in the offices of some corporation that required nearly all her time. The way Jared spoke about Susan—that's how he referred to her, by her first name—made her sound more like his roommate than a parent.

He led me into the living room, where a pink orchid stood on a white marble coffee table between two stacks of design magazines. 'Here,' he said, passing me his paper offhandedly, like a take-out menu, before flopping down on the chrome-framed couch. 'I kind of fucked it up.'

The F on the back was followed by a note listing all the assignments he'd missed and telling him he would fail the class if he didn't submit an acceptable essay.

As he stretched his arms back and rested his head in the palms of his hands, his t-shirt came up off his waist, exposing the blond fluff between his belly button and the rim of his boxers. When I glanced up from his navel, he was looking straight at me. Instantly, I lowered my eyes to the paper.

'What's the matter?' he said laconically. 'You afraid of something?'

My face got so hot I felt almost dizzy. He was toying with me after all. Taking his one-upmanship to another level. If Brett and Stephanie had been there, I could have cut back at him, dumbly or cleverly, it wouldn't matter, any try for a laugh to escape the moment. But we were alone, not high, with no music playing, just the threat of his question burning up all the air in the room.

'Don't be a wuss,' he said. 'You won't get in trouble for helping me, no one's going to find out.'

'I'm not scared of that,' I said. 'It's fine.'

He dozed while I read the essay. Which allowed me to gaze at him all the more. He lay stomach down now, like a big cat at rest, lean and strong, his paws up beside his blond head, his smooth cheek pressed to the pillow.

'It's pretty bad, right?' he said when he came awake.

I didn't want to agree with him, so I asked instead if he'd read the novel.

'Oh, yeah,' he said. 'It took me a long time, but I liked it. And I think I get it. He's supposed to feel more about his mother dying, to mourn better, everyone wants him to be a certain way about that. But he can't, because he doesn't feel anything, he's just drifting through his life. So when he kills the guy on the beach, he doesn't even think about it, he's just thinking about how hot it is. And it doesn't matter if they execute him for it, either. That's what Mrs. Humphrey meant about the antihero. We're not meant to admire him, to think he's a good guy. It's pretty brutal, actually.'

'How come you didn't say any of that?' I asked.

He rolled onto his back and stared up at the ceiling. 'Because it's hard to write,' he said. 'You think I blow everything off, but I don't. I don't know what makes it hard, it's just always been that way.'

He was the one avoiding looking at me now. Which astonished me. That someone so gorgeous could be ashamed of anything. I knew without asking that he had never told Stephanie or Brett this. It was something private, between us.

'If you just keep talking,' I said, 'I could write things down as you go, do it that way.'

'Yeah,' he said, 'all right.'

So that's how it went. We talked about *The Stranger*. About how you could be so caught up in the present moment that you didn't think about the past or the future or the consequences of anything, just the sights and the sounds flooding into you.

'Of course the killing's wrong,' Jared said, 'but the story of it isn't. It could happen that way.'

He flipped through his copy, looking over the passages he'd underlined, saying he thought Meursault refusing the priest at the end wasn't just him being an atheist but his not caring about any conventions, marriage or work or what a son was supposed to be.

We went back and forth for a while and though it took me some time to get it down longhand, into paragraphs, I did it there as he waited, putting our thoughts together on the page, then read it aloud to him.

When I finished, he laughed, but not at me. 'You're good,' he said. 'That worked.'

Out on the back deck, he lit a joint for us. The Cure on the speakers inside competed with the buzzing of the mower in the neighbor's yard pushed by a kid a few years younger than me, back and forth under a row of oak trees, the machine spewing fine grass and the dust of the previous winter's leaves, which I watched as it formed a cloud in the otherwise spotless air and drifted over the fence and into the street.

A few hits in, and my vigilance slackened. I tuned in to the music and the machine and the shadows swaying on the fragrant lawn. Jared got up after a while and I followed him back into the kitchen, where he started goofing around, air-guitaring to the music. I got my camera out of my knapsack and took pictures of him doing it, like an actual paparazzo, which made him laugh and exaggerate his pretending all the more. He even wailed along to Robert Smith's lyrics, sliding onto his knees on the linoleum floor, playing to the camera like a pop idol to his swooning fans.

Afterward, when he headed up the stairs to his room, I followed him there, too. He flung himself down on his bed. I sat on the floor, against the wall. I rested my camera on my raised knees and gazed at him through the lens, zooming in on his bare feet, on the rolled cuffs of his black chinos, the bunching of the fabric further up along his thighs. And then, once more, at that strip of bare belly showing between his waistband and t-shirt.

That's where I had the camera when his hand entered the frame and slid slowly into his pants. I kept very still then and watched as he adjusted himself. A motion that could, after all, just be a sleepy gesture, little more than a drowsy stretch. Until the hand undid the buttons of the jeans, and parted the slit of his boxers to reveal his hard-on.

I hadn't moved a muscle. I'd barely taken a breath. For what seemed like whole minutes, I kept the camera pressed firmly to my brow. Only when the hand was gone, and his dick was still there, out in the open, did I put it aside. His eyes were closed, his head lolled back on the pillow. Carefully, silently, I raised myself up onto my knees and shunted closer, till I was at the edge of the bed. I could tell from his shallow breath, from the pulse of the artery under the skin of his neck, that he wasn't asleep.

'Hey,' I whispered.

He made no reply. But just lowered his hand and touched his hard-on, then let it go again. I sat on the edge of the bed and took his dick in my fist. He made no sound, nothing. His expression didn't change in the least, even as I began to stroke him. As if nothing at all were happening. It lasted only a minute or two. He came without warning onto his shirt and stomach and my knuckles. I looked back up to his face then. His eyes were open now. But right away he covered mine with his hand.

'Whoops,' he said with a chuckle. Then rolled off the far side of the bed and disappeared into the bathroom. I stayed right where

I was, on his mattress, my heart sprinting, and stared down at the pale liquid still warm on the back of my hand. I let myself—just for an instant—smell the yeast of it, then wiped it on the sheet.

I didn't care if he touched me when he came back. All I wanted was to kiss him.

'Hey,' he said, stepping into the room. 'Brett's probably waiting at his house, we should go.'

So we did, and picked up Stephanie, too, and drove to the cineplex and sat through *Lethal Weapon*, the four of us, and afterward Jared dropped me off at home without another word said.

That's how it went that spring, between him and me. Every couple of weeks, he would ask me to help him with an assignment. We would go to his house, work on a paper, then get high and go up to his room, where he'd pretend to be asleep while he let me touch him and eventually give him head as well, all without our eyes or lips meeting. I thought that at least this thing we did together would become a secret between us, a privacy he would acknowledge, however subtly, beyond the walls of that house. That maybe he would give me, now and then, a knowing look. But in fact he treated me no differently than he had before—in school, after school, in the car, in the woods—assailing me with the same casual harshness he'd trained us all to use against one another.

Before that first afternoon in his bedroom, there had been only one place in my life. I hadn't thought of it as a particular location because it was the only one I knew—the ordinary world. But now there was a second place. One where what happened didn't happen. Where I didn't shudder with fear at how terribly I wanted Jared to take care of me always, like a parent cares for a child. Where I didn't start to believe in my secret heart that by letting me touch him, he was doing exactly that, forever, caring for me in the deepest way a man could. Where I didn't cage the shaking in my gut to the point of pain to keep my excitement hidden from him. Where even his coming in my mouth and me in my underwear as I stroked myself didn't happen, because nothing in that room happened. It existed outside the realm of event. This was the place that Jared showed me. Where we didn't do what we did. A place that soon stripped the rest of the world down to nothing for how much I wanted only to be there.

When Vasel shows up for his appointment, having finally texted back, he's wearing yet another new outfit, clothes he must have bought with money from the restaurant. A pressed navy Lacoste buttoned to the top, skinny-fit chinos cut above the ankle, and immaculate white tennis shoes. His hair is even shorter on the sides, the top done up with more product than before, and his skin is clearer too, almost polished. Two months ago he was a sheepish young man hunched in his chair in a gray windbreaker; now he appears more like a New York gay boy working an urban-prepster look.

The owners of the restaurant are opening a new location, he tells me, with a totally new design, and one of them has agreed to check out his drawings for possible inspiration. He announces this nonchalantly, affecting an indifference he seems to have picked up from this new world he's begun to glimpse. You'd think the prospect of his artwork being used practically bored him. But then he can't keep up the act, and he smiles, a Cheshire Cat grin, unable to hide his excitement.

Despite all the requests and reminders I've sent him, the only documentation he's brought with him is a receipt for his airplane ticket from a travel agent in Tirana and a birth certificate so worn from folding it nearly comes apart in my hands. No school records, no medical records, no attestations.

Without any prompting, he keeps on about the restaurant. 'It is good,' he says, 'the people there are okay, I go out with them after my shifts. One of the waiters, there is a room in his share, he thinks it will be free soon. Actually, he is cute,' he adds, trying out a kind of insouciance.

I set the receipt and certificate down on the conference table between us. 'I need a lot more than this,' I tell him, 'and soon. Your application's due in two weeks.'

He checks his phone, then looks away, toward the back of the room.

'This isn't just us going into a courtroom together and you saying, *This is what happened,* end of story,' I continue. 'The judge needs evidence. First, that you're gay, that you're not just claiming it to get protection.'

'What do you want?' he says. 'For me to kiss a guy in front of him?'

I want the statement from his mother, but starting there might set him off, so I begin with Armend.

'I told you,' he says, 'I do not message with him anymore, not for a long time. He went to Italy with his sister. His number probably does not even work.'

'What about Facebook?'

'Yeah,' he says, unhappily. 'He is on it. But it is nobody's business. If they do not want to believe me, then okay.'

'We agreed,' I say. 'You said that you'd help me prepare. I can't do this by myself.'

His expression turns to a sulk. Once again, I'm ruining his fun. He wants to show off the new life he's on the verge of, to excite in me a reaction to this new self—an attractive boy—that he's trying on.

I hear myself telling him that I've been doing this a long time.

That it's hard for every client. No one wants to be forced to go over and over the worst thing that happened to them, let alone ask other people to help document it. Who wouldn't rather forget, if it means being able to live your life? 'But if you don't do this,' I say, 'that life is going to be much harder.'

'You're weird,' he says. 'It's like you believe this shit.'

'Believe what?'

'All this,' he says, gesturing with his hand at the whole office. 'The government, like it means something.'

'It means something if you don't have documents, if they deport you.'

'Yeah,' he says, 'it means some fuckheads have power. Like everywhere. But it is like you think it is more than that.'

He picks up his phone again, bored in earnest this time with where the conversation has gone.

'But what about Armend—don't you want to talk to him?' I ask before I can stop myself.

He looks at me with narrowed eyes, the way I imagine he looked at those men in the lobby of the theater and at the bar, the men who looked at him, he said, like an animal.

'What?' he says, his voice edged with disdain. 'You want to know if I'm still into him?'

For once I'm glad to hear my phone ring. I don't recognize the number but take it anyway, stepping out into the hall. It's Hassan El Moctor. His mother is dying in Rabat. He's needed to know for weeks if he can go back to see her or if it will blow his case, but I haven't gotten around to calling him. The truth is, it's complicated. The department will use the visit against him, to show it's safe for him to return, but there's decent precedent for compassionate leave in circumstances like his. He wants me to tell him what to do, whether to buy the ticket. He has to decide today, his brother says, or it will be too late. I say I can call him by early evening, that we can discuss it then, but he says no, he'll be working, he needs to know now. I tell him if he goes, it has to be brief, he can't leave his mother's house, and he has to get a letter from her doctor.

'I can't promise it won't hurt you,' I say. 'Probably it will.'

'Okay,' he says, and hangs up.

As the call ends, Monica strides out of her office toward the copy machine but halts at the sight of me. We've barely spoken in the past few weeks, outside of staff meetings.

'Hey,' she says, 'can you cover that Phoebe fundraising call for me tomorrow? I found a caregiver for my mother, but if I'm not there, my mother won't open the door for her.' Before I can answer, Monica, glancing behind me, notices Vasel in the conference room. 'For real?' she says, half impressed, half incredulous. 'I thought he ghosted you.'

'I followed up,' I say.

She appraises me skeptically. 'Is he the reason you've been so out of it? Carl said you were a mess the other day in court.'

'You're the one who wanted me to represent him.'

'Excuse *me*,' she says. 'I was just asking.'

'It's under control,' I say. 'And yes, I can cover the phone call.'

'Okay, then,' Monica says. 'Much appreciated. And all I'm saying is, I'm around, in my office, if you want to talk.' With that she continues past me.

When I walk back into the conference room, Vasel is leaned over his spiral notebook, making tiny marks with his black pen. He keeps his head down over the drawing, paying me no mind as I sit opposite him.

'Sorry for the interruption,' I say. 'The point I was trying to make a moment ago is that we need someone to attest to your orientation. And the best person to do that is Armend.'

Vasel's eyes hover so close to the image he is working on that his chest is nearly parallel to the table.

'He watched,' he says after a moment, addressing himself to the page. 'When the kids at school fucked with me, Armend was there. He just watched. But then he came to our house anyway. To be with me. I could have stopped him that night Arbi saw us, I could have said no. Then Pera would be married, probably. And now you want me to message him *Can you please say I am a faggot?*'

He sits upright, to gain perspective on his drawing it seems— another intricate geometry, the tiny shapes densely patterned.

'You don't think he would help you?' I ask.

'Maybe he would,' he says. 'If I tell him I saw dancers on Broadway. He wants to be famous, more than anything.'

'It's important. So I'm asking. Please get in touch with him. And the other person we'll need a statement from—is your mother.'

'No,' he says sharply, shaking his head.

'But she was there,' I say. 'She knows exactly what happened. She can explain it more convincingly than anyone.'

He slaps his notebook shut. '*I* told you what happened—me,' he says. '*I* am the one here telling you this thing, not her. She will not write anything.'

I wait a beat, then say, 'She doesn't have to. I can draft a letter using what you told me. We can have it translated. She just has to agree to it and sign.'

'You think she can't write?' he says. 'That she's ignorant? She is the one who taught me English. But I will not ask her to talk about me this way. To talk about our family. To who? You? Some court person? When she's still living there with them? With Pera. With my brother!'

His face is ablaze with indignation. If I press further now, I'll lose the rest of this meeting, and we can't afford that.

When I ask if he wants water, he shrugs. I get him a cup anyway from the cooler and set it down in front of him. He crosses his arms, fattening his biceps against the backs of his hands so he looks more muscular than he is. I slide a copy of his affidavit across the table.

Without making any concessionary motion toward the document, he peers at the first page. 'What is this?' he says, reading the first few lines.

My name is Vasel Marku, it begins. *I was born on April 3, 1990, in Has, Albania. I am a national and a citizen of that country.*

'You do this for everyone?' he asks. 'You write their story?'

'It's a draft,' I say, 'from what you've told me. We have to present the facts in a certain order, to show the judge you qualify. But it's your statement. Anything you want to change, anything you want to correct—that's why we're here. To make sure it's accurate.'

He picks up the first sheet now and examines it briefly before returning it to the table.

'So this is your job? You say how everyone got fucked, how fucked up their country is? How much do they pay you?'

'I'm trying to help you,' I say. 'I have been from the beginning.'

'No,' he says, 'you thought I was lying.'

'You were,' I say before I can swallow the words, adding immediately, 'I don't mean you were lying, but you weren't telling me everything.'

I have the fierce urge to keep going, to say, *Do you have any idea how many hours I've worked on your case, how many nights of reading, how carefully I drafted these pages that you don't seem to give a shit about?*

But I don't. I hold my tongue, and let the heat in my chest subside.

'And that's fine,' I say, 'I get it. And now you have told me what happened. I just want it to count. To get you your status. Which is why we *have* to get this right.'

I've spoken with too much force, though, or what sounds like it to me. And suddenly I'm afraid that he's going to laugh at me. Mock me for caring.

'You don't have to freak out,' he says. 'I am here, right?'

'Yes, you are.'

'So what do we do now?' he asks.

'I read it to you. Not because I think you can't read it, before you suspect me of that, but because it's better if you hear it aloud. It's easier to hear something that isn't right. They're going to press you on this. The other lawyer. They could question you about any sentence in here, the smallest thing, to get the judge to think you're making it up.'

'Okay,' he says, indifferently.

I read out the formal request for asylum, followed by his background—the family, the small town. Looking up through the glass ceiling, Vasel stares into some imagined distance. When I get to him and Armend going to the bunker, I stop to clarify how many boys appeared that evening and saw them together.

'I don't,' he says, 'it was dark. We didn't invite them in.'

'But you said you went out and saw them running off. Were there two, three, five?'

'Three, maybe,' he says. 'Three little shits.'

And so we move through it, line by line. He seems impressed, if not exactly pleased, at how much of what he told me I have retained.

'This is weird,' he says, using that word again, though more speculatively this time, without the aggression, without the accusation. As if he's actually coming to see what it is that I do.

It is weird, of course—traveling into one life after another, intimacy without intimacy, though I stopped noticing this weirdness a long time ago. *Yes,* I want to tell him, *you're right, it's strange, and awkward, and it always has been.* But I say nothing because I've said enough, and I don't need him to sense more than he already does that right now it is stranger than ever—being in the room with him. Far better to stick to the clear order of the numbered paragraphs in front of me.

'On August twenty-third, 2008, my family attended the

wedding of our neighbor's son. I left before the others and met Armend in the courtyard of our house. Without my knowledge, my brother saw the two of us kissing.'

'Who said we kissed?' Vasel asks. 'I didn't say that.'

'I guess you didn't specify.'

'What is that word—*specify*?'

'You didn't describe what the two of you were doing, exactly.'

'And so you thought we were kissing?' he says, his tone a mix of goading and something closer to disgust—with the idea or with me, I can't tell. 'You said it had to be true, right?' he says. 'So put down Arbi saw me sucking cock. I am on my knees, on the dirt, my brother sees me sucking cock.'

I draw a line through *kissing* and write *having sex*.

'What?' he says. 'Your judge doesn't want to hear it?'

'Let me worry about the judge,' I say.

I wait a moment, then read on: the visit from the old men, the canceled wedding, Arbi waking him in the middle of the night.

He goes quiet again, listening, wearing an expression I often see when I read statements back to clients, a grim wonder at hearing the events of one's life transcribed into such bloodless language.

'From your house to your uncle's house,' I say, 'how long was that drive?'

'Five minutes, maybe. It's close.'

'And in the van, your father, your uncle, they didn't say any-thing to you?'

He shakes his head.

I read my description of his brother taking him from the van, beating and kicking him beside the stream. The muscles of his jaw flex, but he says nothing.

'I need to ask this,' I say calmly, 'because the government might ask: Did you hit your brother back? Did the two of you fight? They're going to try to make it look like brothers fighting.'

He glares at the floor, miserable, and for a moment I think he's on the verge of tears, but I am only imagining this, because when he glances up at me his eyes are clear and dry.

'He used the bar for the tires,' he says. 'I didn't have a bar.'

'Okay,' I say, and note down *tire iron*. 'And was there anyone else by the stream?' I ask. 'Did you hear or see anyone else there that night?'

Again he shakes his head.

I return to his statement. 'My father told me that I was not his son. Then he held his rifle to my chest.'

Vasel's hand floats up to his cheek. 'Here,' he says, 'it was my face, not my chest.'

I make the correction and continue. 'At this moment, I was certain that my father would kill me.'

I wait. Vasel says nothing.

'Is that accurate?' I ask. 'It sounds like a stupid question, I know. But it's important. What you feared then, that's the basis—in the law—of what you can reasonably fear now.'

Vasel stands abruptly and strides to the corner of the room. 'So you are telling me I should say yes?' he says in a raised voice. 'I think he would shoot?'

'You should tell the truth,' I say.

He winces, as if at bodily pain. 'He was so drunk,' he says. 'I never saw him like that. I don't know how to say it. It was not just me, it was like he hated his life. He is the happy one in our family. Always, before this. But whatever, you can say it like you said. I thought he would shoot me.'

I place a check next to the sentence.

Vasel thrusts his hands into the pockets of his chinos and leans his head back against the wall, gazing up at the bright gray sky. For the next ten minutes or more, he remains like that, giving only slight nods or shakes of the head in response to the rest of my questions. I want to read the edited text back to him but I can tell he's had enough, that his attention won't last.

When I say we're done for today but that he has to get me those statements from Armend and from his mother, I expect him to turn and leave but he stays where he is, in the corner.

'So,' I say, 'are you going to move out of Artea's place?'

His frown says maybe.

'If you need a letter saying you worked at a law firm, I still have a copy.'

He doesn't acknowledge my attempt at a joke, but his expression softens a bit. 'At the restaurant,' he says, 'there are lots of lawyers.'

'I bet. And they probably wear better suits than I do.'

This gets a partial smile. 'Yours are not the worst,' he says. 'Not like the ones the Albanian guys wear, all shiny plastic.' He's quiet for a moment. Then he says, 'The waiter guy, he said that I can stay in his room until the other bedroom is free. But I can't tell, is he sorry for me, or maybe he wants to hook up? I don't want to be a bad gay, like desperate. Would you stay there or not?'

'It could be simpler to wait,' I say. 'But it's not for me to say.'

He walks back to the table and, to my surprise, sits again, on the edge of the chair. 'Artea, she found out about me,' he says. 'She saw messages on my phone. I thought she will freak out, tell everyone. And maybe she will. She is just quiet now, like she got bad news.' He pauses, seeming to turn the situation over in his mind. 'Maybe she does not want people talking more about her,' he says. 'Already she doesn't have a husband or boyfriend.'

It occurs to me that I may be the only person Vasel has told this to, it being likely that I'm the only person who has both met Artea and knows that Vasel is gay. 'Don't forget,' Phoebe said once, 'most of our clients are lonely.' Which mostly I do forget, because there is nothing I can do about it.

'I didn't say this to you before,' I tell him. 'But I should have. The things that happened to you, and to your sister, they're not your fault. None of it's your fault.'

'You're lucky if you get to believe that.'

'But it's true,' I say.

'No,' he says. 'I decided to go with Armend. Because I wanted to. My mother—she likes my father now, or she did, but he is not the one she wanted when she was young. Her parents decided. But she didn't complain. There is the rule, and she followed it. Here you have no rules, it is just whatever you want, always. But I knew what the rule was, and I went with Armend anyway. Because of *me*, because *I* wanted it.'

Phoebe enters the conference room without knocking. 'Sorry to interrupt,' she says, 'just to say, you've had someone in reception for half an hour.'

Vasel stands and heads for the door.

'Wait,' I say, 'just for a minute.'

But he slides past Phoebe without another word, and by the time I grab my papers up and follow him into the hall, he is through the waiting area and gone.

It was in the car one morning a few weeks before the summer break, just as she was about to drop us off at school, that our mother told us our father would be moving back to the house. 'You need to spend time with him,' she said, 'the two of you.'

'Why,' Liz said, 'because he's going to die?'

'Because it's important,' she said, coming to a halt by the front entrance, the other cars waiting behind us.

When our father returned to the rectory, he didn't go back into their bedroom. Not that Clare slept there yet—but still. He moved into Liz's room, downstairs, where the hospital bed could be easily rolled.

For so long, he had poked fun at my sister for her various rebellions, almost for sport. But all that stopped now. He wanted to be with Liz more than anyone. And Liz changed too, almost right away. Her hatred of him vanished. She had been sleeping at her boyfriend's house, in defiance of our mother, but now she camped out on the living room sofa in order to be close by in case my father woke in the night. While my mother was at work and I was at play rehearsals, she would come home directly from school to prepare his favorite roast beef sandwiches with coleslaw and sit with him as he ate, and when he had to shit it all out, she helped him to the bathroom.

It was the first time I'd ever thought of Liz as brave. Because even though my father wouldn't have accepted that kind of help from my mother or from me, the fact was my mother wasn't inclined to give it and I was afraid to. But Liz wasn't, and she did give it.

'Did you know Dad was a lumberjack?' she asked me once during those first weeks after his return.

'He wasn't,' I said. 'He worked on a pipeline.'

'Same difference,' she said, 'and he doesn't even like working indoors, but that's all he ever did, which is fucked up.'

I thought nurses dressed in white uniforms and were of a certain age but the woman who came to the rectory wore street clothes and had a sparrow tattooed on the back of her hand. Each morning and evening she checked the bandage that fastened the IV to my father's arm—the IV connected to the bag of clear liquid on the metal pole he wheeled to and from the bathroom and out onto the front porch when he was well enough to walk. He didn't speak to us about his illness, nor did my mother; we were told that it was cancer and that it had spread. The nurse's name was Nicole, and my father flirted with her, or tried to, particularly if my mother was there to watch, though most often she wasn't.

Her routines barely changed. She was busy with church things. She made eggs for me to take to my father before Nicole arrived for her morning visit, and brought leftovers home from various parish functions. It was Clare, sometimes with Roberta, who made us actual meals. They would arrive with canvas bags full of vegetables and canned beans and keep to the kitchen, where my father wouldn't see them, then leave before we ate.

'Clare and Mom want him gone,' Liz said to me. 'They're just waiting.'

When his nausea got bad, he asked Liz for pot. At least that's how she said it happened, unimaginable as it was. Soon the house smelled of it. He'd get up out of the bed, smiling an odd, almost ghastly smile that showed the slackness of his face, how terribly thin he had become. On the porch, he'd grope for the rocking chair, then sit by the railing, gazing fixedly at the big rhododendron in the front yard and the occasional car as it passed. To my amazement, my mother said nothing about it—his getting high, him and Liz doing it together—as though there were nothing to remark on. As though, in his swift decline, he'd become less our father or her husband than a parishioner whose troubles were simply to be borne, his trespasses forgiven.

I ran from it all. To the library to read. To the auditorium to build sets. Into Jared's car every chance I got, going wherever he and Stephanie and Brett were headed. Often we went to Jared's house because we had it to ourselves, though sometimes, late on a weekday evening, if she wasn't traveling for work, his mother would show up in one of her cinched jackets and silky blouses carrying her black leather briefcase and a bag of fancy groceries. As she put them away, she'd pepper us with questions about school and what she called our 'plans.' She was beautiful, like her son, and like him she took great care with her appearance. Even after a long day at her office, her hair still hung lustrous down to her shoulders, as if ready for a shampoo ad, and when she smiled, her teeth were bright and perfect. Brett said she had been a model too, once, and that Jared got a clothing allowance, neither of which was hard to believe, though her being a model might have been more Brett's fantasy than anything he'd been told, a way to say without saying that he found her hot—this woman who was a decade younger than my mother or his, of a different generation, it seemed.

Her confidence fascinated me. How precise her outfits were, yet how casually she wore them, as though she hadn't given them a second thought. That was style, I thought—immaculate without effort. Even the way she moved her body was different than my mother, or any of the women at church. She knew you were looking at her. Her motions were like a character's in a play, considered and somehow meaningful, even if she was just leaning forward over the counter to ask you if her son ever did his homework.

As I got to know her, I saw where Jared had learned how to display himself nonchalantly. How to be coy and indifferent at the same time. And listening to her speak to him, more like a friend than a parent, I sensed, too, an adultness between them, a kind of knowingness, itself alluring, that seemed to have something to do with them being closer in age than most kids and parents were. She admired her son's looks, I could tell that, also. The way she would gaze at him when he was talking to us, approving of his command of our attention, maybe even a little jealous of it. I wondered if she'd intuited already my desire for him, or even what was going on between us, but I could never be certain. She was too contained to let it show. I couldn't imagine her reproaching Jared for anything, though she must have, sometimes. On the rare occasions she sat with us in the living room or ordered us takeout, Jared appeared more annoyed than anything, impatient with her questions to us and with how carefully she listened to our piddling answers.

She didn't mind this. She seemed used to it, even to find it adorable. As if it were part of a charming routine the two of them had, like a couple whose little displays of irritation with each other were just another form of affection. She would hug each of us, over Jared's groaning protests, and say how great it was that we were such close friends, then saunter into her office off the kitchen and keep working.

At first, my father had appointments at the hospital, but by early summer those stopped. After that he didn't go anywhere. Mostly, he slept. In the mornings, I did as my mother told me and helped

Nicole with the boxes of medical supplies she brought in her car. Sometimes, if she asked me to, I would help her shift my father's dozing body so she could check his skin. When he did come awake, he would ask where Liz was, and she'd come in, beatific, almost, in her new role as the favored one. She read the news to him for hours and when my mother wasn't around lit him a joint. They were their own society then, the two of them.

Once, I heard him recounting a story to Liz and stopped to listen by the open door. He was telling her about his own father and the battle that he had fought to defend the castle in Clervaux, the one my father had gone to see on his trip to Europe.

'The Germans were retreating,' he said in his reedy, weakened voice. 'They were broken. No one expected an attack, not in the dead of winter, in the middle of a forest. It caught the Americans off guard. Tanks everywhere, troops all over the streets. That's why people fled into the castle. There was less than a company of troops in there, everyone else had scattered. But the commanders told them they couldn't surrender, they had to hold it. Slow the advance. With rifles. That's all they had.

'Your grandfather told me this story only once,' he said, 'the last time I saw him. About that night he spent in the dark. Tank shells blasting the walls, pieces of the place falling off. You shot at the gunfire, that's what he said. When you saw a flash, that's where you shot. The cooks and the drivers up there with rifles beside him. But the thing he remembered, he said, were two sounds. Kids crying, down in what'd been the dungeon, and someone playing the piano. Somewhere else in the castle, he had no idea who or where. But someone, as the place got shelled, was playing the piano. A melody he'd never heard before. Beautiful, he said. That's why we had a piano in our living room. He bought it when he got back and he learned to play so he could play that piece. But he never found out what it was. He never heard it again.'

'Wow,' my sister said when he was done. 'That's a trip.'

Crouched in the hall by the open door, I decided right then that the reason he'd told my sister this and not me was that he was sick and confused, and except for that, he never would have told it at all.

One afternoon, the last week of school before summer break, Jared picked me up and saw my father on the porch in his bathrobe. After we'd pulled out of the driveway, he said, 'What's up with your dad, anyway?' as though he were the punch line of a joke.

I'd told him and Stephanie and Brett that my father was sick, but offhandedly, the way I thought Jared would do it, as if it were no big deal, so they'd asked no questions and therefore knew nothing of the situation.

'He's dying,' I said now.

At that, Jared turned his head and stared at me. This was satisfying. To have such an effect on him.

Eventually he said, 'How come you didn't tell me?' His voice was different. Calmer, somehow. As if he was actually listening to me, as if he would have wanted to be told.

'I don't know,' I said. 'I don't have you guys over. We're always somewhere else.' We were supposed to pick up Brett but Jared had already missed his street, and he kept going now, past the fire station, out along the railroad tracks, until we got to the road that led down to the woods and the lake, which is where he turned. In the middle of the afternoon, the air was baking hot and still, though I didn't notice this until he parked and the breeze the car had created ceased. Out ahead of us, the sun on the water was nearly blinding.

'That's why my dad left,' Jared said.

'What do you mean?' I asked.

'They found something in his brain, told him that he only had a couple of years to live. So he decided he couldn't wait anymore, there was this woman he wanted to be with in Chicago. And that's what he did, he moved there.'

'Really? He just left?'

'He tried to be nice about it, to me at least. He bought me lots of clothing. Said I could pick out whatever I wanted. I felt bad for him—at first. Like if he didn't have much time left and this was what he wanted to do...but then he came back one time and he told me things had improved. That he'd responded to treatment or whatever, and he wanted me to start visiting him and that woman. He really was sick—my mother went to all those appointments with him—but somehow he got better. Maybe because he was happier. Who knows? I don't want to visit him, though. It would kill my mother.'

When he finished speaking, I let myself glance across the car at him. Part of me wondered if he would look different with his guard down, without a jest or a snarl. And he did. Softer, less like he knew everything, his lips at rest, his eyes gentle. And only the more beautiful for it.

'I'm sorry,' I said. 'That's shitty.'

He rolled his head back and gazed up at the padded ceiling of the car. 'What about your dad?' he said. 'Did they tell you how long?'

'No, but all he takes now is morphine.'

'My dad said all kinds of things when he thought he was dying.'

'Like what?'

'Mostly that he had made all these mistakes. That if there was something I enjoyed, I should just do it. I guess because that's what he was doing.'

His hand moved from the parking brake to the steering wheel. I was certain he was about to start the car again, to cut short this talk, unlike any we'd had before. But he didn't. He just held the wheel. And then I wondered if maybe this would be it—the moment he finally let me kiss him.

'All those pictures you take of me,' he said. 'What do you do with them?'

'Nothing,' I said. 'Just develop them. But no one else sees them.'

'You're strange,' he said. 'I mean, so am I. I wear Japanese clothes nobody understands, and basically live on my own.'

'I like the way you dress,' I said.

'Why, because it looks gay?' he said.

For a second I thought that for once he might not be kidding, he might really be asking, and maybe not just about his clothes but about himself, asking me what I thought of him. Even what I thought about what we did together. Yet when he shifted his gaze from the ceiling, he didn't look over at me but out across the water again, and I wasn't sure. Still, I had to say something, so I said, 'No, I just think it looks good.'

After we picked the others up, we went to Jared's place and hung around until it got dark. His mother was away again, but she'd left the refrigerator full. We got higher than usual, particularly Jared and I, before we ate and then again after. And I told them how my father smoked now, too, and they laughed hysterically, and demanded I show them what it was like, so I did, imitating the way he smiled, too gone to feel more than a passing little death of goodness in me. And when eventually Brett crashed out on the couch and Stephanie started watching some black-and-white movie, Jared shuffled off upstairs, and I followed.

He played Super Mario for a while, cross-legged at the foot of his bed, while I sat against the wall. I had no camera. I just watched the blue and green lights of the game flash over his face.

Later, he put aside his joystick, pulled his t-shirt off, and lay down on the bed, just like he had each afternoon we'd been alone in that room together, as though I weren't even there. Only this time, when I reached the bed, I lay down beside him. His eyes came half open. I leaned over to touch my lips to his, but before they reached him, I felt his hand on the back of my head, pushing me gently but firmly away from his face, down his chest to his belly. And so once again, I took his hard-on in my mouth, crushed and blissful all at once.

This being what Brett saw when he barged into the room to say he was leaving.

Looking through the window above the kitchen sink, Ann spotted Clare on the bench beneath the apple tree. Ordinarily, after Ann's morning meditation, the two of them drank their coffee together at the table, but today Clare had taken herself outside with a book. Whatever she was reading, she appeared absorbed in it, oblivious to the little white blossoms raining silently down all around her.

Ann took a ripe pear from the sill and rinsed it in the frigid tap water.

Yesterday's circle, delayed for a day by Jeanette's visit to the hospital, had been tiring and largely fruitless—a literature professor from Philadelphia very much attached to her suffering and willing to defend it with skeptical questions about which theory of feminism Viriditas subscribed to. The lived kind, Clare had said, letting her pique show, and thus sealing the woman further off from their communion. Her impatience with the younger retreatants had become more pronounced of late, despite her knowing that the center needed them to remain vital. Not just to populate the place, but to teach the three of them where their work needed to go.

Ann cut the pear into segments and arranged them on a small

blue plate, then headed out into the sun. 'I brought you a snack,' she said, holding out her offering.

Clare squinted into the light. 'I'm all right,' she said, 'but thank you.'

Ann sat, setting the plate down between them on the bench. She could wait—an hour, a day—for Clare to bring up what she suspected was on her mind, but over time she'd grown not only less patient with but less fearful of these tensions between them and so instead she just said it aloud: 'You're angry with me.'

'Is that right?' Clare said, continuing to read. 'Funny, I didn't think we were in the business of telling people what they felt. And really, why should I be angry? A woman who lives with us is assaulted in our front yard, or should I say she assaults someone, because in point of fact, that's what I saw Jeanette do. You plainly know the reason for all this but lie to me by omission. In a community we founded on the premise of openness. So why in the world would I be angry?'

The caustic tone Ann could weather. But that word *lie*, it pricked.

Most everyone involved with the center looked up to her and Clare. They were the model couple, the ones who in middle age had given up their attachments to conventional life and become conscious partners in the work of liberation. But that inaugural act—against the grain, hard fought, dramatic in its own way—was a long time gone. They'd been getting by for years, affectionate, grousing, but perhaps above all aware of the need to be observant in the faith in each other that they were admired for.

A lie of omission. Was it?

'If you want to know,' Ann said, 'I made her a promise. Years ago. She said she had something she needed to tell me, but she wouldn't say a word until I promised her I wouldn't speak about it to anyone. Should I have known better than to agree like that without discussing it first? Probably. But there it is, it's what I did,

I gave her my word. If you think respecting that is a lie, so be it. You didn't seem to mind my *omissions* to Richard about us when it meant we could be together.'

At that, Clare stopped reading, or pretending to. 'Wow,' she marveled. 'This runs deeper than I thought.'

'Oh, please,' Ann said. 'You've been hard on Jeanette since she arrived.'

'Maybe that's because she doesn't respect me,' Clare said. 'She worships you, and loves Roberta, but barely respects me. So, yes, that bothers me. It would bother you, too.'

Across the yard, three of the retreatants, two divinity students from New York and the literature professor, emerged from the barn and waved. Ann waved back. The women walked over the lawn to the meetinghouse, where they would find Roberta. Once they climbed the steps and were gone, Ann turned back to face the driveway and the road, on the far side of which the land fell away and the view of the valley opened.

'I suppose it makes me petty,' Clare said. 'To be upset by that. And yes, part of it is that I'm jealous. I can say that. Not of her — of you. That she came to you, like they all do, like they always have.'

'They come to all three of us,' Ann said. 'And there would be nowhere to come to if it weren't for you. This place wouldn't exist.'

'You're not listening to me,' Clare said. 'I'm telling you something, but you're not listening. Is it so unbearable to hear what I'm feeling?'

Yes, Ann wanted to say, but didn't. She'd never known what to do with Clare's envy. But at least when they were first with each other it had been expressed in a doting manner, in that acquisitive way of lovers at the beginning, who envy the other person altogether because they aren't theirs yet. An envy that commitment was meant to assuage. And Ann had committed to Clare. She had left her husband, she had given up the priesthood to found this place. Was that not enough? she thought, recognizing in this flash of anger an older anger that she'd felt for Richard at his smallest, when he'd lashed out at her for simply doing her job, helping others. Was she supposed to apologize for Jeanette's trust, or for the trust of any of the women who came here, for that matter? But then that wasn't what Clare was asking her to do. She was describing an emotion, that was all. It was just a feeling Ann wished didn't exist. Because yes, it embarrassed her, still, after all this time. To be prized for this, whatever quality it was that allowed others to open themselves to her. No one loved her for this as much as Clare did. No one saw it more intimately. And yet, what Clare had said was true, there was something unbearable about the naming of it, something that made her wish this moment would simply vanish.

Besides which, with Jeanette, the idea that Ann had been the recipient of some great unburdening was painfully off the mark. She could still remember the atmosphere in that car at dusk, driving Jeanette back to where she lived then in town. How utterly emphatic her insistence had been that Ann tell no one. It wasn't an opening, it was a demand to remain closed. And why, really, had Ann agreed without even knowing what would be revealed? Was it the pastor in her, used to the ways of confession? No, it had been something else. Something about the kind of violence Ann intuited Jeanette was about to describe. Some disavowed instinct in her—counter to everything she and Clare and Roberta espoused—that such violence should, after all, remain unspoken. That the light of words would only give it life. And wasn't *this* instinct in Ann what Jeanette had *actually* been drawn to? Not to wise Ann—the guide to letting go—but to a keeper of silence. Ann didn't like being made to think this, but part of her knew it was true. And was that what had drawn her so keenly to Jeanette? That she intuited in Ann something no one else did. Something not to be idealized.

'The fact is,' Ann said, 'you're the stronger one, when it comes down to it. You have the courage of your convictions.'

Clare huffed. 'And what good do they do me? I was cruel to that professor yesterday.'

'You weren't cruel,' Ann said. 'You were annoyed.'

'I let myself get in the way,' Clare said. 'After how long? I still do that.'

Ann picked up the plate of pear slices and offered it again. This time Clare took one. For a little while they sat there together, eating the fruit, watching the apple blossoms flurry in the breeze.

'Sometimes I think we ran,' Clare said.

'From what?'

'The world,' Clare said. 'We offer people something, I still believe that. But isn't it best for us, more than anyone? *Always do what costs you the most.* Isn't that the Simone Weil quote?'

'Yes,' Ann said. 'And she starved herself to death.'

'You know what I mean,' Clare said.

Which was true, Ann did know.

The week before Vasel's application is due something strange begins to happen. Something hard to name. The most familiar objects, the ones I live amidst—the beige cloth couch, the dark-veneered dining table, the bookcases and the side tables and the standing lamp, these items that have been arranged in the same layout for years—no longer seem to fit together. It's as though they have become unrelated, like secondhand furniture set out for sale in the mere shape of a room, whatever association that held my belongings together having dissolved. I keep thinking the impression will pass—that it's some kind of reverse déjà vu, an unseeing rather than a seeing-again—but each morning as I awaken and take in the blond wood dresser and caned side chair across my bedroom and each evening when I return to my building and open the front door, this uncanniness greets me, and so I have no choice but to ignore it and carry on.

One evening, as I'm working at the dining table, I get a text from Cliff. When he asked a few weeks ago if we had broken up—teasingly or in earnest—I didn't reply for a day, and when I did, all I wrote was, *Sorry. Busy. More soon.* But now he's here, downstairs. *Okay if I come up?* I consider lying, telling him I'm not home, but I can't.

After buzzing him in, I tidy the pages of Vasel's file into a few stacks and close my laptop. Cliff hesitates at the threshold, then leans forward and pecks me on the cheek a bit awkwardly. Another of his imitations, it strikes me, of a domestic routine we've never had.

Rather than flopping down on the couch as he usually does, he sits upright, legs crossed. His hair is shaggier and hangs down over his ears and he's grown a short beard, which makes him appear both older and younger somehow, older because a beard is not boyish, younger because by the way he runs his hands over its bristles, he seems unused to it. I offer him a drink, but he declines.

'It's okay,' he says. 'You don't have to play along anymore.'

I'm still standing, over by the table. 'It's just that there's this case,' I say, knowing that I'm prevaricating, but too impatient with his sudden visit to do anything more. 'It should be over soon.'

He smiles, and I wonder if he's high, if that's what has allowed him to break whatever loose decorum we have and simply show up. But the smile, as it spreads over his face, is more rueful than glad.

'Do you ever wish there was no internet?' he asks. 'I mean, without web pages to design, I wouldn't have a job, and without the internet, I'd probably have less sex. But it's the situations like this, like you and me. I never would have met you, there's no way our paths would have crossed, not with whatever it is you do and how much time you spend doing it. But we met, and then you just have to make it up. You have to fake it—the closeness—at least if that's what you want. Until you don't have to, I guess. Until it's real. Or until it isn't.' He gazes off into the kitchen as he speaks, as though trying to make something out in the distance. 'I couldn't tell which it was with you. Whether you just wanted sex and so didn't care about not spending any real time together, or if you really were just busy but wanted something more. I guess that's why I kept coming. Because I didn't know. Which I guess meant that I didn't have to know for myself either.'

The way he holds me in his eyes when he does look up is almost alarming in its directness. It's as if I'm seeing him—actually seeing him—for the first time. He is a handsome man, but tolerably handsome. Not so alluring as to put me—or him—in danger of my wanting him too much. He is right—we are strangers. I've let his half pretending that we were otherwise disguise this fact. As I have with other men before him who, over the years, have come and gone from this apartment as he has, for a few months at a time, mostly for the mutual relief of an urge.

'I'm sorry,' I say. 'I know I've been preoccupied.'

'It's all right,' he says. 'You never promised anything more.'

I can't tell if he means this—if he is just here to say goodbye—or if he wants me to protest. But I don't. After a moment, he stands up, and moves toward the door. When I cross to meet him there, he turns to give me a quick hug.

'I hope whatever you're working on goes well,' he says, then nods goodbye.

Later, when my phone rings and I see my sister's name, I'm glad for it. Charlie has gone to bed, she says, so tonight she's able to talk, and she does—on and on—about her Reiki practice starting up again and the dog's chemo and how they've decided to make Charlie clean up his own shit and how the more she reads about General Daniel Brodhead and his exploits in charge of the western front of the Revolutionary War, the more disturbing it is. 'Soldiers,' she says. 'So many of Mom's great-great-whatevers were soldiers. The first guy who got here, in 1664, he was a soldier from Yorkshire, a farmer. He's the one in the group that took Manhattan. It turns out the general was his grandson. And after them there's a whole 'nother mess of lieutenants and captains—the Civil War, the Philippines—a whole parade's worth, and all to produce a big ol' lesbian spirit guide who doesn't give a damn about where she came from. Don't you think that's weird? How incurious she is? But then I guess you are, too.'

For a moment, I try going along with her, picturing some ruddy-faced English farmer in a red coat and tricorn hat landing at the Battery with his musket, a man but for whom, apparently, Liz and I would not be alive, but it is just an image, a Hollywood phantasm, and nothing more.

'I don't get it,' I say. 'What does all this mean to you? It can't just be wanting to tell Charlie someday. Is it the costumes?'

'Fuck you. I'm not some *reenactor*.'

'What is it, then?'

'You'll just be snarky with me,' she says.

'I won't,' I say. 'You're the snarky one.'

She pauses for what is, for her, an unusually long time. 'I believe in spirits,' she says, 'that's the truth of it. Call them ghosts if you want to, that's fine. Dad's a ghost. He's dead but he hangs around in us, doesn't he? And there were the ghosts in him, whoever they were. With the Mom stuff, I might have stopped after some random ancestry googling, but the first time I asked her about it, she went cold as a turkey. Like when I used to accuse her of not actually believing in God, which, PS, it seems I was right about. So of course I had to keep going to find out what she didn't want to talk about. And then you start reading this stuff—all this violence, right from the get-go. I began dreaming about it, seeing some of it. You and Mom will just think I'm some wacko dilettante, but whatever. There's something there, something passed down. We come from the settlers—that's the truth of it.'

'You're serious,' I say. 'You're never serious.'

'Well, you kind of cornered the market on that, sibling-wise. Any-hoo, that's my rant. But what's up with you? Last time we spoke, you sounded wacko.'

'I think I just broke up with someone,' I say. 'But we weren't really together.'

'That sounds on brand.'

'Thanks.'

'Oh, come on,' Liz says. 'You've always been like that. You're like a tortoise crossed with a slut. You sleep around, just in slow motion.'

'That's a loving way to put it.'

'Maybe,' she says. 'But you haven't even mentioned this guy to me. Is he really what's got you looped?'

'Do you remember Jared?' I ask, hearing the timidity in my voice, as though I'm a kid scared to tell my older sister about a boy.

'Of course,' Liz says. 'You think I'm demented? You were obsessed. What about him?'

'I just hadn't thought about him in a long time. And lately I have. But right now the odd thing is the furniture in my apartment. It's difficult to explain. It's like it doesn't hang together anymore, like one thing doesn't belong with the other.'

'Wow. You really are batshit,' she says. 'Though actually what you sound like is Mom. That's what she told us when she threw all our old stuff out, when she moved out of the rectory. Don't you remember? *They're just objects, they have no inherent value. If they're important, you'll carry them with you on the inside.*'

I don't remember this and I doubt our mother said it — my sister has always been the master of exaggeration — but I let it go. And yet, later, after we've hung up and, being too restless to sleep, I go out for a late run, as I'm looking across the canal at the old grain silos with their ghostly spines lit faintly by the lights along the water, it does occur to me there is something about that phrase — *They're just objects*. I can at least imagine my mother saying it. And I can certainly hear the force of the tone she would use, telling me that I was understanding something all wrong.

When he saw me kneeling over Jared that night, Brett gawked at me, stupefied, and without a word uttered turned back into the hall and closed the door behind him. I scrambled up off the bed and stood against the wall. But all Jared did was fasten his pants and roll onto his stomach, as if nothing had happened.

'Jared!' I whispered, my breath fast and shallow.

'What?' he mumbled, sounding half asleep, though I didn't believe it any more than I'd believed he'd been drowsing on any of those afternoons we'd been together.

'He *saw*,' I said.

Jared mashed his face into the pillow and muttered that he was tired.

'What are we going to do?'

'You should just go home,' he said, turning his head away from me.

I remained at the wall, in the faint blue glare of the video console, scanning the room as if for evidence that might still be hidden. Any minute Jared would have to sit up and somehow deal. But he didn't. He stayed prone there on the bed, silent.

Eventually, I had no choice. I put on my sneakers, listened in the hall to make sure Brett and Stephanie were gone, then walked down the stairs and out the front door into the quiet of the dead of night.

I didn't hear from Jared the next day, or in the days after that. When I called his house, his mother said he wasn't there—not the first time I called and not the second.

'What's the matter?' Stephanie asked when I tried her.

If I wanted ever to be with Jared again, I couldn't say anything to her, so I didn't. Still, when I heard in her voice the condescension that she'd shown toward me back before I'd been allowed into the group, I thought: She knows—they all know. Jared's told them that it was me who did it to him, that he was just baked. And now, without saying anything, he's cut me off, and they've cut me out.

The silence went on like this for weeks. Stephanie had a job that summer at a record shop in Boston, and Brett was selling tickets at the little art-house movie theater. Jared didn't need to work so I had nowhere to go where I could try to run into him.

If I stayed in bed before my afternoon shifts at the grocery store, my misery seemed to exist at least just a little outside of me, over in the corner of my room, a separate living creature, which if I didn't move might stay put. But then my mother would come and tell me that it was time to bring my father his breakfast, and as soon as I stood up, the creature would pounce so quickly it threw me off balance, making the room seem to tilt, leaving me dizzy, and I'd have to sit again and breathe before I could put on my clothes and make it into the kitchen.

By then the ordinary flow of time in the house had been suspended. It moved instead at a trickle through those rooms, too weak a current to carry anything more than the stench of my father's illness. All we did was wait.

Liz tried to pretend otherwise, dolling herself up in dresses and putting flowers in her hair, like a nymph who could with pixie dust make things not so. But soon even she didn't believe this, and kept up her costuming as much to ward off boredom as anything else.

As the days went on, my father no longer requested only her company. Sometimes he asked for me, usually only to doze off when I came to sit with him. But other times he stayed awake, and said things. Often just a sentence or two spoken quietly into the air immediately in front of him. About the price that items in the warehouse ought to fetch or various documents that needed attending to. Or sometimes snippets of stuff he wanted me to know: That I should make up my own mind about politics, not listen to my mother or him. That my grandmother was too old to travel, that this was why she wasn't here to be with him, as though I might think there was a different reason.

The air conditioner, the only one in the house, made Liz's room cold, and my father's sheets were kept pulled up over his shoulders, leaving just his gaunt head visible on the pillow. I'd wait till he closed his eyes again before slipping out.

Soon the dizziness that I woke with began to stretch into the afternoons. You're, like, *literally* an airhead, Liz would say when I handed her a tray of food I was worried I might drop. My mother suggested I drink more water, and Clare, who still came and went without ever speaking to my father or going near his room, suggested I take naps. But when I closed my eyes, all I saw was Jared's face and my father's floating together in the darkness.

Late in the day when the heat in the house became intolerable, I'd go into the shade of the backyard and thrash the bushes with a stick till Liz, smoking on the porch, told me to stop being a psycho. Then I'd wander off furious into the neighborhood. One stifling evening when the thunderclouds had rolled in but delivered no rain to break the heat, I kept going, through downtown, through the warren of streets between there and the high school, to Jared's house. I hadn't seen him in a month, and I couldn't bear it any longer.

His mother answered the door. She was dressed more casually than usual, in pleated khaki shorts and a short-sleeved white blouse, though her hair had the same near-perfect luster to it.

'Oh, Peter,' she said, with a slight smile. 'How nice to see you. Come in.'

She led me through to the kitchen, where she asked if I wanted something to drink and without waiting for an answer opened the fridge and took out a fancy bottle of lemonade.

'I'm afraid Jared's not here,' she said. 'He rarely is these days. But I guess that's the age you're all at, bored of your boring parents.'

An endive salad and a nearly empty bottle of white wine stood next to her on the kitchen island. She'd always appeared so put together and so occupied by her job that I'd never imagined how she might be on her own, when she wasn't working. In her shorts and blouse she seemed even younger than before, less like the parents at school than one of the younger teachers whose romantic lives people sometimes gossiped about.

'I don't think you're boring,' I said.

'That's kind of you,' she said. 'But *your* mother — she's an interesting woman, isn't she? A female priest.'

I didn't know what to say to this, so said nothing. When she carried her plate and glass to the kitchen table, I followed, as it seemed she intended me to, and sat opposite her.

'So what is it that Jared told you about me? I'll bet he told you I water his pot plants. Terrible, isn't it? Very irresponsible. His father would be appalled. But then his father isn't here. And letting those things wither would hardly keep Jared from his vices. What do you think? Am I awful? Am I just ingratiating myself with my son?'

She'd addressed her questions to the salad but peered across the table at me now, as she took another sip of her wine. I'd never before been spoken to like this by an adult, as though I were one also.

'Cat got your tongue?' she said with a grin. 'Don't worry, you don't have to answer my silly questions. But why aren't you out with the others?'

When I responded with what was meant to be a shrug of indifference, she didn't seem to believe it.

'What is it?' she said. 'Has Jared not been in touch?'

I blushed and dropped my eyes to the black-and-white tiles, so lacquered and clean.

'It's all right,' she said, her voice gentler now. 'My son's very good at making friends, he always has been. But he's not always so good at sticking around. It's that charisma of his. Drawing people in—it comes too easily for him. His father has it too. I suppose that's where he gets it. Though he doesn't much like his father—to his credit. But who knows?' she said, brightening, returning to her kidding tone. 'Maybe it's my fault. Maybe I spoil him. If he were here, we could ask him! Couldn't we?' she said, as though she and I were in the same comic predicament, here in the house without her son.

'I guess,' I said, sensing she wanted me to somehow join her in the joke but not knowing how to.

Her mind seemed to shift elsewhere then, her gaze floating off into the dining room, where a white globe of a chandelier hung over an oblong white table. 'Of course,' she said, 'it's also true that my son is very good-looking. And I know myself how complicated that can be for a person early in life. When you're still trying to figure out who you are, and people are so often attracted to you.' She glanced back at me as she said this, the playfulness in her voice all of a sudden gone.

She knows, I thought. Even if Jared hasn't told her, she knows.

'In any case,' she said, 'that's no excuse for rudeness.'

'It's okay,' I said. 'I just came to see if he was around.'

'Of course you did,' she said. 'And here you are, having to listen to me prattle on. I can let you go.'

A few minutes later, as we stood by the front door, she rested her hand on my shoulder. 'Don't worry,' she said. 'I'll tell him you came by. I'll make certain he calls you. How does that sound?'

'That's good,' I said. 'I'm sorry if I interrupted you.'

'No, Peter, you weren't interrupting,' she said. 'You're a good person, I can tell that. You're no bother at all.'

As soon as she closed the door, I ran across the lawn and down the empty street, through the cones of yellow light cast by the street lamps onto the warm pavement—the night lit up, then pitch-black, then lit again. By the time I slowed to a walk, it had finally begun to rain. I stepped into the doorway of one of the women's clothing shops downtown to get out of it, watching the water beat against the sidewalk, but I couldn't remain still, so I kept on, letting myself get soaked.

At the house, my mother sat on the living room couch, reading under the light of the standing lamp, her head bowed toward the page. My father could be dying in the other room, yet still it was the printed word that absorbed her. As if this life—our life—were an interruption of the real meaning of things.

'Hi,' I said, when she didn't look up.

'Oh, there you are. Where have you been? You're all wet.'

'It's raining,' I said.

'Looks like you need a towel, and a change.'

I sat in the armchair across the coffee table from her.

My mother knew who Jared was, she'd seen him coming and going, from back when we first started hanging out. She had even asked me about him, what grade he was in, who his parents were, suspicious, I could tell, of his fashionable clothes and the sleekness of his car, the air of materialism about him, that sin she spent her Sundays preaching against in a town full of it. But she wanted me to have friends so had held her tongue. Even after she and my father met his mother at one of the school plays and I could see the judgment in my mother's eyes — of Mrs. Hanlan's snug silver dress and little diamond necklace, her makeup and flawless smile, even her youth — she made no comment on her at all, despite what I knew she was thinking. But if she had taken any notice of Jared's recent absence, she showed no sign of it.

'By the way,' she said, 'I made an appointment for you with the doctor, about that dizziness of yours. I'm sorry I didn't do it sooner. But I'll take you.'

'Fine,' I said.

'What's the matter?' she asked, putting her book down on her lap. 'You sound upset.' Her voice was placid, as it tended to be when she emerged from a long read. Before waiting for an answer, she added, 'That's a rather stupid question, I'm sorry. What you're having to go through at your age, it's a dreadful thing.'

'I don't care about Dad,' I said.

'Don't say that,' she said. 'Of course you do.'

'You don't.'

'How *dare* you say that.'

Her anger — so rare — burst over the room like a thick gas from a ruptured pipe, obscuring the space between us and making me, almost immediately, sleepy. My eyes drooped to the dark braided rug, where, as a child, I had leaned against her leg as she read.

'I'm in love,' I said. 'And I can't stand it. It's too much. Don't ask me who, please don't ask.'

I heard her place her book down on the coffee table, and I knew what she was about to do: turn this into her kind of situation, a priest thing. *Stop ministering to me!* my father used to bark at her when they fought. Any second, she would pose some gentle, measured question, her fear all dressed up as concern.

'I mean it,' I said. 'Don't ask.'

'All right,' she said. 'But I do need to know one thing. Are you being safe?'

'Oh God! Please! Didn't you hear me?'

'Yes, I heard you.'

'No you didn't,' I said. 'You didn't!'

Standing in line at the clerk's office, about to file the Rijals' application, I skim the first page of it and realize that I've missed the deadline. According to the sheet in my hand, they didn't enter the country last May, they entered last April, which means that the one-year period they had to qualify for an interview rather than a hearing expired three weeks ago. It must be a typo, I think. But when I rifle through the documents and find their affidavit, I see that it isn't.

The line moves forward. This can't be, I think. I can't be the reason they are put into court. Suddenly, I'm lightheaded again. The print in the boxes of the form begins to blur, and then so does the room.

'Sir!' the clerk says a moment later as I stand before her at the desk. 'Have you got something for me or not?'

I reel myself back in by focusing on her face — her gloss lipstick, her little diamond nose stud. I have no choice. I have to submit it. The later it is, the less chance I'll have when I go begging the Asylum Office to waive the filing date. I hand the clerk the binder, stricken by the thought of what else in it I might have gotten wrong, then wander out into the hallway, where lawyers and court staff move quickly by, headed home for the day.

At the office that evening, I try to draft a letter, searching for an excuse to ascribe to the Rijals, but each one is a lie. They gave me everything I needed, well in advance. When I call Monica for advice, which I know I shouldn't need but suddenly do, her mother answers.

'Which one are you?' she asks. 'The old leftist or the homosexual?'

'Mama, give me that!' Monica says, taking the phone from her. Then she berates me for calling her at home. 'Just tell the truth,' she says impatiently after I explain the situation. 'Tell them it's your fault, then make your plea.'

So that's what I do, laboring over my words till late in the evening. The whole thing still has me unnerved as I cross the avenue and put the letter in the mailbox, this fuckup beginning to worry me all over again about Vasel's filing. His deadline, which I've now triple-checked, is in two days. Still he's given me no statements. I know I should go home—I'm exhausted, and I can't force someone to comply—but rather than heading for the subway, I find myself walking north up Sixth, then turning onto Houston at the little playground on the corner. I walk on past the Catholic church, past West Broadway, then Broadway, and then on up into Nolita until I arrive at the entrance of the restaurant where Vasel works.

There's a zinc bar up front with big floral arrangements either side of a giant Art Deco mirror. In the dining room at the rear, wood panels with thin metal inlays line the walls and above them runs a strip of black-and-white tile painted with arabesques. The bartender is dressed to match the decor: a short white jacket, black necktie, his hair slicked behind his ears. I perch on one of the stools, waiting for Vasel to appear and spot me. Whatever I do, I can't draw attention to him here.

When I see he isn't among the servers helping the last customers of the night, I guess it isn't his shift. But then, belatedly, he emerges through the door from the kitchen in a pressed white shirt and black dress pants, holding himself stiff and upright, as if he's being scrutinized by every eye in the room, though in fact I'm the only one observing him as he clears away dessert plates from a young couple on their phones, then returns to pour the last of their sparkling water. He doesn't look up toward the front of the house as he comes and goes to the remaining tables, bowing his head slightly at each rather than smiling as an American would.

I ask the bartender for an ice water to cool the heat in my throat, and when he brings it, I steady my hands around the cold glass. Until now Vasel and I have always been across a table or desk from each other. I've hardly ever looked at him like this before, without the pressure of his looking back. At his thin frame and long legs, at the almost delicate motion of his hands as he reaches out for a plate or bowl. It's terrifying, actually, taking him in this way. And it occurs to me now that I have been terrified all along—terrified that I was attracted to him. That all my efforts on his behalf have been a disguise for appetite. A means to draw him to me. Thinking this, even now, scares me. As though even the possibility of my desire is a kind of violence. Yet now that I'm sitting here, unseen, free to consume him with my eyes, to strip him down to fantasy, what fills me isn't lust but something far less acquisitive. Something like sadness.

Suddenly he is approaching the bar, empty tray in hand, and he sees me on the stool. Alarm widens his eyes. And why shouldn't it? I shouldn't be here. A surprise can only mean bad news for him or, as the irritation his expression resolves into suggests, more hassle from his lawyer.

'Not now,' he says, in a whisper, when the bartender isn't looking. 'Go outside, wait for me down the street.' He leaves the tray on the bar and walks off.

Outside, I find a stoop at the corner and wait there. Despite the hour, it takes what seems a long while for him to emerge from the alley. When he reaches the top of the steps I'm perched on, he takes a loose cigarette from his jacket pocket and offers it to me. I decline and he lights it for himself, holding it between thumb and forefinger, drawing deeply on it twice before ashing onto the pavement. Only then does he take a seat on the step below me and begin searching his phone.

'Here it is,' he says. 'I am sending it to you. The letter Armend did for me. He put a date and signed it, like you said.'

The news goes straight to my spine, right between the shoulder blades, where a fist I didn't even realize was there, that has been tightening its grip for months, lets go. I won't fail him. Or, rather, my brain reminds me, I am one document away from not failing him.

'Thank you,' I say. 'This will help, I promise. And now there's just that last thing left—the letter from your mother.'

'No!' he says. 'I told you. I will not ask her that. Why do you not listen? And why are you like this, anyhow? You come to everybody's job late at night demanding things?'

'No,' I say. I need to say something more, to explain myself, but I don't know how.

For the first time that day, it registers with me that it is weirdly hot for the end of May, more like July, and even this late at night the heat hasn't dissipated. The air remains as thick and motionless. I glance at my phone and see the email Vasel just sent.

'You were right,' I say. 'What you said to me last time. I did want to know if you still thought about Armend. It has nothing to do with your case, what your feelings for him are now. But you were right, I wanted to know.'

'What does it matter if I think about him? He is in Italy. He has money. He doesn't need to worry. Probably I will never see him again. High-school crush, isn't that what you call it?' He takes a last drag of his cigarette and stubs it out on the edge of the stoop.

'But yes, sure, I think about him. Now he texts me again. Songs and things. Videos of him dancing. He is still crazy.' He rests his arms on his knees and is quiet for a moment. 'Why do you do your job?' he asks. 'Why not just be a rich lawyer?'

'What?' I say. 'You don't think I live in a fancy tower in Hell's Kitchen anymore?'

'Less,' he says. 'I see the real rich ones now. I bet you do this to feel like a good person, right? Like you're the Statue of Liberty,' he says, chuckling. 'You help all the poor people like me. That's a liberal, no? That is what you are.'

'You make it sound like an accusation.'

'No,' he says, 'but I'm right, yes? Like all the rich white people who vote for Obama. They feel good because they like a Black man.'

'Have you been watching Fox News?'

'No,' he says. 'I mean you. And don't say we only have a few minutes, we can only talk about my case, because it is midnight and you are the one who came here.'

The sound of the traffic coming up Lafayette echoes off the buildings opposite, joining the hum of air conditioners, and the faint whir of a helicopter in the far distance. I am not so much lightheaded now as light-bodied, as if the grid of time and obligation has at last lifted, and my body, so long habituated to its weight, has begun to float.

'I guess that's part of it,' I say. 'The way I was brought up. Don't think of yourself, think of others.'

'Like the priests tell you to,' Vasel says.

'Yes,' I say, 'just like that.'

'I would rather be rich,' he says.

'What would you do with the money?'

'I would send lots to my mother and sister, and then I would buy a big studio with big windows and I would draw.'

A bicyclist with a boom box strapped to his handlebars blaring Sister Sledge rumbles over the semi-cobbled, semi-paved street in front of us and then is gone, leaving the block just a little quieter than before.

'I moved into that apartment,' Vasel says. 'With the waiter guy.'

'How is it?'

'Weird,' he says. 'I thought he was a normal gay. That's what he looks like—clean and cute—and when he goes out, he has nice clothes. But at home he eats only raw vegetables and he kind of stinks, and his room does not have a door, just a curtain. The other people think we are having sex, but it is not true. I want my own room.'

'You know the date of your hearing, right? You have it written down? Or in your phone? It's only a couple of weeks from now.'

'Yeah,' he says. 'You texted me it a million times already.'

I open the attachment to Vasel's email and read in tiny print the first two lines of Armend's letter: *I know Vasel Marku from our town. We went to school together.* I stop there, click my phone off, and put it in my pocket. Across the street, in the display window of a closed boutique, a blue men's dress shirt hangs spotlit against a draped black cloth.

If someone had asked me, *Did you go to Jared's funeral?*, I would have said I didn't remember. Because I didn't. Until now. The service his mother held for him took place at the Catholic church just up from the town hall. An open casket, silk-lined, surrounded by a profusion of flowers. The dark blue suit she'd dressed him in was impeccable. Such a fine garment. His father spoke, but I don't remember the words. When the priest was done, that was it. No reception, no receiving line. His mother just walked out.

'I did meet this other guy,' Vasel says. 'He comes into the restaurant. He's not some gross old person. He's thirty-two. And has his shit together. He texts me now, he wants to go out.'

'That's good,' I say, and then I add, 'I won't bring this up again, but if she did it quickly, there is still time. You could get that letter from your mother. She would want to help you, wouldn't she?'

'You know nothing about her,' he says.

'I know she protected you.'

'I'm leaving,' he says, standing up to go. But a moment later, at the foot of the steps, he pauses and turns back, as if waiting for me. So I get up as well, accepting what seems like his peace offering, and then the two of us walk together in silence back down to Houston, where Vasel heads for his train and I head for mine.

Shortly before he died, my father called me into Liz's room. The hospice nurse had come and gone for the day. My mother and sister were out. He was covered in sweat, his eyes gray and sunken. The beard he'd never had before obscured his mouth and jaw.

'Come here,' he said.

I sat in the chair by the hospital bed. He pressed the button, bringing himself upright. Then with great effort he pulled a pillow down behind his back so he could face me directly. He was gaunter than ever but seemed to be rousing himself for a purpose.

'You think I hate your mother,' he said in a voice that lacked all strength, a thin, reedy voice nothing like his own. 'That I hate her for kicking me out, but I don't. I couldn't if I wanted to,' he said, pulling at the air for breath. 'So don't go hating her, you understand?'

He hadn't said this many words in days, and the finality of them scared me. As the summer had gone on, and I had hung around the house for what seemed an infinite time missing Jared hour after hour and worrying over what he and Stephanie and Brett thought of me, I'd gotten used to my father being sick without imagining he would ever actually die.

'Okay,' I said. 'I understand.'

'And there's something else,' he said. 'Visit your grandmother. I never took you there enough, for one reason or another.' He had to pause before continuing. 'Spend time with her. But you need to listen to me first. Because she told you a story about me, didn't she? About me working up in the woods.'

I nodded. 'A long time ago,' I said.

'Come here,' he said. 'Come closer.'

I pulled the chair right to the edge of the bed. His sweat, which had always had a thick odor to it, had no scent at all now, as if some essence of him were already gone.

'She told you a man broke my arm, didn't she? That that's why I stopped working up there.'

'Yeah,' I said. 'She told us you wouldn't have met Mom otherwise. Because you wouldn't have gone on your trip.'

He grimaced, in pain or anger I couldn't tell, then reached over and yanked his IV out of his forearm. I stood to pick the line up off the floor, to try somehow to put it back in him, but he said, 'Stop it, I need to be awake for this.'

The vessels in his neck were throbbing. He was laboring to breathe. From where the IV had been, a trickle of blood etched its way down the creases of his wrist.

'Your grandmother told you that man up there...that he was a bad apple, didn't she?'

I nodded again, scared not by his tone anymore but by his harrowed stare.

'Well, she doesn't know what she's talking about,' he said. 'That wasn't it, that wasn't it at all.' He heaved to fill his lungs. 'That kind of work, middle of nowhere, in the woods...it's mostly roughnecks, drinkers. I was barely older than you...but I drank with them. Everyone did. Blind drunk. Then you pass out till the next day. That's how we lived.'

He grabbed me by the elbow with uncanny force, and pulled

me close, close enough to see the flecks of spittle in the corners of his mouth.

'That bad apple?' he said. 'He tried to touch me. That's what he did. While I was sleeping. But I didn't let him!' He gasped, tightening his fist around my arm. 'You hear me! I pushed that son of a bitch off. Out that cabin door, onto the dirt, and all those roughnecks watched.'

To get air he had to suck it through his throat like a straw, but still he craned himself up off his pillow and practically shook me. I had never been so terrified of him in my life.

'Your grandmother has no idea what she's talking about!' he hissed. 'That man didn't break my arm. He was a queer, you understand me? I was the one hitting him! He didn't hurt me, I hurt *him*!'

And with that, he collapsed back onto the uptilted mattress, whatever force he had held in reserve to deliver himself of this now spent. I sensed a wetness on my wrist and looked down to see the blood and sweat of his forearm smeared onto mine like the fluid of some dark birth.

'That man,' he whispered, his head lolling back onto the pillow, eyes closing. 'I gave him no reason to think I wanted him to touch me. No reason ever.'

What Ann noticed first was the smell, out by the edge of the meadow, a whiff of shit, and she assumed a bear or some other creature had been by in the night. When the scent was still there the next morning, only more powerful, she thought the rain must have caused it to blossom. It wasn't until the third day, when the meadow had dried and the pungent odor hadn't faded, that she paused on her way to meditate to examine the ground and noticed the bits of brown sludge that had seeped up through the grass—not animal excrement but the remains of their own.

Later that morning, she looked for Jeanette and found her on a ladder up the far side of the barn, taking down an old steel gutter that had been hanging, semi-detached, for months. The bruises on her face and neck had largely faded now and she'd stopped wearing the wrist brace the hospital had given her. From the way she plowed through the early-summer work in the yard and the garden and kept up with this kind of building maintenance on top of it, you would never know she'd suffered bruised ribs and a concussion, injuries she had more or less refused to acknowledge.

'I think we have a problem with the septic,' Ann said.

'Is that right,' Jeanette said.

She didn't stop prying the rusted gutter she'd reached or glance down from her perch, just kept at the task. Ann watched her at it for a bit.

In the days both before and after her altercation in the yard, Jeanette had been spending a night or two a week away from the center, somewhere in town or nearby, presumably, and returning in the early morning. No one inquired where she went, and she didn't explain. It had happened before over the years, her being gone on Fridays or Saturdays for a while. To be with a man, Ann assumed, someone she'd met or knew one way or another. She behaved no differently during or after these periods than she had before them, and soon enough it would be as if they had never happened.

When the gutter was off and Jeanette had come down the ladder, they walked together past the meetinghouse and out across the back lawn to where the grass began to squelch.

'You suppose it's the filter?' Ann asked.

'Could be,' Jeanette said as she moved along the edge of the stained oval, surveying the ground. 'That or the baffle.'

She had this way of not looking at Ann when they were together. She wasn't ignoring her; on the contrary, it seemed a sign of her keen awareness of Ann's presence. Ann had considered it shyness back when Jeanette first arrived, but it wasn't that. It was more like apprehension, which over time she had come to recognize as its own form of intimacy. Everyone else Jeanette looked right at.

They were heading back toward the house in a light drizzle when Jeanette, without preamble, said, 'I want to do a circle.'

Ann came to a halt. 'Has Clare been getting after you to do it?'

'No. Why? You think I'd only do it if she told me to?'

'No,' Ann said. 'I just thought she might have, that's all.'

'Or do I have to apply to be a *retreatant*?' Jeanette said, retracting into sarcasm.

'Don't be silly,' Ann said, picturing the four of them seated in the chairs in the middle of the meetinghouse. Her chest tightened before her mind could name the emotion as fear. 'I'm just surprised,' she said. 'At the hospital, it sounded like the last thing you wanted to do. What changed your mind?'

Jeanette gazed at her foot as it kicked, gently, at the grass. 'A good person in my life,' she said.

'I see,' Ann said. 'And who's that?'

'My cousin. You probably think I go off to town to get laid, but I just go to see Larry. Sometimes he's around, sometimes he isn't, depending on what kind of trouble he's in. He's back now because my aunt's sick, she probably doesn't have long. He always said he'd do that for her, and he's doing it.'

'All this time, you've never mentioned him.'

Jeanette stopped her kicking and rested her hands on her hips. 'He's not the kind of person who would ever come to a place like this,' she said.

'Right,' Ann said. 'But somehow he convinced you to do a circle with us? I don't quite follow.'

It amazed her how quickly ungrounded she'd become, her words little more than a play for time. What if Jeanette did tell Clare and Roberta what had happened to her? What if she let them in on that piece of her past? Would she need Ann in the same way?

'Never mind,' Jeanette said, turning toward the shed. 'I'm sorry I brought it up.'

'No,' Ann said. 'I'm the one who's sorry. I don't know why I'm interrogating you.'

'Really?' Jeanette said. 'You don't think it's because I'm your token local, and that stuff isn't really meant for me?'

'How can you say that?' Ann said. 'That's not true. I love you.'

The words had flown from her mouth, bypassing her mind. She wished, hopelessly, that she could swallow them back again, but they were loose, and the truth of them acted like a lever opening the sluice of a dam, her banked desire suddenly flowing.

She wanted to kiss Jeanette, to hold her, to be with her, with a force she hadn't known since the first time she'd kissed Clare on the back steps of the rectory one winter night after everyone in the house was asleep, the two of them shivering in the dark. How ridiculous, how absurd, and yet here it was, a response over which she felt no control.

Jeanette had gone still as soon as Ann had spoken. She lifted her head now, and stared up into the gray sky. 'What the fuck am I supposed to do with that?' she said.

Ann reminded herself to breathe. 'You don't have to do anything with it,' she said.

For nearly a minute, they stood in silence, there in the middle of the yard.

'You're the one who's supposed to have your shit together,' Jeanette said. 'You're supposed to love Clare.'

'I do,' Ann said. 'But it doesn't mean I don't love you, too.'

This seemed to pain Jeanette. Without ever saying as much, the two of them had, years ago, struck a bargain — that Jeanette would accept Ann's affection as long as it kept its distance, as long as it stayed far enough away that she could tolerate it. But now Ann had forced it close, disturbing their arrangement.

The drizzle they had been ignoring turned into fat-dropped rain. They cut across the gravel to shelter beneath the overhang of the shed. Quickly, the wind picked up, the sky darkened further, and then funnels of water rushed from it, slanting down over the yard, smearing the lines between the ground and the buildings and the trees, everything bleeding together in the sudden downpour. It lasted only a few minutes before softening. Looking up, Ann could see the storm clouds more clearly now as they raced toward the valley.

She thought of hugging Jeanette as an apology, almost, but knew that it would be for her own sake, and so refrained. 'I was being stupid just now,' she said, changing the subject. 'Of course you should do a circle, if that's what you want. Clare and Roberta would be glad for it.'

For a while Jeanette just stared off into the wet air, making no response. Eventually, she said, 'You asked me what changed my mind about it. It was talking to my cousin. That's what got me thinking.'

'How so?' Ann asked, relieved by this bridge back to where they had been before those three little words had escaped her. A relief Jeanette seemed to share.

'When I went to see him,' she said, 'I didn't want to tell him about the fight I got into. Or about going to the hospital, because I thought he'd go after the guy, the way he went after his brother when I got attacked. That's why the guy left back then. Larry hurt him pretty bad, and told him he'd do it again if he didn't leave town. So I didn't want to say anything to him. But then he saw my bruises, so he asked. I was sure he'd fly off the handle, run right out the door and find the guy. But he didn't. And I realized it's because he's got his mother to care for now. He can't afford to get in more trouble. And he doesn't want to. Instead, he just listened to me. And then he asked me how I was doing. And I think that's what got me. Back when I was raped, he never asked me that. He never asked me how I was. He just went berserk. So I told him how I was doing, which isn't great, I'm not doing great right now. And it felt good to say that to him. So maybe that's why I thought I could do a circle.'

'Of course,' Ann said. 'That makes good sense.'

On the appointed afternoon, I arrive at Federal Plaza early, just to be safe, and wait for Vasel by the entrance of the security tent. After a few minutes, he approaches from a distance, hands in his pockets, wearing the same gray windbreaker he wore the first day he appeared at the office, and I wonder why he hasn't dressed in any of his newer clothes. Was Monica right? Will Judge Ericson think he isn't gay enough? I didn't raise the issue with Vasel—I didn't want to make him any more self-conscious than I knew he would already be—but I worry about it again now.

'It's good this one is coming to an end,' Phoebe said at our last staff meeting, and Monica and Carl just nodded, all of them aware of what the case has cost my other clients.

As Vasel gets closer, I begin to make out his features, which is when I realize it isn't him but a man similarly thin-framed and dark-haired, a few years older. He passes the entrance and cuts the corner up to Broadway.

We're not first on the docket this afternoon and I've given us a buffer besides, but I text to ask when he'll be here, then bide my time surveying the lunch crowd crisscross Foley Square. Ten minutes after the agreed-on hour, I call him and get his voicemail. I leave no message, figuring he's on the train.

After another ten minutes, I call back. Still nothing. We should be heading up now. I scan the plaza and the sidewalk and the street for any sign of Vasel. Until finally I can't wait anymore and text him the room number with instructions to meet me there right away.

The waiting area outside Judge Ericson's courtroom is empty. I can just barely make out voices through the doors, the first hearing after lunch reaching its later stages. I don't sit in these foyers much, there usually isn't time, but I sit now and gaze hard at my phone, willing a response. Then I text Vasel again, failing as I type to notice that the voices inside have already ceased until the doors open and a middle-aged Chinese man in a white shirt and tan blazer, fighting back tears of relief, emerges flanked by Tameka French, a Legal Aid attorney with whom I've worked on appeals. She is holding her arm gingerly over his shoulder, letting him know it's really okay. She nods hello to me as the two of them pass by on their way to the elevators.

Inside, it's Sievers. Of all the department lawyers. The man who was so derisive to Sandra Moya during her hearing. Who wears his derision openly, for asylum seekers and for his own job, the one he can't wait to get promoted out of.

But we're repeat players, all of us. You can't make it personal. And it isn't the likes of Sievers who will grant or deny. Yet still, something about him today—dirty blond and pointy-nosed, a jock in early decline, as careless of his body as of his words—sets me on edge. I can't let myself be bothered, though, not in this moment. I nod but otherwise ignore him and put my satchel down on the respondent's table, thankful that Ericson has gone back to his chambers. Five minutes remain before the hearing is scheduled to start, and his clerk is as usual peering over her half-glasses at her monitor. For her, after all, there is nothing unusual about this scene, just two lawyers waiting for the judge, and one of them waiting for a client.

I step back into the foyer and call Vasel's number once more. Then I call the office to ask if he's left a message. After that I look up the number of the restaurant and dial it but get no answer. Finally, I remember I have Artea's number. I try it, and she picks up, or someone does.

I say who I am, Vasel's lawyer, and ask if it's Artea. 'I have to speak to Vasel,' I say. 'Where is he? It's extremely important.'

And then there's nothing, a silence, followed by a click, and the line goes dead.

'*Marku, Vasel,*' Judge Ericson reads off the jacket his clerk has just handed him. He switches on the recorder and speaks the case number into the record.

'Alex Sievers for DHS, Your Honor.'

'Peter Fischer for the respondent.'

'Unless my eyes deceive me, Mr. Fischer, you are missing a client,' Ericson says. 'Is Mr. Marku planning on joining us or have we gathered for naught?'

'I expect him here any moment,' I say.

'I'll give him five minutes,' Ericson says, looking at his watch. 'Which will be ten minutes after we were scheduled to begin.' He puts the jacket aside and turns to a different folder.

Sievers, slouched in his chair, checks email or last night's scores or whatever he does on his phone, Vasel's file closed in front of him.

Between my ears, I sense a rocking motion, as if some heavy liquid is sloshing gently back and forth against the insides of my skull. I sit to calm the sway, the necessity of the task at hand forcing itself through the murk in my head. I must do something.

Before Ericson has the chance to call time, I get to my feet again. 'Your Honor, may I say something?'

'Carry on,' he says.

'Your Honor, I've been practicing in your courtroom for a long time now. I think—I hope—that I've been a responsible, honest counsel. And a well-prepared one. I think I have been that. I haven't wasted your time. That's my job, of course, I know I don't get any kind of procedural credit for that, but still, in this case, I can warrant to you that Vasel Marku is not absent today in bad faith. I'm not going to lie to you and say I know exactly where he is—'

'Oh, come on,' Sievers says, leaning forward to open the file now.

'—but I can say that he has prepared diligently for this hearing and had every intention of being here. Now, I know—'

'The department moves for a final order,' Sievers says.

'Let him finish,' Ericson says gruffly.

'I realize that this would be out of the ordinary,' I say, steadying my legs hard against the table, 'and of course entirely at your discretion, but rather than granting the department's motion, I'm asking you, on my own word, if you would consider adjourning this hearing and permitting Mr. Marku to appear at a later date.'

Instantly, Sievers is on his feet, leaning over his desk. 'Your Honor, if I can speak now—and I won't even address whatever Mr. Fischer just said, because that's just ridiculous—but if you look, this is apparently a gay case, and you've seen plenty of these, we all have, the younger guys who come over here. I'm not talking about the Jamaican guys or the guys from Saudi Arabia, I'm talking about—where is this guy from?' Sievers flips back a few pages and scans the cover sheet. 'Albania. So basically a white guy, right? From *Europe*, who wants to live in America. Fair enough, who wouldn't? But when the time comes, guess what? He decides—surprise, surprise—he doesn't want to stand up in a courtroom and say, *I have sex with guys.* Because frankly, he probably doesn't!'

'Maybe, *just for once*,' I say to Sievers, 'you could try reading the application.'

Sievers turns to me, his head drawn back, as if I've just shoved him in the face, a how-dare-you expression pouring from his widened eyes. 'For the record, Your Honor,' he bellows, red in the cheeks now, 'counsel just impugned an officer of this court! Blatantly impugned me. I have no idea what his *own* feelings about this young man may be, I won't even go there, why he might be putting his reputation on the line in *this* case, but his attack on the department is totally out of line!'

I picture myself grabbing Sievers by the head and grinding that tender vessel of brains against the table, but I fix my gaze instead on Judge Ericson, up there on the dais, in his black robe, a man of sixty or so, salt-and-pepper-haired, thick-jowled, blandly confident in the bland, imperturbable way of a man for whom the world has always been a more or less obvious place.

'It would be out of line,' I say, 'if it weren't true.'

'This is outrageous!' Sievers nearly shouts.

'All right, all right,' Ericson says. 'That's enough, both of you just calm down, it's one case, for God's sake.'

He removes his square rimless glasses and closes his eyes. Leaning back in his chair, he rubs the flesh of his substantial brow.

'Mr. Fischer,' he says, after a pause, his voice dropping into the practiced deliberativeness of thousands of decisions spoken from the bench, 'I appreciate your sincerity. You are correct that I've never had reason to question your representations. The zealousness of your advocacy on behalf of your client is duly noted. However, the respondent has failed to appear for a merits hearing in this matter, which leaves me with no choice but to grant the department's motion, and so, for the record...'

He opens his eyes, puts his glasses back on, and searches the page in front of him.

'The court is entering a final order that Vasel Marku be removed from the United States to Albania, order subject to application for cancellation.'

With that, he leans forward and switches off the recorder.

'Now,' he says, looking out at the two of us. 'Despite Mr. Sievers's apparently jaundiced views on the claims of homosexuals, for all I know your client is stuck on a crosstown bus. So if you can get him here before five p.m., you're welcome to file a motion to reconsider and I will entertain it. And that, gentlemen, is it. Enjoy your afternoon.'

He exits through the door behind his clerk, and I hear Sievers say, 'Watch it, Fischer, next time I'll nail you,' but he's speaking to my back. I'm already halfway to the door.

The northbound 5 doesn't have many passengers at this time of day and moves with uncommon speed, the driver thankfully in a hurry, hurling the train through the tunnel. After Eighty-Sixth Street, there's hardly anyone left save for a maintenance crew in reflective vests gathered at the far end of the car. They get off a few stops later, and then the train shoots up onto the elevated tracks and light floods through the windows and I shut my eyes to hold back the nausea, and it stays bright for what seems like a long time until we dip again underground and finally reach Pelham Parkway.

It's after I walk back south across the tree-lined median and into the neighborhood that the Albanian flags—the black, double-headed eagle silhouetted on solid blood red—begin to appear: decals on rear windows, stickers on street signs and shop doors, and one, on the main drag, emblazoned across the hood of a Hummer.

Vasel never gave me the waiter's address. Artea's is the only one I have. A six-story brown brick building identical to every other on the block. I walk into the foyer and ring the buzzer twice, wait, and ring it twice again, resting my other hand against the wall. Hearing nothing, I try the ones next to it until the speaker finally crackles to life and I call into it, 'I need Artea. Do you know Vasel Marku?'

But no response comes, no voice, however garbled, as if the machine itself turned the intercom on just to prove that no one is home. I push through the front door, and hurry onto the sidewalk, heading back toward the shops. At the corner there's a deli, a fish market, a pizza joint. Across the street a dollar store, a pharmacy. I put my hands to the window of the pizza place and see four men across the room eating under a black-and-white portrait of Mother Teresa, all of them dark-haired, all in their fifties, heavyset, foremen by the look of them, clipboards on the benches beside them but no dust on their Carhartts, all old enough to be Vasel's father, none of them speaking, none of them uttering so much as a word. Vasel wants to say what happened. I know he does. So that he can stay here, yes, but more than that, simply to tell the truth, and to be believed. But he thinks he won't be, so he's pretending again. That none of it matters, that none of it exists, that if he just doesn't look, the truth won't be there.

Artea's uncles, I think. Their vegetable market. I find one a couple of blocks down, Dodaj Pick and Pack. Fruit in boxes on the risers out front. A stout woman in a white grocer's jacket behind the counter. Two teenage boys in their own white jackets sorting trays of potatoes at the back.

If I'm not careful, I'm going to be sick. An old woman leaning on a wheeled cart deliberates over the lettuces. A bearded man in a gray suit emerges from the back, speaking into his flip phone. He waves to the boys, who stop what they're doing and disappear through the door he came out of.

'Excuse me, sir, excuse me,' I say.

'Yes? What do you need?' he asks.

The fluorescent lights above him are nearly blinding.

'There's a young man,' I say. 'A young man I need to find.' And then I thrust my arm out to keep myself upright, but the pile of fruit gives way, spilling, and I fall toward the man and down onto the linoleum, everything spinning fast now—a sickening carnival ride approaching full strength.

III

The path is the dirt and the pebbles and the motion of the shade of the leaves. It is the woods on one side and the lake on the other. Bugs dart weightless by the shore. Ahead of me Jared swats at the verge of weeds with a stick, the dates of a Smiths tour listed down the back of his t-shirt. His denim shorts hug his thighs. The spirit of God, my mother preaches, lives in the beauty of the world, and in the beauty of the human form, it does not exist to deny us these pleasures, though of course she doesn't mean Jared's beauty: God in the motion of his legs, in the proportions of his arms. God didn't create Jared for me to long for, He didn't create him at all, I don't even believe in God, but I thank Him anyway, grateful that Jared has allowed me into his presence again, that I am permitted to follow him on this path, dirt and pebbles and now pine needles soft and dry between the exposed roots of the trees. August, evening, still light. I'm walking a few feet behind him, close enough to see the soft blond hair of his calves and the rims of his Converse smudged gray. On a curve in the path, the lake opens before us, columns of the setting sun stretched over the water, and then as the path cuts inward we are back in shadow, in the hum of insects, the light dappled over Jared's shoulders.

When we reach the little inlet, he lights the joint and doesn't ask if I want a hit, just holds it out to me from where he sits on the ground by a fallen tree. I pinch the rolled paper from beneath the moist skin of his thumb and finger. There is the sandy earth at his feet. There are his bare white knees. The stick he was swatting the weeds with rests in the crease of his hips.

Two days ago, my father died. In the late afternoon, with the air conditioner going and the shades pulled and his eyes closed and my mother standing by the bed holding his hand, gazing down at him almost impassively. The nurse had called us in an hour earlier, when his body had begun to rattle, and Liz and I had stood against the wall as the nurse tried to steady his arm to get more drugs in him, and when she couldn't, Liz helped her, holding his wrist down, and I'd thought, She shouldn't have to do that, my mother should do it, but my mother had stayed where she was on the far side of the bed, always the minister, never the doctor. Once the morphine had been given, my father's body went still and his jaw hung open, and all the nurse had left to do in the time that remained was to swab my father's tongue every few minutes with a wet dipper to keep his mouth from drying to the point of pain. When his breathing finally ceased, my mother held his hand a moment longer, then set it gently down on the bed, nodded to the two of us, and walked out into the hall to phone the undertaker. His body was gone in an hour.

Afterward Liz and I sat on the back steps. She smoked a cigarette and we stared together at the uncut grass and she told me she wanted to move somewhere far away. I couldn't bear being at that house a moment longer. I walked down the side yard and out into the street, then kept going past the other houses and yards, and turned onto the street that led downtown. I wanted to go to Jared's house, to bang on the door and force him to see me, but I didn't. I just continued through the main intersection, past the town hall and the library and my mother's church, then out along the route my father used to walk to work.

It wasn't until the next evening that I called Jared and left him a message telling him what had happened. And earlier today, at long last, he called back.

Now there is the spreading of his collarbones as he leans his shoulders against the tree trunk. There is the lengthening of his throat as his head rests back. The touch of his fingers as we pass the joint. Since he picked me up in his car, we've barely said a word.

'Where were you?' I ask, still standing over him. 'Two days ago.'

'What do you mean?' he says, his body splayed out in front of me.

'I'm asking you, where were you the afternoon my father died?'

'I don't know, out maybe. Why?'

'Because you killed him,' I say. And as I say it, I mean it.

'You're crazy,' he says.

I move to grab the stick from his lap, and he whips his arm down trying to get it first, but he's too late, I've got it, and I brandish it over him, ready to strike.

'What the fuck!' he says, leaning away from the impending blow. Never before has he paid me such complete attention. Not staring into my camera, not in his bedroom, never. 'You need to chill the fuck out,' he says.

Blood thuds in my ears. My face is hot. I bring the stick down, grab it with my other hand, and break it over my knee, then turn and hurl the pieces into the lake.

It takes the sun forever to disappear. I sit a little ways off, cross-legged on the pine needles, watching it go. Jared has closed his eyes. The underbellies of the clouds turn pink, then gray.

After a while, Jared sits up again, pulls off his sneakers and t-shirt, and steps into the water. I gaze at his back, the bow-like curve of it. He wades deeper, then dives in.

When I step into the shallows myself, the water is black and warm as the air, nearly indiscernible against my skin. I dip my head under and coat myself in it. Jared is farther out already. I see only the motion of him, and swim toward it. We hug the shore for a bit, then he turns toward the middle of the lake and I follow, the two of us swimming, first crawl, then backstroke, switching from one to the other. When he pauses to tread, I keep on, brushing past him, my arm grazing his stomach before I let my legs drop and paddle around to face him and the shore.

He rolls onto his back and arches his neck, gazing up into the darkening sky. 'You're a lunatic,' he says. 'You know that, right?' He's tracing a slow arc in front of me, moving only his arms at his sides, as if making a snow angel on the water's surface.

'You never called me,' I say. 'After that night with Brett. I left you messages. I came to your house.'

'Yeah,' he says. 'My mom told me. Things just felt too weird. Like maybe it was better to chill for a while.'

I want to be furious, to call him an asshole, to tell him he has no idea how cruel he's been, but his presence overpowers my anger, and all I feel is longing.

'Does that mean it's still weird?' I ask.

'I guess not,' he says, continuing his slow loop. 'Brett probably thought he was tripping anyway, when he saw us.'

Us. He's never uttered the word before. My legs kick faster, pushing the tops of my shoulders above the surface. There is nothing but the gathering darkness, and the water, and *us.* No edges, no gravity. Night swimming on a quiet night. I'm hard and practically naked, and feel suddenly as alive as I've ever been.

'Do you like me?' I ask.

Jared comes upright in the water to face me. 'What do you mean?' he says.

I need to see his expression, but I can't in this light.

'You know,' I say. 'Do you like me?'

'Sure,' he says. 'Why wouldn't I?' Then he takes a deep breath and plunges downward. A moment later, a current pulses against my abdomen as he glides past. It's many seconds before I hear him break the surface again, back in the direction of the inlet.

He reaches the shallows first. Through the dimness, I watch him grow taller with each step out of the water. At the lake's edge, he slides his shorts off and standing in his drenched white underwear wrings the water from them. I walk up beside him, until our arms are almost touching.

Once he puts his clothes on and we leave here and drive back into the world, this moment will cease to exist, like all the others with him have. Unless I do something. I step around in front of him, and leaning my head forward, I close my eyes and touch my lips to his. They're cold, but softer than I'd long imagined.

When I draw my head back and open my eyes, I say, 'That's what I've always wanted to do.'

'How come?' he says, a tremor in his voice I've never heard before.

'Because I love you.'

'No, you don't,' he says. 'You just think I'm cool. And you like the way I look.'

'No, that's not true,' I say. I reach out my hand, gently cup the back of his head, and again bring my lips to his. His body goes still. But then his lips part, and I feel at last the warmth of his mouth. He lays a hand on the center of my chest. I open my mouth wider, tasting the lake on his tongue. And then we are kissing, it is happening—the saving thing.

His hand is firm against my chest, his other holding my arm. I lean into the pressure, and so does he, his hard-on pressing against my belly, and mine against his. Then his lips come away, and his hand on my chest is more than firm, it's pushing, pushing me backward, hard, and I have to grab his arm to stay upright, which pulls him with me. Then suddenly both of us have lost our balance in the rocky sand and are toppling into the shallows together, my elbow landing first, my back scoured by the stones, as he falls on top of me, shouting, 'Get off, get off,' and we're lashing at each other, writhing, tangled, until he manages to scramble to his knees and straddle me. He's sitting on my chest, using his hands to pin my arms down by the wrists, holding me down in the water, so that I have to crane my neck to keep my head above the surface. I batter my knees against his back, flailing, trying to wriggle free. When his hand slips off my wrist, I swing my arm up and grab him by the neck. Then, straining my whole body upward in a sudden rush of force, I shove him sideways, hard.

The sound of his head bouncing off the rock is like boulders knocking in the surf. A dull thunk. His whole body goes limp. An instant later, his arms spasm, splashing in the water, then his legs too, all of his limbs jiggling unnaturally. And then just as quickly it stops, his limbs go still, and he sits up, raising his hand to the back of his head, wincing.

I stand and reach down to help him up, but he waves me away.

Thirty seconds, a minute, several minutes, I don't know. Some time goes by. The two of us remain there in the water, the little waves of the lake lapping against Jared's scraped shins.

'Are you all right?' I ask.

But he doesn't answer.

After a bit, he pushes himself upright, then takes a few steps onto the shore, wobbling as though drunk, still just in his underwear. He makes it to the fallen trunk where he left his t-shirt and sneakers and sits again on the ground in front of it.

'Jared,' I say as I come across the clearing to him. 'Are you okay?'

When he doesn't answer this time, I can't tell if it's because he can't hear me or is too pissed to reply.

'Say something!' I nearly shout.

He reaches for one of his sneakers, slips it on the wrong foot, then the correct one, then painstakingly ties the laces. 'Like what?' he says.

Eventually, he stands, pulls his shorts on, and his t-shirt, then starts walking toward the path. I grab my things and follow him barefoot. We move slowly. It's hard to see the way in the dark. The dirt and the pebbles and the pine needles are all but invisible now, just textures pricking my feet.

It's not until we get into the car and the ceiling light comes on that Jared runs a hand down the back of his head and we see blood on his fingers.

'Great,' he says. He reaches into the back seat, finds an old t-shirt, and wipes at the back of his skull, staining the white cotton red.

'Let me drive,' I say.

But he doesn't reply. He just starts the engine and pulls onto the road.

I begin to shiver. It starts in my chest and spreads down into my gut and up into my jaw until it seems every muscle in my body is shaking. When it begins to rain, Jared doesn't turn on the wipers. I reach over to do it for him. I expect him to swipe my hand away, but he doesn't. He doesn't even seem to notice.

At the rectory, he leaves the car running after he parks, neither looking at me nor uttering a word. He pats the back of his head again with the t-shirt. The bleeding seems to have stopped.

'You should come in,' I say. 'To clean that up. Really.'

He opens his door, leans out of it, and vomits onto the driveway. Then he pulls the door shut again and wipes his mouth with his forearm.

'What the fuck was that?' he says.

'I mean it,' I say. 'Come in.'

'No,' he says. 'Just get out.'

Scratch-scratch, scratch-scratch, that little dog scratching behind my neighbor's door. And when no one comes to let it out—a bark, singular, like a single shout. Still no one comes. So the barking begins in earnest. *Yap-yap, yap-yap, yap-yap, scratch-scratch,* desperation taking hold, the struggle to escape bound onward toward exhaustion.

I paid this noise no mind before. It was merely a thing outside me, from that other apartment down the hall. A distraction like any other voided by the will to work. Yet lying here now in my darkened bedroom, in the spiral of vertigo, I can't deny it. It enters at my temples, echoes in my head and chest, until the vibrations seem to issue from within, the distance between me and that animal seized down to nothing.

Until, at last, it ceases. Then, if I remain very still and breathe only lightly, the bedroom's swirling motion calms to the pace of water above a slow drain, nearly imperceptible. And I can float for a time, at peace, almost. Unmoored, unresistant. Until I must haul myself up to use the bathroom or the scratching at the door starts up again, and the speed of the gyre once more quickens to nausea.

There is no question of working. The pills the doctor prescribed help, but not much. I wobble from bed to bathroom and back again, eating only when the hunger is worse than the retching that follows. Sleep, when it comes, does little. In dreams I spin faster yet, a centrifuge whirling in the dark, until I wake gripping the mattress for balance.

'I'm sorry you're so unwell,' Monica says, in a studiously neutral tone, when she calls to talk about the coverage of my clients. Phoebe has already told me that the cases can't wait for my return and that, at least for now, a leave is best. I hesitate to ask Monica anything about Vasel, yet ask nonetheless, and she says there has been no contact. It isn't him she's called to talk about. I hear her words, but it's as if they're addressed to someone else, some mutual acquaintance, who, for decorum's sake, I'm still pretending to be. As soon as she hangs up, the words and the person to whom they were spoken seem to disappear.

In the moments when it doesn't hurt my eyes to look at a screen, I check for messages. But from Vasel there are none.

By the fourth day, I'm able to sit upright on the couch. This is somehow worse. In the bed I was simply ill. But here in the living room, unable to focus, I'm caught in some dreadful in-between place, amid these pieces of furniture, which no longer seem merely unrelated to one another but, more than that, never to have been mine at all. As though I've been living for years on the set of a play. And now the performance is over and the theater is empty.

Acting. That's one of the things we did together. Jared and Stephanie and Brett and me. In those high-school productions. Our teacher was eccentric and wildly ambitious, given what he had to work with. He once cast us, absurdly, in an abbreviated *King Lear*. We could barely memorize our lines. The first time Stephanie used ketchup for blood to gouge out Jared's eyes, none of us could stop laughing.

Eventually, I make it to the store, moving down the aisles like a convalescent, heavy-limbed and still woozy. When I get back to my building, my neighbor from down the hall is there in the lobby, her wheeled basket half full of groceries, the little gray schnauzer held on a silver leash. She is not an old woman but is hunched like one, her shoulders folded forward as if to shield herself from some imminent blow. I follow her into the elevator and she doesn't so much as glance at me or say a word as we ride up together. It is the dog who eyes me warily. In the hall we go our separate ways and the two of them are shut up again behind that door.

The silence in the apartment is complete now, a kind of substance of its own, a beingness that has lurked here all along, waiting for me to discover it.

The night Jared left me at the rectory and drove off, I was still shivering. There were no lights on inside. I passed through the darkened hall, and the darkened living room, searching for my mother. It was in her study that I saw her, standing with her back to me at the open sash window, looking out on the driveway. She'd seen Jared drop me off, she'd heard the front door open, she must have. But she didn't turn to face me. She simply remained there, silhouetted against the glass dotted with the rain just ceased, cool air flowing through the screen into the darkness between us.

'Your grandmother,' she said eventually. 'She called this evening. She told me that she wants your father's funeral to be at the family church in St. Paul. Also, she would like him to be buried there. That's what he would have chosen, according to her. It's quite an assertion, when you think about it.'

'Mom,' I said. 'I hurt Jared. I think it's bad.'

'So tomorrow morning,' she went on, 'we'll need to talk, you and Liz and me, about what it is that you want. In terms of a grave site. Whether having a place nearby is important to you. It is for some people. For others, less so. As for the funeral, I told your grandmother no. The service will be here. She can have a memorial if she wants one. But his funeral will be in my church.'

'I mean it,' I said. 'He was bleeding.'

'What is it you're talking about?' she said.

'We got in a fight. I hurt him.'

She switched on the lamp that stood on the table beside her and only then turned into the room. Seeing me there, she approached, and touched her fingers to the side of my neck, along the welter of a bruise.

'What happened to you?' she said. 'Did that boy hurt you?'

'You're not listening,' I said.

'I asked you a question!' she yelled, her voice wild, uncontainable, an extreme of pitch I'd only ever heard her use against my father, the sound of utter exasperation, of no room left in her for a single thing more. 'Did he hurt you!'

Instantly, my shivering ceased. I was still cold — very cold. But all motion inside me stopped.

'No,' I said.

Her fingers, seemingly unconnected to her mind, caressed my arm, feeling along the scratches that the rocks in the water had left on my skin. 'You're all dirty,' she said, her tone altogether calm again, as if she hadn't raised her voice at all. 'You need to take a bath. You need to clean yourself. And then you need to get some rest. We all need rest.'

The next morning, for the first time since we were children, my mother made pancakes with all the fixings. Fresh fruit cut up in a bowl, warmed syrup, powdered sugar, freshly whipped cream. She didn't sit with us, though. She stood by the stove, watching.

Across the table, my sister heaped the bounty onto her plate. 'Dad should have died more often,' she said.

Ignoring Liz's provocation, my mother asked why I wasn't eating. Rather than answering her, I picked at a loose thread in the tablecloth.

'The question,' my mother went on, 'is whether you two want

a place to visit, a gravestone and so on, somewhere nearby. Which you may well want, though who knows where you will be in the future.'

She was dressed more brightly than usual in white espadrilles and white cotton pants and a sky-blue oxford shirt—a men's shirt—the sleeves rolled to her elbows, as though she were about to go cruising on a sailboat.

'How about one of those mausoleum things?' Liz said. 'Like a stone temple with a big black gate, and gargoyles.'

The phone on the wall above the counter rang and I leapt from the table to grab it.

'Peter!' a voice sobbed. It was Stephanie. 'Peter!' she cried. 'It's Jared—he's dead.'

More words, other words—lots of them—tumbled out of her then, and into my ear, but I didn't hear them. They were blotted out by a different noise, a loud, disturbed fluttering, like the flailing wings of some giant bird.

I gazed at the countertop, at the white Formica, where beside the hand that held me upright—my hand—there was a faded circular mark where some earlier minister of the church or member of his family must have set a hot saucepan down, leaving the hard plastic calloused and slightly raised. The counter whose surface and shiny steel edging was otherwise perfectly intact.

'As for me,' my mother said as I swerved around to find her face, 'I think memory is the thing. The places we go back to, that we associate with people, and what we feel when we're there. Rather than words chiseled in stone. But he was your father, and you should have a say.'

When she saw me glaring at her, she stood upright and tilted her head forward, as if listening for a barely discernible sound.

'He didn't wake up,' Stephanie said through the phone. 'He just never woke up.'

My eyes fell to the table, to my sister's plate. To the glisten of the moisture on the strawberries' raised skin and the blank white nothingness of the pillowed cream.

'Did you talk to him?' Stephanie asked, through her tears. 'I haven't seen you in so long.'

Which is when the beating of the bird's wings, which had kept on in my ears, stopped, and everything went silent, and nothing my eyes saw made sense. I removed the phone from the side of my head, hung it back up on the wall, and ran out of the kitchen. I didn't know where to go. I found myself rushing into my mother's study, to the window on the far side with the sill covered in old paperbacks.

'What on earth is the matter?' my mother said, coming in behind me. 'Who was that?'

'I told you!' I said. 'I told you last night, you didn't listen! And this is what happened—I killed him, he's dead.'

She shut the door behind her and stood with her back against it. And then, in a torrent, I told her everything—my pictures of Jared, doing what we did in his bedroom, being caught, trying to kiss him the night before, the two of us fighting—all of it, and she listened, her face going pale.

When I stopped, she crossed the room, opened her arms, pulled me to her. 'Oh, my dear,' she said, 'oh, my darling.' She cupped the back of my head in her palm and pressed my face to her shoulder. 'How awful. How terrible. For you—and for that poor boy's mother. But listen to me,' she said, clutching me tight, her voice down to a whisper, her lips at my ear. 'You will get through this, you will get through it. But right now you're confused. Of course you are. That's what happens when someone close to you dies, you lose your bearings. You feel so guilty, you imagine things, it's what people do. They imagine it's their fault.'

'No,' I said. 'I'm not imagining it. I did it. It was me.'

'Listen, listen,' she said. 'You're in shock, of course you are, how couldn't you be? All of this at once. But Peter, you have to

251

understand, you would never hurt someone like that. You never would, you know that. It's not something you would ever do.'

She was holding me so close it was hard to breathe.

'So you have to listen to me, Peter. This is very important. Because if you tell other people what you're telling me right now, they going to get confused about it, too. They're going to think it's your fault.'

'But it is!' I cried. 'It is!'

'No, no,' she whispered. 'I can't believe that. That can't be.'

The phone at Viriditas rings four times before the answering machine picks up. On the recording, it's my mother's voice. I don't hear the words, just their rhythm. That calm, patient, deliberative rhythm. The tone of wisdom her parishioners were always so entranced by.

'It's me,' I say after the beep. 'Peter.'

Once the bus from Port Authority makes it out of the city, I lean my head against the window and am gone, waking only intermittently to the sense but not the memory of dreams, before dozing off once more. There's a wait and a switch in Albany. I close my eyes again but don't sleep. When I open them, we've left the interstate and crossed into Vermont, passing fields and farms and hills in the distance.

It's the end of the afternoon by the time I get off in the town that's a twenty-minute taxi ride from the center. The driver doesn't need to be told where Viriditas is, he's driven the route plenty of times. We climb into the hills along densely wooded roads, the sun still hours from settling in this northern latitude in June, its light dappling the mass of leaves and the grassy verge and the creek beside us, all very pleasing to the eye.

Close to the top of the rise, the house sits on a cleared bluff overlooking the valley. A woman in a plaid shirt and baseball cap is pushing a mower around the base of the big tree in the front yard. She comes to a halt, stops the engine, and watches me as I step out of the car and take my suitcase from the trunk. She doesn't have that beatific expression I associate with my mother's admirers.

There's something harder about her, more suspicious. But when I say hello and tell her I'm Ann's son, she smiles wryly, apparently satisfied by my appearance—I have no idea why—then introduces herself as Jeanette.

'So you're Peter,' she says. 'I've heard a lot about you.'

It's cooler than it was down in the valley. The air is so fresh it feels like a different substance altogether from the atmosphere of the city. The cut-grass scent reminds me of the rectory yard.

'Ann's off meditating,' she says. 'But that probably doesn't surprise you.'

'No,' I say, 'it doesn't.'

'She's been at it all day, actually. Maybe because you're coming.'

I can't tell if she means to be pointed or is just speculating aloud. Am I being warned, blamed for causing a disturbance?

My first visit here was also in summer. I remember boxes everywhere, and lots of women smiling with a kind of sustained relief as they painted and cooked and cleared the yard. All promise, all future. And nothing to do with Liz or me or my father. As for the last time I came, I honestly don't remember. Though I know the place looks different. There's a new building between the barn and the house, the house is a different color, and a meadow has replaced the trees at the back. Things have moved on here, too. My mother has been living a different life, with people I've never met. Like this woman, who clearly knows something about my arrival that I don't.

'You probably want to get inside,' she says, parking the mower next to the tree we're standing beneath. She leads me across the yard to the kitchen door and holds it open for me.

When the woman at the sink turns to see who's come in, I almost don't recognize Clare. I do, of course—the tall, thickly built woman Liz used to call a Druid, earthen and strong—but not the gray skin, the bones of the face beginning to protrude. She smiles and looks at me with that cool, knowing wonder I had forgotten, the childless adult taking in the child intimate, and to my amazement, my pulse quickens. I'm a kid again, wanting her gone.

'My goodness,' she says, staying right where she is. 'You are actually here.'

'You're lucky,' Jeanette says to me. 'Clare's cooking tonight. She's better at it than Ann.'

'Oh, he's eaten my food before,' Clare says, 'so we can let him be the judge of that. But thank you, Jeanette,' she adds with elaborate politeness. 'That's kind of you to say.' The kitchen is twice the size that I remember it; an extension has been added to the back, with skylights and a wall of windows. Did Liz tell me this? Probably she did.

Jeanette is already gone, the screen door banging behind her.

'It was such a surprise, to hear you were coming,' Clare says.

She may be older, but that supposedly neutral tone hasn't changed: the preemptive defense of my mother's time.

'In any case,' she says, 'let me show you where you're sleeping.'

I follow her through into the living room, where the upholstered gray couch from the rectory sits in front of our old braided rug.

'The last time you were here,' Clare says as we head up the stairs, 'we were still using the guest room for the center. But it's just for our friends now. And family, of course. It's where Liz and Norman stay. In fact, I think he's left a monitor in here for his video games. He never stops playing them—it's remarkable, really, for someone his age. But what do I know?'

She stands aside to let me enter the room. The pale blue carpet, the flowered wallpaper—I have a vague memory of it, apparently one of the unrenovated spaces.

'Ann will be back in time for supper,' Clare says. 'She's been overdue for a retreat, but at least she got a day out at the studio. Come to think of it, the studio wasn't even built when you last visited. She'll want to show it to you, I'm sure.'

I put my suitcase down on the bed and turn to face her.

'Look at me,' she says, 'I forgot to give you a hug.'

But she doesn't step forward or open her arms, not at first. She waits for me to come toward her, and then we each lean in awkwardly and touch our shoulders together. She has a dry, floral smell, some scented talcum powder, and her frame is stiffer than it looks, not frail—yet—but not the stolid, commanding presence her body once was in our house.

When we separate, she steps away, over to the dresser. There is a row of books along the back of it, against the wall. From atop one of them, she removes a desiccated moth, pinching its wing between her fingernails.

'The one thing I would mention,' she says, 'and maybe it's not my place—though I suppose that's never stopped me—is that you not visiting here for so very long has obviously been hard on Ann. Of course she's glad you're coming, and maybe she would have said nothing, so maybe I'll be in trouble already for speaking of it. But she does think of you, so you staying away like you have—you can imagine how it's made her feel.' She drops the moth in the wastebasket and wipes her fingers of whatever detritus remains, the effect of her performance being the opposite of her words, leaving me with the sense not of time gone by, but of none having passed.

'Thanks for letting me know,' I say. 'It may have been a while, but you seem much the same.'

'Oh,' she says. 'Have I offended you?'

'No. It's just that I'm here to see my mother, that's all.'

'Of course,' she says. 'And you will. And I won't trouble you anymore now. I'll let you settle in.' With that, she walks out the door and closes it behind her.

I take my shoes off and lie down. When I close my eyes there is still the faint swirling at the center of my head, which mixed with the fatigue of the journey feels like a swoon back into the sickness. I rest awhile, waiting for the sensation to subside.

A little later, before going downstairs, I check my email for anything that needs to be forwarded to the office while I'm away, and see a message from Monica. No text, just an attachment. Judge Ericson has issued his opinion in Sandra Moya's case, and Monica's sent me a scan of it. I fiddle to enlarge the tiny print and scroll past the cover page until I reach the final line of the summary: The respondent's application for asylum from Honduras is granted.

First comes a familiar relief: I didn't fuck up. I worked hard enough. I did my job right. But reading on into the body of the opinion, this falls away, and it isn't even Sandra that I'm imagining, but Felipe. I picture him in that apartment in the Bronx that I have never seen, in the room he shares with his little sister, weighted to his bed by the stone of depression and a fear too big to let in—that he will lose his mother and, with her, everything. A child on the rack of the state. Felipe knowing he won't lose her—it's a relief of a different order.

Sandra picks up on the third ring.

'Oh, esto es bueno,' she says when I tell her. 'Esto es bueno.'

She's surprised, taken aback, but also distracted by children playing in the background and what sounds like a baseball game turned up loud on the TV.

I tell her she can apply for a Social Security number now, and a driver's license, eventually a green card. And if she wants, one day, citizenship.

'Sí, una licencia, eso será bueno,' she says. 'We're in Florida now, everywhere's far.'

They're staying with her brother Herman, she tells me. It is better, mostly. She misses New York, her girlfriends there, but the apartment was too expensive. Down in Florida, though, Felipe isn't in school anymore, and it worries her.

'But he will be happy to hear the news,' she says. 'He wants this for me, por mucho tiempo. Who knows? Tal vez vuelva a la escuela. I can hope, right?'

'Yes, you can,' I say.

Maybe it's the phone, or the noises behind her, or the way she seems to be listening to me and others at the same time, but I'm embarrassed in a way that I've never been in all these years, as if I'm overstepping somehow, experiencing more relief than she is. She's in the middle of an evening with family, in the midst of her life, her ongoing life. I'm the one whose mind is back in the alley behind her father's house, the alley in the narrative I wrote with her, where her brother lies naked and dead. I'm the one imagining, absurdly, that this news I'm delivering to her now is the redemption of this horror, of all that she has endured. And all that her son has endured as well. As if a story, once it is believed, could undo what it is about.

'Pero lo siento,' she says, 'I have to go. Eres una buena persona, Mr. Peter. Really. Muchas gracias.'

Approaching the house on her way back from the studio, Ann saw Peter through the bank of kitchen windows, and her easy pace immediately quickened, as if rushing to reach him in time (for what?), her composure from hours of meditation undone in an instant. But then, a few yards on, she did as she'd trained herself to do, noting the sensations of her walking, the muscles in her thighs and calves, the pressure on the ball of one foot and then the next, and this more ordered attention allowed her initial shock to pass through her and out into the spaciousness of the early-summer evening, leaving her sufficiently present to note the coolness of the back door's metal handle as she took hold of it, and the warmer air of the kitchen.

And then there he was, her son, on the far side of the room, his face so much thinner than she remembered it. Was he sick? Is that what had brought him back here at last?

'Peter,' she said, and crossed toward him. 'You made it.'

He stiffened as she grew near, standing more upright—she'd forgotten how much taller he was than her—his posture warding off a hug. She rested a hand on his arm instead. He wore a soft black sweatshirt, dark blue jeans, and blue sneakers, which, despite how much older he looked, struck her as boyish.

'I'm so glad you're here,' she said.

He nodded, politely, and reached for his glass of water on the counter. It wasn't just age, either. He looked somehow confused, as if he weren't quite sure where he'd arrived.

'Turns out he took the bus!' Clare said, rattling loudly in the drawer for a corkscrew. 'How was the sitting?' she asked. 'I was saying to Peter you're overdue for a retreat, you should have had three days, but you can't tear yourself away from the guests.'

'Clare, please,' she said.

'Well, it's true,' Clare said. 'But there we are. Dinner's ready. I forget, Peter, do you drink?'

'I won't, thanks,' he said.

Ann was still taking him in. The fact was he'd never looked so like his father as he did now. Around the eyes, across the forehead, a certain concentration that had become habitual in Richard. As though his mind were fixed on a problem perpetually unsolved. Such completely different people, he and his father were, and yet here it was right back in front of her—that same look of consternation, a look she had more or less forgotten.

'Here,' Clare said, handing her the salad bowl and a plate of garlic bread, which Ann carried over to the table.

Once they were seated, Peter facing the two of them, Clare lifted the lid of the Dutch oven and steam clouded her glasses.

'Curried lentil stew,' she announced. 'Ann's favorite, and there's plenty of it.'

'Thank you,' Peter said as Clare filled his bowl.

'Oh, you're welcome,' she said. 'Anytime.'

To Ann's amazement, Peter ate no faster than they did. He'd always wolfed his meals and rushed for seconds, but now he paused between bites and seemed at moments only half aware of the food in front of him.

'So,' he said after a few moments, 'this place has changed.'

'How do you mean?' Ann asked.

'There's a whole new building.'

'Oh, you've seen that before,' Ann said. 'It's been here a long time now. You're probably just forgetting.'

'No,' Clare said. 'It wasn't here the last time he came.'

'That doesn't seem right,' Ann said. 'But it doesn't matter. We can have a walk around in the morning. Tell me about work,' she said. 'Your cases, how is all that going?'

The length of the pause that followed gave Ann the uncanny sense that despite his being only three feet away, Peter had somehow failed to hear her question.

Finally, though, without looking up, without the slightest change of expression, he said, 'Do you actually want to know?'

Clare, who'd just lifted her wineglass from the table, placed it down again. Ann picked hers up, took a sip to clear her throat, then held the glass with both hands in front of her chest.

'Yes,' she said crisply. 'I do.'

He glanced up then, holding her gaze for the first time since she'd entered the house. 'Well, officially,' he said, 'I'm not working. Officially, because I got sick. Vertigo. First time since I was sixteen. You might remember—my dizziness, you called it. So, officially, I'm on leave.'

'I'm sorry to hear that,' Ann said.

She put her glass down and moved her hand across the table, as if to reach for his, but he either didn't notice or pretended not to, and leaned back, away from her.

'My sister has vertigo now and then,' Clare said. 'Sounds like hell to me.'

Neither Peter nor Ann said a word to this.

'Mostly stress-induced,' Clare went on. 'For her, I mean. If it weren't for her tedious fundamentalism, she might do something about it other than pray.'

'Are you feeling any better?' Ann asked. 'Are you still having symptoms?'

'I'm not flat out in bed anymore,' he said. 'If that's what you're asking.'

His aggression—it was palpable, and poorly veiled. Like his father's. That caustic manner to which Richard had surrendered at the end. Which whenever Ann had called him out on, he had denied. An old instinct flexed in her now, the temptation to state aloud the emotion that was going unnamed. But Clare was right—telling people what they felt never worked, even if it was true. She noted the urge arising, burning momentarily, and then blessedly falling away.

'Well, I'm glad to hear that,' she said. 'This is a good place to come, if you need rest. We're all set up for it.'

'Oh yes,' Clare said, 'we're a regular spa, minus everything you might associate with the word.'

'You know what I mean,' Ann said. 'People tend to sleep well when they're here.'

'That much is true,' Clare said, and began to clear the plates despite the food still on them.

She walked behind Ann across the kitchen, and soon the sound of a knife scraping china, then water rushing from the faucet, filled the otherwise silent room.

'So how does this go?' Peter asked. 'Me being here, a male, at Viriditas.' He had his arms crossed, his chair pushed back from the table, one leg draped over the other.

'You're behaving as if you've never been here,' Ann said. 'You know perfectly well there's no issue about that. Norman comes all the time.'

'Here you go,' Clare said, handing Peter a slice of blueberry pie. 'It's fresh from the grocery store.' She told the two of them to go with their dessert into the living room, and she would bring the tea.

Peter followed Ann through and perched on the edge of the couch. He glanced about the room, eyeing the blond wood sitting chairs, the faded black cloth of the magazine rack, the quilt of the tree and its roots that hung above the mantel, all of this familiar to the point of invisibility to Ann. Yet through her son's eyes she now found herself disaggregating the objects into the tables and lamps that Clare had brought with her, the sofa and rug that had come from the rectory, the artwork they had acquired together in the years since. An oddly alienating exercise—to unwed their possessions like this. But then, of course, it wasn't her own alienation she was feeling. It surprised her that after such a long time Peter would still experience the physical reality of this place at such a remove, as if the furniture had arrived yesterday rather than two decades ago.

She asked about his trip up, about whether he'd seen a doctor for his condition, about when he'd last spoken with Liz, but no question got more than a few words in response. Eventually Clare took over, going on about the work at the center, how the meeting-house had come about, and what it allowed them to host, sounding more positive about their mission than Ann had heard her be in a long while.

When they were done, and Clare had gone back into the kitchen to tidy up, Ann walked Peter up to the guest room. His suitcase was still on the bed. He began to unpack it.

'I meant what I said,' she told him, hesitating at the threshold before saying good night. 'I'm glad that you're here.'

'Thanks,' he said. He removed a pair of pants from his jumble of clothes, peered at them as if they belonged to someone else, then put them aside. 'I didn't know I was coming,' he said. 'Until I did. I just called to talk, and then I heard your voice on the machine.'

'That ancient recording. I'm surprised you can still make it out.'

'It's clear enough,' he said. 'It's your priest voice.'

'Oh, dear,' she said, 'that sounds ominous.'

Giving up on the suitcase, he sat on the edge of the bed and glanced about the room like he had at the objects downstairs, as if taking it in for the first time. 'I talked to a client earlier,' he said. 'A woman from Honduras. She comes from a town called Potrerillos.

I looked it up again, after we talked, to see if there were any new photographs online. I do that sometimes, when a case ends. You picture a place for so long, trying to assemble it in your mind, and then the person's deported or allowed to stay, and you don't imagine it anymore, you don't have time. Did you ever go to Potrerillos? On those mission trips you and Clare used to take?'

'I don't recognize that name,' Ann said. 'We always went to the same village. We had a very limited view of the place, looking back on it. But this woman? How did it turn out for her?'

'She got asylum today.'

'That's terrific. You must be very glad.'

'It's good news,' he said flatly. 'Good for her son, too. He was afraid he was going to lose her. He had kind of shut down.'

'When I think of all the people you've helped,' she said.

'Please,' he said. 'Don't.'

'Don't what?' she said, more forcefully than she had intended. 'Am I not allowed—even from such distance—to admire what you do?'

Peter's eyes widened, his upper lip flared, some sharp retort about to leap out at her. But nothing came, and a moment later he leaned back on the bed and pressed his hands to his face.

'I'm sorry,' Ann said. 'I know you're tired. You need rest. I'll let you be.'

Low cloud covered the valley and hung over the field across the road and along the road itself. They walked in silence at first, which was fine by Ann, good even, for the two of them just to be together, and it seemed good by Peter, too. He wore the same sweatshirt and jeans he'd been dressed in the night before, making her wonder if he'd slept in them, though she wasn't about to ask. She simply watched him gazing down the hillside, the view appearing and disappearing as they moved in and out of the mist.

They walked at a good clip, which they always used to—Richard, too—a pace Ann was glad she could still maintain. Soon they were passing Gerry Connor's place, where the coiled snake of the DONT TREAD ON ME flag hung limp from a pole erected amid the yard of dead vehicles. And then on past the field of goats he kept, and the stand of oaks at the edge of his property.

'Was that the guy's house?' Peter asked. 'The one who cursed you at the beginning?'

'Yes, good memory,' Ann said. 'He stuck to his word, too. He hasn't spoken to Clare or me since. Though Jeanette did get him to lend her his cement mixer when she rebuilt the shed, so I suppose that's progress.'

'That woman, she lives here, right? She seems to know you pretty well.'

'Yes, she does live here,' Ann said, wondering what sign of intimacy between them he'd noticed.

Farther along, at the back entrance of the Tibbett farm, the gates hung open, the paddock an expanse of mud, but no cows in sight. On the roof of the old hay barn a tarp had come loose, exposing a patch of missing shingles, the downturned flap idle in the still air. At the end of the grazing meadow they came to the intersection, where Ann decided not to turn right toward the usual loop that led eventually back through the woods but to carry straight on instead, out along the ridge. The fields here had been green for weeks and were already getting eaten down.

Soon she heard a car coming from up ahead and recognized the sound of Roberta's old Subaru. It slowed to a halt as it reached them, the window already down.

'Hello!' Roberta called out with that solar smile that after all these years still warmed Ann each time she received it. 'Peter!' she said. 'I haven't seen you in an age. How are you?'

'I'm okay, thanks,' he said unconvincingly, as though accosted by some old relative, which in a sense Roberta was.

'It's great to have you here,' she said. 'I won't bother you two now, but later, I hope.'

Ann waved, and Roberta smiled again and was off, tapping her horn as she went. They watched her go, then turned and kept walking.

The fog on the hillside was dispersing, but still hung thick over the creek below.

'You see,' Ann said. 'You've been missed.'

Peter had his hands in the pockets of his jeans. He stared not into the distance any longer but at the wet pavement in front of them.

'Right,' he said.

'And me,' Ann said. 'I've missed you.'

When he made no reply, she reached out and placed a hand on the middle of his back, but as soon as he felt it there he flinched, and then Ann flinched too, and withdrew her touch, taken aback by the instinctiveness of his retraction from her.

An image flashed up in her then—of Richard wincing at the sight of Peter as he'd emerged into the lobby of the high school after the performance of a play, still in his costume and his makeup, the tightening of Richard's mouth at seeing Peter's painted face up close, making Ann fear momentarily for his love of their son.

How long had it been, she wondered, since he'd been touched?

She waited till they were most of the way down the gentle slope toward the wooded section of the road before saying, 'I'm sure you don't want me asking you this, but of course I think about it—whether you're with anyone.'

As at the dinner table, she just had to assume he'd heard her, given his failure to register the question.

'What do you want me to say?' he asked eventually.

'Nothing,' she said. 'Only what you want to share.'

After another silence, he said, 'You know, when I used to tell people you left Dad for a woman, they'd ask, So does that make it easier with her, you being gay? And I never knew what to say. The question seemed obvious to them. But I didn't get it—what the one thing had to do with the other.'

'I suppose we didn't really talk about it,' Ann said. 'In those terms. You were still quite young at the time.'

'Is that what you think?'

'It's not a question of what I think,' she said. 'You were fifteen, sixteen, you were in high school.'

They had reached the end of the field and were passing along a wooded stretch of the road.

Peter kept his eyes turned away from Ann, gazing into the trees.

'If what you're asking,' he said, 'is whether I have someone you'd call a partner, then no.'

'I'm sorry to hear that,' Ann said. 'He'd be a lucky person, whoever he might be.'

At the bottom of the slope they'd been descending, water had collected into puddles, and the two of them had to part to get past. There was mist here again, and it was cooler. Cool and quiet. Ann never failed to notice the quiet when she went on her walks, or failed to appreciate it—the mute forgiveness that it was for whatever troubled the mind.

'Do you even think of Jared—*ever*?' Peter asked.

'Your friend Jared? Of course I think of him—now and then. It was an awful thing that happened.'

The look he gave her at that moment went well beyond the consternation on his face the night before. It was a look of complete incredulity.

'An awful thing?' he said. 'That's it? Really?'

'How do you mean?'

'I *believed* you,' he said. 'Don't you get it? You told me that what happened didn't happen. And I believed you—for so long I forgot I was even doing it. But you lied. You told me I didn't do anything wrong.'

'Oh, Peter, no,' Ann said. 'Please tell me you don't still harrow yourself over that, after all these years.'

'What are you even saying? Can you hear yourself? You told me to lie. You were a priest, and you told me to hide what I'd done.'

For once, Ann was relieved by the grinding noise of the tractor as it rounded the corner and crept down the slope they were now climbing, its green frame rusted half brown, Jim Tibbett's teen son, in a baseball cap and tan jacket, erect behind the wheel as if he were driving the lead vehicle in some somber procession. He nodded hello, eyeing Peter as he passed them slowly by.

Ann knew she had to resist the instinct to listen to her son as she would to one of the retreatants, whose spirit it was her job to intuit more clearly than they intuited it themselves. And yet how not to feel for a way through the strain in him?

'Dear,' she said, after the sound of the tractor had begun to fade. 'You're talking about something that happened almost twenty-five years ago. You were a boy. You'd just lost your father. You and Jared—you got in a tussle. You told me that yourself. What happened was an accident. I can't stand to think that you've been torturing yourself like this for so long.'

'But I haven't!' he called out. 'Don't you get it? I work—that's all I do. I get people to tell me their stories, I try to prove what they tell me, then I do it again. That's it.'

'That can't be true,' Ann said. 'I'm sure there's much more to your life than that.'

'You can't listen to me, can you? Still. You just can't bear it. I'm telling you I didn't think about Jared for years and years. Not till this young guy came into the office, and I kept needing to know more about him.' At the crest of the slope, he came to a halt and turned to face her. 'We lied,' he said, 'you and me both. I know the police came to the house—Liz told me. I know you spoke to them. What did you say? Why did I never have to talk to them?'

It amazed Ann how young his voice suddenly sounded, as though he were speaking to her from back then, some part of him still wandering the rectory halls. What she remembered of that time had little order to it: Clare helping her pick out a suit for Richard's corpse, Liz stoned and eating oranges on the back steps, and of course Peter getting that phone call and running into her study.

'Peter,' she said, 'do you remember what you told me that morning? The stream of words that came out of you? About Jared, yes. But about your father, too. A story he'd told you about when he was up in the woods. Some man he'd fought with. You were absolutely distraught about it. You said he must have known what you and

Jared had done together. And that was the reason he had told you the story. Do you not remember this? Saying to me that what you and Jared had done is what killed your father?'

The disbelief on his face morphed as she spoke, as much inward now as outward. He broke his stare and started walking farther up the road toward the sign for the village. Ann gathered herself and followed a few steps behind. They passed the entrance of the dairy, then the dark blue grain silos, then a pasture where in the far corner part of the cattle herd sat clustered by the wire fence, by which point she'd come up alongside him.

'You're doing it again,' he said. 'You're trying to make it go away. But you weren't there that night. I was. And you wouldn't believe me.'

An old anger flared in her, one she used to harbor for Richard — for his insistence, his obstinacy — but directed now at Peter. And in the rising of that feeling, the span of her life came abruptly into view: From that day Richard had approached her in the courtyard of the youth hostel in Paris to walking this road now with their son. And she saw more clearly than she ever had how sharp the divide was between the cutoff person she had been, married to a man and raising children, and the living person she had become here with Clare and Roberta and Jeanette. What chance had she ever had to know her own desire in the onrush of Richard's? So full of passion he was. For years she'd thought, How can I blame him for my own ignorance of what moved me? Blame the culture, maybe. Patriarchy, maybe. But the person she woke up next to every morning — devoted, hardworking Richard? How could he have known what she herself hadn't for years: that being with a woman would feel like discovering she had a body. And yet she *had* blamed him. Because he'd idealized her. Confined her to a pedestal for admiration. And then he'd refused to relent, even after the move to a town and a state he didn't want to live in, for her job. All that admiration — it was irreproachable, until you understood what it really meant: *Unless you're still the person I fell in love with, you're betraying me.*

Is this what Peter wanted? To force her back into that earlier self, so he could argue with her as the person she'd been then?

As they rounded the bend, the steeple of the Congregational church down in the village came into view, along with the cloudy sky beyond it.

'There's something I need to say to you,' Ann said. 'I know that you never wanted me to be with Clare. And you didn't want me to leave our house and move up here. I understand that. I don't blame you for it. And I don't blame you for not visiting more, though I would have liked that. But this is my life, the one I chose. And this isn't easy to say to you, but being a mother—being a wife—that was *part* of my life. But it couldn't be all of it. It's hard to understand that if you're not a woman, let alone a woman of my age. You can't open your mind just once, just cut the fetters and that's it. You have to do it over and over, for years. And I'm sorry, I am, for what that may have cost you, when you were young, and I was caught up in all the changes I was trying to make.

'And you're right,' she said as they continued, several feet apart, though still side by side. 'I wasn't there that night. I didn't see exactly what happened. But imagine for a moment all the things you were telling me that morning, that onslaught of guilt—about your father and that you'd been intimate with your friend, weeping to me that you'd killed him. What mother on earth would say, *Oh, well, fine, then, if you say so, it must be true, off to prison you go.* Your father wasn't even in the ground. You were hysterical with grief, as well you had the right to be. I didn't tell you to lie, Peter. I told you you weren't a murderer. Because you weren't. You aren't. And I said to the police what I needed to so the world wouldn't mistake you for one. If that's what you've held against me all this time, then so be it. I would do it again. For you, and to be honest, for myself. Because it wasn't just your life that would have been torn up if I'd let your guilt overcome you.'

She had sped up as she spoke. They were walking fast now, both of them, racing almost toward the dilapidated houses at the near edge of the village. The more she'd said, the more frustrated she'd become. He'd succeeded, he'd dragged her back into a story-line she'd done her best to drop, but that apparently he never had.

The yards they passed now were unkempt, strewn with weeds and children's toys left out to bleach in the sun. Not the rural idyll many of the center's visitors imagined the entire state of Vermont to be, a notion most of them were soon disabused of.

'Is that what you've come here for, Peter?' she asked. 'To wring a confession out of me?'

He didn't answer. He just took his hands out of his pockets to let his arms swing at his sides as he tried to keep up with her.

We pass a pizza shop, a post office, a gas station, the general store. I don't know where we're headed, and I don't think my mother does either. Opposite the church, there's a green with three enormous spruce trees along one edge and an old granite monument in the middle. There's not a moving car in sight. This place is as silent as the fields we've just walked through. My mother crosses onto the green, comes to a bench, and turns around as if we've reached the end and it's time to go back, then seems to change her mind and sits.

She's aged—I know she has—but I can't take it in the way I did with Clare. It's as if her face is so deeply imprinted on my mind that the pattern obscures the surface. All I see are the rounded cheeks and big owl eyes, as lucid as they've ever been. The force is with her, Liz used to quip when we watched her enfold one troubled parishioner or another in the cloak of her attention. She's lost none of that presence. If anything, it's stronger than it was before. Standing over her, I'm not dizzy or nauseated, I don't have that swaying sensation between my ears, none of the symptoms of the illness, but in its place there is a bewilderment far more profound: that my mother is barely troubled by what happened; that all this time

I have been avoiding it on my own. I somehow thought, without thinking, that she and I were bound by the things we had done then and left undone, and that because of that it didn't matter how long I stayed away from here: whenever I returned we would return together to this. As if in the realm of a life's meaning, time doesn't pass. But it does.

I sit beside her on the bench, not sure what else to do with myself. For what seems a long time we stare together at the gray obelisk at the center of the green, and my mind drifts off, away from the argument we've just had.

On the monument's dark copper plaque, a short list of names is etched above an inscription: *To the Memory of the Lamoille County Men Who Fought with the Green Mountain Boys at the Battles of Hubbardton and Bennington, 1777. Erected by the Sons of the American Revolution, August 16, 1899.*

'Did I ever tell you about my boss, Phoebe?' I ask.

'You tell me very little,' my mother says. 'But yes, I remember that name.'

'She reminds me of you, actually. If she hadn't been a lawyer, she'd probably have been a priest, or at least a therapist...sometimes she takes us to these workshops for immigration attorneys. They asked us, at one of them, to go around the room and tell our family's own migration story. I realized that all I had were generalities—about Dad's German ancestors and your English ones. But now it turns out Liz has done all this research.'

'Oh, don't tell me,' my mother says. 'She's full of questions.'

'So you know about Brodhead, the general.'

'Yes,' she says. 'She's been particularly keen to point him out. Apparently, he's famous for killing large numbers of the Seneca and burning their villages. Which is horrific, obviously. But what I don't say to her, because I don't want to argue or hurt her feelings, is that family genealogy has always seemed sentimental to me. I could have as easily been descended from someone of no particular note, but that wouldn't make me any less a descendant of what Daniel Brodhead did. We all are. It's the history of the country.'

'So it doesn't mean anything to you? Your connection to it.'

'She's traced the male line,' my mother says, 'because that's what's in the record. What about all the women?'

'Fair enough, but does that make what she's found irrelevant?'

'The point is that history's a mess. Who even knows if the documents are accurate, or who had an affair with who. I just don't see the point in looking narrowly backward like that. If we don't live now, in the present, we don't live at all.'

'That's a convenient theory, if you've done something you want to forget.'

'Ah,' my mother says. 'So we're not actually talking about ancestors. We're still talking about Jared.'

'Apologies. I didn't know the subject was closed.'

Another long silence. I watch a large crow land at the base of the monument and begin ordering its wings, flicking off moisture or stiffness, or simply flexing them for the pleasure of it.

'What Liz seems to forget,' my mother says, 'or maybe she somehow failed to notice—maybe you did, too—is that if there was anyone in our house talking about American colonialism, it was me. Your father hated it when I talked like that. He preferred his patriotism, his father fighting the Germans in the Ardennes. That's why he went to Europe looking for that castle. For some essence of his father that his father wouldn't give him. And instead he found me.'

The crow, settled now, begins to peck at the dark soil, stepping between the memorial flowers that someone still plants here.

'He told us that story so many times,' I say. 'About the two of you meeting in that hostel.'

'Yes,' my mother says. 'It meant a great deal to him.'

'Do you regret it? Marrying him?'

'I can't,' she says. 'There wouldn't be you or Liz. But do I regret I couldn't know myself better at a younger age? Yes.' She uncrosses her arms, sits up slightly, and joins her hands in her lap in what looks like an almost meditative posture. 'And even with AIDS,' she says, 'and all that backlash, I did hope it would be easier for you than it was for me.'

'You've never said that before.'

'No, I suppose I haven't. Probably I should have. Maybe if it had been Liz.'

'What do you mean?' I ask.

My mother's gazing at the crow now, too. Its black feathers shine even in this dull light. Looking up from its feeding, it tilts its head as if to listen to us.

'Men,' she says. 'Men and boys. The way they want things, the way they need them. Maybe it's my upbringing, or my dated feminism, but it's always seemed foreign to me, and not exactly safe.'

Hearing these words feels like her inserting a key into a lock in my chest and turning it open. My collarbones widen, my head floats up and back, and I find myself gazing up into the trees, up into what seems now to be a great spaciousness. 'Wow,' I say. 'You never said that to me, either. I wish you had.'

'Why?'

'Because I think I've always felt it—that you were afraid of what I wanted.'

My mother doesn't move as I say this. She remains almost perfectly still in her contemplative stance. The only motion is a slight narrowing of her eyes.

'In that case,' she says, 'I'm sorry that I didn't.'

The air around us is likewise motionless, as are the branches of the trees. Until another crow lands on a high branch, which dips and rises under its solid weight. Then out of nowhere a revving noise fills the square, both birds lumber into flight, and a large black pickup speeds past, barely slowing as it races to the pump at the gas station across the way. A bearded man about my age, wearing sunglasses despite the overcast sky, gets out, walks around the back of the vehicle, and begins fueling it.

'That story that Dad told me,' I say, 'about when he worked up in the woods, the one you said I was going on about the morning Jared died, did he ever tell it to you?'

'Just that he helped to build a pipeline,' my mother says. 'Which he always seemed very proud of. And which I'm sure I failed to appreciate.'

'What he told me is that a man in his cabin had tried to touch him—sexually. And that he beat the shit out of him for it.'

She turns her head to look at me for the first time since we sat down. 'Your father said that to you?'

'A couple of days before he died. He really never told you?'

'No,' she says, seeming to cast her mind back. 'Probably because he would have been ashamed to. To tell me he'd been violent like that. It may seem outlandish to you, but he never stopped wanting my approval, to the very end.'

'Why would he make such an effort to tell me that if he didn't sense something about me?'

'There's no way to know,' she says. 'He may just have needed to tell someone because he was dying.'

'What I remember about it most,' I say, 'is that he kept saying it wasn't his fault. That he'd never wanted to be touched by a man. And you know what? I think after he said that to me, that's who I thought I was—a person like that man in the cabin, a creep. For wanting Jared so badly. If I'd wanted him less, he'd still be alive.'

'Don't say that,' my mother tells me. 'You can't think of it that way.'

Across the square, the bearded man pushes the gas cap shut, then climbs back into his truck. The rumble of the engine is low at first, a growl, but then the roar of exhaust explodes from the tailpipes, ripping through the air, echoing off the church, and out across the valley.

Back at the house, I go upstairs and lie on the bed to rest my eyes for a few minutes. When I come around again, sunlight is streaming through the windows from the west, the morning clouds gone, and I realize that I've slept right through the afternoon. Even once I get up, the drowsiness persists, all through the early evening and into dinner with my mother and Clare, for which I'm only half awake. I haven't felt so drugged by slumber since I was a teenager. After the meal, I head back to bed and sleep another twelve hours.

When I come down the next morning, the house is empty, Clare and my mother long since off into their day. They've left out their muesli and the bread and jam. I eat, ravenously, then head out for a walk, to try to wake myself up, but by the end of the afternoon I'm upstairs napping again. This time, when my eyes come open, I hear voices from downstairs, one of them a boy's.

'Rip van Winkle lives,' Liz says as I enter the kitchen. My sister, having materialized seemingly out of nowhere, is sitting across from Jeanette, a nearly empty wine bottle between them, Charlie wriggling in her lap, his head tossed all the way back, looking at me upside down. 'See who it is, duckie?' she says. 'It's your uncle, risen from the dead.'

'How long have you been here?' I ask.

'Not half as long as you've been comatose, apparently,' she says. 'Mom called to say you were here so I figured this was my chance to see you in the flesh. She said you'd been sick. You sure look it.'

Jeanette, appearing a bit tipsy, fails to suppress a grin.

'It's okay,' Liz says to her. 'He's used to it.'

Charlie scrambles free and rushes toward me, but pulls up a couple of yards short and gazes at my face with great seriousness. He's wearing little sneakers and little blue pants and a little knit sweater. His brown eyes appear overlarge, as if they have grown more quickly than the rest of his features, though perhaps this is just his resemblance to my mother, which I can see clearly now.

'It's okay, duckie,' my sister says. 'He's harmless.'

'Hey there,' I say.

'Hi,' he says. 'I'm Charlie.'

'I know you, Charlie. I'm Peter. I'm your mother's brother.'

'Why?' he asks.

Jeanette lets out a little cackle.

'Well,' I say, 'that's just how it happened. Your grandmother is your mother's mom, and she's mine too.'

He seems to doubt this, then find it joyous. Giggling, he sticks his tongue out and darts past me toward the refrigerator, which he tries to pry open with both hands, though to no avail.

'Mom and Clare are off preaching to the choir,' Liz says. 'So we're just drinking and failing to make dinner. You didn't even tell me you were coming! After me trying to get you here all this time!'

She's dyed her hair jet black since I last saw her, a look I remember from a brief goth phase she had in high school.

'It wasn't really a plan,' I say.

Jeanette, who's been observing us as though taking in a scene she's long imagined, gets up now and fetches a third wineglass, which she sets down at the head of the table. I thank her and she nods, curtly. Liz empties the bottle into my glass, filling it far too full, then, enjoying herself, bangs the empty on the table like a saloon barmaid. Her neon-green tank top reads in spangled letters *Want a Pony? Become One!* If the two of us had met as strangers at no matter what point in our lives, the chances of our becoming friends would have been virtually nil. And yet here we are.

'Where's Norman?' I ask.

'At home, approaching level three hundred, if I had to guess. Or at the oncologist with the dog. Poor Maisie. Who you've never even met. But then you've only met Charlie like five times.'

'That's not true,' I say.

'Have you noticed,' Liz says to Jeanette, 'that's one of my brother's favorite lines? He says it all the time. Mostly when things are true. It's part of his schizoid charm. He and my mother—remembering basic shit about their lives just isn't part of the program. Which makes you think they'd get along just hunky-dory.'

'Well,' Jeanette says to me, 'Ann's definitely glad you're here.'

'You probably wouldn't know if she weren't,' Liz says, picking Charlie up off the ground and placing him once more astride her lap.

'I'm not sure,' Jeanette says a little suggestively. 'I might.'

At this, even Liz doesn't joke. There's a brief pause, all three of us collectively ignoring her comment. Charlie tugs at Liz's shirt, reveals a nipple, and aims his mouth at it, but it's covered again before he can make contact.

'Okay!' Jeanette exclaims, pushing her chair back. 'I'm going to cook. I never cook, but I'm going to cook for everyone!'

For the next little while, the four of us hang out, Jeanette busy at the sink and stove, Liz and me watching Charlie careen about, then circle back to beg his mother for this or that before growing bored of her refusals and turning to me again, considering the idea we might be related.

When my mother and Clare return through the back door, it amazes me how matter-of-fact Liz's greeting of Clare is. Their hug may be perfunctory, more knowing than warm, but it's familial.

'What's all this?' my mother asks as she crosses the room to Jeanette. 'I was just coming in to start.'

'Too late,' Jeanette says. 'I planted these fucking vegetables, and now I'm going to cook them. Whether it's good or not. So have a drink'—she puts her hand on my mother's arm—'talk to your kids, and let me handle it.'

Clare and my mother exchange an indecipherable glance, but right away there's Charlie again, running up against my mother's leg, gripping it like the mast of a storm-tossed ship, and whatever tension the moment held melts in the shift of all eyes to the boy with his face pressed to the cotton of my mother's drawstring trousers. She brushes her mottled fingers through his dirty-blond hair, which stands on end from the static energy between them.

'Well,' she says, 'I guess that's that.' She gets out cheese and nuts, potato chips for Charlie, then opens another bottle of wine and hands a glass of it to Clare.

I drink for the first time since I've been sick, not all of what Liz poured me, but enough to suspend for a while the discombobulation of waking to my sister being here, of all of us now in one room, eating the goopy vegetable stew Jeanette eventually produces, and afterward a poppy-seed lemon cake that Clare seems genuinely pleased to hear complimented, the conversation running on happily without me.

When the meal is done, I try to help Jeanette load the dishwasher but she won't have it. 'I don't have gifts for anyone,' she says, as though she's come to a birthday party empty-handed. 'So let me do this.'

Charlie dozes in Liz's lap. Clare and my mother tidy the rest of the kitchen, the evening coming to an end. Eventually, I follow my sister into the study. Its walls are lined with my mother's books, more of them than ever, though in better order than they used to be. Fewer stray stacks, fewer of them piled sideways. Liz sits on the edge of the foldout couch and tucks Charlie into the cot beside it, then takes a storybook from her bag and starts reading. When she's a few pages in, Charlie's big eyes close and he begins to drool.

'Should I go?' I ask.

'No, he's down for the count,' she says. 'Stay.'

I swivel my mother's desk chair around and take a seat facing the foot of the bed. Liz closes the book on her lap and puts it aside. For a moment we're quiet, watching my nephew sleep.

'So what kind of sick are you anyway?' she asks me. 'Chronic fatigue?'

'No,' I say. 'But I guess I haven't been sleeping well enough for a long time.'

'Well, you stirred up something coming here,' Liz says. 'Mom's definitely less Yoda than usual. But maybe she just wasn't prepared for how old you look.'

'So tell me,' I say. 'When your son's a teenager, are you going to be as mean to him as you were to me?'

'I wasn't mean to you. Someone just needed to liven that joint up. You were all so fucking earnest. Except Dad—and he was teasing *me*.'

Charlie's eyes have begun to twitch beneath his closed lids, and his mouth hangs open. For all the drama of her complaints about his use of the toilet and her seemingly offhanded parenting, Liz is more devoted to him than she's ever been to any person or pursuit. It's not that I didn't know this. But I haven't experienced it as clearly before. I haven't watched her gaze at him asleep or seen her allow herself the undefendedness of wonder.

I've judged my sister for so long, judged her enthusiasms and her jokes as shallow. Just like my father did, until he was dying. But what has her joking been, really, but a way to tolerate loving people who didn't take her seriously?

'I should have visited you more,' I say. 'Since Charlie was born, and before that too. I'm sorry I didn't.'

'It's okay,' Liz says as her son's little body squirms around until he's lying flat on his stomach. She reaches down and wipes the moisture from his lips. 'I know you're busy saving the world—you and Mom both.'

'I mean it,' I say. 'I've missed you.'

She looks up from the cot to make sure I'm sincere. 'That's unlike you, *brother*. But thanks. I've missed you, too.'

It's finally dark out, on one of the longest days of the year, and from the open window beyond the cot, cooler air flows, along with the humming of New England in the summer.

'Mom told me you were getting on her about the family history stuff,' my sister says. 'Have I converted you?'

'You should send me some of what you've found,' I say. 'I should read about it. I read history all the time—just other people's.'

'Are you going to keep doing that forever—your lawyering?'

'I don't know,' I say. 'It's basically all I've ever done. It becomes the way you see everything. I look at Charlie and think: He's a citizen. He'll never need someone like me to argue that he deserves the chance to be one.'

'Which is why,' Liz says, 'I want to teach him how we got here.'

'But you said it was more than that. You said you believed in spirits.'

'I do,' she says. 'And maybe Mom's right. Maybe they don't haunt us down tidy family lines. But does she really believe all that violence just goes away? That it doesn't show up somewhere in us? Call me crazy, but I kind of wouldn't mind knowing what's rattling around in me—and in him,' she says, nodding toward Charlie.

The door of the study creaks open just wide enough for my mother to poke her head in. 'Oh, there you are,' she whispers toward me. 'I didn't know you were in here with them. I won't disturb you, you two carry on—please. I'm just saying good night.' She blows us a kiss, we say good night to her, and she presses the door closed again.

I never get to smile knowingly with anyone about my mother—I didn't even know that I missed being able to—but I get to do it now, with the one person I ever could, a grinning acknowledgment of the little comedy of her ways.

For another few minutes, I stay with Liz and Charlie, in the most pleasant and unbothered silence I remember experiencing in a very long time. Then I go out into the quiet of the hall. I've slept so much the past two days I'm not sure I'll be able to now. Rather than going upstairs, I pass through the darkened kitchen and out the back door into the yard. A three-quarter moon in a clear sky lights the grass and the apple tree and the bench beneath it, which is where I sit. Either I have failed to remember or never quite took in the grade of the land that this place rests on. How the ground slopes down from the trees at the back, through the new meadow, and across the slanting lawn to the driveway that bends down to the road. There is a suggestion of motion in the angle of it all, a gentle unfurling.

You look away from one thing—and so much else gets lost with it.

Like the memory that floats up in me now with a bodily fullness almost uncanny. The memory of a night I'd forgotten entirely. My first winter in New York, freshman year of college. Someone on my hall invited me to a party down in the East Village, which turned out to be crowded with mostly older guys, in their twenties and thirties, where I hovered awkwardly at the edges until it was late and I was drunk, and one of the guys, handsome in his white t-shirt, came over to me and said, 'You should come to my place.' And so I followed him in a kind of trance to a railroad apartment nearby, terrified that I'd catch the virus, and he pointed me through a door into his bedroom, lined with bookcases, and told me I could take off my clothes. Then he took off his, stepping out of his jeans, and glanced at his watch before putting it aside. The two of us knelt together on his futon on the floor. He kissed hard, like he wanted to swallow me whole, then rolled me onto my back, slid on a condom, and lifted my legs over his shoulders.

He had a cat, or someone living there did, a pale gray creature with large yellow eyes who watched from the little desk as the man pressed himself into me, more painfully than I could have imagined, and I clamped my teeth and tried not to wince because I didn't know how to tell him that it was my first time, and I wanted him to like me. So I fixed my eyes on the animal instead—upright and motionless, its thick tail wrapped around the columns of its front legs, perfectly indifferent it seemed to the jerking bodies in front of it, taking the scene in like a servant bored at the folly of its master.

When we had both come and the jerking motions were over, the cat leapt to the floor and wandered off down the hall. The man followed it, returned with a glass of water, a plate of clementines, and a towel.

'You're welcome to shower,' he said. 'There's no rush. My boy-friend's out of town.'

When I got out onto the sidewalk, it was draped in an early snow, and snow covered First Avenue as well, where the taxis glided almost silently past the darkened high school across the street. I wanted to talk to someone. To say what had happened. On the opposite corner there was a pay phone. The only person I could think to call was Liz. She picked up, but as soon as I heard her voice, I lost my nerve. I said nothing. Just asked how she was.

Across a stretch of lawn, through the study window, I can see my sister now, still perched on the edge of the bed beside the cot where my nephew sleeps.

How full of shame it is to be lonely.

At noon Ann and Clare and Roberta joined the retreatants in the meetinghouse for the final gathering of their stay. It was, as always, a chance to weave together the themes that had emerged in conversations and circles during their time at the center. The eight women in the group that week were members of an alliance for the public schools in Albany—social workers, teachers, a nurse, and a principal. The work had turned out to be helping them to strengthen the bonds already in place, reflecting on the sustenance of friendship—ways to offer it, ways to receive it. They were thankful, as so many who came to Viriditas were, for the attention and insight of its founders.

Ann sat between Clare and Roberta in the circle, contributing little, gazing instead through the windows that looked toward the house and barn, out into the heat of the day. Toward the end of the hour, she spied Charlie dashing from the kitchen door and racing across the grass to the flower bed along the barn. A moment later, Liz appeared and followed after him, dressed in a surprisingly conventional red sundress, which, on her, seemed like a costume of normalcy. The two of them did a little jig, Liz pretending to be Charlie's dance partner, then she lifted him by the wrists and, twirling like a shot-putter, spun him round and round. The two of them would be returning to Portland at the end of the afternoon, a long round trip for a short visit, but Liz had wanted to see her brother, who now emerged himself, through the same door, but remained by it on the step, squinting into the sun. How long Peter would stay, Ann had no idea.

Since their walk, she had pressed on her memory of those days right after Richard's death, recalling, as she hadn't in years, having to bicker with her mother-in-law in St. Paul over the burial arrangements, and manage Clare, who wanted to be at the rectory every minute to help, which was the last thing Liz and Peter needed. And then the news of Jared's death.

It was in the welter of that August heat that, late one morning, the police had come knocking on the door. Two clean-shaven white men, the older of whom, Michael Ryan, was a parishioner of Ann's, a fellow about Richard's age with one son in the confirmation class and another in Sunday school. She remembered him dressed in a suit too warm for the weather, but of his younger partner, all she could picture now was his blue uniform belted above the waist and that he'd held a small pad in one hand and a pen in the other. She had known well enough why they'd come but waited for Michael Ryan to explain. He began by apologizing for disturbing her at a time like that, with everyone at St. Stephen's aware of the grief she and the children must be experiencing, leaving unstated what everyone at the church also knew—that she and Richard had separated only six months earlier—and, more unstated still, what many of them suspected: that it was because of Clare. It would be brief, he promised. They were just speaking to a few of Jared's friends before closing things out, the boy's death having been, it seemed quite certain, an accident. Apparently he'd been swimming at the lake on his own and had knocked his head coming out of the water. That was what he'd told his mother when he saw her that night.

'You can never tell with a head injury,' Michael Ryan said, his bald pate beaded with sweat. 'She couldn't have known there was a brain bleed, but of course she's torturing herself for not taking him to the hospital...it's an awful thing. I can't imagine if it were one of mine. We just came by because Mrs. Hanlan mentioned that Jared and Peter were friends.'

Friends, Ann had thought. That would be fine with these two policemen. To them, friends would make easy sense. And so would roughhousing, or even a scrap between teenagers that led to a terrible mishap. But what if Peter were to tell these men the things he'd told her? About what had happened in Jared's bedroom. About trying to kiss him that night. How they had fought. What then? What would these fathers—for Ann felt certain the younger man had children, too—make of her son's appetite for another boy? And what would their system do to him in the light of that boy's death?

That Peter wasn't at home just then was no lie. 'Certainly,' Ann added to this simple statement of fact, 'Jared did used to come by. But he hasn't for a couple of months now—or hardly at all, I should say, since summer began. And this last while, since my husband's death, the three of us—we've mostly just been here.'

'Of course,' Ann's parishioner had said. 'I really am so sorry about Richard—we all are. I almost didn't come, but we're just crossing things off our list. We won't need to bother you again. If you could just tell Peter that if he thinks of anything we should know, he can give us a call.'

There was nothing more to it than that. No grilling, no need to mount a defense. A matter of a few minutes. Not a moment she was proud of, and one—it was true—that she had never dwelt on, because what good could come of that?

'Are you all right?' Roberta asked after Clare had accompanied the group out and it was just the two of them in the meetinghouse putting away the chairs. 'You barely spoke.'

Ann made no immediate answer. When they were done tidying,

she walked to the windows she'd been gazing through, and Roberta joined her there.

'How has it been?' she asked. 'Having Peter here.'

'Hard,' Ann said. 'When he called—when I heard his voice on the answering machine—I thought it meant he had let go of something, that he wanted to let me back in. But I had no idea how angry he's been with me.'

'About what?' Roberta asked, direct as always.

'I protected him from something,' Ann said. 'A long time ago, when he was a boy. Protected him from the wilds of his own heart. And it turns out he's never forgiven me for it.'

Roberta raised her hands and placed them flat against the glass, as if holding that invisible barrier up. 'Never forgiven you?' she said. 'Those are strong words. Is it something you want to talk about?'

'I should have talked to you about it back then,' Ann said. 'But I think I just put it out of my mind.'

'Is it about that boy? The one who died?'

Ann, astounded, turned to behold her friend. 'What makes you say that?'

'You said *the wilds of his heart*. Wasn't he in love with that boy? Isn't that what you told me?'

'I said that to you?' Ann asked, less in doubt than in amazement at having no memory of it.

'You didn't like that kid,' Roberta said. 'You thought he was arrogant, that he treated Peter poorly.'

'That's true,' she said. 'I did. But that wasn't it. Peter thought it was his fault—the boy's death. And I couldn't let him believe that. Or go around saying it.'

'His fault?' Roberta said.

'He was with him, the night he got hurt.'

The two of them were still looking at each other, their faces just a few feet apart. In her dear friend's eyes, Ann intuited a question.

For once, however, Roberta didn't ask it. Instead, she remained quiet. And then, after a pause, said, 'It's still good, though—isn't it? That he's come back?'

'Yes,' Ann said. 'Of course.'

After Roberta left, Ann remained by the window looking into the now empty yard. She needed to return to the house to spend time with Liz and Charlie before they departed, but an image that had pushed its way into her mind's eye fixed her where she stood: Jared's mother in her flawless black dress and veil sitting in the front pew of the Catholic church, gazing at her son's open casket. All through that service, as Peter sat stone-faced beside her, Ann had found it hard to look away from Susan Hanlan. Roberta was right, she had never taken to Jared—or to his young mother. There was a prettiness and a finery about both of them, a regard for appearance that she distrusted. But watching that woman walk from the church at the end of the funeral without greeting a single soul had shaken her.

It was a few weeks later, heading into the supermarket at the end of the day, that Ann had seen her at a distance, leaving, dressed in a pantsuit and sunglasses, pushing a cart that held a single bag of groceries. As a minister, she knew well how the busyness of a death tended to occupy the bereaved at first, but also how soon the quiet set in, and with it the real absence. In the store, she tried to focus on her list but couldn't. She kept thinking of that woman returning home to eat by herself. Instead of her own groceries, she grabbed a quiche, some fruit, and a bouquet of flowers, and after borrowing the store's phone book to look up the address drove over to Susan Hanlan's house.

The rooms inside were immaculate, as much like a chic hotel as a place anyone lived. The two of them sat in thickly cushioned white chairs either side of a low marble table with an orchid at its center. She accepted Ann's condolences with the faintest of smiles. It was kind of Ann to come, she said, under the circumstances—Jared had told her that Peter's father had died, and she was sorry to hear it. When Ann thanked her and explained that Richard had been sick for some time, Susan Hanlan seemed to pause, uncertain how to respond. And then, as people often did in Ann's presence, she said a great deal all at once. That her husband had been sick too. That they had thought he didn't have long to live, which was when he had told her there was another woman in his life, and that he needed, in what time he had left, to be with this other person.

'Part of me couldn't blame him,' she said. 'We'd married so young. I'd gotten pregnant in college. Having a child at that age—it's not how he'd pictured his life. But then it turned out there was a treatment, or he wasn't that sick after all—it was never really made clear to me. Just that, in any case, he wasn't coming back. And I do blame him for that—for leaving Jared.'

When she was done, she apologized for saying so much, as people also often did, and Ann assured her there was nothing to be sorry for. In the silence that followed, Susan Hanlan looked at her with a kind of beneficence. It was a warmth beyond the usual thankfulness and relief that came with unburdening oneself.

'Your Peter,' she said. 'He spent a lot of time in this house. It wasn't so long ago, actually, that he came here looking for Jared. We got to have a little chat. He seems like such a kind boy. The truth is, I think he and Jared were quite fond of each other.'

Which was when Ann realized that the woman knew. Not that Peter had been at the lake, but that there had been something between their sons. And what disarmed her so completely then wasn't just this implicit acknowledgment, but the lack of any judgment in it—the generosity of it, as though she were letting Ann know not only that she understood, but also that it was all right.

And in that moment, Ann sensed that she could trust her, she could explain what had happened, how it had been an accident, and Susan Hanlan would understand, and she would see that blame made no sense, that it would help no one. But then she thought, What good is there in it—to tell a grieving mother all this? And she let the moment pass.

Monica is working on an appeal due that afternoon and says she can't talk long. 'We haven't heard from Mr. Marku,' she adds. 'If that's what you're wondering.'

'No,' I tell her, 'it isn't.'

'Well, for the rest, we're asking for continuances. And Phoebe's taking their calls. You got lucky on that Nepalese couple. The Asylum Office said they'd waive the deadline. They'll get their interview. I don't know about all the others.'

'I'm sorry,' I say, 'that you're having to do all this.'

'Yeah, the timing's not great,' she says, though not in an angry or aggrieved tone. The opposite, in fact—a tender one that I haven't heard from her before.

'Are you okay?'

'I thought you were too dizzy to stand up,' she says. 'You're really asking?'

'Yeah, I am.'

There's a pause on the line. Then she says, 'I'm not so great, actually. I guess I thought my mother would live forever. I guess that was the plan. But now she's dying in our living room, and she won't go to the hospital. And all I can think is—I never got her the house I promised her, with a yard. She never got to plant her vegetables. So what did I give her, bringing her here? An apartment in a city that meant nothing to her? A daughter without a husband? Who's going to make me feel bad about being single when she's gone?' she asks, her sarcasm returning to fill the cracks in her voice. 'I'll have to do it all by myself.'

Looking out over the drive and across the road, I remember teasing Monica about her vacation, how unlikely it seemed that, having never taken a break in all the time I'd known her, she would choose to come to Vermont. I imagine her for a moment as a guest at Viriditas. Sitting with Clare and Roberta and my mother in the meetinghouse, explaining to them how her father was murdered by a dictatorship, and how despite the U.S. supporting the remnants of that same regime, she has made her life here, helping others, almost despite herself, to stay. What would she think of their encouragement to self-forgiveness?

'I'll make you feel bad about being single,' I say. 'If you do the same for me.'

'I can't wait,' Monica says.

'What are you going to do?' I ask. 'Will you get hospice?'

'My mother says she isn't in pain, but she's lying. She just doesn't want strangers in the house. My cousin's helping, and a couple of the neighbors. And Phoebe knows. I'll take time when I have to, whether you're here or not. What's another forty cases delayed in the scheme of things? Other than people's lives.'

'Did I ever tell you what Carl asked me the day I met him, at my interview? What if in the big picture you aren't actually helping? What if you're a bureaucrat in an endless moral disaster, but if you walk away the disaster will be a tiny bit worse? Will you still do it?'

'Sounds like Carl,' Monica says. 'Dramatic.'

'That's what Phoebe said. She told me I didn't have to answer the question. So I didn't.'

'I stopped thinking about the big picture a long time ago,' Monica says. 'In more ways than one, I guess. The only person my mother wants to see is the priest.'

The morning after Liz and Charlie depart, I wake early for the first time since arriving at the center. Through the open kitchen windows comes a chorus of birdsong. Which birds on what migratory path, I have no idea. It's a sound I haven't heard in ages, and one I hadn't noticed here until now. Outside, the song is louder still. Listening to it—listening and doing nothing else—I hear the music but also sense the space that it fills, the vast, borderless air, into which it seems almost possible to dissolve.

At the top of the sloping lawn a path into the meadow begins. It leads through the high grass and along a short, wooded stretch into a clearing surrounded by fir trees. The studio is smaller than I'd pictured it, more solidly built than a shack but still a modest structure. Approaching the window to the left of the green door, I peer inside, where my mother is seated on a rectangular black cushion in the middle of the room, facing the far wall. There's a woodstove to her right and a simple desk and chair to her left. On a low, shrine-like table set against the wall sits a small bowl of water and another of herbs or incense. Between the two is a miniature framed version of the tapestry that hangs in the living room: the Viriditas symbol—a tree and its visible roots. It's at this that she gazes.

Like a kid again at her study door, I hesitate to disturb her. Though apparently I already have, because she turns on her cushion and, seeing me at the window, brings her hand to her chest.

'You startled me,' she says when she opens the door.

'I didn't mean to. I can go.'

'No, it's fine,' she says. 'I wanted you to see this anyway. Just slip off your shoes.'

The room is simple, a pinewood floor and plain white walls, with no sign of electricity or running water. Just the furniture and the cushion at the center.

My mother goes to a shelf above the woodstove and takes down two mugs. Looking at her reach up like that, I'm able to see, as I somehow couldn't before, that of course she has aged, being slighter around the shoulders and hips, and thinner in the legs. There is less of her.

'So this is the place,' I say.

'Yes,' she says, unscrewing the lid of her thermos. 'Nothing fancy. Still, I wasn't sure we could afford it. But Clare insisted—even though I'm the one out here most.'

I cross to the desk and glance at the little stack of books: Pauli Murray, Adrienne Rich, Thomas Merton, Thích Nhât Hanh. My mother's books. Beside them a journal lies open with an entry dated that morning.

'It was good of Liz to come,' she says as she pours the tea. 'I'm glad you got to see her.'

'I want to visit her in Portland sometime,' I say. 'And see Charlie again.'

'I'm sure she'd like that,' she says, handing me a mug. Then she returns to her place by the stove.

'It must be freezing out here in the winter.'

'It's fine once the fire gets started,' she says, then pauses. 'I suppose you might think that it's selfish of me—given the work you do—to spend so much time quieting my own mind.'

'Isn't that the idea?' I say. 'Quiet the mind to help others do the same.'

'Indeed,' she says cautiously, apparently uncertain of my sincerity. 'That is the idea. And I will say, it has changed me, over time. I'm of better use to people now than I was trying to prove myself as a priest.'

'Oh, I think you were a good priest. Everyone loved you. You were their hero.'

To this she gives no response, just takes a sip of her tea, abiding in her familiar calm.

'I have to go back soon,' I say, placing my own mug down on the table. 'I can't leave my colleagues to do all my work.'

'I do wish I had a better sense of all that,' she says. 'What the work is actually like for you. You've told me so little.'

'Is that right?'

'Of course it is,' she says. 'We barely talk.'

'What do you want to know?'

'Peter, it doesn't have to be like this. I'm not your adversary.'

'Well,' I say, 'there's a lot of violence. That's one thing. My clients have lives, obviously — families, jobs, plans for the future. But that's not what I talk to them about. Mostly it's the violence. The details of it. They don't want to have to remember. But that's what I do — mostly. I make them remember.'

'Do you ever talk to the other lawyers about it? It must be hard, holding all that.'

'What is this? Are you ministering to me now?'

'You sound just like your father.'

'And you sound like you're talking to him.'

I walk to the window along the back wall. The clearing that I have just come through is covered in fir needles, russet brown.

'I'm sorry,' she says. 'That was unfair. I just want to understand better. You may not want to think of it like this, but what you and I do, it's not so different. I know a thing or two about

298

listening, as a profession, and what comes with it. Needing to let go of things.'

I hear her words but don't follow them. My mind has moved outside, where the roots of the firs protrude from the earth, gnarled like the backs of ancient hands. And what I find myself wondering is whether that clearing in front of that loggers' shack up in the North Woods of Minnesota looked anything like this one. And wondering this, I wonder something else, something I've never let myself consider before: Who *was* that man my father beat? Was he a drunk? Was he an abuser? Or might he have been a scared young man himself? A boy who thought his touch might be welcome. Like the boy I once was.

What if the story were told that way?

Shaping narratives. Presenting events in a particular order. It's what I've spent my adult life doing. Whittling stories down into the patterns that the law can see. And all of them written for precisely the same purpose: to justify to the system a person's fear of returning to the scene of a crime. And yet in that shaping, what violence is done to the fullness of an actual life.

'We talk about the cases,' I say, eventually, my eyes still fixed on the clearing. 'Phoebe's always telling us that's what we have to do—find a way to let what we hear move through us. I thought I was okay at it, that being okay at it was why I could keep going. Until this kid appeared, and showed me I was wrong.'

'How did he do that?' my mother asks.

I can hear the suppressed hope in her voice. The desire for me to finally give a part of myself back to her. I hear it and I resent it. And in the sharpness of that retraction, the obstinacy of it, I understand clearly, for the first time, the kernel of fury that has kept me away from her: If you would not see me then, you will not see me now. And yet what has it been worth—this absence of mine?

'It's all right,' she says. 'You don't have to tell me if you don't want to.'

'He turned the tables,' I say. 'That's how he did it. He made *me* remember. Just by telling me his story. That he was together with a boy at school. The shame of it for his family. He didn't want to tell me the truth about it, not at first. But eventually he did. And then at the last minute, before I could help him, he disappeared.'

From behind me, I hear my mother approach. I want to tell her to stop, but she is already here, standing only a couple of feet away.

'I just keep thinking about what happened to him,' I say.

'What about it?'

'His brother and father—they tried to kill him. To guard the family's honor. But his mother went to where they were going to do it. I don't know how she got there. She didn't have a car, and it wasn't close. Maybe she rode a bike, maybe she ran, I don't know. But she got there, and she stopped them. Knocked her husband down. And then she got Vasel out. Out of that town, that country. She saved him.'

My mother comes a step closer and I feel her hands on the backs of my shoulders. And I feel too the flinch that doesn't come.

'And I know,' I say, trying to steady my voice. 'You were trying to save me, too.'

Her arms come all the way around me now, her hands clasping my chest. 'But I didn't,' she says quietly. 'I see that now. I was too afraid that people wouldn't understand.'

I lean my forehead against the window's cool glass, determined not to cry. 'I just thought you were ashamed of me.'

'Oh, my dear,' she says. 'No. It was never that.'

'I was so scared of what I'd done. But I couldn't even talk about it.'

'I know,' she says. 'And I should have found a way to let you.' She presses the side of her face to my back and I sense the warmth of her cheek through my shirt. 'I don't think I knew it then, but I was afraid of more than just the police,' she says. 'I was afraid of what you wanted, because part of me was ashamed of it in myself—for wanting Clare.'

I lay a hand over her hands on my chest.

'But that wasn't your fear to bear,' she says. 'And I'm so very sorry if I made you bear it.'

I can't prevent it any longer—the water in my eyes wells over. 'So it's not just men and boys, then? The way they want things.'

'I guess not,' she says, crying a bit herself.

In the clearing I see my father, a young man fighting on that hard ground. A boy who went home to his mother and said nothing about what had really happened. Because he, too, was ashamed. What a waste a closed heart is.

'The thing I've never known,' I say, 'is whether Jared was—or would have been—gay himself. If he was just fooling around, or if he was scared like me of what he was attracted to. If I'd been braver, I would've ignored you. I would've gone and spoken to his mother. Even if she could only hate me.'

Slowly, my mother releases her embrace and takes a step back, giving me room to turn and face her. 'She didn't hate you,' she says.

'What do you mean?'

'I spoke to her. A little while after Jared died.'

In her wide-open eyes, I can see my own amazement registering. 'You talked to his mother?' I say. 'What did you tell her?'

'Nothing,' my mother says, glancing away. 'I agreed with her that the two of you were close. But she knew that already.'

I step away, back toward the table and chair.

'You were still so upset,' she says. 'And the case was settled. Nothing I could have said—to you or to her—would have brought him back.'

At the sight of her open journal on the desk, my gut twitches, and a sudden vengeance rips through me: my mother in all her wisdom deciding who should know what and when, up here on this green hillside, with her reading and writing and meditating, while down below the world grinds on and people are ground up in it. She wanted out of our old life, and she got out. And she didn't let my father's death or Jared's stop her.

'You should have told me,' I say. 'You should have let me talk to her.'

My mother crosses the room to stand in front of me once more. On her face there is a look of such terrible sadness. 'I don't want to lose you again,' she says. 'Please.' She puts a hand on my forearm. 'You must know, Peter, whatever was or wasn't said back then, you didn't kill him. You have to know that.'

A tingling—pins and needles—spreads from the top of my head, down over my face, into my neck and chest. The narrow band of space between my mother and me seems to oscillate or shudder, like the sudden release of a vacuum.

Crossing my chest, the tingling reaches down into my gut, and as it does some deep clench releases, and that wanting creature in me that I have been terrified of ever since I wanted Jared, that thirsting creature coiled so long beneath this inner grip, unfurls itself up into my lungs, up into my throat—a bird of prey rising into the air above my mother and me, where it spreads its dread wings and, meeting the open air, dissolves.

No danger after all. Just space. Ordinary space and love.

I open my arms, and then my mother is in them.

IV

Hart Crane, 'To Brooklyn Bridge,' opening stanza: *How many dawns, chill from his rippling rest / The seagull's wings shall dip and pivot him, / Shedding white rings of tumult, building high / Over the chained bay waters Liberty—*

The book, it turned out, was still on my shelf. I found it there the week I returned to the city. Some of the images in that opening poem I could make no ready sense of—'A rip-tooth of the sky's acetylene,' an 'unfractioned idiom'—but the reading of it gave me pleasure nonetheless. And there was that penultimate verse with the lines I'd remembered: *Under thy shadow by the piers I waited; / Only in darkness is thy shadow clear. / The City's fiery parcels all undone, / Already snow submerges an iron year...*

When I started back at the office, I decided to begin my days by walking across the bridge in the early mornings, before the heat set in, and catching the subway at Chambers. I was glad for the view and the light and the time to think before the rush of work, and on the days I finished early enough, I walked the whole way home, not in protest, as my father had, but for the calm of it, and the sight of the water and the ships, and of distance itself, of the openness of the sky.

It wasn't until a Saturday in the middle of September, while I was finally rearranging the furniture in my apartment and considering replacing some of it, that I got a response to one of the periodic texts I'd been sending Vasel.

Things are all right, he wrote. *I'm okay*. Without my prompting, he suggested we get together later that week, before his shift at a different restaurant at which he now worked in the West Village.

I arrived a few minutes early where we'd agreed to meet, at the renovated Christopher Street Pier. It was still summer weather, people running and strolling in shorts and t-shirts, some lying out on the neatly tended grass in the full sun, some beneath the rows of fixed white shades. Curved benches lined the edge of the lawn. Beyond them was a stand of locust trees. The place bore no resemblance to the dilapidated dock I had cruised, drunk, now and then, years ago, after frustrating nights out, accusing myself of being unattractive and therefore lonesome, before returning to my apartment on my own. Gay Pride banners hung from lampposts, a chrome balustrade protected visitors from the water, and along the sides of the pier, decorative mooring bollards had been installed to evoke the ships that had once docked here to disgorge their cargo into the city.

'Hello,' Vasel said.

I turned to see a young man whose appearance had once again changed. The preppy look was gone. He had tiny diamond stud earrings, a hint of eye shadow, and was dressed in a dark blue tank top and denim shorts with a knapsack slung over his shoulder. Right away, I sensed an ease in him altogether absent before. In the office or at the diner, he had scanned his surroundings as if for spies, but now he seemed barely to notice the gaggles of queer kids laughing into their phones, the white guys in skimpy swimsuits tanning on the grass, or even the beat cops slouched against the railing, as though he didn't need to, because the city was now — in some way, at least — also his.

Neither of us seemed sure what to say next so we just started strolling out along the pier.

'You have a new job,' I said.

'The other place wouldn't let me be a waiter, but now I am. And it's better money. Also, I got my own room.'

'That's good,' I said. 'Do you have space for the drawings?'

'Ha,' he said. 'You remembered.'

'Of course.'

'I have a wall,' he said. 'So, yeah, I can work on bigger pieces. And I get to take the courses I want now — it helps to have a teacher. It's just a dream, I get it. But I do it every day, so who knows.'

A svelte white woman in a gray unitard jogged toward us pushing a stroller with wheels the size of a bicycle's, a determined look sealing her face shut, only to be passed by a girl in a red unitard, twirling by on roller skates, bobbing to whatever tune played on her earbuds.

'I'm sorry,' Vasel said. 'Not showing up for the court thing, or answering your messages. You worked a lot on that stuff, I know.'

'I did,' I said. 'But that was my job. That is my job.'

'I was going to come,' he said as we kept on out toward the end of the pier. 'I even got dressed up like you told me to. But then I kept thinking that if I do this, I can't go home. Not for years, or, who knows — with your system, maybe never. My sister, my mother, they are still there. And I know you said get your papers and then you can help them, but it isn't like that. They will live there all their lives.'

The old instinct to explain — to quote the law, the timelines for citizenship, the process — rose up and faded away.

'I get it,' I said. 'A lot of people hesitate for the same reason.'

'But it wasn't just that,' he said.

'What?'

'You'll think I'm stupid,' he said, looking down at the paving stones.

'No stupider than I am.'

'You told me that in the court they would ask about every detail,' Vasel said. 'About everything that happened that night at the stream. And I thought fine, who cares? But there is a thing I didn't tell you, because why should I have to? Yes, Arbi hit me, like I said. But before, when he got me to the water, he made me take my clothes off. My underwear, everything. And whatever—he is an asshole, he is disgusting, I don't give a shit about him. But my mother—' he said, then bit his lower lip, as if to arrest the words about to escape him.

'Your mother saw you like that,' I said gently, finishing the thought for him.

'Yeah,' he said. 'She saw me naked. And she had to help me. With my clothes. She had to touch me like that. If I ever kill Arbi, that's what I will kill him for. That day I was supposed to meet you, getting ready, getting dressed, I thought, they will make me tell them this. It's stupid, I know.'

'It isn't stupid,' I said. 'It's human.'

We had passed the locust trees and reached the large, open area at the end of the little park. When he'd texted, I thought Vasel was contacting me as his lawyer, wanting me to pick up the pieces of his case again. Which is what, I suppose, I should have wanted for him. Yet in that moment, as we crossed to the balustrade and looked out over the river together, it wasn't his status in the eyes of the law that I was thinking about but rather how each of us had come to be there.

My caseload was no smaller now than it had been before I took my leave. Every week the number of people calling the intake line asking for help only increased—the need for shelter from violence and ruin growing ever more vast. But mostly now I left the office no later than seven, and didn't take files home. Sometimes on the weekends I read books that had nothing to do with work. Like those poems, and even a biography of Crane that I found in a bookstore, about his days in New York scraping by with ad-copy jobs, living in Brooklyn Heights with a view of the bridge, his short life spent often drunk, often fighting, cruising in the Navy Yard. And then one night on a ship returning from Mexico he was beaten up, by a man he'd made a pass at, apparently, and in shame or drunkenness or both threw himself into the sea. A poet who had been determined to forge an optimistic vision of America, of its bright technological future. Thinking of that life now, I thought how all along, well before I'd ever met Vasel, from the time I'd first listened to Tesfay Kidane describe his torture in a shipping container in the heat of a Red Sea port to the time I'd spent transcribing the account of Sandra Moya finding her faceless brother in that alley, I had been trying, through their suffering, to reach my own, to know the current of violence that flowed through me, from my grandfather to my father to those moments with Jared at the shore of the lake, where unbeknownst to me my soul had remained while my body and mind moved inexorably on through the necessities of time.

Out in the shimmer of the Hudson, a Circle Line tourist boat motored south toward the Statue of Liberty, while two men on jet skis flew by in the opposite direction, kicking up great plumes of water.

'I thought you would be pissed with me,' Vasel said.

'Maybe I was, at first,' I said. 'Or just worried. But that's me. I'm not the one who has to live your life. Or the one who gets to live it.'

A tugboat's bass horn sounded in the distance. Boys on skateboards rumbled past.

'Thanks,' he said.

'For what?'

'I don't know. I just wanted to say it.'

'Well, you're welcome,' I said. 'For whatever it is.'

For a few moments more, we stayed there at the railing, Vasel casting his eyes out across the water to the apartment towers lining the far shore, then we turned and walked back along the other side of the pier.

Ann steps out of the woods into the meadow and the sugar maples across the field fill her vision: brilliant yellow against brilliant blue, the mass of leaves against the morning sky, a sight so radiant, so piercing it makes her eyes water the way the sight of food waters the mouth. Gratitude isn't the word. What this beauty fills her with is joy. A sharp, spontaneous elation. She knows this almost celestial burning will pass, the vividness will wane, or go unnoticed, and yet her mind does not grasp at it, but rests, letting the brilliance lighten her.

On the path, the grass is still dew-tipped, as is the grass of the lawn, which wets the tips of her canvas shoes as she comes down the slope. Clare, in a puffy blue jacket and one of Roberta's red wool caps, sits with her back to Ann on the bench beneath the apple tree, laden now with fruit. She has a cup of coffee in one hand and a book in the other. Ann slows her pace but keeps on toward her.

It was only a few days ago, as the two of them ate their breakfast, that Ann finally told Clare about her feelings for Jeanette. She wasn't telling her, she'd made clear, because of any intention to act on it, even in the unlikely event Jeanette would want that. She was telling her to make good, however belatedly, on the promise they had made to each other and to the community: to be open, to be forthright. She'd braced herself for Clare's envy and anger, but the first thing Clare said was 'Did you really think I didn't know?' Of course it hurt, she'd told Ann. But it had *been* hurting. And how many times did she have to say that her jealousy wasn't of Jeanette but of Ann, of how others were drawn to her. 'For such a good listener,' she'd said, 'you can be terrible at it.'

Approaching the bench from behind, Ann stops a few yards short. Clare is still absorbed in her book and hasn't noticed her. Her red wool cap sits unevenly on her head, holding in more of her hair on one side than the other, and from her frayed jacket collar little bits of down feather escape into the breeze. Clare was right. For all Ann's capacity to ground herself in the present, how often has she used her focus to avoid what she found intolerable? And nothing, she realizes, has been more intolerable to her than aggression—the evidence of it in Peter that she wanted nothing to do with, the reality of what had happened to Jeanette, which she kept at bay. Its presence in her own wild heart.

Gazing now at the woman she came to this place with, in love, twenty years ago to found a retreat from the subtle and unsubtle violence of a patriarchal world, she marvels at the violence she brought with her.

'Hello, dear,' she says, coming up to put her hands on Clare's shoulders.

Clare mumbles an acknowledgment, her eyes remaining on the page.

'This jacket is ancient,' Ann says. 'It's time we got you a new one.'

'Right,' Clare says absently.

There is work to do. Tomorrow a new group will arrive. They need to tidy the barn, make up the beds, get to the grocery store. And when all that is done, and they have eaten their dinner, and Clare has gone upstairs, Ann will try Peter. They haven't spoken for a week, and she wants to hear her son's voice again. But before any of that there is this morning's circle.

In the meetinghouse, Roberta has already pulled the curtains back and turned on the heaters. Together she and Ann and Clare arrange the chairs and place the low table at the center. When the knock at the door comes, Roberta is the one to answer it.

Jeanette has dressed for the occasion, which is to say not in jeans and a work shirt, but a pair of dark blue corduroys and a black pullover sweater. By the look of her damp hair, she's just showered, too. She takes her seat with the three of them but remains on the edge of her chair, crossing her legs, which she almost never does, and clasping her hands over her knee.

'We'll begin as we usually do,' Roberta says. 'With a moment of silence.'

One of the other things that I read—at last—that September was
the package of papers and articles that Liz had sent me back in the
spring. Among them was a capsule biography of General Daniel
Brodhead, written in 1883. There was one passage in particular,
about this man from whom I was descended, that I couldn't get out
of my head:

'Washington, by sanction of congress, issued an order,
dated March 5, 1779, directing General Brodhead to proceed to Fort Pitt, Pennsylvania, and take charge of the western department, extending from the British possessions, at
Detroit, on the north, to the French possessions (Louisiana)
on the south, a command and responsibility equal to any in
the revolutionary army.

'Gen. Brodhead established the headquarters of his
department at Fort Pitt, now Pittsburgh, Pennsylvania. In
1779 he executed a brilliant march up the Allegheny with
605 men, penetrating into New York, overcoming almost
insurmountable difficulties, through a wilderness without roads, driving the Indians before him, depopulating
and destroying their villages all along his route, killing

and capturing many. This expedition began August 11 and ended September 14, 1779, between 300 and 400 miles in thirty-three days, through a wilderness without a road. Gen. Brodhead received the thanks of congress for this expedition, and the following acknowledgement from Gen. Washington: The activity, perseverance and firmness which marked the conduct of Gen. Brodhead, and that of all the officers and men of every description in this expedition, do them great honor, and their services entitle them to the thanks and to this testimonial of the general's acknowledgement.'

I believe in spirits. That's how my sister had put it. Something is passed down.

The weekend before Thanksgiving, later that same fall, I rented a car and drove up to Longfield. I hadn't been there since the summer after I graduated from high school, when my mother had moved to Vermont. The town appeared little changed. Some old stores had gone and new ones had come in, but the facades along main street were much the same. As was the brick town hall and the brick library and their kempt lawns. What was different were the trees. The poplars in front of St. Stephen's had grown hugely and were now as high as the base of the church's slate-covered spire. The trees around the rectory appeared enormous too—the trunks of the oaks twice as thick, the Japanese maple, whose leaves still clung, covering half the porch in shade. The only thing missing was the big rhododendron in the front yard, where a jungle gym now stood. I considered knocking on the door to see if anyone was at home and telling them who I was but decided against it, and kept on through the neighborhood and then out along the road that ran past the lake. The trees here were more mature as well, the tops of their bare branches arched together high above the pavement, the winter skeleton of what in summer would be a canopy of leaves. The entrance to the path Jared and I had taken along the shore had disappeared in the growth, filled in by bushes and vines, obscuring the view of the water.

On the other side of downtown, along the street that led toward the high school, the red Colonial with black trim looked much as I remembered it, though it too appeared more hemmed in by the cedars at the back and the holly bushes bordering either edge of the property.

It had never occurred to me that Jared's mother would still be living in this house. To the extent I had imagined her at all, I'd pictured her long gone. But this is where she had remained. In response to my email asking if it would be all right if I came to visit her, she had thanked me for writing and said I would be welcome.

Having arrived early, I parked across the street rather than pulling into the driveway, and waited there. For all the attention and money people in this town lavished on their houses, there was so rarely any evidence of the people themselves. The street was as empty now as it had been back then. I wondered why she had stayed in such an isolating place. As if she were the parent of a missing child, not a dead one, and wanted to be here in case he returned.

The same evergreen shrubs, trimmed flat, lined the stone walkway. The same potted boxwoods, higher now, stood either side of the wide white door. I climbed the steps and knocked. A few moments later the door came open.

How beautiful Susan Hanlan still was! The lustrous hair, the heart-shaped face! She was no longer young — a woman in her early sixties — but what vitality, what brightness. More, even, it seemed, than I remembered.

'Peter,' she said, stepping aside to let me enter. 'Do come in.'

The carpet in the front hall had been changed — Oriental, not beige — and the color of the walls, too, not plain white anymore but a blue and yellow floral print. As I followed her into the kitchen, I saw that the whole floor plan had been altered, the wall between the kitchen and dining room removed, the space opened up. The sleek, pale-toned furniture was gone as well, replaced by Shaker chairs around a farmhouse table.

'Thank you for letting me come,' I said, still getting my bearings.

'Of course,' she said. 'It's good of you to make the trip.'

'The house looks so different.'

'Oh, it's been like this a long time,' she said. She poured two glasses of water from a pitcher on the counter. 'It's funny, I'm trying to think if there's anyone who still visits who remembers it the old way. I barely do myself.

'Dear?' she called across the room into the hallway. 'Are you in there? He's here.'

A moment later, a balding white man about her age in rimless glasses and a green crewneck sweater appeared and waved hello.

'This is my husband, Sam,' she said. 'Sam, this is Peter Fischer.'

'Pleased to meet you,' he said as we shook hands. 'I'm always glad to meet people who knew Susan before I did.'

'He was only a boy!' Jared's mother said as this man came up beside her and put his arm over her shoulder. 'He wasn't paying any attention to me.'

'Well, it's good to meet people who knew Jared, too,' he said.

'Indeed,' Susan said, looking directly at me for the first time since I'd entered the house. 'That is good.'

The man asked if I'd like wine with lunch and when I said yes, he took a bottle from the fridge, poured me a glass, and then helped Susan carry a salad and plates to the table. As we were about to sit, I heard footsteps on the staircase and looked over my shoulder to see an apparition of Jared: a boy in his late teens with blond hair cut short on the sides and parted down the middle. He wore jeans and a Joy Division t-shirt. The hallucinatory recognition that filled me didn't end until Susan said, 'This is our son, Dylan,' and the boy, as he approached, held out his hand. 'Dear,' she added, as I took his palm—real, not imagined—in mine, 'this is Peter.'

The boy walked around the table and took the seat diagonally

opposite me, beside his mother. She handed him the platter of sandwiches, he chose one, and then the three of them began to eat. For
the next little while, Sam asked me about my work, and I did my
best to describe it, entranced though I was by the uncanniness of
the mother and son sitting across the table. But as the meal went
on, and Susan asked after my mother, and I told her about the center, slowly my astonishment lessened. When I first met her, she had
been, it occurred to me, the age I was now, if not a little younger.
Why shouldn't she have had a future? And as I watched Dylan
listening to his parents' questions and listening patiently to my
answers, I saw that for all his resemblance to the boy who had once
meant the world to me, he possessed little of Jared's self-assurance,
much less his bluster. In fact, he seemed shy, deferential even, quietly intrigued by this stranger who'd known the brother he'd never
met. It wasn't until the end of lunch that he spoke a word, and only
then when prompted by his mother to describe his first semester in
college. Dutifully, he obliged, saying he was taking mostly literature classes.

'You think that'll help him get into law school?' his father asked
with a chuckle.

When I demurred, his mother ran a hand through Dylan's hair,
despite his trying to avoid her touch. 'He just got there,' she said.
'He's working it out.'

She brought in coffee and cookies, and Dylan remained at the
table throughout, looking up at me now and then as the three adults
talked.

When eventually we all stood, he said to me, 'Sorry I have to
go. I'm supposed to hang out with some friends. But it was nice to
meet you.'

'Likewise,' I said.

Then he headed back up the staircase.

As her husband started to clear the dishes, Susan proceeded
into the front hall and I followed her. I had worried that coming

here was selfish: to disturb, after so long, this person's understanding of her son's death, and for my own sake; to say at last what had happened and all that I was sorry for to the one person to whom it could really matter. But I'd come to see a bereaved woman, alone with her memories. I'd thought she was the one who'd remained, as if for Jared to come home. Yet it turned out I'd been the one waiting, mistaking his death for the meaning of my life. And a narrow life it had become.

But it didn't need to be. Not anymore.

When Dylan came back down wearing a gray puffy jacket, his mother walked up to him, reached down to his waist, and zipped it up to his chin.

'Mom,' he said. 'You don't need to do that.'

She kissed him on the forehead. 'Text me when you get there,' she said.

Without offering a response, her son was out the door.

Susan handed me my coat and lifted her own from a chair beneath the window. 'Why don't you and I go for a walk,' she said. 'The air will do us good.'

ACKNOWLEDGMENTS

But for the extraordinary talents of Ben George—the most astute and caring editor a writer could ever hope to have—this book would not exist in its final form.

For their considerable work on my behalf in bringing this book into the world, thank you to Ben, Amanda Urban, Sabrina Callahan, Liese Mayer, Byran Christian, Maya Guthrie, and Mike Noon. Thank you to the many immigration lawyers who gave me time they did not have to describe their work lives in detail, and most of all to my friend and law school classmate Amy Meselson (1971–2018) for giving me the chance to see the remarkable things she did up close. Thanks to MacDowell for time and space. Thanks to Steve Paulikas and Julia Macy Offinger for answering my church questions. For their close reading of my work when I most needed it and the wisdom they offered in response, deep thanks to my friends Mark Breitenberg and Amity Gaige. For her friendship, her care, and her permission, I am forever grateful to Jenna Chandler-Ward. Thanks to friends Andrew Janjigian and Melissa Rivard for food and comfort. Thanks to my sister, Julia, and my mother, Nancy, for lifetimes of support. And finally, my deep gratitude for the love, patience, and comradery of Daniel Thomas Davis.

ABOUT THE AUTHOR

Adam Haslett is the author of the story collection *You Are Not a Stranger Here* and the novels *Union Atlantic* and *Imagine Me Gone.* He has twice been a finalist for the Pulitzer Prize, as well as a finalist for the National Book Award and the National Book Critics Circle Award and a winner of the Los Angeles Times Book Prize. He is the recipient of a Guggenheim Fellowship, the PEN/Malamud Award, the Berlin Prize, and the Strauss Living Award from the American Academy of Arts and Letters. He currently directs the MFA program at Hunter College in New York.